THE FIFTH DAY LADY

CAN SHE MAKE IT WORK?

THE FIFTH DAY LADY

SHE CAN MAKE IT WORK?

L.J. Golicz

ARPress
45 Dan Road Suite 5
Canton MA 02021

Hotline: 1(888) 821-0229
Fax: 1(508) 545-7580

Ordering Information:
Quantity sales. Special discounts are available on quantity purchases by corporations, associations, and others. For details, contact the publisher at the address above.

Printed in the United States of America.
ISBN-13:   Paperback   979-8-89330-803-7
                eBook   979-8-89330-804-4

Library of Congress Control Number: 2024901937

Dedication

This story is dedicated to the memory of my brother Kenney, as well as to my friends, and all of my family.

Contents

Dedication...V

Chapter One
    The Meeting...1

Chapter Two
    Josephine Plays Polo................................15

Chapter Three
    At The Hospital......................................29

Chapter Four
    At The Plane Alive..................................39

Chapter Five
    Making The Estancia Alive.....................57

Chapter Six
    On The Pompas For Ponies...................66

Chapter Seven
    Dinner For The Generals........................81

Chapter Eight
    Off To Spain Under Cover.....................93

Chapter Nine
    On Target In Paris.................................106

Chapter Ten
    St. Petersburg's Russian Help................121

Chapter Eleven
    Let The Games Begin............................136

Chapter Twelve
    Surviving The Ride................................151

Chapter Thirteen

A Volvo 167

Chapter Fourteen

Changing Saddles 180

Chapter FiFteen

Back To Bogota Undercover 190

Chapter Sixteen

Getting In Deep 202

Chapter Seventeen

And Deeper..211

Chapter Eighteen

Building The Bomb 227

Chapter Nineteen

Penthouse Party Disaster 239

Chapter Twenty

A New Boss At Tridexan 253

Chapter Twenty One

Day One At Monserrate..266

Chapter Twenty Two

Making Cartegena..278

Chapter Twenty Three

Day Three Sailing On Papillon 285

Chapter Twenty Four

Day Four Mexico City..294

Chapter Twenty Five

Day Five Death And Destruciton 305

Chapter Twenty Six

What's Next? 319

Chapter One

The Meeting

"It is black and unmarked, just behind us, not even 300 feet above us. Dios Mio, hand me my pistol!"

long west Florida's lush green, well-trimmed barrier islands with sugar sand beaches lapped by the Gulf of Mexico, the obvious resident carriage trade constantly cruises their expensive cars to celebrate their playful living. Day after day, parties at million-dollar beach condominiums can't overcome one simple but strangely repeated gossip among the women. At sunset, a rum soaked drum beating circle on the beach, with one well-endowed lady doing a sinful belly dance, screams out to a gaggle of gigglers, "Why do we need a dentist?" They cheerfully reply, "Oh, is it because he is so painless, in so many ways!" The gaggle then sings out with a choral cheer, "Who is your dentist?"

After all of that fun in the sun, dental work might be needed. A slight tooth ache may lead to a new adventure. Will well-heeled women, slightly fat with too much make up, or sleek and slim, with the latest plastic adjustments, seek to amuse themselves at a unique dentist's office, especially designed for the ladies? And a modestly designed dentist sign swinging from a full-columned portico and veranda of a two-story Plantation Greek Revival house overlooking the beach beckons such a visit. The double door entrance of inlaid beveled diamond-shaped inserts offers an attractive and guaranteed expensive visit. Once inside, the reception area engulfs the eye with the peculiarities of a Victorian parlor, packed with Chinese porcelains, jade statues, bronze sculptures, century old massive portraits in oil, gold leaf wallpaper, and heavy gold encrusted framed mirrors.

Still, one wall in the sumptuous reception area displays educational awards and a dental college degree, even a Harvard business degree. To top off the display, on a black and white laced marble console, gleaming in a spot light from the ceiling, two large, highly detailed bronze horses in a gallop with a rider bending over and swinging a mallet to the ground at a ball offers an impressive trophy display. On a turn to the counter, there to greet a prospective patient and, to no great surprise per the gossip, is a very good-looking young man, with bulging upper torso muscles. With a promiscuous grin, he gently escorts the lady patient to register and take a seat in a Napoleonic chaise lounge.

Soon a prospective, adventuresome patient will encounter another attractive possibility. A well-poised man in a tailored white jacket and black tie without speaking approaches her without apprehension. His charcoal dark eyes, endlessly deep, sink into a sharply chiseled face framed by a sea of curly jet-black hair just skirting his neck and forehead. Tall with square shoulders and tanned olive skin, he profiles a smile with a perfect set of pearly white teeth. And in a deeply mellow confident tone he introduces himself, "Greetings, dear lady, I am your dentist, Julio Juan Verelez de la Vega." With an aristocratic family name he is thee dentist, the one who is attracting the wealthy women of the beach.

The gossip on the beach also includes a second floor waiting room separate from the dental office on the first floor and accessed by a quaint, also Victorian, wrought iron enclosed two-person elevator. After a constant buzzing sound, once up to the second floor, it opens to a large twelve foot ceiling room with a golden chandelier, a wet bar, a wall sized TV and music system, a chaise lounge set, and a small work out area with a bike and treadmill. The double French doors open to a furnished balcony overlooking the beach. To the right, a ladder leads to a loft with a king-sized bed draped in silks. This special patient "waiting room" also includes a Bianco Carrara marblefinished bathroom with a roomy walk-in tub and shower, easily for two, well accented with wall and ceiling mirrors. It is all to be enjoyed while waiting or recovering. It no doubt serves as an overnight for the doctor and guests, if desired.

Back on the first floor the bronze polo trophies on display advertise an athlete. How many lives does this dentist live? These hard won trophies don't come without a fight with La Passion de Hombre, a man of passion. Today, he's leaving the office to train his team for a championship match at West Palm Beach. Then, almost out the door, an equally striking figure catches his eye. His greeter announces her name as Mrs. O'Connor, a new patient, just there for making an appointment. Julio turns his head over his shoulder to watch her lean over to sign the information sheet. From where he stands, his eyes turn into magnets attracted to her well-outlined hourglass figure and shapely breasts, exposing an inviting separation along the rim of her blouse. When she stands up, her tall and limber physique leaves no doubt as to her athletic tone. She smiles and extends her hand to him as he turns to face her with anticipation in his eyes.

Softly with a comely smile she greets him: "Hello, my name is Josephine O'Connor. I assume you are my dentist." For once in his life, Julio is lost for words, stumbling into his standard gracious greeting that truly reflects his inner mind. With an ear-to-ear smile, he cheerfully replies, "Ah yes, my dear lady, I look forward to being of service to you." For a brief silence they search each other's eyes. Almost hypnotized, Julio gazes in awe as she floats across the room toward him. She then turns to the veranda looking out to the Gulf and remains quiet with a slight smile. Not to let her go so easily, Julio quite clumsily calls for her attention, "And uh." Josephine swivels around to face him and answers. "Until next week, Wednesday at 9:00 a.m.?"

Regaining his composure, Julio, now fully forward but still gentle and friendly, expresses a standard come-on without even thinking, "Why wait until then? I am leaving for a polo tournament in Palm Beach. Would you like to join me?"

Josephine, not really taken aback, looks as if she expected some kind of invitation, and his awfully forward invitation came forth with overwhelming confidence. With a pretend surprise and some hesitation, already with a tone of familiarity, she replies, "Oh! Polo, I love horses but know nothing of the sport. Is it an important match?"

With energy and an inflated chest, Julio replies, "Yes, we will ride for the Gold Cup Trophy, a US Open match. My team from Argentina comes up against our greatest competitor from Columbia."

Then Julio begins to beg off as he finally notices a large karat set of diamond rings on her left hand. Apologetic, he searches for an opportunity to steady his stride, and wisely states, "I see that you are wearing a wedding ring. Would your husband like to come along also?"

Acting with an undisguised admiration for Julio's polo venture, Josephine still smiles. "My husband is a developer building high-rise apartments in Dallas. We vacation here but he has had problems with finishing the 41st floor. We stay in touch by cell phone and hope he can get away, but not likely soon. And staying at our beach condo waiting for a chance for him to get away can get boring including most of the beach life."

Julio is lost for words. With some thought but much enthusiasm, Josephine breaks the silence, "I should like very much to watch you lead your team to win. And my husband would be happy to know I will not be bored at the beach. And please call me Josephine."

With a mild smile, Julio offers his hand. "Yes, I love your name, Josephine. Please call me Julio. Please inform your husband of your new adventure in Florida and you can stay as my guest at our ranch near Palm Beach and..."

As they walk down the steps together toward his car, he continues, "There is no need for you to pack. My aunt managing this part of our estate will provide you with your personal needs, clothing for the ranch, and for the polo match."

Now in the parking lot, Julio opens the passenger side of his Aston Martin. Josephine, slightly hesitant, grins as she enters the car, and Julio, with a hint of arrogance, no doubt about his vehicle, brags a bit,

"We will be there in no time. My aunt will have dinner waiting for us."

Once in the car, Josephine comments. "This leather interior is very well done, and look at all of those gauges."

Before turning the key, Julio cannot resist detailing the car's features. "This is a 2002 Aston Martin Vanquish V-12, the same car driven by James Bond in the movie Die Another Day. It has a 5.9-liter engine, generating 460 horsepower, a six-speed auto-manual transmission, a drive-by-wire throttle, independent suspension, and anti-lock brakes. I can go zero to 60 in five seconds with a top-end speed of 190 miles per hour." And off they go with a squeal.

Since the ride covers 130 miles, taking maybe two hours, Josephine and Julio have time to get to know each other with "just friendly" conversation. Laced with curiosity, relaxing at 90 mph on Alligator Alley, Julio looks slightly sideways at Josephine and asks, "Do you ride horses?"

Just waiting for the question, Josephine proudly proclaims, "Oh yes, I am Arizona born and lived near Sedona on a ranch in the Verde Valley. Our family loved and raised well-bred horses for rodeos and jumping."

Julio, stunned by hearing what he never expected, now needing to know more, yells excitedly, "Wonderful! We train the best horses for polo. How have you ridden?"

With some show of humility, Josephine answers, "I earned a few trophies at rodeos. I gave up barrel racing and then tried for jumping, and with the help of my dad, I was able to compete at the French nationals." Not to change the subject but to change the direction, Josephine asks, "And how did you start in polo?"

"Oh, I grew up on my grandfather's estancia in Argentina. He raises polo ponies and manages a large herd of cattle. For me, it means riding with the gauchos tending the herd. I also worked with the vaqueros breaking and training his breeding horses. Of course, I also rode with his polo team to victory in Buenos Aires with a ten-goal handicap, winning trophies when I was 16 years old."

Josephine diplomatically, yet quizzically probes further, "Well, dentistry is a long way from polo. What happened?"

Julio exclaims, "Ugh, my mother. My grandfather joined the junta with Juan Peron and insisted his daughter marry a military man. My mother wanted a professional in the family, but not like my father, an arrogant, temperamental general in the Argentine army. For all of my riding and polo skills, I am thankful to my grandfather, not my father. He would rather have sent me to the military academy, but my grandfather saw my talent as a rider in polo and would not allow it, as long as I learned on the side, to fly his airplane and gained the shooting and fighting skills of the army at a nearby base, which I did."

Julio, with a smirk, continues, "My father, well known for his large ego, along with a few other generals like him, failed to defeat the British over the Falklands invasion. He wisely resigned under pressure. My mother initiated our family move to Bogota, in Columbia. My father agreed, I think because of his fear of disappearing. Sadly, for him, but better for my mother, he also had to give up the pleasure of his la Niña. So, his failure in the Falklands and leaving the country solves the la Niña problem. But, more than ever, he still pretends importance."

Being familiar with Spanish, Josephine asks, "Your father has a daughter?"

Julio backs up a bit, with an uncomfortable answer. "A la Niña is a gorgeous young lady, who makes an older man laugh, and is very willing to please that man who cares for her every whim and desire. She is always there for him and he knows she is with her real boyfriend when he is not. No matter. He gives her a car, an apartment, clothes, and an allowance which she saves for her boyfriend, the one she would likely marry."

Josephine, slightly puzzled, nods with a sympathetic smile. Julio then brings his mother back into the picture. Starting with a growl, "My father squandered a great deal of money on his mistress. My mother, well aware of his dalliance, tolerated it for my grandfather's sake, but once in Bogota, she took over the family funds and investments to start a business."

With that earful, Josephine tries to change the subject, "But Julio, how does all of this come to bear on you becoming a dentist?"

Julio now gains some composure. "Once in Bogota, my mother, very much disappointed with my father, and being away from my grandfather, took over my life with a vengeance. She sent me to study with the Jesuits in this country at the University of Detroit in Michigan, where I best learned English and took up my studies with enthusiasm. Very much interested in medicine, I entered their dental school. And during all that time, my mother started a veterinarian pharmacy that catered to horse breeders and farm animals so that she could compliment my grandfather's polo horse training and selling, and at the same time maintain a team at my grandfather's estate. After graduating with a dental certificate, she then insisted that I go to Harvard to get a master's degree in business."

After a moment of silence and making a true confession, Julio feels an incredible relief and is very comfortable and at ease with Josephine. His curiosity intensifies about this lady of mystery that just drops into his life, and he wants to know more. He begins his questions in his most delicate chair side manner. "So much about me, how have you come to Florida after Arizona?"

Josephine bites her lip and shows some pain as she speaks. "My dad flew for the airlines. He earned his spurs flying a B-17 for the 8th Air Force flying over Germany. After the war he remained in Europe working as a freelance pilot. In Paris at a cabaret, I think it was the Moulin Rouge, he met Gamal Abdel Nasser of Egypt and signed on as his personal pilot."

Julio interjects, "What was Nasser doing in France at the Moulin Rouge?"

Josephine backs in with a cautionary voice, "Dad laughed about that. He said he was directed by the OSS to meet him there. But that is all that he would tell me."

Julio thought and adds, "Well, he bravely flew the gauntlet with his B-17 and survived those very dangerous missions."

Josephine continues, "Yes, but he said Europe was just as dangerous after the war, flying C-35 cargo planes to Berlin. And the Nasser job had its problems. For one flight, Nasser's opponents paid an Egyptian air force pilot acting as an escort to shoot his plane down near his landing at Cairo. Dad saw him coming head on, forcing him hard to port and their plane went into a stall. He regained control in a forced dive and just cleared the desert dunes. Some heads rolled after that. But things kept getting worse in Cairo with additional coups and military juntas popping up along with major political and religious uprisings. With Nasser's blessing, and I suspect an ok from his other boss, he left with a suitcase full of British Pound notes and flew to Phoenix."

"Born and raised in Arizona, he bought a horse ranch, met my mother, and here I am. Dad taught me how to ride and even to fly his airplane. That was my joy as well as his. The three of us pitched in keeping the stables clean, training the horses, and traveling to rodeos and auctions. We lived the good life."

Julio's enthusiasm for Josephine becomes readily obvious. "Josephine! You are amazing. I also have a pilot's license and we both grew up on ranches with horses."

Josephine then replies with a sullen look, "Yes, but our good life didn't last. On a Friday I will never forget; my Dad invited my mom to fly with him to Las Vegas to meet with a dealer about horses for breeding. He radioed a May Day with engine failure over the mountains. They died in the crash."

Julio, while scanning for pythons and gators on or near the asphalt, quickly blurts out a mournful response to interrupt her, "Oh, Josephine, I am so sorry."

"That was the end of the ranch. Their flight was for a deal to save the ranch from foreclosure. My Dad had everything he owned in it. So, I moved to Dallas looking for work. I ended up a secretary in a mortgage broker's office. One day, one of the broker's clients waltzed in and sat on my desk. His name was Mathew I. O'Connor."

She continues, "As wealthy developers go, he was not bashful but kept a very serious business-like manner. He said, 'You are a proper, well dressed, good looking young lady. How would you like to earn $500 tonight by going with me for dinner to meet a client?'"

"He then blurts out in a strict way, 'this is a strictly business proposition. At my side, with your office knowledge of financing, and I suspect your quick wit, you will fill in the gaps in our conversation. I need to pitch this client to buy my forty-four million dollar downtown high rise apartment project. After dinner, I will take you home with your five one-hundred-dollar bills. No strings attached.'"

Josephine quips, "And my boss just laughed and said it's ok with him. And, that starts the beginning of a permanent round of dates to show me off to his clients as his administrative assistant, always with a slight, you know what I mean, grin."

Julio listens with sympathy as he readily identifies how life's circumstances provide a path to follow while at the same time being led. After her telling story, they finally arrive at a cast iron gated entrance to a large estate outlined by typical horse breeding pastures with double fenced, three tier and wood boarded, beautifully green pastures.

Julio taps his phone and the gate opens to a winding drive that leads past air conditioned stables, a covered training ring, an open training coral, a large caretakers home, and a sprawling brick, tile roofed, ranch style house with an extended veranda and a five car attached garage. As they approach a staircase to the veranda and main entrance, a servant comes out to welcome Julio with a surprised look, then a knowing smile, when he sees Josephine.

As they leave the car, once again Julio is overcome with desire as he watches Josephine slowly walk up the steps to the entrance. Her flowing blonde hair drapes over her shoulders waving lightly in the breeze, highlighting her nicely tanned shoulders as she moves with the elegance of a model and an exciting intelligence. Julio suffers a near melt down, but again recaptures his composure as the door opens. To greet him, there stands his aunt with a cast iron grimace, and she is not so pleased to see Josephine.

Once indoors Alessandra, with arms stretched to the ceiling, screams, "Julio, my handsome nephew, the big match is in two days. Who is this lady? What is she doing here?"

Julio somewhat shrinking from her loud voice and her overbearing demeanor, in an almost apologetic tone replies, "This is Mrs. Josephine O'Conner. I invited her to come with me to watch me win the match. She is a rider like me and competed in the national jumping competition in France."

Alessandra thought for a moment and inquires, "Well, where is her luggage, does she have her saddle with her?"

Julio now on the defensive, "No, it was all short notice. Would you take her shopping for overnight and clothing to attend the game and for riding with me on the ranch and the team for practice?"

Alessandra calms down, "Well, we can put her up in the guest suite. I will give her some of your mother's clothes as they are about the same size. Where is her husband?"

All Josephine can do is hold onto her smile while Julio strokes his aunt's arm for acceptance, but it is time for the lady to chime in. With assertion, Josephine takes the stage. "My husband is working in Dallas while I am staying at our place in Florida. I met your nephew for a dental appointment. I have no other commitments, and with horses we have something in common. I consider it a great courtesy for him to invite me to watch a polo match, and yes, I can ride well enough to help with his team practice, and of course watch your nephew win the championship. I will call my husband to let him know where I am and am involved helping a polo team in this national competition."

Alessandra without hesitation exclaims, "Well of course you are most welcome to stay with us but I should like to speak with your husband to insure him that you will be well cared for as our guest."

Without hesitation Josephine reaches into her purse punching her cell phone, "Of course Senora, I'm on my husband Mathew's private line. I'll put him on speaker. Hello Darling, how is the tall building going today?"

Mathew O'Conner speaking busily, "Josephine, my love, there is always a problem on the 41st floor. How is beach life treating you?"

"Well, I now have a diversion. I am in West Palm at a new friend's family ranch. His name is Julio Verelez. He is also my dentist of all things, but also is in a national polo match here in two days. And I am going to help with the horses, training, and practice for the match." Mathew curtly responds, "AOK my darling, just don't fall and break any bones. I have a call coming in. Keep me informed and thank the lady of the house for her gracious hospitality."

Alessandra grabs the phone and interjects, "Of course Mr. O'Conner, we will ensure that your wife is well cared for and will appreciate her assistance with this important polo match for my nephew Julio."

After ending with satisfied smiles, with her typical curt direction, Alessandra almost pushes Julio and Josephine to the dining room where dinner is waiting. Toasting with a glass of wine, Julio especially smiling at Alessandra, "This is a good time to tell Josephine about polo, our country's most important game and the oldest team sport in the world."

Alessandra looks at Josephine and speaks with more than a little pompous tone. "Oh yes, we are all riders, even into our 60's and women now play the game as well, and also play in mixed teams with men in this country. It is a dangerous sport full of injuries to be had. And Julio has had his."

Josephine picks up on the trend and plugs her culture of the West. "Yes, while barrel racing, I suffered a broken clavicle and my horse Comanche Jane, an appaloosa, broke her leg when we made a hard turn to pick up a few seconds on the timing."

Julio adds with enthusiasm, "Yes riding at speed is dangerous in any event. Your barrel racing has given you an important skill in Polo. Fast, hard, and tight turns are an important talent for capturing the ball in a face-off between riders facing each other when the umpire tosses it between the teams to start the game."

"And like hockey, with flat end sticks to hit a puck, we have long handled mallets to hit a small plastic ball three inches in diameter, trying to drive the ball between the goal posts located behind our opponent as we gallop from each end of the field pursuing a score."

"For polo we are riding in a crowd of eight, usually bunched together and often going thirty-five miles an hour on a field as large as nine football fields, all trying to control and hit the ball between the goal posts. Like football, it is a team sport. We have six timed periods to score goals, each running seven and a half minutes but longer to fifteen minutes, depending on penalties. And although there are penalties, polo has always been a gentleman's sport."

Josephine interrupts, "Wait a minute. You are telling me there is no rough stuff in this sport?"

Julio shrugs his shoulders, "Like a hockey puck, the ball when hit will reach 90 miles per hour and travel 100 yards."

Alessandra confirms, "And yes, Julio was hit. I nursed his broken ribs for a month after that."

Julio adds, "Riders can steal the ball when they maneuver their pony to brush and shove from the rear or at the side of the pony whose rider has control of the ball. They can also hook the mallet of the rider getting ready to make a swing at the ball. Sometimes in a crowd with all eight riders, a pony may fall. And you know a fall can break bones, but worse can happen when speeding and under the hoofs of others.

That is why we wear helmets, leg protection and elbow and knee pads." Alessandra stands up and then concludes in her commanding air, "Well that is enough for tonight. We all have to rise early to train the ponies and have some field practice. Our team is from Argentina and is staying at our ranch manager's house. Josephine, I will show you to your room and we can go over some clothing of Julio's mother for your stay here."

Julio gazes a moment at Josephine. "Good night Josephine. Tomorrow you meet our players and train and limber the best polo ponies in the country."

Josephine being rushed ahead by Alessandra turns around looking at Julio. "Thank you for a great day. I can't wait till tomorrow morning!"

Julio enthusiastically replies, "Me too!"

Alessandra leads Josephine down the guest wing to a very large bedroom with full bath and there are French doors to a patio overlooking the paddock. She opens the closets and dresser drawers filled with Julio's mother's clothes.

Alessandra with a friendlier tone, "Rest and be comfortable, my dear. Draw a warm bath and for tomorrow choose riding clothes. These boots should fit you and there are also leather leggings to wrap above your shoes. I will be knocking at 5:00 A.M. for breakfast. Tomorrow we begin work to win the match. Good night."

Josephine echoes the same as Alessandra closes the door. She then grabs her purse for her cell phone and punches a number. With three rings, a voice answers.

"How did it go today?" It's Matt, Josephine's husband at large.

Josephine jokingly replies, "What? No 41st floor problems?"

Matt now impatient for her story, "Ok, Ok, how did it go today?"

"The car ride was great, the dinner was great, and tomorrow we train with the ponies for the match."

Now, also with a playful tone, Matt quips, "Well don't let a horse bite. Remember to get on the saddle from the left side."

Josephine now sassy, "Hah, I lived on horses, and over here they call them ponies. Since you are so big on construction, make sure not to miss a walking plank over that elevator shaft!"

Matt replies with his mouth half open on one side, "AOK, sleep tight and sleep right. Keep me posted, my Darling, love and kisses."

After a hot shower, sorting the miraculously fitting clothes for the night and the next day, she climbs under the silky sheets of a king-size bed and quickly falls asleep.

As for Julio, under a great deal of pressure, to foster family honor and name, regardless of his dental practice, he trains his Argentine team for several months to win this national trophy event. Although with the wealth of his family, Julio enjoys the best, he has to show the best as well. Regardless of his distracting fascination with Josephine and his dental practice, viewed as a side line by his parents, Julio always sleeps uneasily when it comes to defending the family name in Polo and Argentina's world events in Buenos Aires."

Chapter Two

Josephine Plays Polo

Alessandra pounds on Josephine's door calling out like a drill sergeant, "Five A.M. breakfast served in ten minutes." Startled by her booming call, Josephine sprints out of bed and dons her riding clothes, gloves, boots with knee caps and hard riding hat, all to show a fine profile as she tips her hat to herself in a tall dressing mirror. She then opens the door to meet Julio in the hall walking briskly to the dining room. Julio, equally dressed for riding, turns and greets, "Good Morning, Josephine, you look like you are ready to ride and train for the day!"

At the table Julio motions to Alessandra, "Is Carlos ready with the team to practice?"

Alessandra looks at Josephine and in her commanding voice replies, "Of course, and I suggest that he take your lady friend over to the stables and help her choose a mare to make a back-up set of six ponies for game rider replacements."

With Julio taken aback by his aunt's outburst, Josephine sees the need to smooth out the beginning of a management conflict. With a half-smile she interrupts, "Oh. That would be great. Do you have barrels to practice hard turns? I did of lot of that with barrel racing in Texas and Arizona, always turning on a dime, cutting into cattle and horses."

Josephine's remark backs off Alessandra and gives Julio a good stage entrance for his game speech. "Our pre-match practice regime includes strategies for passing, cutting into a clutch, stealing the ball, bumping a rider, and hooking a mallet. All of our ponies are quarter horses 15 and 16 hands high. They are hot blooded, quick, and agile, as well as excellent sprinters, and my pony, Cleo, I clocked at 55 miles per hour."

Julio finally with the certainty of a competitor, "Our best effort is to ride off on the side of an approaching opponent to steal the ball."

Alessandra, a self-appointed coach, blasts a warning. "We are under a great deal of pressure to win the tournament. Julio's grandfather and my father is El Patron. He supports our team deficit and provides our thirty-two polo ponies at a typical value of $40,000 each."

Julio interrupts her, "Yes, but our greatest worry is from Colombia's polo team captained by El Machismo, patronized by drug cartels out of Bogota. An attacker for his team, he readily accepts a penalty for the many injuries made by his ruthless charges across the front of his opponents, or he hard side bounces a horse to knock a rider off the saddle, often tripping the horse, all to gain possession of the ball. Openly bragging, both on and off of the field, about his questionable legal hits in a game, he is a master of intimidation that we can't ignore."

Julio worries about El Machismo's unending ambition to do anything to win. And for beating Julio, the motive must go much deeper than just winning a game. Enough said, Julio rises from the table to escort Josephine to the stables to meet Carlos. While walking, Josephine asks expecting an answer, "How much do you know about this Machismo?"

Julio stops walking and holds Josephine's hand firmly as he slowly speaks in a very low and guarded voice. "In English his name means the machine. We played his team in Argentina a few years ago. Carlos, my best rider, was very young then, but his family lived in Columbia. The drug cartel hacked his parents to death with machetes, leaving their bodies in the street gutter in front of their house. It was a message, their reward for cooperating with the DEA and Columbia's drug enforcement agency. Miami is more than a home for a polo team from Columbia. It is also a drug depot for Machismo."

Josephine stands frozen for a moment, silent and aghast. "Carlos, I am sure, is looking forward to meeting him on equal ground, a Columbian representing the people who killed his parents."

Julio agrees. "Say nothing to Carlos about this. He wants no sympathy, just the opportunity to meet El Machismo on the field."

Now at the stables, Carlos comes out to greet Josephine and Julio. "Hola, Senora O'Connor, welcome to our stables. This pony to your right is called Loco. He is bright and spirited but doesn't like to take orders. Do you think you can rein him in?"

"Well, thank you Carlos, we are all riders. Call me Josephine. And I will do my best to bring this pony in as a team player."

Things start well. As Josephine strokes his diamond face, Loco nudges Josephine's head bringing laughter to Julio and Carlos. They know the powerful bond between a rider and pony grows into a partnership and they could see it happening with Josephine.

Josephine smiles and opens the stall to bring Loco out for a saddle and his first training session with neck reining. As she strokes him below his main, she whispers to Loco with respect, "You are well built with a good deep girth and strong hind quarters. I know we can turn on a dime, stop to hit a ball, and out run on a chase for the ball."

Julio watches Josephine mount with her excellent posture and notes, "This pony loves to compete and if he likes you, he will help you."

Josephine rides off with a speedy canter and starts her maneuvers. Carlos now looking at Julio, "I know what you are thinking. She has no rating in Polo."

Julio speaks cheerfully, "Yes, but look at her ride. She has great posture and with that hot blooded three-year-old she can make a goal for our team. Her heart and mind are one with Loco's. Look at her smile, and at his alert ears. They are pleased to help each other. And I think we can list her as an alternate."

Carlos with a grin, "And how did you know this when you invited her here?"

Julio thinks a moment. "I felt it. I had to know her. And now I know why."

Carlos agrees in a knowing tone, "Si Senor."

Elsewhere, on the other side of the coming challenge, practice is also the rigor of the day. A short, stout man with square shoulders and a grim face fenced in with dark straight hair, Raul Dominguez, aka El Machismo, demands and commands attention from his team at practice. Raul plays an attacker position and knowing his competition from Argentina being Julio, his goal to defeat him goes beyond a score board. He has clear orders from Bogota to take him and his family out of the game. As he mounts Zeus, his sturdy equally short pony, he looks to his teammates to practice a maneuver for a gang attack on Julio.

Raul yells to Sanchez, "I want you to cross Julio to steal the ball. And Rodriguez, I want you to foul hook his stick at the same time. That will confuse him while I engage him at an angle to knock him and his pony to the ground."

Sanchez growls back, "That won't take him out of the game; his horse will counterbalance and not fall on him."

Raul looks shocked, "What? Look! Here is what I am putting in my boot."

He reaches down and pulls out a long pencil-like object with a red button on the top.

"See this button? When I push it, a needle shoots out."

Rodriguez, familiar with hypodermic needles, shouts, "You will get him with a poison?"

"No, stupid. I can't do that. I would be caught. What I can do is make him dizzy. The drug in this needle will quickly disappear in his blood stream. When he loses his balance in a run for the ball, he will fall forward and cause his pony to roll out, throwing him into the air, head first, to break his neck."

"How do you know that he will break his neck?"

"I don't, but I know, if he doesn't, he will still be out of Polo for a long time, Hah, a very long time."

With an ear-to-ear smile Rodriguez agrees. "Si Patron"

Back at Julio's ranch, after two solid days of hard work exercising and training the team's ponies for all of the typical practices on the field, the next morning, up at 5:00 A.M. after a team breakfast, all are out loading the ponies on trailers for a short drive to the gated field at West Palm. At last beyond the gate to unload at their end of the field, they are pleased to see a filled grandstand with tented areas set up to serve drinks and snack items, along with loud speaker music, there is a recognizable gossip buzz, no doubt about the teams and records of wins and losses. The dress for the day includes the best of ladies' hats with white and colorful light dresses and swank casual tops and bottoms, and a very high casual for the men with special straw hats, and binoculars to aid for close ups on the mallet action, hits, hooks and bounces. With perfect coordination, Julio and Josephine quickly marshal the unloading of the ponies, while Alessandra supervises the team saddling up their steeds for the first round of play in five minutes.

With an air of excitement in the crowd, the loud speakers announce the players as they enter the field and line up their ponies in the center field, four in a square against four in a face off as they set up for the first of six periods called chukkers. Julio's team watches Le Machismo's four with one eye and with the other they watch for the riding field umpire's turf drop of a three-inch plastic ball between them. Julio playing number one, and Carlos playing number two, plan to attack the scramble and shove, tap, and slam the ball 150 yards from the center to the opponent's goal posts at the end. Pedro and Alejandro, numbers three and four, both playing defense, plan to interfere with Machismo's team's access to the ball by riding into them and by their side and crossing in front of them while distracting them with faked swings at the ball.

With the toss of the ball, the players cram into each other. Julio gets it loose with the side of his mallet and slams it to the boards at the sideline of the field. Julio moving in the same direction at a full gate reaches and hits the ball to set it up for a single thirty-yard shot for the goal posts. Raul riding Zeus at full speed to meet Julio before he can take his goal shot gets bumped hard by Carlos running defense for Julio. But Zeus holds speed and bumps back with greater force, and bounces Carlos off of his horse. The umpire blows the whistle to stop the play for an illegal move by Carlos.

Carlos cannot get up from his fall. Julio returns and dismounts to reach for Carlos. "Are you ok? Why did you do that?"

Carlos speaking quietly, "I heard his number two, he said it was time to get him, they meant you, and I wasn't about to let it happen."

The medical staff with a doctor arrives at double time to check Carlos. After a few painful shouts when the doctor gently moves his arm, he proclaims his diagnosis. "Well, you are a lucky one. You have a broken clavicle. It will heal in a month or so. In the meantime, there will be no riding ponies."

To resume the game, the umpire cites illegal bumping by Carlos and awards a 30-yard shot at the goal to Raul. With a very pompous approach, Raul stands his pony firm and with a full and heavy swing of the mallet, fires a clear shot, straight and high, between the posts, and the sideline referee flags a score for Raul.

With some time left in the chukker, Julio has a few minutes to reset his team. He rides to the other side of the field where their ponies are stationed, pointing at Josephine and jumping down from his pony.

"Josephine, we need you, now!"

Josephine yells back, "And what am I to do?"

"Carlos is injured out of play. You practiced well and your pony is your ready partner. You are taking the place of Carlos as my number two attacker. We need to score and I know we can beat that moron, Raul. Work with me closely and watch out for Raul. Carlos thinks he is up to dangerous plays. To keep his teammates from setting him up for one of his bumps, we have to avoid bunching. Passing is our best play to keep them separate on the field."

Enough said, Josephine nods yes, and mounts with one hand and a mallet in the other. For another bowl in by the umpire, they ride back to the center. This time Raul breaks the ball loose and makes a tail shot toward, instead of away from his goal. Josephine gets the jump on the hit, getting to it before Rodriguez, and takes possession with the side of her mallet and makes an offside open shot passing to Julio to her left. Julio with a perfect set up under the neck of his pony, takes his shot toward the goal with the ball reaching Pedro and Alejandro waiting off the side of the goal, and then pass it to approaching Josephine heading straight for the goal from the side line. She hammers the ball under her pony as she rides past the posts. With a flag for a goal by Josephine, the first chukker ended. The announcer lauds Josephine, an alternate without a goal rating, for executing a miracle shot. With a great deal of cheering approval and clapping, the crowd's excitement gains momentum and the sun glare off the hundreds of binoculars in the stands reveals a fully attentive band of fans.

At a fifteen-minute break to change ponies between chukkers, Raul rants wildly. "What are you fools doing? We are not here to play fair. Why weren't you there with that woman when she took a pass? We are here to win and to put Julio and his family to shame and getting him out of the game and his family out of our way. Bogota shows its anger over failure, you know, with chainsaws! Comprender?"

Sanchez is gulping to speak, "I think that Carlos is on to us. He bumped you to keep you away from Julio."

Raul said, "He is out of the match now. And that woman in his place makes a goal because you let her."

Sanchez in defense, "She rides her pony like the wind. She scored that goal with a trick shot and yet she has no rating for even playing polo!"

Raul stopped to think about that, "Yes, who is she? We have not seen her on the circuit. Is she a shill? Whatever! Show her no mercy in riding to meet her, bump her, and high hook her. You must roughen her up a bit to show her we are the boss." Rodriguez chimes in. "What about penalties?"

Raul loses patience, "Dios mio! So that the umpires don't see you, always act in bunches of two or three. That slows the game down, but we can afford that. My pony Zeus and I will carry the day."

For the second chukker, the umpire's drop finds Raul with a straight hit toward his opponent's goal, going over fifty yards. Josephine's faster pony beat Raul and Sanchez to the ball and tail hit it back to Julio pacing behind her for a passing chance after the ball. This time Raul's defense riders, Sanchez and Rodriguez crowd around Josephine to keep her from helping Julio by moving up for a pass. Now riding side by side, Raul's Zeus challenges Julio's pony with grunts and snarls and moves to cross Julio before he could hit the ball on his right-hand side toward the goal. Even though Josephine breaks loose from Sanchez and Rodriguez, it is too late to assist Julio. Raul recovers the ball without a penalty call on his bump and makes a clean shot through the goal posts for his second score in the match. The second chukker expires and a fifteen-minute break allows for regrouping at the replacement pony site. Raul pointing his finger at his team, "Now you see how we slow them down, enough for me to make a goal. Keep bumping the woman, every chance you get with at least two of you on one, intimidate her."

Raul then thinks to himself, "Julio is smart and rides well to avoid me. But when the time is right for my needle to do its work, I can still ride Zeus astride him for a bump."

With the horn, the game resumes for the third chukker. The umpire bowls in the ball. A heavy scramble with entangled ponies with small hits leaves the ball at the edge of the field. Josephine brakes fast along the wood barrier to keep the ball in bounds, and makes a hard full swing hit to the opponent's goal. Julio and Raul ride out of the scramble to take possession of the ball. Riding nearly side by side, Julio sensing a bump move by Raul, turns off to the right while hitting the ball under Raul to the center of the field empty of players.

Josephine's pony, Loco, resents the blocking to center field by Rodriguez and Sanchez and begins bucking and kicking the other ponies. To Josephine's surprise, Loco breaks away on his own, to give her a first call on the ball for a shot to the goal with Julio and Raul racing to meet it. Josephine's ball hit the goal post on the left side and bounced back to the middle area in front of the goal. Julio making the best speed, had to slow his agile pony, Cleo, to make a turn-around performance that allowed him to tap in the ball between the goals and ties the score two to two. The crowd, amazed with the dexterity of the play, cheers louder than the announcement for the score by the Verelez captain, Julio.

For the fourth chukker, few words erupt at the break when the field is tamped over to fill in deep hoof marks and torn grass. And the wear and tear of the game also weighs heavily upon the riders and ponies.

Julio's team now anticipates Raul's blocking plan of attack. With the best ponies needing a rest, including Loco, the hero of the first half of the match, changing the last set of ponies requires more riding skill with more effort. On the other side, Raul's team makes quick changes with assuring glances and affirming nods and smiles.

With a tie game, the crowd in the grandstand mulls and speculates over who is going to win after seeing so many good plays and tricks to cover foul plays, the pros and cons of any game. With the goals now reversed to equalize any wind or field advantage that might exist in the beginning of the game, the crowd grows silent with anticipation as the players move back to center field for another face off. The umpire bowls in. With the bumping and pushing of ponies in the scramble, Zeus's kicking forces the ball out toward Raul's goal. Josephine rides to retrieve with Raul's defense riding on each side of her and closing the gap on her for a double bump. Just as they make the move, she pulls on her reign to stop her pony which kicked up his front legs, letting Raul's defense team slam into each other, unhorsing the two in the process. The crowd roars with laughing approval, and the umpire calls a penalty, giving Josephine a twenty-five-yard shot to the goal. With the accuracy of a sniper, her overhead swing lifts the ball thirty feet into the air in a straight line between the goal posts for a score, giving Julio's team a lead of three to two. The crowd favors Josephine with shouts of "Great Game and More! We want More!" a definite boosting sensation above the usually more sedate atmosphere of polo fans.

Playing out the remainder of the chukker proves a boring series of moves and counter moves with bunching and knocking the ball in and out of groupings, accomplishing nothing on the field but jumbled movements ten to twenty yards at a time. With the sound of the horn ending the fourth chukker the teams quickly retreat to their replacement ponies. With all working at quick changes, whispers echo among the players.

Raul grabs Sanchez by the arm while he is synching his saddle. He warns, with his eyes wide open in a heavy whisper full of venom, "This woman makes you and Rodriguez look like clowns. She and Julio are matching our moves and playing our game against us. This chukker must eliminate Julio, for if we go after the woman again, the crowd will boo us off the field!"

Julio stops by Josephine as she moves to mount and puts his hand on her shoulder. With a broad smile and a face full of appreciation, he crows, "Your fantastic quick recovery from that bump charade brings us back into the lead. On this chukker, I'll haunt Raul to give you a chance for another goal."

Josephine is looking over her shoulder at Raul mounting, "No, he is after you. All you will be doing is giving him a chance to hurt you. Let me ride him down."

Julio stiffens up with an obvious posture of pride and asserts, "No! I will not have you doing my work. I will not give him a chance to hurt you instead of me. I can handle him!"

The tension in the crowd grows obvious with yells of "game on" as they absorb the venom of the battle in the field. All ride to the center of the field for the bowl in for the fifth chukker. Raul's heavy shouldered Zeus moves him in for a whack on the ball out of the set up. Josephine along-side Sanchez, gives chase. Julio rides ahead of Raul toward Josephine. Sanchez gets ahead of Josephine and takes a shot for the goal. The ball hits the post and bounces back. As Sanchez rides past the goal, he side mallet sweeps the ball back between the poles for a score. The score is now three to three. With a short break, for the fifth chukker, all ride to the center of the field for the bowl in. Raul's Zeus again gives him a chance to whack the ball out of the set up. Josephine, always along-side Sanchez, gives chase while Julio hangs back to guard Raul, who with a grim smile, bumps into Julio and extends his leg to match Julio's. With his needle extended, Raul jerks his knee into Julio's thigh. Julio, feeling a pinch, yells at Raul, "Is that the best you can do?" He then rides off at a gate toward Josephine.

With an out-of-bounds hit, the teams assemble back off-center for another bowl in. There are only two minutes left in the chukker. Julio and Josephine take possession when Julio at a full cantor moving down line, suddenly begins to weave with his body swaying side to side. Josephine yells, "Julio, Julio, what is wrong?" Julio looks up at Josephine with a blank face. His eyes fall back into his head yelling, "Josephine, I can't...." Then his head falls forward onto the neck of his pony. Josephine yelling, "Julio, Julio!!!!"

Julio's pony Cleo panics and falls forward in a roll. Unconscious Julio flies over her to hit the turf. Whistles blowing, the umpire and medical people run to help, yelling at Josephine, already there, "Don't touch him." Julio, unconscious, lying on his side, the doctor checks his pulse, lifts his eye lid. "He has suffered a concussion and neck injury. From bruising it looks like he fractured his right arm and he snapped the femur on his left leg. We need to get him to a hospital immediately."

As the ambulance rides onto the field, Julio's aunt Alessandra, running furiously from their pony station, screams, "My Julio, what have they done to you?" The umpire determines there is no interference; Julio was riding on his own following Number 2. Alessandra replies, "Raul bumped him earlier, why did you not call that?" The umpire replies, "There was no possession at hand, just some roughing."

After the staff loads Julio into the ambulance, Alessandra pulls Josephine to the side. "We must not let that evil captain Raul, win this game! My stable manager, Alvaro can ride in Julio's place. He is older but can handle one chukker with no trouble. Like a general in the field, Alessandra emphasizes, "This last chukker is up to you. You are like Julio; you think in the saddle. You can do it with Pedro and Alejandro. Alvaro will keep track of Raul. Like Carlos he has a sad past with his kind and will readily address the man with determination and force."

Josephine, with tight lips and a firm tone, "For Julio and you, I will do my best, and more than ever, I will see that Raul will not bathe himself with a victory. But he will need a shower!"

Alessandra replies, "Hah, I believe you will make him sweat a great deal. Go, my dear lady, and have fun! Make the pig go oink, oink!"

The umpire accepts Alvaro as a substitute to finish the match. As the ambulance leaves the field the spectators stand and clap for Julio and then give a loud cheer for Josephine, announced the new team captain.

The mood is set for a final battle. In place at the center of the field for the bowl in for the last chukker, Raul with Zeus, again powers into the center and whacks the ball hitting Josephine's pony in the leg.

Josephine along-side Alvaro, both split to give Raul a bump on each side with a smile, as she breaks loose from the scramble for a line in possession of the ball toward Raul's goal. Alvaro holds back but remains in front of Raul while Sanchez and Rodriguez bump and hook with Pedro and Alejandro. Josephine takes a long shot and misses to the left of the goal. Riding to recover, she passes back to Alvaro who now is riding along-side Raul.

Raul's defensive riders give chase to the goal to block their opponents from getting a clear shot between the posts. At a full gate they make the end of the field. Alvaro moves to block Raul with a cross over and recovers the pass from Josephine, and hits the ball between the goal posts. The sideline umpire waves the flag for a goal. Josephine's team now leads four to three. The grand stand is shaking with applause and a chant for a win. Only three minutes remain in the chukker for the end of the match. With the umpire bowl in at the center of the field, Alvaro side hits the ball to Alejandro turning in a circle to place his hit to Josephine already riding down field to make a goal. Raul yells, "Idiots, follow me!"

Following is a problem. Rodriguez and Sanchez struggle with Pedro and Alejandro pacing them side-by-side, limiting their maneuverability toward the goal posts. Raul avoids the bunch and makes it to Josephine's side, gritting his teeth in an ugly smile, countering Josephine's every move, and bumping her with each turn she makes to aim her mallet at the ball to the goal. One minute remains, Raul surges with a heavy hit toward Josephine's goal. The ball stops between the posts just a few feet from the line. Raul points his mallet to the goal and yells to his team, "Get there first!"

The crowd screams with excitement anticipating a race to get to the ball, with all eight-galloping neck and neck. Josephine, the lightest rider leads by a head against Rodrigo, while Raul on Zeus is the heaviest rider with his short-legged pony running last. Only a few seconds remain as Josephine arrives straight on to the ball and in passing it going into the goal with her mallet hits the ball under her pony's belly to the left side boards away from the goal. In a few seconds all players bunching along the board struggle to retrieve the ball. The grand stand is on its feet in utter excitement. With all of the concern for who is who doing what, the horn sounds for the end of the match. As the best in a series of matches, the announcer declares Julio's team the trophy winner to a lasting applause from the grand stand with special recognition with the announcer's generous thanks to Josephine O'Connor, also announced the most valued player in the match. The crowd stands with a three-time Hoorah for Josephine.

At the trailers for loading the ponies, Raul, more than depressed, expresses to his team, a great deal of fear over his loss to Julio and his clan in Argentina and Columbia. "This will not go well with our friends in Bogota. Last year, our Columbia team also lost to Julio's grandfather in the Argentine World Cup at Palermo in Buenos Aires. We may not be getting another shipment for a while. But this is not over for me. I think that woman Josephine is one of Julio's hired assassins. Hah, we shall see who the assassin shall be."

All of El Machismo's men reply aloud. "She is dead as we speak."

Chapter Three

At The Hospital

Alessandra leads a parade to Julio's room. Escorted by Pedro, Carlos, Alvaro and Josephine bring up the rear in a halftime march with Alejandro carrying the championship cup. Opening the door to room 177, Alessandra bursts out, "We won the cup! The whole match is video-taped and plays on TV in Argentina. Your grandfather sends his congratulations and asks, "Who is she?" Julio now sitting up, "Where is she?"

Alessandra pulls Josephine from behind and pushes her to Julio's bed.

Trying hard to look unemotional Julio gestures with his left hand, "How did it go?"

Josephine is beside herself with joy. "It was great; we are the machine defeating El Machismo."

Julio cannot contain himself, "You made our team a peer among the best, gracias!"

Alessandra interrupts, "It is more than thanks that she gets. My father, your grandfather, wants you, your team, and especially Josephine to come to his estancia in preparation for the world cup in Buenos Aires next month."

Julio replies without hesitation, "But I have a dental practice to maintain!"

Alessandra dismisses his excuse. "Your practice is the best and I am sure you can get a substitute for a month or so, maybe even a partner."

Julio looks at Josephine with a question mark, "Josephine, would you be able to go to Argentina for a month?"

Josephine thinks for a minute and taps her cell phone on speaker, "Hello darling, we won the cup. Julio's grandfather wants me to be his guest at his estancia in Argentina for a month to work with their team for the World Cup in Buenos Aires."

Matt exclaims, "Whoa, you just said a mouthful. That is a long time in a foreign country and your Spanish is not so good."

Alessandra hears his remark and grabs the cell phone, "Mr. O' Conner, you can be sure that I will chaperone your wife and take full responsibility for her safety and comfort. It is a matter of our family pride that our guests shall not experience any discomfort or danger."

Matt calms down a bit, "Ah, yes, I remember you from our last conversation. You sound like the boss. I will need the name, address, and phone number of your father and I will get back to Josephine to talk it over again. Please pass me back to Josephine."Alessandra, "Si Senor!"

Matt signals to get off the speaker and in a quiet tone, "Joe, what do you think? Is it going anywhere?"

Josephine puts the phone back on, cheery and loud, "Matt, I think it is a great opportunity, and I promise to keep you going on our progress. There is so much to do and learn. This world cup competition includes winning teams from Argentina, Brazil, Mexico, England,

France, Germany, Pakistan, and Australia with a total of twenty-four countries competing. It is an Olympic sport that we enter. What fun!"

Matt with equal enthusiasm and support, "Your excitement is contagious. You are back in the saddle and that is good. I look forward to your calls on progress. Unfortunately, I am so burdened with the 41st floor it will be at least six months before I can get away to be with you. So go for it. God Bless and Keep you, my love."

"Thank you, my love, until we talk again." After hitting the offbutton Josephine declares with her hands in the air, "I am on track with you for more polo in Argentina!"

Cheers coming from all, Julio asks Alessandra, "Who did the video of the match?"

Alessandra held out her palms to quiet the talk, "It was your mother. She came here with your father while on their business trip to Miami."

Julio much deflated, "What? She couldn't come to see me at the hospital, and after this great victory?"

Alessandra in sympathy, "Yes they are always at every match with expectations of your success. Unfortunately, after the match they had urgent business at the Miami airport as they left for Bogotá."

Julio sadly disappointed concludes, "It is always business for them, but not for me. What do they do that is so urgent!?"

After everybody left to tend to the ponies, Julio's mind wanders. El Machismo got to him somehow. And his team somehow has something to do with people competing with his mother's business. Oddly, the owner's name is Alexis Brontinoff, a middle aged wealthy Russian entrepreneur with a Merchants Certificate in Columbia. Is this Columbian competition so deadly, leaving him with a crushed body and Alessandra having to put down Cleo so injured by her flip? Julio is used to attacks in the game, thinking his loss of balance this time went beyond a singular motive to win a match. And his blood pressure starts increasing.

Changing channels, his heartbeat also increases as his thoughts wander to Josephine, and haunting thoughts of anticipation of being with her. Why was this happening? It doesn't make sense to him. All of his affairs are "let's try it and see" and "let's have some fun." In fact, Julio by this time has become fairly cynical about women and the ease with which he is able to obtain their favors. As an egotist and with his own Spanish born machismo, he doesn't think that women might be taking as much advantage of him as he is of them.

Now he runs into this mystifying lady who is just as hard with polo as he is. Even though married, is she just as lonely as he is? He thinks, "Wealthy, but not happy."

If she lays herself bare in his bed, will he have flashbacks about his other women? He concludes, "Sex with Josephine is not my prime drive with her. She haunts me with a new yearning just to be with her." He has to know more about her husband.

The next day, with visitor hours beginning at 10:00 A.M., Josephine knocks and enters Julio's room with a basket of fruit, some flowers, and Julio's lap top. Full of ginger, with her eyes wide open and fixed upon Julio, she ends a pleasing moment of silence between the two. "Julio, you look much better today. Did you sleep well?"

With a happy to see you tone, Julio exclaims, "Wow. All I could do is dream of the great match we played, your stunning moves with the mallet and your ponies, and how Raul got to me. How is it going at the stables and grooming for our winners, including Loco?"

With her familiar but poorly disguised anxiety "Carlos can't sit still and Alvaro is doing a wonderful job of brushing the ponies and giving them gentle walk down exercises. But your aunt, after speaking with your mother, fears Raul is still after you. She wants you away from here, up and about to make the flight to Buenos Aires, as soon as possible."

Julio interrupts in a rage, "Why does my mother care about me, but does not speak to me? Am I an object on a shelf to dust once in a while? She never wishes me a happy birthday or gives me a party or present, always pushy and then condescending even when I succeed for her!"

With Josephine's "no time for this" look on her face, Julio settles down. "I am sorry to expose you to my problems. We are having so much fun doing the ponies together. We seem to be at our best when working together. I can't wait to get back on my feet."

Josephine is at a loss on how to comfort Julio and his lifelong mother problem. Rather she moves to discuss getting to Buenos Aires. "Julio, the doctor says you have a mild concussion. Your fractured arm will heal in a week or two. Your broken femur is in a strap-on cast that will allow you to walk with crutches for about a month. He will release you tomorrow. Alessandra, Carlos, and I will be here tomorrow at 10:00 A. M. sharp to take you back to the ranch. We have a flight booked out of Miami at 2:00 P.M. Now I must leave to go with your aunt and get better fitted for riding and street clothes, boots, and equipment."

Julio immediately sits up straight. "Josephine! We have our own airplane. It is a DC-3 that we bought from the Columbian Air Force, an "avion fantasma," a ghost plane, what in Viet Nam was called 'Puff the Magic Dragon', now an old taken out of service gunship."

Josephine in disbelief, "That plane's production ended after World War II, and it still flies?"

Julio assuredly, "Oh yes, it flies very well, is very stable, and easy to control, with a capacity for 6000 pounds, it has been very popular in South America for cargo duty. We installed stanchions for transporting our ponies to fly five, three-year-old ponies weighing 900 to 1,000 pounds each."

Now Josephine, scratching her head, "But that plane is over sixty years old!"

Julio showing a great deal of confidence, "Reliable and rugged, that airplane is overbuilt to last a hundred years. At my grandfather's estancia, with its tail dragging wheel, I can land on grass pastures. It flies 1,500 miles at a cruising speed of 200 miles per hour at 10,000 feet. With it we fly to auctions from Brazil to Mexico and bring ponies to Florida for our use or for sale."

Josephine interrupts, "Ok, but Julio, for that great distance you can't fly with your injuries."

Julio insists, "With one hand and both my legs to work the foot pedals for the rudder I can fly that plane. And we have auto pilot as well. Besides, you told me you learned to fly with your father on a twin engine plane. Relieve me as needed, but also be my co-pilot. Just like in polo, we can do it together as a team."

"I keep my flying time up on weekends where I store the plane on the west coast at the Venice airport. I will file a flight plan with my laptop including a fueling and rest stop in Cartagena in Columbia with stops in Peru and Chile as needed. There are no creature comforts, except for the original passenger rest room, canvas seats, and cots; the open interior is fitted with aluminum pipe with floor anchors for the horses. Get me with Alessandra, Carlos, and yourself with all of your luggage and a suit case of clothes and riding gear for us all to drive back to Venice where we will board our plane and fly to Buenos Aires."

Josephine with renewed excitement throws Julio a kiss as she turns to leave, "Julio, copy that, and I can't wait to start flying!"

With the afternoon all on his own Julio fires up his laptop to file a flight plan. He also needs to know more about Mathew O'Connor. His Google name comes up with a list of items and photographs. He shocks himself out loud, "Josephine's husband is 55 years old! Josephine must be in her middle twenties." Now silently absorbing an impressive resume with photographs of presentations and speaking engagements, he mumbles, "He appears athletic and trim. And building a high-rise apartment building requires energy."

And like many wealthy men, Julio is sure Mr. O'Connor is at the top of the heap for anything he wants to do or be. And given his financial position and a man who looks and acts more like he is in his forties; Julio believes Josephine is loyal to that man. He confirms his respect and admiration for her with the thought, "If needed, she will go home to him."

Out loud, Julio makes a promise to himself, "I will do more with Josephine as long as I can. With her at the estancia in Argentina, we will come closer to each other, I am sure, as we pick new ponies for the international match at Palermo. Better to have her as a friend than not to have her at all."

On the other side of the fence, in Miami at his kingpin mansion on a bay harbor island, in Miami, Raul's mental recovery includes him having Sanchez checking the hospital about Julio's health. Sanchez reports to Raul. "Julio is being released today. What should I do?"

Raul replies, "When they leave, follow them and call me when you know where they are going. I know his mother was in Miami doing business. He has his plane in Venice on the Gulf but I don't think he can fly now. But with him going to Columbia to be with his mother to get better can be a problem for our business. We need to stop him on the way."

Sanchez with a hollow query, "How will you stop him? He has a fast car!"

Raul is in a vengeful mood, "He won't be driving his fast car with a leg cast. You will follow him and cell phone us his highway location. Wherever he goes, I will send out a friend of mine with his helicopter to drop off a present."

Sanchez, "Ahhhh, Si Patron, I am sure it will be a very welcome present."

Where Julio in a wheel chair waits, Carlos driving an SUV carrying Alessandra and Josephine and a lot of luggage, pulls up to the emergency entrance ramp. Alessandra jumps out of the vehicle to greet him with a hurried look, "Julio, you look great, but we must get moving now."

Julio objects, "What is the big hurry?"

Alessandra, in a hushed voice, "My dear nephew, Raul is still out to hurt you. He is ruthless and unforgiving, even with a legitimate loss in polo, but it also goes beyond that with his patrons in Bogota who are friendly enemies of your grandfather and all of his family, especially your mother and me!"

At this point Josephine, with fixed attention, holds back with any questions, believing that Raul is a never go away problem. Carlos helps Julio load himself into the front seat of the SUV with his crutches. Alessandra and Josephine go to the rear seat and Carlos drives a quick exit from the hospital north to State Highway 70 to drive around Lake Okeechobee heading west across Florida to Venice on the Gulf. Sanchez is quick to follow, but fearful of losing Julio he drives too close. Carlos, speaking out of the right side of his mouth, "Julio, we are being followed."

Carlos adjusts the right-side mirror for a rear view for Julio to look. "Yes, I can almost make out one of Raul's soldiers. Do you think it is Sanchez?"

Carlos squints, "Si, but he is looking upward to the sky. What is up there to look at?"

Julio now opens the sun roof window and looks skyward and sees nothing, but, "I can hear a helicopter." He pushed himself upward to get his head above the roof line. "It is black and unmarked just behind us, not even 300 feet above us. Dios Mio, hand me my pistol!!!"

Carlos opens the center counsel and grabs a loaded Springfield 1911 45 caliber, semi-auto pistol, "Are you going to shoot it?"

Julio immediately empties eight rounds, yelling, "There is a man leaning out and aiming an RPG grenade launcher at us! I got him to duck back in, more ammo quick!"

Carlos nods back to Josephine, "I'm zig-zag steering, get the extra magazines to Julio."

Josephine reaches over and stands up to hand the magazines to Julio. When she looks down again, she sees a machine pistol, a 9 mm Uzi, grabs it, sits back down and rolls her window down, asking Alessandra to hold onto her legs while she sets her back on the window frame and forces herself out of the vehicle looking skyward with the Uzi, aimed, locked and loaded.

Julio yells, "Josephine! Get back!"

Josephine looks toward him and with a half-smile turns upward, aims and unloads the whole 30 round 9mm clip on the chopper, while Julio shoots at Sanchez and the windshield of the pilot.

As fast as it happens, it is over. The chopper peels off with the shooter wounded and Sanchez drives off the road with a broken windshield and blown front tires. For a short while, just staring in silence on the road at 80 to 90 miles an hour and then slowing to 35 just before entering the cowboy town of Arcadia, Julio breaks the silence, "Where are the state troopers when you need them."

Josephine quips, "They attacked us in the middle of nowhere, land in every direction growing sugar cane, cucumbers, and no traffic. We are lucky. And thank you for carrying these weapons. Was it Raul?"

Josephine then looks at Alessandra, remaining calm and stoically silent, and asks, "Has this kind of ambush happened before? You have the look of experience on your face!"

Alessandra offers a platonic response. "We are successful among many striving kingpins in Miami. Some we call a hoodlum who makes his wealth by drugs, force, intimidation, robbery and murder. The commodity of Raul's wealth is drugs, prostitution, gambling, protection, extortion, and killing for hire. When it comes to Raul seeking social acceptance with his illicit wealth and his mansion in Miami, for those of us who make him look cheap and crooked on the polo field, we make ourselves his enemy just the same as in any gang war. Yes, this has happened to us before and Julio has a permit to carry a weapon. Gracias a Dios, he took the time to learn to shoot well. And Josephine, Santa Maria! Where on earth did you learn to shoot that machine pistol?"

Julio speaks up, "La Tia, Josephine is the daughter of a WWII bomber pilot. He taught her a lot more than we know, and we are now learning some of it." Then Julio looks at Josephine with a very sincere smile of appreciation, "Muchas gracias, you save us in our odd fields of battle on the road and on the polo field. We would be lost without you. I hope you can fly as well as you can shoot."

Chapter Four

At The Plane Alive

At the Venice airport and on-board the DC-3, Julio and Josephine enter the cockpit, sit and buckle themselves in with Julio on the left as pilot and Josephine on the right as co-pilot. At this point Julio begins speaking as an instructor, "Josephine, I know that you know that we are in a tool room with a lot of tools that need a lot of attention. In the cockpit, we only talk tools. The airlines call it a sterile cockpit rule. We begin with a check list, the all-important checklist, and your job is to scan all functions constantly and the horizon for any other flights in our corridor."

Josephine agrees with a nod. "As a co-pilot, I often flew with my father and am familiar with all of the items on the checklist, as well as being a practiced eagle eye in the sky. In Las Vegas with a confused tower using two different channels, we had a near collision, and with that experience, I am forever vigilant."

Julio emphasizes, "Yes, especially checking that the flaps are extended for take-off, the brakes and all gauges, radio, and transponder are functional, the elevation adjustment is correct with our charts, the oil temperature is up to 140 degrees, the checklist must be confirmed before take-off. In 1998 at the airport in Buenos Aires, a pilot with thousands of hours flying experience, with permission granted for taking off, at reaching lift off speed of 90 miles an hour he rotated upward. Without the flaps extended the plane went into a stall and came back down with a belly flop on the runway with only a few hundred yards left before crashing at the end and killing 60 people. With airplanes, there are no second chances for mistakes made."

Julio looks back at Alessandra and Carlos telling them, "You two are passengers and do not enter the cockpit except for bringing coffee and sandwiches. The cockpit is not a chatter box."

Alessandra chuckles, "Oh, this is one time you can tell your aunt to shut up? Ok, Julio, I love you still."

Carlos pulls up the ladder and closes the hatch. He and Alessandra buckle up in the canvas window seats behind the cockpit bulkhead. Julio confirms with Josephine that the checklist is completed with no problems noted, all fuses hot, and breakers closed. He starts the two 1200 hp engines with a roar and throttles them to warm up at idle, asking Josephine to check all gauges and fuel and oil pressure read-outs. With her "all systems go", he calls the tower, "This is Delta Charlie one zero one ready to taxi" The tower replies, "Delta Charlie one zero one, you are cleared to taxi to runway twenty-three." In a few minutes, Julio advances the throttles to steer the plane to a position facing into the prevailing winds from the southwest off of the Gulf of Mexico.

Julio calls the tower, "Delta Charlie one zero one ready for runway clearance." The tower replies, "Delta Charlie one zero one you are cleared for take-off to 3,500 feet on course 230 with a course change to 170. Maintain 9,000 feet for Cartagena."

With Julio's nod, Josephine pushes the engine throttles to full power, double checks the flap indicator for take-off and releases the brakes as Julio firmly holds the yoke wheel with one hand while taping his other arm in its cast onto the wheel to help control it with his shoulder while, without much pain, using both legs for rudder pedal changes with the full weight of his left leg cast helping with the port rudder pedal. The 1200 horsepower Pratt and Whitney Twin Wasp engines roar and pulse the entire plane with its power vibration and thunder. With Julio's firm guiding grip of his yoke, the plane runs straight and true down the runway. At lift speed, Julio calls, "Josephine! Rotate!" Simultaneously they pull back on their yokes and the nose of the plane points skyward. Once airborne, Julio takes control and eases up on the yoke and power to gently climb to 3,500 feet before making his turn to 170 degrees, a straight route to their fuel stop in Cartagena. At a cruise speed of 200 miles per hour, he increases altitude to an elevation of 9,000 feet to cross the Caribbean.

Josephine looks at Julio. "This ten-ton plane is a lot more work than flying my Dad's little twin."

Julio replies, "Yes, but in the sky, she is gentle and easy to fly. Are all systems, ok?"

Josephine, on a second check assures, "All systems go."

Now only eighty miles from Cuba, Julio announces, "We are now coming up to Cuba and will be flying over Havana. I am switching to their Havana tower channel."

Julio clicks the yoke mike switch, "Jose Marti Tower, this is Delta Charlie one zero one seeking permission to fly over Cuba en route from Venice Florida to Cartagena."

Tower replies, "Delta Charlie, we have your plane registered for permitted passage per your commercial license to land here. Who is the pilot?"

Julio snaps back, "Copy that, I am Julio Verelez, the person who applied for the permit."

After a short silence the tower replies, "Delta Charlie one zero one, you are cleared for passage over Cuban air space at an altitude of 7,500 feet. Be advised that a Pacific storm front is now over Panama and Costa Rica moving northeasterly at 15-25 miles per hour."

Julio replies, "Roger Jose Marti tower, now entering Cuban air space for fly over, increasing altitude to 7,500 feet. Thank you for the weather alert."

Josephine has to speak, "I didn't know you needed a permit for a civilian fly-over?"

Julio smirks, "Cuba's communism has a 'scratching the wall economy' trying to get pennies wherever it can. In Castro's days, they worried about a spy fly-over, but now with satellites, the US military can read license plate numbers. And today, the permit is free for tourism. Otherwise, they charge."

Josephine starts digging a little deeper, "Is it that much trouble to fly around Cuba?"

Julio is happy to answer with his expertise but cautions her with a wagging finger about chatting in the cockpit. "Well, this is cockpit information so I will answer. It is not trouble; it is fuel consumption. We carry 830 gallons. Our range is 1,500 miles while our straight-line distance is 1,300 miles. But with a storm or strong head winds we could run out of fuel before reaching land if we do not have extra flying time in reserve. For this flight per Cuba's tower, we now watch for an approaching Pacific storm front. In four hours, we may encounter the front or back of that storm. Our cabin is not pressurized and we cannot fly over the storm and we will encounter winds up to a gale force over 45 miles per hour. In just a half hour those winds will suck up a lot of gas."

Josephine, now with a serious concern, "I am glad you are on top of this. You must have a lot of experience flying over the Caribbean."

Julio elaborates, "We fly all over the Caribbean and around South America for horse-trading and I also fly for my mother's veterinary medicine business. And on pharmacy deliveries I have landed in Havana over the last several years. Our foreign registry in Columbia also helps with getting over flight permission at a reasonable cost, zero."

Julio thinks for a second, anticipating Josephine's next question and continues, "And no, we are not communists, but we are not anticommunist. We have farmers on the easterly side of the island. They grow herbs for our medicines. Fidel did appreciate our business and allowed us to use a confiscated farm house to manage the farming with my cousin who lives there. With my mother's business competitors equally as active there, I wonder how he is doing."

All goes quiet for two and a half hours and Alessandra brings forward sandwiches and coffee. She jests, "Here you go Julio, your un-favorite ham and cheese. And how is our co-pilot doing? Are you hungry for a sandwich?"

Josephine replies with a singing voice, "I feel fine as wine, and ham and cheese are great. This flight is a new Julio adventure for me." The relaxed mood abruptly changes when Julio raises his left hand and yells, "Madre mia, look! a thunderhead is on our starboard side, fast-moving cumulonimbus clouds over 10,000 feet ramping high winds. We can't fly over them. Josephine, get ready to steady the yoke pedals with me. Don't let them knock you out of your seat. Carlos you first, then help my aunt fasten her seat belt. We are in for a bucking bronco!"

With the heavy rumbles of thunder and blinding flashes of nearby lightning producing a cracking sound louder than cannon fire, the roar of the engines fights the hard shifting winds and down drafts. The plane bounces violently, swinging side to side with Julio skidding the plane sideways to keep on course and fighting to keep level, often dropping hundreds of feet from the swirling down drafting wind.

Julio yells to Josephine, "For going through this heavy turbulence, just hold on to your yoke and move it with me as we fight the twists and turns. Josephine nods affirmative, jamming her teeth and growling at the storm and the heavy control torque changes. Both show no panic and a great deal of grit. Fighting the storm is like sailing into the wind, making little headway but staying on course remains the task. After a half-hour, they passed through the storm front. The sun also went down at the same time. Then Josephine, finally letting up on the yoke and taking a deep breath, checks the gauges, "Julio, the fuel is down to less than two hundred gallons! Our GPS shows we are 210 miles from the Cartagena airport!"

Julio tightens his lips, "It looks close. Click me to the airport traffic control frequency A." Julio hits the button, "Cartagena CTG, this is Delta Charlie one zero one on a flight line 170. Do you read me?"

The tower controller responds, "Delta Charlie one zero one we don't have you on our radar. You are cleared to land on runway 19 just off the water coming from the north on your flight line. There is a northeasterly wind crossing you near land. Hold your altitude till you approach for a landing."

Julio is now thinking, "Cartagena CTC, we are low on fuel and may arrive with a dead stick."

"Delta Charlie, keep us posted as you approach. We will have emergency vehicles standing by. We will notify our coastal police of a possible crash landing on the water off our runway. We will keep them posted with our frequency."

Julio, "Roger, Cartagena. Proceeding as instructed with clearance to land."

Julio side glances at Josephine, "We have a chance to save on fuel consumption, by the minute, if we can pick up some speed with a possible tail wind approaching land. Go tell my aunt and Carlos to break out life jackets and the inflatable raft. Think positive. However we land, with no gas, we have no fire or explosion."

Josephine, "Yeahhh, That's positive alright."

Josephine un-belting and going behind the bulkhead, "Alessandra and Carlos, we have a problem, low on fuel. Julio wants you to break out the life raft and life preservers."

Alessandra immediately standing up, but not shaken, "My dear Josephine, it is time for us to form a circle and pray to the Lord for a safe landing."

Josephine and Carlos and Alessandra reach out joining hands to pray. "My Lord, we pray you for your help for our safe landing. Our faith in you is our strength in this time of need. Our thanks for all that you have given us as we live our lives in your name with the grace and blessings you have given us. Amen." Carlos makes the sign of the cross, "Amen." Josephine, with her right hand on her heart, repeats with gusto, "Amen!"

Julio yelling back to the cabin, "What is going on back there?

Josephine, I need you up here, now!"

Josephine jumping back into her seat buckling up, "What's up?"

Julio, now worried and excited, "I can see the compass showing the wind pushing me off course. Watch my pedal action for the rudder. I will skid the plane to get back to our course!"

Josephine watching Julio's muscles strain reaches over to wipe sweat from his brow. Julio approaching physical exhaustion, asks in a huff, "What is our air speed?"

Josephine loud and clear, "Wow, we are going 225."

Julio asks, "Am I on course with our GPS?"

Josephine squirming a bit, "There is a slight squiggle off course but we are back on our line."

Julio asks again, "How far are we from the airport?"

Josephine clear as a ringing bell, "One hundred miles."

Julio now very nervous, "How is our gas?"

Josephine with a frown, "We have less than 150 gallons."

Julio estimates, "That would give us 80 miles. We are out of fuel 10-20 miles from our landing. I am backing off the skid with the tail wind. We need to pick up five more minutes of flight time to get to the airport. Say a prayer!"

Josephine jitters with a razor voice, "They are praying again, and so am I!"

As the lights off the coast become visible on the approach, the engines start coughing with some back fires, and the fuel pressure gauge bounces up and down.

Josephine with hope in her eyes, "I can see the airport beacon. We are ten miles out!"

Julio. "Dios Mio, the starboard engine just quit. Feather the prop to reduce drag. We can land with one engine."

Josephine scared but calm, "Oh shit, the starboard tanks are empty. And the port tank needles are bouncing on empty!"

Julio offers some hope, "I can pick up some tail wind to roll a turn to make my 19-degree approach. I'm nosing her down now and loosing elevation and airspeed for a landing."

Josephine gleefully crows, "There's the runway!"

Julio in full command, "Pull back to half throttle on 2! Lower landing gear! Flaps down now!"

Josephine does her job with conviction, "Gears down, flaps down!" Now frozen and braced for a crash, she yells, "Oh my God! Number 2 is quitting, just one more mile, please!"

The Caribbean waves offshore at the foot of the runway glitter with reflected moonlight as Julio guides the plane down to one hundred feet, coming up to the beach perpendicular to the 1.58 mile runway. Carlos and Alessandra, closing their eyes with hands held tightly, continue to pray.

Julio, now with clamped and exposed teeth, "Hold on to your wheel, we are going to drop down hard!"

Five seconds later, the DC 3 hits the runway pavement with a bang and a big bounce up and another bang down, and then a minor bump up as it settles into a solid landing with the tail dropping down its rear wheel to the ground. With the sudden dropping, the plane stops less than halfway down the runway. Sirens break the silence on board as trucks approach the plane. Julio looks at Josephine totally exhausted, but happy. Just sitting there is all that they can do.

The tower calls, "Delta Charlie, is there a need for an ambulance?"

Julio, "We are ok. We landed just when our engines quit. We need a truck to pull us off of the runway."

The tower, "Delta Charlie, we will tow your plane for refueling to slot 15 in our open tarmac."

Julio, "Roger, tower control. Thank you. Over and Out."

Unbuckled and standing together at the hatch, they all cheer with joy, "Hoorah, Happy Days! We made it!" And after climbing down the ladder from the plane, they wantonly kiss the ground. Julio, barely being able to walk, "Time for a meal and a good night's sleep. There is a bed and breakfast behind the passenger building. We can ride back with the tow truck."

Booking is no problem at the Hostal Arrecites. Julio and Carlos share a room and Josephine and Alessandra another. Without much to say, they hungrily scarf down a cold meal and drag themselves to their rooms to sleep.

Alessandra, almost asleep, "No need to undress, just lay down and sleep."

Josephine, in a hollow voice, "I am so tired. But happy we made it.

And Julio, I am happy to say, boosted my energy with his confidence."

Alessandra replies, re-awakened as a proud aunt, "My dear, you are one among many women that he has impressed with his strength and courage."

Josephine, "Yes, I can understand that he is gentle and accepts women as an equal partner, in our case with me as a team member. Yet why does he speak so harshly about his mother?"

Alessandra now offers a cautionary background on his mother. "My sister Lucia is a mountain of stone. I have never seen her cry. She shows no emotion or love for him and never has. Life is all about her. Julio is a burden that she fences in and owns like a dog. I have my sister's assigned duty to look after him almost as a prison guard. And yes, he also overwhelms me. And I love him as my son, not hers."

Josephine, "And he has no respect for his father?"

Alessandra, "His father is a pompous, arrogant fool, but dangerous with a temper. At a squash match, he beat a player unconscious with his racket for making a shot that lost him the game. After watching you play polo, for him you can be sure that you are more than a curiosity. Even though you are a married woman helping Julio, you may want to keep your distance from his father. He has had many affairs which Lucia tolerates while she masterfully leads him around with her leash."

"Regarding you, his mother is unpredictable and you should be wary. Regarding me, she will not be happy over this near crash tonight. She knows that Raul tried to kill him in that match, and she did nothing for Julio. I think that attempt is caused for some business reason, about what, I don't know."

Josephine confirming her commitment, "I am here because I like Julio, Carlos, and you. I am doing what I like with horses, which I have missed now for many years. I hope my presence will not create a problem for you or Julio. And I will leave if you tell me to."

Alessandra offers a compliment, "You make Julio happy and that makes me happy. We will work it out. His grandfather is a fine gentleman and will shield us from his oldest daughter's daily domineering cruelties."

Josephine sighs contently, "Thank you. Now I can sleep much better. Good night Alessandra."

The next morning, fully rested with a breakfast, coffee and a basket of sandwiches the Julio crew makes their way to their fully fueled plane. With little said and very business-like, they board the DC-3, to take their positions. Julio starts the engines, Josephine runs through her checklist and Alessandra and Carlos, with belts buckled, once again make the sign of the cross. With tower clearance for taxi and take off, Julio announces, "We are off to Lima, our next fuel stop. For the next seven hours we have clear skies and boring views of endless, seamless green, tree-topped jungle."

After two hours in the air Josephine could no longer stand the silence and speaks up, "Julio, do you think we can relax your silence rule in the cockpit for just a little while?"

Julio scans the horizon and then looks at Josephine softly saying, "I will put our ship on autopilot. We can talk for a while before we get to Lima. What would you like to know?"

Josephine starts with a big question, "I have never been to South America. And I know nothing about Argentina. What is Buenos Aires going to be like when we get there?"

Julio begins with the big picture. "Argentina is like the United States. With people from all over the world settling here in the last hundred years, it is a melting pot. Our climate also includes subtropical and sub-Antarctic temperatures with our land stretching 2,360 miles north and south and 880 miles wide east and west at its widest point with our borders in the shape of an upside-down triangle. Buenos Aires is our cultural capital and frankly the cultural capital of South America. Our food is the greatest and our steaks can turn a vegetarian into an ardent carnivore."

Josephine breaks in, "What about art? I like going to the theatre."

Julio begins with a boast, "Oh, Buenos Aires has three hundred theatres playing in different languages, with plays popular on Broadway or Japanese traditional dance and stories. Cinemas are also everywhere. The people of the city demonstrate and support the arts with art fairs and many independent cultural centers reflecting the many different ethnic backgrounds of our people. Music with special bands and concerts are everywhere. The broader European cultural influence is very strong, including authors and poetry. And Che Guevara was born and grew up in Argentina and was a part of our social democratic movement."

Josephine interrupts him again. "Che Guevara! He was a violent revolutionary!"

Julio continues, "Yes, that goes to another part of our culture for which I must prepare you. The country's mood revolves around a very expansive freedom, in many ways unruly, yet very friendly, some say even wild. We have laws but enforcement is weak, or lacking. There are no security cameras posted to watch traffic or street scenes in commercial areas. And there is minimal restriction on public and private behavior."

"Crime often goes unsolved. Petty theft is everywhere. You have to watch out for pickpockets and purse stealers, cutting your straps and running away with no one to stop them. Out around Plaza de Mayo, a giant walking boulevard, on the subway, busy streets, buses, going into banks and at ATMs and even in restaurants, you have to watch. But for important people, wealthy people, especially foreigners who come here to play or work, the greatest fear is kidnapping for a huge ransom. We have foreign automotive executives managing our many plants for making cars and car parts for different companies. They often travel in armored limousines with bodyguards and are provided well-secured residences."

Josephine wonders, "My God, how does the city survive with such uncontrolled crime?"

Julio very seriously states, "Our city harbors extreme poverty concentrated in Cuidad Oculta, the "Hidden City" with over 16,000 people and many well-trained children and youngsters who learn the arts of stealing just to survive. To me, the chaos of crime committed against anybody and everybody is a kind of warped freedom and tolerated. I believe that in the end, it will be our downfall with massive and destructive riots, many of which we have already had in the past. This behavior led to the dictatorship of Juan Peron and the Junta, and now our current situation with a poor economy and a failing government, another dictatorship can always be at hand."

Josephine still a little skeptical with Buenos Aires being a large metropolis, "Your frankness is well appreciated, but how bad is bad?"

Julio is digressing a lot, " Like it is in the states, the dark side of our culture is drugs. Argentina is plagued by an addiction to readily available Paco, a toxic, raw cocaine processed with kerosene. It is a cultural habit chewed for energy and to feel good. But without moderation, that poison can cause delusions and rage leading to self-destruction. Our problem is also compounded with Columbians operating in Argentina as a sanctuary escaping Columbia with army and DEA crackdowns. In our jungles and northern hills, they operate well-hidden and seek to corrupt the police and government officials. Smuggling tons of cocaine from Columbia they process it with gasoline, then crystallize it and crush it to powder for packing in their labs along with methamphetamine. But Peru, Bolivia and Chile also make and distribute cocaine and simple coca a native plant leaf. Finally, marijuana is also very popular and like your country, Argentina is eliminating its use personally as a crime."

Josephine, now very concerned, "Can the Columbians be stopped?"

Julio is almost giving up, "Our borders are porous with no border patrol. Active smuggling from Bolivia, Chile, and Peru goes on with no difficulty."

Josephine now incredulous, "How can it be? Doesn't the government do anything?"

Julio hardens his tone, "Oh, with four million of our people in poverty, cocaine is just for the better to do and those who steal to buy it. Actually, our country is open to smuggling to and from. It is also a transit point for cocaine by the ton received and delivered all over the world. Sadly, many people are calling our plague a benefit to our economy. It is called cocaine tourism, attracting visitor users from Europe, the US and Canada."

Josephine with a shrug said, "If you could, would you try to stop the smuggling?"

Julio lowers his head, narrows his eyes, and thoughtfully speaks in a low tone, "Josephine, I see it all around me and I despise it. I have seen how it destroys people's lives and lowers the quality of life, such a good life that it can be in this blessed country. Yes, if there is something that I could do, I would do it. The warfare that follows me is not because of my dentistry and polo; I believe it is because of what my mother does. I am suspicious of her, for I cannot believe the competition for veterinary medicine is deadly, yet everywhere I go I am confronted with violence because of my mother's business. And she tells me nothing about her business and orders me to fly her goods when she can't arrange her own transport. But say nothing about my feelings to my aunt. She is a wonderful person but utterly loyal to my mother Lucia."

Josephine quietly nods to assure Julio of her silence. And their conversation ends with a dreary silence.

The only other break for seven hours is a pleasant conversation that comes with Alessandra cheerfully greeting her favorite pilots. "Good afternoon, I am flight attendant Alessandra, coffee or tea and a sandwich? We have smoke cured ham on brick oven baked rye bread, and Swiss cheese."

Julio cracks a smile, "Yes, my dear lady, I would like you with my meal as well?"

Alessandra snaps back, "Oh, you warm my heart, but how could you want this old lady with such a lovely co-pilot sitting next to you?"

Josephine chimes in with a laugh, "Aha, I am a married woman and my husband is always watching over me, even at 7,500 feet."

Alessandra sighs, "It is still nice for a woman to feel wanted. Thank you, Julio."

After flying over the Andes between mountains going up to 20,000 feet, Julio makes a short stop at Lima for gas and some leg stretching along the runway. In an hour they are back on track for another seven hours to Santiago and on to Buenos Aires. The engines become a welcomed droning sound with a calm flight, gentle winds, and a clear blue sky. Josephine keeps checking the gauges, GPS, and the horizon for other aircraft. The view is now from offshore along the coastline going south and the sun is getting close to setting as they near their next change in course going east to Argentina.

Julio calls into Santiago's Airport tower control for his approach to their air space on their channel frequency, "Santiago tower, this is Delta Charlie one zero one, do you read me?"

Santiago tower controller, "Delta Charlie, we read you. Have you on our radar approaching from the north. What is your destination?"

Julio, "We departed from Lima en route to Buenos Aires. Are we clear to fly over Santiago?"

Santiago tower, "You are cleared to fly due east at 7,500 feet. Traffic occurs at 3,500 and 5,000. The weather is clear with calm winds at ten to fifteen miles per hour. Keep up your visual at all times for emergency flights with the military or unregistered private traffic."

Julio. "Roger, Santiago tower. Thank you, keeping a channel open." Then he looks at Josephine, "That statement about unregistered traffic can be black ops for anything illegal."

Josephine nods with disbelief and a question, "Oh my God! You mean we could crash into a plane flying illegally? What kind of smuggling would that be?"

Julio replies, "Drug traffickers from Chile, Columbia and even Argentina. Commercially this airport is the sixth busiest on the continent, serving as a hub for all traffic including international lines worldwide. With their heavy traffic we are fortunate to gain a clear corridor."

Josephine looking past the city horizon with a worried look, "Are those mountains around the city?"

Julio familiar with the landscape, "We are on the skirts of the Andes at 2000 feet. With our good weather we will be crossing the tail of the Andes near an old volcano at 6,500 feet. We will be approaching the mountains with a light tailwind and an updraft. If we experience bad winds, the downdraft would be deadly and we would be flying to the north to follow the highway through the passes between the mountains."

Josephine with preciseness, "Our GPS indicates we are 706 miles from Buenos Aires."

Julio, getting weary but cheerful, "Aha, at last, in a few hours we will be arriving at the Paris of South America!"

Alessandra shouts from the cabin, "We hope so."

Breaking over the small mountain range proves no problem with an hour of desert encountered before flying over the lush green Pampas for which Argentina's beef production is famous. At this time, Alessandra enters the cockpit asking Julio, "Are you going to inform Ricardo of our arrival?"

Julio agrees, "Oh, yes, it would be good for him to meet us with the estancia car."

Josephine queries, "How are you going to call him from up here?"

Julio proudly exclaims, "No problem, we have our own monitored short-wave frequency at the estancia. Please turn to channel 7."

Julio now speaking charged with authority, "Estancia Vega,

Estancia Vega, Estancia Vega, this is Delta Charlie one zero one, over."

Estancia, in a dull tone, "We read you Delta Charlie."

Julio coolly replies, "Please put Ricardo on."

Estancia returns in a vibrant voice, "Ricardo on, what are your instructions?"

Julio confidently requests, "Meet us at our destination in two hours with the estancia security vehicle."

Estancia's Ricardo reliably confirms, "It will be done, over and out."

Josephine now curious, "That was short and sweet."

Julio, with a wary tone, "Yes, the airwaves are constantly scanned for chatter by smugglers and thieves. We don't want to give away where we will meet and who is coming to meet us or we could be in trouble. Oh, and the word security is a give-away describing an armored car with weapons at hand. And we are even safer also speaking in English."

Josephine in disbelief, "Yikes you do this all the time when traveling by air?"

Julio. "People that exhibit wealth, from clothing to cars to airplanes are targets on foot, in cars, at train stations, and at events, especially polo, the sport of the wealthy in Argentina."

Josephine now curiously looking down over the pampas, "Amazing, the pampas is all green with large squared off fields."

Julio expresses a great deal of pride and then some sourness, "Those are part of the large estancias. Look over to the right. There is an estancia of several thousand acres with a winding road and culde-sacs. That used to be an estancia and ranch, now a subdivision for wealthy residents and their million-dollar homes."

Josephine looking across the horizon to Buenos Aires, suddenly sees an incredibly sprawling view of civilization, "Is that Buenos Aires, a mass of squared off, road-defined blocks of land, all filled with homes all along our horizon? From up here, it looks like a white carpet speckled with red roofs."

Julio confirms the immensity of the view, "Fifteen million people have to live somewhere and land is a precious commodity. All of those homes are side by side with narrow walkways between. Please place the radio on channel 8."

Julio now in Argentina speaks with an imperial voice, "Buenos Aires Airport tower, this is Delta Charlie one zero one, approaching from Santiago at 7,500 feet requesting permission to land."

Buenos Aires Tower, "Delta Charlie, make your pass at 3,000 feet over to the water for your approach to runway 13. You are cleared to land and cleared to taxi to your hanger on the tarmac at the end of the runway."

Julio confirms, "Roger tower, proceeding as instructed."

Julio and Josephine land the plane like pros and on this last leg, Carlos and Alessandra did not make the sign of the cross. Julio taxies the plane to the twin-engine commercial hangars at the end of the runway where two airport security vehicles keep guard. With the hangar door already open and Ricardo at the ready, he flags Julio to the opening and signals to cut engines. Carlos opens the hatch and drops the ladder and all come down to the open arms of Ricardo, "Bienvenido a casa, we have missed all of you and are anxious to prepare for the international polo match at Palermo. I have brought the armored car fully gassed and loaded with your preferred arms just in case." He looks to his side and with great surprise, "I see you have brought with you this wonderful senora. Mi querido Senora O'Connor, your performance in West Palm has made you a star for our team here in Buenos Aires. Bienvenido a Argentina!"

Chapter Five

Making The Estancia Alive

As everybody boards the four-door six seat converted Cadillac Escalade SUV, Josephine notices the hangar full of stacked boxes on three tiers of heavy metal shelving and looks at Julio asking, "Is there any room for your plane with all those boxes in the hangar?"

Julio punches his reply, "For safe storage space, there is no better place to store goods than at this airport. Our mechanic will park the plane in the hangar and work over the plane. With living quarters in the back, he also carries a gun and radio for the airport police."

Josephine asks, "Is your estancia on the pampas?"

Julio nods, "Yes, we are in the Province de Buenos Aires on the northeast side, away from the city via route 9. Water rights are important to us and our location borders a small river."

Ricardo interrupts, "Si, the estancia is beautiful. We have a polo field and oval track for speed development, ample stables for our horses, a wonderful hacienda, and we groom our fields to raise cattle traditionally with our vaqueros. After a moment he continues, "On the way, please keep your eyes open for bad traffic."

Julio fills in with, "Bad traffic means trouble like we had before."

Josephine stiffens up and Carlos and Alessandra once again make the sign of the cross. Julio is a likely target for kidnapping. And Julio's family has quite a bit of influence in Argentina because of his mother's business and his father's military connections, some of which go back to the bad times when kidnappings and murder by the police and military were commonplace. Once out of the airport compound, the airport police escort waves off, and Ricardo proceeds northeast on Ruta 9. Once past the downtown area Julio becomes nervous, and passes a word of caution to Ricardo already looking hard. The street suddenly looks like an unused movie setting, too empty with no walking traffic. Coming around a bend in the road, Ricardo spots a road block of old cars. With the brakes slammed, a hard wheel turn, and a floored accelerator, he reverses direction. A second too late, a flatbed truck blocked the rear. Julio pulls out a grenade launching M-16, opens his door standing on the running board and shoots at the vehicle. The hit blows it to pieces with the gasoline in its tank creating a giant flaming ball. At the same time AK 47's opened up on the SUV from the rooftops on both sides of the street.

The Suburban, containerized with two-inch plate steel and bulletproof glass stops the plinking steel rounds to the roof and sides with ear deafening intensity. Julio jumps back into the vehicle as bullets slammed his door shut over his hand. Looking at Josephine he yells, "Jump over the seat and grab this automatic rifle."

Ricardo demands, "Does she shoot?"

Julio in pain screams, "Si, she shoots! Drive like a demon and open the sunroof for her to stand up in."

Ricardo floors the engine to run through the shattered parts of the destroyed truck as Josephine grabs the Kriss Vector, with a high rate of fire and 30 round clips. Josephine pops out of the roof to her shoulders and suppresses the AK 47's with a broad sweep from one side of the street to the other. Then a fool with an RPG on the roof of a two-story house took too long for his aim and Josephine brags with a huge growl, "I got that bastard!"

As she empties her rounds, Julio passes her another clip and yells, "Keep shooting!" Reloading with click lightning, she targets with sureness and precision, all that she learned from her Dad in clay competition in Arizona. Five of the attackers are down, and three are now running.

With the road cleared, Ricardo drives at speed to get away from the ambushing neighborhood. Josephine quickly drops down and holds Julio while opening the door to free his crushed right hand. Shaking violently, Julio starts going into shock.

Josephine asks Ricardo. "Is there a hospital nearby? Julio needs emergency first aid now!" Ricardo replies, "There is a clinic one mile away. I will keep speeding. The local police will be coming soon."

Alessandra prays and cries at the same time while Carlos takes Josephine's seat with an M-1 Carbine to watch for any more attackers. They make the clinic in five minutes.

At the emergency room a diffident doctor concludes, "Senor Verelez, you have had a serious break in your wrist. I see you are recovering from a broken leg and fractured arm. I don't know what you do for a living, but you will need bed rest for at least a week. Our x rays show no serious damage; however, there is no sense in taking chances. I will send a nurse tomorrow to check on you. "

The doctor then looking at Josephine, "Senora O'Conner, is it not?" Josephine, "Yes."

The Doctor continues, "You are indeed a heroine this day. Senorita Alessandra said you killed five terrorists single-handedly and saved Senor Verelez, the grandson of one of our prominent citizens whom we appreciate and respect. It is fortunate for Senor Verelez that you know how to shoot. Is this your first visit to our country?"

Josephine rather clumsily replies, "Yes, I came here to help Julio select new ponies for his polo team....."

The Doctor interrupts, "Ahhh, polo, a great sport."

Then he directs his next comment to the both of them. "As is the case for this kind of incident, no news has been released and as far as the clinic is concerned you had a road accident. The military police will take care of all other matters."

Looking at Julio, "Our ambulance will take the both of you to your father's estancia with a police escort."

Julio thanked the doctor as the nurse wheels him out of the emergency room to the loading ramp for the ambulance. Julio is still awake enough to thank Ricardo as they wheel him to the ambulance.

Captain Garcia of the special home guard greets him with a wink and closes the door to the ambulance behind Julio and Josephine.

Julio, with his eyes fluttering, "Josephine, it all happened so fast."

Josephine grimaces a bit, "Why you, why me? This was planned and they knew we were coming by time and place. What is it about you that brought this on?"

She finally lets loose, "Do you know we barely survived?"

"We are just lucky to be alive now," as Julio kisses Josephine's hand, "and it is because of you that I am alive."

Josephine now reverses her tirade realizing something good also happened. "I have never been so close to being really alive or dead, than when I have been with you." And then she thinks to herself, "I never felt more alive than now."

Julio, with intensity, tries to answer her questions. "It may be because of my parents, the attack, that is. That was no kidnap attempt. They want me dead."

Julio's parents flew in from Columbia the day before Julio landed his plane. With his grandfather they anxiously await Julio's safe arrival at the hacienda, and to meet the lady who saved his life. As the police escorted the ambulance and Ricardo, driving the SUV, approach the gate, Julio's mother Lucia and father Adolpho, headed by his grandfather Damian Vega de la Dega stand at the columned portico hacienda entrance, waiting to greet Julio and his team. All are looking sharp for the occasion including formally dressed vaqueros, with sombreros in hand. Lucia, dressed in a stylish black and silver threaded ghoulish twenties-looking Parisian gown, draped with a multiple stranded diamond necklace, stands there speaking irately and loud enough for her father Damian to hear, "Why must Julio always bring trouble and attention to us? His escapades never end. Someday this will be the end of him!"

Adolpho, dressed in a military style jacket, sheepishly agrees, "Si, he is just so careless."

Julio's grandfather with a tight-lipped smile replies, "Oh, after defeating the Bogota team in the Florida championship, he is a hero. That woman with him delivered great goals to help win the match." Lucia picks up on the last comment as the ambulance stops, "Si, she is a married woman. Where is her husband?"

Adolpho, with a broader smile, couldn't resist applying his false wisdom. "She is very interesting for Julio, I am sure."

As the driver opens the rear door, Josephine looks out and smiles while the attendants slide-out Julio on his wheeled gurney up to the porch. Josephine steps out to follow.

Julio's Grandfather Damian, with arms outstretched, "Greetings my grandson and greetings to you Mrs. O'Connor. We are relieved that you survived that road attack without any injury, but Julio, your hand, will it heal for the world tournament at Parma?"

The attendants lift the gurney end for Julio to speak, "Grandfather! We have worked hard to get here for this great event. And we will do our best."

At that moment Alessandra and Carlos come up from the SUV with Ricardo, "Greetings my daughter, and Carlos, it has been some time since you played for us here. Mrs. O'Connor, I would like you to meet my other daughter Lucia and her husband Adolpho."

Josephine nods her head with a formal smile, "Please Senor Degas de la Vega, call me Josephine."

"Agreed, with pleasure, and please call me Damian."

Josephine looks Lucia straight in the eyes with a slight nod to Adolpho, "It is a pleasure to meet you Senor and Senora Verelez"

Lucia, also with a formal smile replies, "Since we are being presented as a family by my father, call me Lucia and my husband is Adolpho."

At that point, Damian ushers all into the main hall to meet for a late dinner.

Two vaqueros take over the task of moving Julio's gurney, with one whispering to him, "Where did you find her? They tell me she killed five attackers shooting from the sun roof of our SUV. Is she from the military?"

Julio painfully laughing, "She is the daughter of a WWII veteran and used to ride in the American rodeos. She knows horses and is here to help pick our ponies for the tournament and may ride with us. And yes, she knows how to shoot very well without hesitation and with the focus of a combat veteran."

The vaquero replies respectfully, "Your choice is our choice. We have never worked with a woman, but why not? We saw her playing on the video, and are impressed."

At the dinner table, Lucia directs a question to Josephine, "What do you do to be so good at killing people and riding ponies in polo?"

Josephine picks up on the attack, "Oh, you have seen me ride as you videoed our win in Florida. I grew up on a ranch in Arizona where we bred and breathed horses and horsemanship. Now, I am the wife of a wealthy developer who supports my activities while he is busy making money. And you know how much time making money takes, I mean with your business, especially when it interferes with seeing your son in a hospital after our win in Florida!"

Lucia replies haughtily, "Well, I have never been so insulted. How dare you question my concern for the welfare of my son! You have no place here to speak that way to me ...especially since you are here with my son without your husband!"

Adolpho snickers a bit and is about to speak when Damian interrupts Lucia, "Now, now, Lucia, we all know how devoted you are to Julio and your business. And we thank Alessandra for her helping Julio at the ranch in Florida. Josephine is also a helper and a very good one. She now has had firsthand experience with the drug syndicates arriving here from Columbia to do their business and for some reason thinking we are their enemy, or at least at this point, their competition for polo fame."

Josephine speaks up, "Yes, our last tournament involved a battle with a drug kingpin in Miami called El Machismo. After we beat him at polo, he ordered a helicopter attack on us as we drove to Julio's plane to come here. But that aside, my cell phone doesn't work here. Do you have a telephone that I can use to contact my husband to assure him that I am in good hands at your estancia?"

Damian signals to a servant to bring a hard-line phone and insists to speak to Matt as well.

Josephine takes the phone in hand and dials the US entry number and Matt's direct number for his cell phone. And that takes about a minute to achieve.

Josephine hears the buzzing ring and the click, "Matt, this is Josephine."

Matt surprised and excited, "Josephine, my darling, it is so good to hear your voice. I was beginning to think you had forgotten about me. Are you OK? How was the trip and where are you staying?"

Josephine in an assuring tone, "Matt we arrived in Buenos Aires today and are now at the Estancia de Vega de la Dega in the Province of Buenos Aires. Tomorrow we start choosing the ponies and then train them for the international tournament in the city." Damian motions for the phone.

Josephine, "Honey, Mr. Degas would like to speak with you."

Damian in his broadly confident voice, "Mr. O'Connor I want to thank you for allowing your wife to assist us with this most important tournament. She has been a God send for us. We are amazed with her riding talent and horse knowledge and know that she can help us win the championship."

Matt replies in a calm and controlled voice, "Mr. Degas, Josephine is full of surprises with her talents. I trust you will be sure to keep her safe. I cannot come to be with her at this time and rely upon your hospitality to include a meaningful and successful visit for her."

Damian, "Mr. O'Connor, my hospitality includes my duty to make my guests safe, comfortable and free to pursue their activities with us here at the estancia. We have the best vaqueros to watch, guard and help her with the ponies. And Julio is at her side at all times." Damian hands the phone back to Josephine.

Josephine, "Matt, all is going well. You have the phone number here and I will keep in touch."

Matt, "Ok darling, I am sure you can work things out and make the trip worthwhile. Just don't get hurt. Take extra care, you are in a foreign country in a city which has a high crime rate, especially with tourists."

Josephine bites her lip, "OK my darling, I love you." And she shuts the phone off.

With the dinner ending, after a long day they all bid good night and are escorted to their rooms. Alessandra had the room next to Josephine and Julio went to his old room down the hall, while Carlos went to stay with the vaqueros in their quarters in the next building by the stables. After an exhausting trip including some air lag, all slept well.

Chapter Six

On The Pompas For Ponies

The next morning, as usual, Alessandra bangs on Josephine's door, "Josephine, wake up we have work to do!"

Josephine springs to the door, opening it with "Aha," fully dressed in her riding gear including knee boots.

Alessandra, "Bueno! You are ready to come to breakfast with me. I will be your guard as we sit with Lucia and Adolpho. Julio is already up and out at the stable to get the horses for your ride and camping overnight on the river."

Josephine, "How can he ride with all of his injuries?"

Alessandra, "He still needs to recover and you will be going with Carlos and Guillermo. They will show you the herd and help round up your choices. Julio will join you with a four-wheeler at the end of the day to go over the pony choices with you. In a week you and he will break and train them along with Carlos. We have short wave radios to keep in touch while on the pampas."

At the breakfast table all is not friendly.

Lucia, "Ah, there she is the heroine of the day, and without your husband to cheer you on? I am amazed about your ability to do so much, fire weapons, ride ponies, fly airplanes and yet you do so little as a wife. How does that work for you?"

Josephine, slightly on edge trying to eat a fancy Argentinean specialty, a candied cake, "Oh, you must agree that love includes trust and commitment. We love each other and are committed to each other for our happiness based upon shared desires to live with each other knowing that even when we are apart, we are together in soul and heart."

Lucia, now very skeptical replies, "Is that what marriage is all about, or is it his money?"

Josephine, "He trusts me and I trust him. Is that something you don't understand?"

Lucia, now showing a temper, "I understand that you are a gold digger and still looking around for another money roost, perhaps because your money man is running out of change."

Josephine with contempt, "My husband could buy this estancia for cash and would turn it into a resort with condominiums, a club, restaurant, golf course, shooting range, and for his friends in Texas, also a landing field for private jets."

Lucia, now shut down a bit, "Oh really, I want you to know I am watching you and warn you to keep your eyes and hands off of my son. He is not for your entertainment!"

At that moment, Adolpho speaks up, "Por favor, but you are welcome to entertain me all you want."

Lucia, "Shut up you fool!"

Josephine, "While we are at it, why don't you tell me about your business that takes so much time away for your family and son?"

Lucia, "My business is none of your business. And I will be sure to keep it that way!"

Alessandra breaks in. "Enough of this, Josephine let's go to the stables."

Josephine nods, takes one last bite, and leaves the table with her arm out stretched with a famous Italian arm gesture.

With all others out of the room Lucia in a lower voice speaks to Adolpho, "I do not trust her. She is up to something and taking control of Julio. That means trouble for us and we cannot allow it to happen."

Adolpho, no longer consumed with his pretension of self importance, "Of course, mi querida, what would you like me to do?" Lucia, "Not yet, but start thinking about an unfortunate accident, after the polo tournament. After all we still want to win and she is obviously good at that, as well as her gold digging."

Adolpho, "Si mi querida, there will be many opportunities around Palermo after the tournament from there to here. Perhaps even at the stadium."

Lucia, "Muy bueno! But keep your hands off of her until then. Comprender?"

Adolpho is not looking back. "Si mi querida." as he walks away to watch at the stables.

Just then, Damian comes down for his breakfast and sees Lucia pensively staring at herself in a mirror on the wall. "Lucia, mi querida, what are you thinking on this bright Monday morning?"

Lucia smiles falsely. "Buenos Dias mi padre. I was just thinking about all that has happened and am concerned about Julio. He has had so many injuries and close calls. I wonder if he should go back to Florida to recover."

Damian is incredulous. "Que? He is our only chance to win the tournament."

Lucia, "I understand, but I think that woman is a bad influence on him. She shouldn't be here."

Damian, "Are you serious? You saw her play. Her strokes, her posture, her aggressive moves and body language, it's as if she talks to the ponies without speaking. On top of that, Julio's riders all want her on the team. They are a true team working for each other to get a goal. There is no high riding in their action, just great coordination and a spirit to win."

Lucia, "Si, padre, but I still think she will be trouble for us."

Damian, "Es absurdo. And you make yourself sure to show more common good behavior. I will not allow you to upset a winning applecart. Comprender?"

Lucia, "Si, mi padre."

Lucia has no intention to make life easy for Josephine.

With Carlos and Guillermo, the chief vaquero, and two other riders, and Josephine, select five range horses and two pack horses for camping equipment and food. Saddling goes quickly and quietly. As Josephine mounts, Guillermo cautions her, "Senora O'Connor, that chestnut horse has a mind of its own. It always wants to go back to the stable. He sometimes breaks away with a gallop."

Josephine, with her standard, "I know what I am doing tone." used at rodeo's, "Gracias Guillermo, that is why I picked this horse. He is well built like the Andalusian horses of Spain. He is tall, well shouldered with a straight back, arched neck and full hind legs. He has good conformity for balance and I like his blaze face. Is he a threeyear-old? And I respect his strong mind that will make him a winner. He knows I know it. We will work well together."

Guillermo, "Si Senora, we just broke him in last year. Many of our native horses have Spanish blood. That is the reason why we bring them together in a herd to do their own breeding. Given his aggressive behavior, he will not be intimidated on the polo field."

Josephine replies, "Bueno, he may well be my ride for the cup. Does he have a name?"

Guillermo, "No, as he is now your friend, feel free to pick a name for him."

Josephine has some thinking to do on that one. After she and the crew take a half day ride out to a slightly hilly, heavily grassed area when once over a knoll, they come upon a small heard of mares, fillies, and foals, dominated by a mature black stallion. Guillermo speaks quietly, "Don't move suddenly or make any noise. The stallion is watching around."

Josephine whispers into her horse's ear as she rubs his neck, "Be calm my friend."

It did no good. The stallion gives out a smart snort and whinny call reaching the perked ears of the dominant black stallion, no doubt challenged by Josephine's horse.

As the herd starts to run away from the crew, Guillermo yells, "Time to ride. Force them to the river directly in front of us."

For Josephine this is no different than herding cattle, but the speed and maneuverability of the horses doubles the challenge.

Carlos, riding alongside Josephine shouts, "I am going to cut out the stallion. Keep pushing the herd."

With his whip and the skill of a Spanish picador, Carlos separates the black stallion from the herd. At the ridge just before the river, the chase ends as the herd settles down at the river bank in an open-ended spacious coral.

Josephine whispers, "I will ride slowly up with my horse. Without the black stallion he will calm them down even more. Come up slowly and stake yourselves around them and start bringing in the gates to close the corral."

Guillermo motions to the other vaqueros and they quietly gather the gates on the ground at the open ends of the coral. In fifteen minutes, the herd is safely contained. And another vaquero brings up the pack horses under his reign. Carlos shows up later after a lengthy battle keeping the black stallion away from the herd. After staking, unsaddling the drive horses, and settling back for making a meal with a camp fire, the conversation brings the group back together as a team. Guillermo offers a compliment to all, "It was a good drive." The others voiced loudly with a laugh, "Si, and we did it with a great rider." and with a bit of a friendly jibe, "And she is a woman."

Just then the sound of a four-wheeler can be heard and their walkie-talkie barks, "Vega riders this is Julio. Do you read me?"

Carlos replies, "We read you. We are at the river. Drive up to our campfire."

Julio confirms, "Roger, Vega riders. I see your light, over and out."

It is getting late and with Julio's arrival, after a full day, they all agree to turn in to their pup tents for the night. Julio walking Josephine to her tent quietly lets her know his feelings for her, "I missed you. Could we talk for a while at the campfire?"

Josephine softly responds, "Sure."

Julio asks, "How did it go today?"

Josephine, "It was great! Your vaqueros showed great skill and I didn't know that they use short whips to direct the herd and to keep it together."

Julio, "Yes they always carry whips. They are called rebenque. Did they give you any problems?"

Josephine, "Oh, they have been good and showed me their appreciation as a joke, with us doing so well, with me, a woman, and we all laughed."

Julio, "Do you think we can be a team with you as number 2, me as number 1, and the other four as defense and Carlos to back you and me for offense?"

Josephine, "Yes, and I now have a name for the horse I've ridden and choose to be my polo pony, his name is Bandit."

Julio, puts his hands on Josephine's, smiles and whispers, "That makes me so happy. Tomorrow we pick our new set of ponies to be. And I want to tell you that after all our time together; you make me happier than I have ever been. I like being with you. Is that ok with you?"

Josephine now pressed to speak with a smile but with slight watery eyes, "Julio I know what you mean and I can only be with you as a friend. I know it happens this way, but you must understand. We can work and play polo together, but I am bound to my husband and will not disappoint his love for me. Again, I understand your feelings for me and they reach deep into my heart. Please, I need to sleep."

Josephine stands up and walks away without looking back as she enters her tent. The next morning after some hot coffee and firewarmed bread with meat and cakes, the riders go to the coral to pick out eight horses, usually two young stallions, just under age to be with the herd, with the rest two to three-year- old fillies. Julio prefers dark horses, so the buck and pinto marked horses he ignores in favor of chestnuts and sorrels for offense and bays for defense.

Josephine asks, "What kinds of confirmation are you looking for?"

Guillermo speaks up, "No short necks, no long necks. As you said with picking your horse, for polo we want arched necks with straight backs that flow into the hind quarters for balance and efficient maneuvering."

Julio adds, "Si, I look for Arabian blood, with big eyes and dished heads to favor endurance and large nostrils for a better supply of air for speed."

Carlos adds, "Don't forget to look at their jaws. Large jaws reduce quick direction changes."

Josephine concludes, "Well that ends an education in choice. Is there anything else?"

Julio adds the last word, "Ears, we like ears that rotate front to back in order to hear from where the play comes."

In two hours, the horses are picked and the vaqueros tie on ropes and headgear to trail them back to the hacienda. Once there they put them in a corral for training and for a relaxing evening they walk to a barbeque on the veranda behind the hacienda. Light guitar music highlights a fabulous beef meal, some drinks and then they retire after another long day.

The next week is a matter of finding out if it all comes together, despite the problems with Lucia. It takes another week for Julio to get back on his feet. Josephine and Julio go out into the pastures to run the horses they collected and finally select the final sixteen pony string for the international tournament. They have another two weeks to train and practice on the polo field at the estancia and the large oval track to work up speed and endurance.

On the northern side of the world in Texas, Matt, busy as ever, keeps thinking about Josephine and how she is doing. In the back of his mind Matt has a blind spot. He knows nothing about the Vegas clan and this Julio, the leader of the polo team. To keep things on the quiet side, he thinks to contact an old friend, Mannie Landren, disability retired with battle scars from the DEA. Matt sends him an email, "Hey Mannie could you do some checking for me on the QT of a guy named Julio Juan Verelez (de la Vega)?"

Ten minutes later Mannie emails back, "Julio Juan Verelez (de la Vega) has a dual citizenship, in Columbia and in the US. He has a degree in Dentistry from the University of Detroit Dental School and has a practice and residence in Sarasota Florida. His parents own a veterinarian pharmaceutical business in Bogota, Columbia."

Mannie then adds more questions than answers. "This Julio, he's a dentist and yet from a wealthy family. And yet how does a dentist afford a ranch in West Palm, a polo team, and keep an open account from an off shore trust fund that basically pays him whatever he wants, whenever he needs it, to do whatever he wants to do, including owning a commercial airplane registered in Columbia?"

Matt nods and quips to himself. "Hmmm, horses are what is going on?"

Mannie adds another email with some amusement, "And I understand he's being paid one million dollars a year to maintain that polo team, and that his grandfather Damian Vega de la Dega owns a large estate, an estancia, in Argentina near Buenos Aires that basically raises beef and also polo ponies for a profit."

Matt is getting more quizzical emails back asking, "How often does he go down to the Argentinean estate, I mean estancia, to buy polo ponies?"

Mannie replies after another ten minutes of checking, "Well, at least once a year, I think. But this guy comes and goes without leaving tracks. He keeps his plane in Venice, Florida and records flights to Mexico and from there we don't know where he goes. Oh, he also lands in Cuba now and then."

Matt emails again, "Isn't that an awful lot of flying for polo ponies? What kind of plane is he piloting?"

Mannie quite interested about it, checks the registration, "He flies a DC-3, a former Puff the Magic Dragon gun ship salvaged from Vietnam, and sold to the Columbian Air Force. He bought it decommissioned and registered it back in Columbia. With a decent cargo capacity, the plane is rigged to carry horses. I guess he gets his ponies every year because he runs them to the ground, and then sells them for pleasure or any other purpose."

Matt gets clinical, "That's interesting and who maintains the ranch, I mean estancia, down there?"

Mannie, totally engrossed in this research, emails back, "It is owned by his grandfather, a former general in Juan Peron's army. His father Aldolpho Verelez is also a former general in the Argentine army."

Matt impatient finds the emails too much and calls Mannie on his cell phone, "Hi Mannie, that's quite a story. I would like to know more about his parents and their pharmaceutical factory in Bogotá. I want you on site. Go to Bogotá to research their operation. Raising cattle and horses can't support a polo team. It's his parents, not his grandfather, that rack up the money."

Mannie replies showing interest, "Matt, I am just a broker in real estate, ahhh but not very busy......."

Matt interrupts, "Ok, this is unofficial, an off the grid assignment. Mannie, your experience with the government people in Columbia fighting the cartels, as well as your fluent Spanish make you a prime candidate for some undercover work. And it is the kind that you are used to doing. I will open a black box account for you with an open budget. No limitations. I know your blood hound instincts and you won't stop sniffing till you find out what is going on in this situation."

Matt adding a point of honest concern, "Please understand, this is for a friend, Josephine O'Connor. She is at the estancia in Argentina riding with a polo team for an international tournament. I believe she is getting into deep water with the Verelez people. I need to find out how deep the trouble might be and then to get her out of there before problems erupt."

Mannie shrugs his shoulders, "As long as it is ok on your end, I can do that. Might be some fun, but it's not going to be without sticking my neck out. Violent crime is still a heavy prospect and those people solve problems personally."

Mannie arrives in Bogota on the 15th at 2:00 A.M. Juan Valdez, his old contact with the DEA, meets him at the gate. They sit down at a table in the airport to set up logistics for the next week.

Juan opens up with, "How's it been going with you, Mannie?"

Mannie a bit dull from the flight, "Oh I am doing well in real estate brokerage in Las Vegas. I try to stay away from the tables but every now and then I do lose a commission. Juan, how is your family?"

Juan proudly smiles, "We are doing fine, we have another child that makes four. My wife is very busy these days and with me too!"

Mannie, ready to change the subject, "Hey that's great. How are you doing with the drug enforcement business?"

Juan recovers with a straight face, "The federal government is not giving us enough money and the US is not working as hard to keep the "wanna be kingpins" at bay. We have killed the biggest pig, Pablo Escobar, but now they come out of the jungle trying to replace him. They still murder people who get too close to their operations. So, you are interested in finding something about one of our illustrious families?"

"Yes", replies Mannie, "Verelez, the man I am investigating is Julio Juan Verelez."

Juan perks up, "Ahh, the Verelez family, yes I know of them but not personally, the wife is of an old Spanish heritage, the de la Vega family, but they moved to Columbia from Argentina because Adolpho Verelez, formerly of the military junta that ruled the country, foolishly lost the war in the Falklands. The Junta was overthrown by a popular revolt in the streets with a democratic government established. The Argentine people still fume over the loss of the war. And Senor Verelez was lucky not to be shot. But his wife over the last twenty-five years, with the help of her father in Argentina, and his contacts in Spain, developed a pharmaceutical business and Adolpho, a general who couldn't run or win a war, pretends to be running it."

Mannie asks for more, "Well, what kind of business is it?"

Juan continues, "They manufacture veterinary medications for dogs, pigs, horses, cats, even parakeets."

Mannie sharpens his question, "What kind of shipments do they make, what kind of volume do they do?"

Juan starts to wonder himself, "It's really kind of strange. They basically ship between Spain and Columbia by air cargo and they also ship to most of South America. But a lot of shipments go to Argentina because of the husbandry industry there with, hogs, horses, and cattle."

Mannie raises his eyebrows. "I see, so do they have a network for distribution?"

Juan continues, "We investigated this company because of its great sales volume. There are two blind corporations owning 60% of the company, with the rest owned by Julio's family, his father, his mother and her sister."

Given the basics, Mannie keeps on, "Where do they manufacture these pharmaceuticals for veterinary?"

Juan replies, "We are not completely sure. We know they import medicines from China shipped out of Shanghai. For doing medicine research and for quality control of the shipments they receive from China they have a small lab here in Bogota. After receiving raw shipments from Spain, and assembly of components into pill or liquid form, they route product to Argentina for quality control and labeling. From the pharmaceutical company and their manufacturer in China, shipments go out to all parts of the world under their label."

Mannie captures a better frame to make a picture. "They have a fairly complicated network of marketing and production. But these links, are they just business or cultural, like the Spanish speaking people for the link in Spain?"

Juan replies with a counter, "You would think so, but the names on the shipping company from Spain, coming through customs, are Russian. I don't think it is strictly cultural. There may be some other ties with Russian distributors or producers. With Julio's fame as a polo player, we discovered that there is a Russian polo team in Azerbaijan, sponsored by Georgian's that produce off-the-shelf medicines that may be another positive link."

Mannie is gravely certain. "Ok, ok, this is starting to sound like a drug story."

Juan smiles nodding in agreement, "We have done all of this investigating because initially we were suspicious of that link as well. We have found nothing, nothing at all coming from Spain that implies they were shipping drugs from Turkey to Russia or from Russian contacts. That would be opium trade that we would be concerned about. But with low labor costs and government preferences, Bogota has ten of the world's largest pharmacies operating here doing the same thing, importing low-cost components for over the counters by the gross, re-tabulating them and shipping elsewhere all over the world."

Mannie, undiscouraged, continues on the same track, "But what about cocaine?"

Juan rebounds with an interesting detail, "After our persistent shut down of most of the processing labs in Columbia and our constant raids into the jungle, the lab operators migrate to less stringent countries to the south including Peru, Chili and Argentina. Those borders are not patrolled. With a trumped-up sanitation inspection of the Verelez labs here, we could find no evidence of cocaine processing. But odd to us is the very large pills they develop for large animals. Finally, the Verelez location here makes sense with other larger pharmacies in the city. As for horse medicine, Columbia also has a fondness for polo and horses. We have a regular Cavalry Guard in the capital that we put on parade and use for ceremonial occasions. And our polo team always competes internationally in Buenos Aires. Even so we have checked those kinds of shipments and found nothing incriminating."

Mannie grows unsure about everything, "Ok, let that rest for a minute. Let's go back to China."

Juan proceeds, "Ok. We have checked China shipments too and those basically are legitimate veterinary medicines for heartworms and other ailments for four-legged animals."

Mannie still trying to close some gaps, "But you don't check anything being shipped out of Columbia, do you?"

Juan admits without a problem, "No, we don't really have a reason. We basically verified the legitimacy of the business and have not been monitoring shipping out from Bogota. They basically get shipments in, they re-label, re-package large quantities of pills in smaller doses and with the Internet they sell those through their distributors around the world."

Mannie finally feeling sure about what to do, "From the ground up it looks like a legitimate and profitable business with a pretty sophisticated marketing network with some big money backers in the 60% ownership. They have a product that links them with all the medicine producing areas of the world and their network of consumers is worldwide."

"For veterinary medicines that is correct. It is all straight forward." confirms Juan.

Mannie roundly concludes, "No, no, I am not talking veterinary medicines. Juan what I am thinking is they are using veterinary medicines as a cloak to ship illegal drugs and the business helps launder the money they make from primarily cocaine and other bad stuff including heroin and meth."

Juan still shakes his head in disbelief, "Well, there is a drug that they do ship that we don't really have any control over. That is morphine."

"Aha, morphine is a bi-product of opium." quips Mannie.

Again, Juan confirms. "Yes, and it is totally legal for pain in horses and other animals."

Mannie agrees to disagree, "It is all too clear to me. They have one heck of a racket going on. We've just got to figure out how it is working. Let's take tomorrow as an opportunity to go and investigate their pharmaceutical lab."

Juan scratches his head, "How do we do that without being too obvious? I need a good reason or I will hear about it from above."

Mannie agrees, "No, we don't want to alert them. I think we need to go under cover. How about pharmaceutical salesmen? But for them to even talk to us, we would have to be a big company rep. Do you know anybody in town that might be helpful in that respect?"

Juan answers quickly, "Noooo. I have no contacts in that area. You might have to go back to the United States for some credentials that could be used."

Mannie agrees again and with little ado he bids Juan a farewell as he books the next flight back to Texas with the intention of forming a plan to dig deeper under cover.

Chapter Seven

Dinner For The Generals

Julio, now confident with team preparations and training, still carries lurking doubts about his mother and father's veterinary business. Today, he and Josephine prepare for a formal dinner for ten special guests arranged by his grandfather Damian. With a long dinner table fully set with fine china, crystal wine and water glasses, gold candelabras and silver service, the hosts patiently wait at the entrance steps of the hacienda as chauffeured limousines approach the circular drive. As each vehicle unloads its passengers, Damian, dressed in his former uniform full of medals and ribbons, hails a welcome to equally dressed full uniform military men with their wives in evening gowns. Damian introduces Julio and Josephine as they reach the foyer of the hacienda. (Because of Adolpho's past history in the military, he and his wife Lucia do not attend.)

One after another the officer core of Argentina in full regalia makes its presence felt as they move into the large expanse of the lounge area in front of the dining room for a service of cocktails and hors d'oeuvres. The center of attraction is the Generalissimo, the supreme commander of the Army, Navy, and Air Force. The other three generals act as his aides de camp. Another important gentleman is Colonel Vegez, in charge of the internal security for the country and related to General Hidalgo, one of the aides in charge of the Air Force.

Random groupings fill the room with pleasant chatting. Julio's grandfather then announces that dinner is served. Everybody with their partners seats themselves at the long dinner table with their names lettered at each location. Julio and Josephine sit near the head of the table close to Damian, and the Generalissimo. The dinner progresses with the servings appropriately focused by Argentina's legendary steak, grilled asado sausages, chimichurri salsa, empanadas, and alfajores, sweet shortbread biscuits, all with a variety of grilled vegetables, and a table full of sweet cakes, cookies and pudding breads.

After the pouring of wine, the Generalissimo rises and offers a toast, "To Argentina. May its government live long and provide for the people."

All rise and repeat the toast in a very military fashion. With that being done Julio's grandfather stands up to make one more toast. "For the winning of the international polo competition at Parma, this toast is for us. Against the best polo players in the world, may our polo team win the honor and the cheers of our people."

With that, all stood and loudly repeated, "For Argentina! To the best polo players in the world, Salute!"

With a broad smile, the Generalissimo turns to Josephine and winks, "So, you are the woman who saved the life of our polo team captain. I am impressed with your good shooting. My security officer tells me you killed five men, including one with a rocket launcher on a roof."

Josephine politely replies, "Yes sir, we had no choice but to defend ourselves. Julio also launched a grenade from his passenger side before they opened up with AK 47's."

The Generalissimo leans closer, "Be assured Senora O'Connor. We are concerned for your safety, Julio's, all of the polo team, and this estancia. We can't have an American woman polo player harmed at any time let alone before and part of a world event."

Josephine with more confidence, "Safety is an issue. And we very much appreciate your concern."

The Generalissimo goes on, "What you are doing, is for the people of Argentina. Our creditors like to see success in many ways, including sports. We have loan commitments with the World Bank supported by your country and many Americans invest in us with their plants that keep our people better employed."

Josephine sees the light? "I didn't know how important Argentina's image in the world could be."

The Generalissimo now increasing his voice to be heard by all, "Winning this tournament will help us grow our economy, increase pride in our country, and give our democratic government our military support to overcome the many problems we have here."

Josephine asks in frustration, "Do you know who and why they attacked us?"

The Generalissimo's eyes roll back, "We have many discontented groups. Some are violent. We suspect outside influence from Columbia, Chile, or Peru. Not the governments, but the kingpins of smuggling who want to keep our country weak for their own thriving business in drugs, guns, or the human trade. If our team wins, our ability will be increased to fund improved patrols and law enforcement. In this area, our credit report has not been good. And it will be better with a polo win."

Josephine very respectfully asks, "How does your President and Legislature move to deal with these problems?"

The Generalissimo raises his right eyebrow, "Senora O'Connor, I swore to uphold our constitution. They are counting on us to help them maintain order and stability when needed. They are developing new laws, rules, and regulations to deal with our poverty, illiteracy, illegal drugs, street crime, and terrorist combines. And we are always ready to carry out their orders and enforce them as needed."

Josephine now turns her shoulders to him and with a pretty smile and an upraised voice and a salute, "My dear Generalissimo, you are my hero. God bless you."

At that moment, the entire table stood up and in unison cheered, "God bless our hero!"

That cheer ends the dinner. The women withdraw to the lounge area and the men withdraw to the smoking room with a billiards table and comfortable chairs. At the gentlemen's smoking room, Pedro, a lifetime servant with the family, brings in a selection of the finest cigars and distributes them along with a very old single malt scotch. With glasses full, once again a toast is made. This time it is simply, "To us, Salute!"

The Generalissimo engages small talk with Julio. "It is very fortunate that your team mate helped you stave off your attackers. She is indeed a beauty with the kind of talent we need for this game."

Julio responds, "Her hitting that RPG saved our day. I think they meant to kill us."

The General agrees. "This is not typical. We have run convoys and patrols up and down that highway for years staving off those predators who seek to kidnap and collect ransoms, but never using grenade launchers. They melt into the mountains, hillsides and neighborhoods without a trace, if we catch them at it, we fight them to the death, for they will not surrender."

Julio's grandfather is looking sideways to listen when Julio asks the next question. "It was indeed unfortunate that your special military police were not on patrol. But it seems like an odd time of the day for a convoy to be running the highway."

The General responds, "Nonsense, we change our schedules constantly to try and catch them off guard. That's the end of it. We continue to make our patrols to capture or kill them."

Julio's grandfather, Damian, in an attempt to change the subject interrupts. "How are you doing in selecting your horses for your polo team?"

Julio enthusiastically answers, "I have two good black stallions. They ride well and are very alert. They have a lot of energy that will make my team more aggressive. We captured six-, one- and two-year olds with a lot of energy. For those along with your current stock, Josephine, Carlos and Guillermo train them with patience. For the game the ponies are proving themselves to be excellent choices."

Although the billiards table starts raising the level of noise in the room, little do the men know that in the second story room over the smoking parlor, Lucia and Adolpho have their ears to an opening in the floor, listening intently, as best they can, for what the Generalissimo is saying. His very deep base voice can be distinguished from the others, but the cracking of the billiard balls and exclamations of "Bueno, a good shot!" make it difficult.

Adolpho is having no luck listening and asks Lucia, "Can you hear anything?"

Lucia whispering, "It sounds like they are talking about sixteen. I think it's polo ponies."

Just then the Generalissimo looks at Julio's grandfather and speaks gravely, "Don de la Vega, we are concerned for the safety and success of your son and his team, including Senora O'Conner, especially at the tournament. We will be posting plain clothed security at your ponies next to the field, near your vehicles and around the grandstand. They will be following you wherever you may be going."

Damian agrees. "Si, that is an excellent idea. We really need to be more careful. There is no sense in taking chances."

Adolpho upstairs impatiently whispers, "What are they saying now?"

Lucia with a scowl whispers back, "They are going to put surveillance on Julio and the team around the clock."

Adolpho admits, "That is a problem for me."

Lucia stands up and speaks with her commanding tone, "You have a new job. Make sure Julio is safe. We now have to worry about the Columbia people winning the tournament or somehow keeping Julio from winning. Is that Miami pig El Machismo coming to the tournament?"

Adolpho shrugging his shoulders, "I don't know, but what about Senora O'Conner?"

Now lethal, Lucia with her tight lips and nasty tone, "We must wait on her!"

Julio concerned more than ever about the violence of his current visit to Buenos Aires, questions the Generalissimo, "I don't understand. I never had problems visiting Buenos Aires, no problems with the people in the hills, or the city. Where is Argentina going now?"

The Generalissimo consoles, "Times are changing. It's not our people. Terrorist agendas vary but are ludicrously radical. They ruthlessly attack and discredit the social and government structure of our country. They are preaching anarchy, confusion, chaos and fear in order to gain power by a revolution in the streets. One day they attack an embassy of the United States. The next day it's Brazil or the French embassy. Then they ambush a military convoy. It is all designed to appear random but the lesson is classic guerilla warfare per Chez Guevara. The pattern is disruptive to cause a lack of confidence in our government so they can take it over in the name of the people but really for themselves."

At the Ladies Lounge on the other side of the hacienda Josephine sits with the military officer's wives drinking lightly. Polite conversation starts out and then falls quickly to gossip, the interesting kind. In this case, Julio, a famous polo player at Parma becomes the topic of interest. Pointing at Josephine, they tell her with a snickering kind of admiration, "You are lucky, you with such a man, as a friend that close to you with your husband so far away. Of course, it is obvious that Julio is smitten with you!"

Josephine with all her skill holds her breath and with somewhat of a smile, "I certainly am lucky to ride with him, all for the game of polo!"

The Generalissimo's wife unloads a ton of gossip, "Mi querida, I am so happy that you have been spending time with him. It is so nice to see him with a real woman instead of a Niña. I know he had one in Buenos Aires last year. He would leave the hacienda for weekends at a time. And you ought to know that Julio has been doing this for many years and will probably continue to do so. It seems to be a habit amongst our men to think that they have to have younger women with them at all times."

Josephine being mildly amused, "Julio seems to be fairly interested in me for my polo skills, and I am so happy that he is. I enjoy being with him and it has been wonderful to be riding with him. Maybe there is a change in his life coming, about that, he could leave me in his past. Our time together is something we never want to forget. And you must know that I take him into my heart but not into my bed. I am true to my husband."

The other military officer's wives giggled a little bit. "We agree and play the interest game with our husbands all the time, despite a Niña."

The evening grows late and the hacienda is more than large enough to host all of the guests overnight and such is the plan. The military officers with wives withdraw to their rooms. Julio bids his grandfather good night as does Josephine and both Julio and Josephine retire to their rooms.

Not much later, a woman laughingly knocks on Julio's door, "Are you there?"

Julio with an equal laugh, "And who is knocking on my door?"

The woman stands patiently behind the door, "It is a lady fair wishing to be with you. Would you like me to come in?"

Julio guessing it is Josephine "Mi querida senora, you realize you will be entering the boudoir of a man very receptive to your wishes."

"All the more to be interested in you," she responds. "Would you open the door for me please?"

"Mi querida la senora, with great pleasure I would do such a thing."

He quickly opens the door. Before him stands a most beautiful lithesome woman. Her long hair drapes over her shoulders and flows playfully around her breasts and down to her waist. Her most inviting hips joined her thighs beautifully. Her smile says I know what you want and I am giving it to you. She introduces herself, "I am Tina. I am a present from your mother."

Back in Dallas, Matt anxiously reflects upon Josephine's touchy situation. It's like holding on to a phone waiting for a delayed answer with music playing. She just isn't calling every day or even once a week. Just then his cell phone rings with a foreign exchange on it. Matt slaps it to his ear, "Hello, is that you Josephine?"

Josephine speaks in quiet tones, "Hello my love. I am speaking on a house phone. It is difficult to call you from here."

Matt, happy to hear her voice, "I understand darling. How is it going with you?"

Josephine opens up, "I have learned a great deal about polo and am going to ride in the international competition with Julio's team. With getting that done, there are problems here with people who want us to lose at polo and with the loss to interfere with his mother's business for some reason."

Just then Lucia picks up the house phone extension, "Who is on this line?"

Josephine cracks, "This is Josephine. I am speaking with my husband!"

Lucia retorts. "Bien, get off the line now! I have important business to conduct."

Matt rudely interferes. "Hey, with such a big mouth, from where did you get your lack of manners?"

Lucia screams, "How dare you! Your wife is our guest for polo, certainly not you."

Josephine's voice cuts in, "I'll call back later darling. Bye for now."

That call toughens Matt's suspicions about Julio's parents, hoping Mannie's investigations prove very interesting. He assures himself that Josephine is on top of the situation as much as can be expected. Somehow, someway, Julio is tied in with his parents' business and he will learn how through Josephine.

Matt then calls Mannie who is back in Bogota. "Mannie, I just talked with Josephine and Julio's mother rudely cut us off of the only hard-line phone at the estancia. How does the Verelez business look in Bogota?"

Mannie unloads a lot, "The Verelez family operates around the world. Juan and I are under cover clerking in their shipping department. Loading and unloading barrels and boxes of this and that and various containers, we are noticing a pattern of interest. On certain shipments, there is always an orange-colored band around the wrapping for a loaded pallet that would be moved by fork lift into a separate corner in the warehouse."

Matt showing a special interest, "Mannie, let me know when you find out more. Be careful. I don't want you to stick your neck out." Mannie assures Matt, "Don't worry too much; the Columbian agent working with me is now more interested in the Verelez operation than you."

Matt concludes, "AOK my friend, steady as she goes."

Mannie ends, "Copy that!"

In Bogota at the Verelez Tridexan Pharmacy warehouse it is siesta time. The warehouse is not air conditioned and quickly empties out for a few hours. Even the labs are shut down for this time of the day. With this opportunity, Mannie and Juan, also taking their break, walk over to a corner of the warehouse where the orange striped pallets are located.

Mannie notices, "Juan, these various packages originate from Spain and China."

Juan contemplates aloud, "We have never paid much attention to them because basically they are already pre-packaged and preformed pharmaceuticals for husbandry animals primarily horses and pigs, including some antibiotics."

Mannie wonders, "Did you ever test the antibiotics?"

"Si, although they looked harmless enough, we pulverized them and found nothing that indicated cocaine or heroin. We sent a package to the FBI coming back with negative results."

Mannie thinks it out. "If these are all prepackaged and preformed drugs, why do they take these back into the lab. Do they remanufacture the pills?"

Juan remembering, "I did not notice that it was being done. When we saw these in our original inspection, we assumed they were just being held for reshipment."

Mannie adds a negative direction, "No. I saw the lab technicians coming out here and taking one of these boxes back into the lab."

"But that must be just testing for quality," figures Juan.

Mannie now hardens his words, "No, they came in the next day and took another container. In fact, they have been taking a large container each day from the same lot and I don't see them returning the same containers. They end up outside for recycling."

Juan plaintively replies, "I don't really know where you are going with this, because we do have our dogs to sniff for cocaine and heroin on every shipment that comes through. We check for materials that would even cover a scent such as coffee. We have not found anything except the clean shipments that have come to this facility. They are branded and named and used as branded for veterinary pharmaceuticals."

Mannie at this point getting edgy, "Yeah, I know. I know. That's what bothers me. The pattern is there but we can't find the material. We can't find any clue of what's really being passed."

Juan replies, "Bueno, maybe it is just our imagination overlaying something on a standard business in Columbia that looks suspicious because it is pharmaceutical. It looks suspicious because it runs from Spain to China and ships all over the world."

Mannie with a striking idea, "Yes, we need to go to Spain to find out from where the Spanish shipments originate."

Juan delightfully agrees, "Bueno, I would be happy to accompany you to Spain. I have not been to Madrid for many years and it would be a very pleasant experience for me, even though I know we are going there for a fairly dangerous reason."

Mannie, now the blood hound, wants a covert approach. "Let's not make contact with Interpol and the Spanish authorities and set up our own investigation for next week. We need to track down the source of the Spanish shipments and don't want to alert the shippers that they are being watched."

Juan agrees. "It makes sense. I will go back to my superiors and make the proposal. I am sure they will agree. But I am getting some political pressure because what we are doing is beginning to leak upwards. I suspect that the Vega de la Dega family will soon be informed of our work at their Tridexan plant. That means Senora Verelez, the rude woman you heard on the phone, a demon, a screaming banshee, a herald of death and destruction, may present us with what has happened to many young people here in Bogotá and that is a death squad."

Mannie replies without even thinking. "We shoot first. But why take chances here with your system catching on to our game and passing it to our suspects. I'll put you on my budget. Why don't you take a vacation or go to see a sick and dying relative so we can stay undercover without your superiors."

Juan knows Mannie barely survived a kidnapping in Bogota. The Wall of Honor at the DEA headquarters displays eighty-four agents killed in the line of duty. DEA agents, especially undercover, risk torture and murder from cartel bosses operating in Columbia who get feedback on them from the criminal investigation system.

What started out as a simple private investigation already has left a footprint with the drug enforcement agency in Bogota and the DEA. Worse than that, the CIA, investigating several families in Bogota for their ties with terrorists of the Che Guevera kind, start to sniff out Mannie. Back in Dallas, his one-man real estate office experiences a break in, rifled records, and a missing computer hard drive.

Juan gets personal time off from his agency and proceeds to get undercover IDs as well as arranges for pick-ups in Madrid for pistols with silencers, Uzi's, some C-4 plastic packages with timers, and miniature hand grenades that are about the size and appearance of a pack of cigarettes. Ipod style communicators also keep Juan and Mannie in touch with a range of three miles. At a very high frequency they can penetrate concrete walls.

Mannie warns, 'I am glad we will have hardware to carry with us in Spain. We are going to need it. And I like your pen name, Manfred Witherspoon, Hah!"

Chapter Eight

Off To Spain Under Cover

Back on track, Mannie and Juan arrive in Madrid looking for the warehouse and manufacturing facility that ships to Columbia. The facility they quickly located by return address contains one hundred thousand square feet of space. As they drive up to the rear loading gate, they see suspicious features.

Mannie in a miffed voice, "Hey, there are only three loading docks to provide for shipping and receiving for a place that big?"

Juan glibly adds, "Of course, when you don't want people seeing what you are doing you have a rail line into your building with an inside, secured, loading dock."

Just then a heavy steel rail door opens as a diesel yard switcher rolls into the building. A few minutes later coming out, a box car trails behind it.

Mannie notices, "They must have just taken a delivery of something. That box car from Germany is empty with its doors open."

Juan now getting excited, "They just released that empty to roll onto a side track. The switcher is picking up another car on the other side. This one bears Italian markings on it for the City of Turin."

Mannie more excited and now aggressive, "Juan, the outside of the plant has no workers around. The workers need to be where the box car moves into place at the dock! Let's run down to the track and grab onto the back of the switcher to get inside the door and drop off before anyone sees us."

Juan disagrees, "If we had those overalls that the other workers have, we would have a pretty good chance but I just noticed a rifled guard sticking his head out of the track door. Let's go back, get some coveralls and come back tomorrow."

Mannie not hesitant, "Oh sure, it would be legitimate for the operation of a pharmaceutical company to have armed guards around valuable cargo like medical supplies. But we need to take the chance now. That guard will be walking back to the box car by now to watch the unloading."

Juan replies, "Let's go back to the hotel and get ourselves some clothing that would match, then come out to work on the boxcars tomorrow and see if we can get in that way."

Mannie not giving in, "It's now or never. Lock and load. Let's go now!"

Mannie jumps up and starts to run to the step rail at the back of the switcher.

Juan now ticked off, "You bastard, I'm coming," as he runs hard to catch up to Mannie.

Shoulder to shoulder they grab the step-up rail, climb up to the platform and crouch down as the engine noses the box car into the plant.

Mannie whispers as the engine makes its way in, "Jump now!" They leap and bounce up after they hit the pavement and crouch behind boxes along the inside of the wall.

Juan whispers, "You are right. The guards need to watch the workers to keep them from lifting the goods."

Mannie now looks around, "Hey, that fully enclosed office with air conditioning over there is no doubt for shipping and receiving. Quick, let's go."

The two-creep military style along the wall to the office enclosure and crawl on their hands and knees to the door.

Mannie with a deep breath, "Great, we are in. Start looking at all this paper work. It will take them an hour to unload that box car."

Juan is not joking, "What? They are using a fork lift. I say twenty minutes. Start shooting with your iPhone"

Mannie grabs a clip board, "What's this, a tank car full of benzene? Why do they need benzene?"

Juan still looking, "I don't know. They show a lot of fluids for cultivating vaccines. This stuff is from France, Russia, Germany, and Iran"

Mannie, "Ok, I'll shoot all of the wall mountings."

Just then they hear the switcher fire up its diesel engine as the track door slowly reopens.

Juan, "Ok, let's go now!"

Too late, the floor supervisor walks in and baulks, "Hombre, Que hace aqui?"

Mannie pulls out his gun, "Ciera la boca! No te muevas!" Looking at Juan, "Grab those cords, tie his hands and legs, and stuff this paper towel in his mouth"

By now the switcher is slowly moving toward the door. Mannie hits the supervisor on the head to knock him out and they both run, track style, for the rear of the switcher as it moves outside.

Mannie with Juan on board bellows with an open smile, "We made it!"

Just then rapid-fire AK's are bouncing bullets off of the engine as guards run to stop them and the engine.

Mannie motions, "We need to run for our car." It is just outside the gate about twenty yards. "It's time for a left right hook run. Bet I beat you!"

Juan is the sprinter, "Sure, come and get me."

They run, dodging bullets tracing their steps by a few inches into the dirt or ricochet off to the right or left. With their zigzag rapid evasion maneuver, including a few hops over a line of ricochets in front of them, they get out of the gate and the shooting stops.

Back in the car, Juan shows his sprinting talent with wheels as they peel rubber in a wide turn to the main street, racing back to their hotel.

Mannie whimsical about Juan's crazy ticket style driving, "Where is a cop when you don't want one, good thing, nowhere!"

Now in their room they have a lot of work to do going over all the paper work that they photographed. For finding interesting information about benzene, a product of oil refineries producing gasoline, Juan fires up his lap top. "You won't believe this. They use benzene to make fenbendazole for de-worming animals and also for humans as a cancer treatment."

Mannie frowns, "Yeah, and I'll bet they use it for making cocaine. Kerosene also works fine with coca leaves."

Juan adds, "They could ship it as a medication with some simple distilling at the receiving end. But everything looks legitimate. Their web page indicates special treatments for foals, mares, ponies, and breeding stallions and de-worming all warm-blooded animals."

Mannie scratches his head, "We need to talk to a chemist. Do you know somebody here in Madrid that can tell us about processing benzene?"

Juan puffs up a bit, "We have cooperated with the forensic lab at Interpol which has an office here in Madrid. Let's go there tomorrow and see what they can tell us."

Juan and Mannie slept well after gorging themselves at the bar with tapas and croquettes. The next morning after a brief breakfast they board their car.

Juan announces, "We are off to Paseo de la Castellana to the Comisaria de Policia Nacional. We can also stop by the British Consulate if needs be. We will be near embassy row for any country including Uzbekistan which also has a polo team that competes in Buenos Aires."

Mannie now thinks, "Hmmmm. Is that a possibility for another connection?"

Juan happily announces, "Look, a parking spot on this side street behind the forensic lab, what luck!"

After presenting Juan's credentials at the main entrance his friend, Arsenio held out his arms with a greeting, "Juan! Que pasa? It is so good to see you again after our last investigation with your country."

Juan replies, "Bien, Arsenio it indeed has been some time. Allow me to introduce my American compadre, Mannie Landren."

Arsenio shakes Mannie's hand, "Si, Mucho gusto. Let us go to my lab where we can talk."

At the lab Juan poses a question. "Arsenio, can drugs be extracted from a soluble solution and not be traceable in that form?"

Arsenio did not hesitate, "De curso, a drug like cocaine, heroin, or the THC of marijuana can then be extracted from a solution through a fairly simple distillation or refractory process to crystallization without any difficulty."

Mannie asks the same question differently, "How does one go to a solid form, like a pill, that could not be detected and shipped anywhere in the world and in our case to Columbia."

Arsenio thinks a minute, "I see that we are looking at a potential smuggling system for illegal drugs using a pharmacy cover."

Juan speaks up, "We know they are using benzene for making pills for various legitimate treatments. We are concerned there may be a sideline to it all. From our inspections and observations of a company, what they are doing and using makes all the sense in the world and is totally legitimate."

Arsenio answers cautiously, "And to go to solids requires significant technical skill and heavy lab equipment to avoid adverse contamination. The process now involves dissolving a solid and then again distilling out the elements smuggled in with the solid. But once the chemical balance is made solid, I doubt that a drug like cocaine could easily be detected, especially if the pill is constructed in layers with the cocaine inner laced and covered by the legitimate pill function. Manufacturers of candy do it all the time, including the famous jelly bean."

He continues after a thought. "You see, to combine the pill they would need a state of art platform generating high levels of drying component transfer to room temperature stable tablets. With a high through put this is standard for most pharmacy production with industrial tablet casting equipment. Given all the work to create the transfer and recover the distillate to a powder or crystalline form they might recover 40-50%."

Mannie notes, "When we investigated a plant named Tridexan, the ventilation stacks reminded me of white labs with separate ventilation, negative air pressure, and noise suppressors. I find that to be the technical expertise of which you speak."

Arsenio agrees, "Si, I have had a liaison with drug enforcement, and I can contact him to at least meet with you and talk about your problem. I think you can trust him to be discreet about the situation, but don't expect him to start an investigation."

Juan, "Ok. What is his name?"

Arsenio, "His name is Dimetri Lopez."

Mannie "Dimetri Lopez? That sounds a little Russian to me." Arsenio "That's true. He has a Spanish father and Russian mother. I will arrange for you to meet him on neutral ground at your hotel at 9:00 A.M., say the restaurant for breakfast and coffee?"

Juan agrees, "That would be fine, I remember working with him on one of our cases."

Arsenio ends with a warning, "Be advised, the company here in Madrid that you have mentioned is what in the US you call "big pharma." To investigate them openly will lead to political complications which will likely lead to your being forced to leave Spain or finding yourselves having an unfortunate accident,"

Mannie adds, "That's an interesting thought, does this company have a polo team?"

Arsenio. "Why yes, it is famous and will soon be playing at the international competition in Buenos Aires. Why do you ask?"

Mannie with a grin, "Just a thought."

On their way-out Juan concludes with Mannie, "There could be more to this situation than meets the eye. The boxes in the warehouse are labeled in Russian and shipped from Paris. And to Paris they are routed from Moscow to St. Petersburg, through Germany and Poland. And it had to come from another direction, probably Georgia and Uzbekistan, the name on one of those tank cars with benzene. So, let's meet this man from the policia tomorrow and try to get some names."

The next day, Mannie and Juan meet with Dimitri, a short, stout man, slightly tanned with dark hair and dark eyes. He recognizes Juan immediately and hails him with his hand as he walks over to their table.

Dimitri a bit loud, "Como estas Juan?"

Juan stands up and offers his hand for a firm shake, "Bien. I would like you to meet my friend Mannie from the United States."

"Mannie, Mucho gusto." Juan offers Dimitri coffee. A waitress promptly brings a platter of munchies from which they all grabbed a handful. Juan then goes to the chase, "We are investigating Tridexan in Columbia, a possible part of a wider pharmaceutical company here in Madrid."

Dimitri pops, "Tridexan! We know it well. They produce many products, a lot of opioids that are addictive. They also produce a lot of morphine from the opium poppy. Our involvement includes an inspection once a year. We use a dog to sniff outside the production labs where they convert opium to morphine."

Juan wonders, "Can we assist you when you make your next inspection?"

Dimitri shrugs, "Oh, I am no longer in the division of the drug control service. I am promoted to investigations for Vice."

"Well, maybe you can give us some insight. The reason why we have asked to meet with you is because I believe we can trust you to keep quiet about what we are investigating."

"I will do my best," said Dimitri. "Of course, I have my responsibilities, but at this point I can certainly reflect upon what you are doing and help you as much as I can."

Mannie interrupts at this point. "We think the plant we are investigating here is also a wholesale and intermediary processing facility for the same pharmaceutical company out of Bogota, Columbia. And Tridexan produces a considerable amount of morphine for animal pain relief. But we believe they are also converting it to heroin and are shipping illegal drugs as pill form medications for animals."

Dimitri disagrees. "Oh, I am not sure that you are on the right track with Tridexan. The owners are very influential people and they have very high contacts in our government, including the Spanish army. Tridexan cooperates with many South American companies in providing equipment and training. I can understand your suspicion, but how do you think this could possibly be?"

"Well," Mannie grumbles. "We know that you can take heroin and opium in a raw state and dissolve it in a carbon-based solution like a petroleum byproduct and then reconstitute it after shipping it in a liquid form. We know that this is possibly what's happening in terms of shipments that are coming from Russia to Paris to Spain and then going from Spain to Columbia."

"Yes, but producing heroin from opium is a complicated process involving many chemicals. We know that this can be done but the Tridexan labs don't have the set up for the chemicals nor that level of expertise. And we have checked their shipments from Madrid to various locations, including Columbia and have found no trace of any illicit drug in any of the commodities that they are shipping. They typically ship vaccine treatments in pill form for internal problems like de-worming."

Mannie keeps on coming, "Have you checked the benzene that was being shipped to them?"

Dimitri is now defensive, "No, whatever for? Benzene is a common commodity used everywhere for many things. And as much as we have drug issues here in Madrid, nothing has ever traced to this operation."

"Well, we know that the shipments are coming from Paris. Have you done anything in those areas as to the origin of the shipments?" asks Juan.

Dimitri admits, "Ok, in the beginning we pursued deep screening. The connection there comes with Sergei Ivanoff. A former colonel, he operates his shipping out of Moscow. Sergei has a contact in Paris named Anatoly who basically handles the inter shipment to Spain. We learned this from a contact at the Moscow metropolitan police. It is a woman named Anna. We don't know her real name. She works undercover and alerted us that Sergei is part of the Russian mafia's many illegal businesses, including drugs. Anatoly is a middleman who takes Sergei's shipments and distributes them throughout Europe. Watch out for him. He is also an enforcer."

Suddenly Dimitri becomes nervous. He recognizes a man across the dining room. In a jitter, he whispers, "I must go now. I have given you as much information as I can. If you need to know more, go to Paris and seek out Anatoly. Just follow the shipment labels that you discovered and go from there. I can't help any longer. I must leave." He stands up, military swivels, and walks double time out of the restaurant. A man sitting at a table on the other side of the room gets up at the same time walking as fast to keep track of Dimitri. Juan notices immediately and says to Mannie, "I think we may have caused some problems for this man. I hope he will be ok."

Mannie queries, "Is this thing under such tight wraps? Are we being watched also? I think we need to decide now, make official contacts or go deep undercover."

Juan's thinking, "Developing a network to offer us some protection risks our losing our leverage investigating. I already have slippage on my side of the fence. If word gets out as to what we are up to here, the circles will close in on us and we will either be shut out or found dead in a sewer."

Mannie still intent on going on, "Well, there is no sense in us sitting around here. Let's go to Paris and stay under cover from now on."

The next morning, Mannie and Juan check all the photographed papers and find a tank car from Paris, shipped from 61 Le Rue de Point Neuf. They rent a car with all of their new weapon's gear and drive to Paris without stopping.

Back at the Estancia, with the tournament only a week away, Alessandra, again practicing her drill sergeant technique, goes up and down the hall at 5 A.M. as she bangs a pot with a big stirring spoon yelling, "Breakfast is served. You only have ten minutes." Josephine already dressed for riding, jumps out of her room and cheerfully adds, "Where have I heard that before?"

She walks briskly to the dining room and enters with an astonished face, "Me soprende, Lucia what are you doing here this early in the morning?"

Lucia tightens her lips, "Josephine, some of us need to do real business. I have associates in different time zones with a need to talk on the phone. Oh, by the way, don't try to call your husband in Texas, because of our need for security I have had a scrambler installed on this phone, on all out of country calls."

Josephine looking a bit perplexed, "No matter, I will make my calls when we go to Parma for a practice game."

Julio, equally dressed for riding enters the room singing, "Buenos Dias, Josephine y mi madre. Josephine looks ready to ride and train for the day. Doesn't she mother?"

Lucia bunted loathsomely, "Yes, at least looking as ready as she can be."

Alessandra, ready to shepherd the two off from a batting match, in a commanding voice replies to Lucia, "My dear sister, of course she is good, and better than you on a horse any day and Sunday."

With Julio taken aback by his mother's sour remark, Josephine sees the need to smooth out another family conflict.

With a half-smile she interrupts, "Oh, I am here to do my best, but I do hope my riding as well as by my playing, I will encourage more women in this great sport."

Josephine's remark backs off Lucia and gives Alessandra an opening for her coach's game speech.

"We have the finest ponies, the best trained and ready to play. They will perform with their commitment to our excellent team of riders. We, as well as the ponies, are hot blooded, just as quick and agile, and alert for every opportunity to strike the ball in our favor."

Just then Guillermo walks in, "Pardon my interruption. Senora Verelez, there is a long-distance call for you in the library."

Lucia jumped up in a huff looking at everyone, As she hustles out of the room speaking with her back to everyone, "Thank you Guillermo, this conversation is getting a bit boring."

Alessandra laments, "Ah, my sister, she is so pretentious. Off we go to the stables to trailer our ponies for the ride to Parma."

With no further words, the room empties and, in the hall, as they leave, they can hear Lucia yelling on the phone. In the library, Lucia's face turns red with anger, "Sergei, what do you mean somebody is investigating our plant in Madrid?"

Sergei is serious to the bone, "Yes, one of the Spanish police investigators was seen meeting with a known Columbian drug investigator."

Lucia fires back, "What is his name?"

Sergei backs up, "At the plant two men broke into our shipping warehouse. Our guards saw them as they left the building and fired on them hiding behind our diesel engine as it left the dock after unloading. They escaped before we could kill them. We know one of them is Juan Valdez."

Lucia now unnerved, "I know him! He and a team searched our plant for drugs and harassed us for months. They failed. And in Bogota I know how to get to him"

Sergei continues, "Through one of our insiders, we found out about a Spanish investigator who later met with them. Our enforcers met the investigator. He spoke after persuasion. The Columbian and an American named Mannie suspect that a drug ring is working through our plants. They got hold of our shipping bills of lading, leading them here to Paris, on to Moscow and down to Kazakhstan. This could be the DEA. We have to take them out, here and now!"

Lucia now planning, "They are no doubt already in Paris. Adolpho will send three of our enforcers to your plant. Until they get to you, stay clear of the business."

Adolpho comes alongside Lucia, "I heard you yelling. What is happening?"

Lucia now calmed down, "We have trouble in Spain and France. Juan Valdez and an American snooped into our plant and copied shipping documents. They are in Paris to snoop our shipping point. Send three of your best men to Sergei to eliminate them."

Adolpho saluting, "They will be on a plane within the hour."

Chapter Nine

On Target In Paris

In Paris, Juan suggests, "I don't think we want a tourist place like the Hotel de la Tour Eiffel. Even off-season Japanese and Italian tourists fill the lobby and restaurant. Let's go to Saint-Michel. I know a concierge at a bed and breakfast who only takes cash. If we are being traced, they won't find us there."

Mannie remarks like a good old boy, "It sounds like you have been around the block on pleasure as well as business."

Juan thinking back, answers, "Gracias, you just reminded me that I was involved with a case involving heavy cocaine shipments from Argentina. I ended up catching a smuggling ring with over 860 pounds shipping it from the Russian Embassy in Buenos Aires to Paris and then to Moscow. A corrupt senior police officer worked ,with several embassy workers to get luggage uninspected for air delivery to Paris. It worked but in advance the cocaine was discovered and replaced with flour to find out who was doing the business. Arrests occurred on both ends."

Mannie no longer scratching his head, "Now that you mention it that way, dealing with Moscow, I think we are also dealing with a twoway street, one way with opium, the other way with cocaine. My God, this is incredible! I need to make a call now."

Matt gets a jingle on his private line, "Hello Mannie. How is it going?"

Mannie talks fast, "We are busy, just out of Madrid and now in Paris, finding out a lot of possible tracks leading to a two-way drug running ring from Russia to Argentina."

Matt issues a warning, "Well thanks for the heads up, but be on the look-out. The lady boss of the plant in Bogota may be acting on an alert. We monitor a couple of her enforcers. They just booked a flight to Paris. She may have found out about your presence in Madrid and her solutions are nothing less than a death squad sent to look for you two."

Mannie ends with a covering your back statement, "Copy that, this is just like the good old days. I will keep in touch. Bye."

Juan asking, "What did he say?"

Mannie turns and looks hard, "The lady boss from Columbia is likely on our tail with a death squad. We need to act fast. If not here now, they will be here soon."

Juan provides a knee jerk reply, "Let's go now. We can catch the shop closed up and check out their files."

Mannie and Juan now in the car, "Ok, what's the address. Juan answers, "Aha, Go to the Place de Pont Neuf. There is a quay there along the river where heavy barges tie on for semi-permanent docking."

Juan adds more detail, My GPS locates the address on an island with the Cathedral of Nortre Dame and the island is the seat of the national court system and the Monnaie de Paris is next to the quay. It mints all of the coins for the Euro money system. What a great place to locate a cover. Oh my God, the address is a barge on the river."

Once there, they experience towering office buildings and apartments with typical temporary street markets with a usual stream of tourists. Taking steps at street level they look down to the Seine River and see a series of barges tied up alongside the bulkheads. They casually saunter down a stone set of steps to the quay on the river side lined with the barges.

"Look!" Mannie points, "That one has a Russian flag. It must be the place."

A gangplank leading to it is chained off. It looks like the barge is uninhabited. And being later in the day in the summer with all the other occupants in the barges either on vacation for a month or just a few lounging on their decks cooling off.

Mannie suggests, "Let's look like we own the place. Just unchain this thing and we'll walk aboard looking busy."

Juan backs off, "I would rather wait until nightfall and enter the barge unseen."

Mannie baulks but then relents. They keep on walking past the barges and up back on to the street, Quai de Conti. They take a leisurely dinner at a sidewalk café, Le Pixel, and walked back towards the barge as the sun sets. Because they drove, they were able to bring their weapons from Spain with no border checks going into France. Mannie brought a 9-millimeter semiautomatic and Juan has an Uzi 9mm machine pistol. Both weapons fit nicely under their windbreaker jackets which are appropriate for evening wear as Paris gets cool at night by the river.

It was at this time that Mannie and Juan, approaching the steps to the quay at the bridge noticed three men across the street breaking up and crossing over to the quay side. Looking at each other with a nod to the street, Mannie poses a possibility, "If those are the bad guys looking for us, I'm going down and hang back under the bridge. You go right to the barge. Let's see what happens."

Juan agrees, "Ok, let's do it."

They both peel off in different directions at the bottom of the stairs. Stopping and looking back, none of them show up.

Mannie walks back to Juan, "If it's trouble they are taking their time. Let's go to the barge and be ready for them if they come."

Mannie keeps talking as they walk. "They must have gotten to our informant in Madrid."

Juan surmises, "I think it goes back to Bogota."

Mannie agrees, "We have been compromised. And it was someone with the Spanish Policia who turned Demitri in as an informant."

Juan also agrees, "It could have happened that way. And I know the ones we saw today are not the Serrate. They would have grabbed us instead of watched us."

Getting on the barge no longer troubles Mannie, "Let's get on with it. It is dark enough now. There's the barge and what? Lights are on!"

Juan notes, "Those are motion sensor activated, but I see no activity, probably frogs. Keep going to get on board. But get your gun out. We may need it."

Mannie readies, "Roger that, lock and load"

Mannie and Juan also watch a group of tourists crossing the bridge past the steps to get on board the river tourist boat just ahead on the island quay. As they approach the barge, one of the loaded tourist boats comes up the river with the lights out and the spotlight shining on the bank of the river to expose young lovers hugging and kissing.

Mannie laughingly comments, "I'll bet those lovers are paid by the skipper to be there when they come out at night."

Juan scoffs, "In Paris there is no place to go on the cheap to kiss and hug. Here you have to pay to sit on a park bench."

Once the tourist boat passes, Juan and Mannie approach and lift the chain across the planking that leads to the large cargo barge on their side of the quay. They walk on the plank and quietly board the boat to a stern below deck entrance.

Juan whispers, "Do you see anybody out there watching us?"

Mannie looks far and wide, "It looks clear around us. Shine your flashlight on the door so I can jimmy the lock."

Juan moves his light, "Here is the door handle."

Mannie jokingly discovers, "My God, a cheap brass lock. I can pick that with the wire picks I keep in my wallet."

With the door soon open, a cascade of light comes out from the cabin below and they see no one in the large windowless space. Without a word, they step down below deck.

Juan motions, "Ok, go forward to the cargo hold. Open the hatch and stand back and I will shine in the light."

With the hatch open Juan motions, "Looks ok, I'll keep left and you keep right. Do you see anything?"

Mannie disappointedly remarks, "Hey, no cases or containers, this place is empty."

Juan figures, "It ought to be empty. They just sent a shipment to

Madrid a few days ago. Let's look for paperwork. How is your Russian?"

Mannie now looks around in the cabin, "Yes, I spent some time in Moscow in the old days. I still remember their Cyrillic alphabet, but I will need a dictionary. That filing cabinet in the corner is a good start."

Juan walks over, "It isn't even locked. Here, take this drawer's files to the table and I'll get the rest."

Mannie almost jumped for joy, "Now we are cooking. Look at all of these bills of lading. They are all coming from Moscow with back up billings coming from Uzbekistan and Georgia. Benzene is the commodity with a reference to a Formula D but some include a Formula C."

Juan comes over to look, "Yes, these other files go back a year and they all have the same cargo benzene marked with Formula D and C. What is this formula referring to?"

Mannie adds, "I am not sure but I think it has something to do with the transition in the shipping from benzene to a more potent product like morphine. It may also add proprietary secret elements into the benzene. That would make it more potent in terms of some other characteristic for the petroleum product involved, maybe even including disguised components."

Mannie could at least read some of the billing statements, "These shipments are ten-to-twenty-thousand-gallon tankers."

Juan adds, "That confirms what we saw in Madrid and recovered from their shipment schedules, but nothing showed a formula designation like these?"

Mannie concludes. "Ok, we've seen enough. Copy everything with your cell phone and let's get out of here."

Juan changes the subject, "You know if we just wait here long enough maybe Anatoly, full name now including Caramazov, will just show up and we can have a very private and personal interview to find out where, why and how these shipments are coming."

Mannie thinking out loud, "Well, that might be a good idea but should we expose ourselves to this middle link at this point in time? Do you think maybe it would be better if we backed off at this point and try to keep going back towards Moscow to see if we can locate the source of this shipment?"

Juan just about to answer out loud whispers, "Did you hear those steps? The barge is also listing on one side. We've got boarders!" Juan pulls out and cocks his Uzi.

Mannie waves Juan to back off to the side of the bunk area behind curtains as they hear steps with loud voices coming down to the cabin. The lock and handle turned and the door opens with steps now in the cabin. A large black bearded hulking silhouette of a man with a heavy throated mumble speaks, "Anatoly, I know we need not worry about that warning from Sergei. We need to be concerned about the next shipment to make sure that it clears properly so that there are no delays. Delays are costing us time and money and they will make our customers and bosses extremely unhappy."

Anatoly agrees. "Yes Boris," We have a great difficulty with shipments out of Moscow. They want more money. They will not be satisfied without a greater share of the prophets."

Anatoly continues, "This is not wise on their part. Sergei does not tolerate such greed. They are not that strong that they can overcome Sergei and his Georgian group." The two men enter the room and take off their jackets and are sitting in the chairs in the pen area.

Boris no longer talks like a muscle man, "You know, if we knew the formula, we could bypass all these fools from Spain and get into a larger market ourselves. Is it that difficult to find and do it ourselves?"

Anatoly now sighs, "Ah, you cannot possibly understand it. It is a very difficult and complex system. I am a chemist myself trained at the University of Moscow and I cannot fathom the complexity of this compound and the catalysts that are used to change the compound into an inert product that cannot be detected as a source of drugs."

Mannie's eyes light up. 'Drugs,' this is the first time he hears the word drugs.

Boris understands, "Well, it is not that we do not make any money. Quiet and easy to do, this has certainly been very profitable for us for two years without any problems whatsoever."

At that moment a cell phone rings and Anatoly pulls it from his pocket. He listens, "Dah, we will be cautious. Ya ponimayu. Spasiba." Then Anatoly hangs up.

Anatoly points to Boris and turns his head sideways nodding over to the side of the cabin with a wall cabinet after pointing to the file cabinet with open drawers and papers opened on the top. Boris walks over to the cabinet, opens it to pull out a 9mm Makarov PM, and an auto 9 mm AR9 with a 31-round magazine. He keeps one and tosses the other one to Anatoly.

Mannie elbows Juan and jumps out from the curtain, "Drop it, you are covered"

With their backs turned but guns in hand they spin around. Boris yells, "Strelyat'v."

An immediate burst of fire without aiming comes from Anatoly and Boris. As they turn Mannie yells, "Hit the deck!"

Both Mannie and Juan throw themselves to the floor and roll over. Juan yells, "Take'em down." Shooting upwards also leads to poor aiming. And now with the lights shot out, Juan tries to crouch up behind the corner of a cabinet and before he could fire a return in the dark, he takes a hit in the shoulder knocking him back to the floor. Mannie remaining calm, rolls over one more time to the wall of the cabin and waits for a gun flash to return fire.

Boris yells, "Where are they?" And begins shooting blindly.

Mannie rises up slowly and aims his gun at the gun flashes for a double tap. In three seconds, it is over for Boris with Mannie's comment, "Thanks, I got your friend." as Boris groans a last nothing, and falls hard to the deck. Mannie's ears now ringing from the gunfire can barely hear Juan in pain from across the cabin.

Mannie commands Anatoly, "Surrender, sounding in Russian like svodotzen."

Anatoly, knowing Boris is dead, again opens fire at Mannie's voice yelling, "Swinia, I will get you. I will not surrender." That last message gives Mannie a head to chest points of fire and with a double tap Anatoly is down and out.

With all the gunfire there is plenty of commotion at the barge within minutes. Mannie goes over to Juan crouched on his side on the deck. "Are you ok? Can you walk?"

"I'm hit in the shoulder. I can walk fine. Just help me up. Mannie grabs his shoulder. The bullet went clean through. Mannie needs to stop the bleeding. "Let me patch you up with these table napkins." He then tightens his shoulder under the arm with his belt.

Juan is in pain, "Ok. We've got to get out of here."

Mannie helps Juan and they stagger out of the cabin up onto the deck. As they look around, they see nothing on the quay, but police car lights are shining from the bridge steps.

Mannie is exasperated, "We can't get off on this side. We have got to go in the water."

Juan pleads, "Aw, Mannie, I don't know if I can swim."

"Juan, you have to at least kick your legs and hold your breath to float. We can't get off this side of the boat. There is going to be traffic here in a second."

They both lower themselves down a riverside ladder and grab a line that is used to tie the barge to the other barges and cleats on the bulkhead. They rope their way along ten feet with their legs and three arms along until they come to another barge.

Mannie smiles, "Look there's a dingy underneath the bow!" There they hide in silence as they hear footsteps and muffled sounds going across the plank to the barge they just left.

Mannie whispers, "Those aren't police. They would be there with all kinds of noise and racket."

Juan stretches his neck for a look, "Yeah, I think they are friends of the friends we just killed."

Mannie chimes in, "OK, it is time to get moving again. Let go the tie line for the dinghy, we'll just drift along the river's bank until we can find another stairway up to the street."

With no moonlight and a slow current, they move unnoticed in the dark. A slight glitter on the water reflects the lights along the river road above. After traveling a few hundred yards, they come up to a set of built-in peg ladders that rise up to street level. With Juan climbing first with his one arm and Mannie behind with a push they make it to the top. By this time, they can see the blue lights from the gendarme's cars on the street and two security boats alongside the barge. Mannie wonders, "Do you think those bad guys got away before the gendarmes?"

Juan, half joking, still in pain, "We will read about it tomorrow in Le Monde, that paper loves crime stories. Two dead men found in a barge. Yikes. They were Russians."

Mannie leaves Juan on a park bench, no charge for sitting after 9 P.M., to get their car and drives to a Pharmacie Odeon in Saint-Michele for bandages, a shoulder sling, aspirin, and antiseptic salves, and then picks up Juan. He bandages him in the car putting his arm in a sling. Back at their room after waking their grumpy concierge for a room who joked with them saying something about bar fights, Mannie and Juan hit the sack dead asleep as they fall.

Back at the Hacienda, Lucia now muses, "Very strange, too many things go wrong since that women Josephine comes along. By the way, is that idiot from Miami going to be in the tournament?"

Adolpho dialing long distance, "Ha, I just got an email that El Machismo was found in his mansion entrance hung upside down from a chandelier, cut in half with a chain saw. Our team practice game at Parma today includes Columbia's team as an opponent."

Lucia, now talking to herself as Adolpho makes his call, "Hmmm. I think the Bogota ponies need some veterinary medicine to get them into shape for the tournament. Gasterophilus Intestinalis will do fine."

Larcenous Lucia has more orders to give, "Adolpho! Call our lab and have them ship us a canister of equine bot fly eggs, at least five hundred."

Adolpho quizzically, "What do we want with them?"

Licentious Lucia with a smirk, "We want to make a present of them to the Bogota ponies. I want you to find someone to plant a cluster of eggs inside the lips of each of their ponies."

Adolpho is still doubtful, "Bot flies are a common pest, using horse flesh for their eggs to hatch and mature. They attack the stomach and the stable people will know the symptoms in their manure or with a loss of eating and they no doubt have our medicine to eliminate them before the game."

Ultimately lethal Lucia now speculates, "Maybe yes, Maybe no. With their gums infected instead of their stomach, the infection will go unnoticed and their teeth will loosen, and irritated gums make a pony less willing to respond to reigning. It will take a few days to a week and if they don't check their teeth, their ponies will not play well. That would make one less competitor in the field. And they would have no one to blame but their own carelessness. And that would also suit our business partners by helping our team or their team to win."

Adopho asks, "What other team are you talking about?"

Lucia, "Never mind! Bogota's ponies are likely stabled at the race track near the international field. Pass out some Paco to the stable boys and you can pet the ponies' faces, Si?"

Adolpho also now smiling, "Si, I will enjoy doing it myself."

Back at the estancia stables getting ready to leave for Parma, Carlos comes out to greet Josephine and Julio coming to load the ponies for today's practice game. "Hola, Senora O'Connor, we have loaded most of the ponies but I left Bandit for your handling."

Josephine warmly greets him, "Bien, gracias Carlos, and por favor call me Josephine."

Julio politely breaks in, "Josephine, for my grandfather, and yes my mother and father, it is a matter of tradition around the estancia to maintain formality among staff. When on the road, on the field or at a party, the formality quickly vanishes."

Josephine agrees with a smile. After quickly loading the trucks and trailers, the ride to Buenos Aires with horse trailers attracts no attention on the road. Once in Parma, they arrive at the south end of the polo field and set up the trailers in an open corner, unload the ponies and set up posts for securing their reigns. Julio goes to the grand stand to inquire about the other team for the practice.

Julio greeting the counter attendant, "Buenos dias Senor, I am here with the Vega de la Dega team to practice. Who will be our friendly competitor?"

The counter clerk replies, "Ah Si Senor, we have the team from Columbia stabling at the Lago Hippodrome. They should be here shortly."

Julio is taken by an OMG surprise, "Gracias."

Back at the setup, Alessandra the coach bows to the captain. Julio announces, "Everybody listen; we are practicing with Columbia. We have practiced our passing, and drives with defense. What we want is to learn their passing and drives. So, in this case we play as a lady and gentlemen with normal practice passing and defense, but no special moves. OK?"

Carlos opens up with disgust, "You mean we don't get to beat them here?"

Julio, "Bien, no, we can still beat them, but only with their mistakes, not our edge from special training, including under belly shots and cross fronts on the run."

Carlos hardly agreeing, "Si, it would be a greater win without working too hard."

Josephine asks, "They are not here yet. I am all saddled and ready. Before we play, I would like to call my husband from the grandstands. I'll only be a few minutes."

Julio hesitates a bit, "Of course, we won't start for at least ten minutes."

Alessandra then makes her pitch, "And tell Mr. O'Conner how much we appreciate him for supporting your being here to help us win this tournament. He is a good man."

At the grand stand Josephine dials up Matt's number with her credit card.

Matt answering his private phone, "Hello, is that you Josephine?"

Josephine in a hurry, "Yes, my darling, we are about to start a practice. All is going well but Julio's mother is having problems with her business. She is definitely committed to beating the Columbian team. She definitely hates me and I am beginning to suspect her of violence as a solution to her problems."

Matt now concerned, "Yes, well her Columbian competition in Miami was found cut in half hanging from a chandelier at the entrance to his mansion. You need to be very, very careful. I have a friend helping me out here. I am concerned that everything works out ok for you. As soon as the competition is over come back to Dallas."

Josephine looking at the field, "OK, I must go. Good bye my darling."

Matt wishes her, "God speed, play well, until then, my darling."

Now all saddled and ready to go, for the entire team, it is hard to hold back their excitement riding out to the center drop in the field. For a practice, only one umpire and another timer at the grand stand control the pace of the game. With the first bowl in by the umpire, Columbia's #1 makes a hard mallet hit toward their goal on the Vega side. Julio and Josephine ride hard to guard the Columbian defense team riding shoulder to shoulder. Carlos playing Vega #3 breaks away and beats the other team to reverse hit the ball back to the center of the field. Josephine stays back to pick off the hit with a cross court shot to Alejandro who taps the ball along the sideline toward the Columbian goal. A Columbian offense paces Josephine to the center about twenty yards to their goal. Alejandro hits the ball in front of the two and Bandit breaks away like a race horse out of the starting gate. Josephine intercepts the hit and taps the ball in between the goals with the side of her mallet. Score 1 for the De La Vega team in the first chukker.

Back at the staging place for a break, Alessandra scolds the team, "What are you doing? You are showing them our best moves?"

Josephine throws her hands out, "I was ready to lose it, but Bandit just took off. He loves to compete. And I don't want to hold him back in practice."

Carlos adds, "I will make it easy for their number two. Julio and I will play one of our easy practice passing games."

Alessandra accepting the proposal, "Very good, now easy does it."

Josephine plays defense and runs Bandit every other chukker. The game goes on and in two hours per Alessandra's instructions, the team is loading up the trailers with the Columbian's sporting a win with four to one goal.

Before the team returns to the hacienda for a planned fiesta barbeque, Lucia is in the process of receiving more bad news on a circuit protected phone call. "What? Sergei and Boris are dead! Three Columbians are arrested for shooting them at the business place? How can that be?"

Vladimir, at the Moscow Embassy in Paris, exclaims, "Those idiots. They came too late. The intruders were already there and were discovered by Sergei and Boris. They ended up firing at each other in the cabin in the dark. One of them is an excellent shot. According to the news, Sergei had a hole in his forehead and one in his heart. Boris had three in his chest. When your Columbians came, they went into the cabin, picked up the weapons, and started to leave when police boats and National Police surrounded them. Did they look guilty? In France you are guilty until proven innocent. I doubt your Columbians will look innocent, since they also carried their own stolen weapons. They are under arrest for a ruthless murder of two ordinary Russian businessmen."

Lucia, not so commanding with Vladimir, who represents a sixty percent owner, proves apologetic, "We hoped to get our enforcers there before the intruders and we warned Sergei of their coming and told him to stay away from the business until our enforcers get there. I regret this happening. And we still have the intruders to deal with."

Vladimir orders Lucia in no uncertain terms, "Do nothing! We will deal with these tracers. They are making waves with the CIA, MI6 and the French General Directorate for Internal Security. You should have called me before making your foolish decision to use foreigners in France. Win the tournament. Our partners thrive on good publicity and are willing to accept a few blunders to gain it. Do you understand?"

Chapter Ten

St. Petersburg's Russian Help

The next day at Charles de Gaulle airport waiting for their plane to leave for Berlin, Juan and Mannie take breakfast after passing up the fungi scary meal at the bed and breakfast, bidding au revour to the concierge who corrects their French pronunciation as they leave. Once out the door Mannie complains, "We never corrected his bad English." Juan laughs and confirms, "Going to Berlin is a stop-over. We really need to get to Russia. Our passports are neutral so we should have no problem getting to St. Petersburg first and then on to Moscow. I have worked under cover more often than not. I suggest that we go as buyers looking for special herbs for our health supplements. Just as well we left our weapons on the barge. Look at this paper with the pictures of our Columbian hit men under arrest. How slick can we get?"

Mannie is rustling through the bills of lading in his lap, "How about being lucky as we can get. We should investigate St. Petersburg first. There are a lot of shipments from there."

Juan thinks for a second, "That is a good idea. They will be waiting for us in Moscow coming in on a flight from the west. It seems a lot safer to divert to St. Petersburg and train from there to Moscow instead."

Mannie remembers, "Oh I once had a flight from St. Petersburg in a Tupolev, a converted military transport plane. Their TU 154 had seven fatal crashes that we know about. On secondary routes they fly old planes. The engines can blow up or the controls go wrong."

Juan laughingly replies, "Oh, come on! It can't be that bad."

Mannie agrees, "Ok, that's the wiser move. Hopefully the flights have improved. So far, no government agency is after us. This way we just have to watch out for the bad guys."

Once in Berlin, they transfer to a St. Petersburg jet and arrive there in three hours.

Juan and Mannie debark and walk from the terminal onto the street with their carry-on bags. Juan asks with a slight jest, "Now we need a taxi. How is your Russian?"

Mannie cringes a bit, "It has been a while. But most cabbies speak English. Write down the address and try to copy the Cyrillic letters for the street name. That should work."

Opening a door to a cab, Mannie smiles, climbs in and hands the cabbie the address saying "Da?"

The cabbie looks at the address and replies in Oxford English, "There is no such address here. I can guess that it is across the river by the old tank plant in the Kalinsky district by the train yard along Arsenainaya on the river. Historically this was a secret military district with a blanked-out area for the maps of the city."

Mannie is taken aback, "Where did you learn such good English?"

The cabbie continues looking straight ahead out the windshield, "My name is Mikhail, under the Soviet regime I was a military attaché at our Embassy in London. With the failure of the system my good life ended and I was transferred back to Russia with no need for a military attaché uniform. What money I had, I invested in this cab, to make a living. But I can tell that you two are not tourists. You are an American. Your friend has a Hispanic look, from South America? Whatever way I can help you, I am willing for Euros."

Juan speaks up, "My name is Juan and I am from Columbia. Can you take us to this place in Kalinsky?"

Mikhail now gets friendly, "Of course, but it is getting late and traffic will be difficult. Let me take you to a small hotel along a canal where you will not stand out from the thousands of tourists that come to see the Hermitage."

Mannie and Juan agree and Mikhail drops them off at a small hotel along a canal near the square facing the Hermitage. As Mannie pays Mikhail off with Euros, "Will you pick us up tomorrow morning at 9:00 A.M?" Mikhail smiles shaking his head, "You bet! Is there anything that I can get for you that you cannot get yourself?"

Mannie looks at him, "I think you know what we want. Can you get us a couple of Makarovs?"

Mikhail with a slanted smile, "Of course, for a price I can get you that handy pistol for self-defense, how about two hundred Euros for each one including two full magazines?"

Mannie jumps back as Mikhail drives away. "It's a deal. Tomorrow 9 A.M.!"

Tourism makes the situation easier than expected. The room is neat and clean and the meals are filling, although Mannie warns Juan, "Don't order water or a drink with ice, and drink only bottled water. It is safer with beer, since the bottled water can be fake."

Juan agrees, "Ok, but where are the potatoes on the menu?"

Mannie chides, "Enjoy the cucumbers and tomatoes grown in hot houses. The potato crops go for vodka."

The next morning, Juan and Mannie are getting ready to meet Mikhail for a drive to the tank plant area on the other side of the river, when suddenly there is a knock on the door. With no weapons, Mannie motions to Juan to stand off from the door as Mannie standing sideways backs up as he opens the door. With his mouth wide open, Mannie exclaims, "How may I help you?" Standing in all her glory is a ravishing Russian woman with a message. Her neat uniform with her hair bound up high under a nice tight cap tells him she is a cop. The badge in her hand is an inspector for the Metropolitan Police of Moscow.

She introduces herself. "My name is Anna Matrinov. I am here to assist you."

Mannie quizzically replies, "Assist us to do what?"

Anna in true Russian bureaucratic style, "We are well aware of what you are doing. We are informed of your encounter with Anatoly and Dimitri."

"Who is we?" interjects Juan.

Anna speaks with pride, "The Metropolitan Police of Moscow, of course! I am with the bureau of narcotics and am assigned to assist you with finding the network that kept Anatoly busy in Paris. We have been watching him and are aware of his trafficking but have been unable to backtrack from Paris to Moscow."

Mannie is obviously overwhelmed, "But how did you know about us?"

Anna after walking in and closing the door, "Regrettably, you are not very good at concealing your investigation. Our cohorts with the Spanish and the French keep us informed of your bold but poorly concealed adventure. Our sources also indicate your American CIA showing an interest. Most seriously, what you call our Russian Mafia is looking for your elimination. Then with a smile she reaches behind her back, "Oh and here are the weapons that you requested from Mikhail."

"Great," exclaims Mannie. Without hesitation he offers his hand to the lady cop. "It is indeed very nice to have you on board."

Anna almost in jest, "I do not sail. I am committed to ending this business and doing it with you. You narrowly escaped death from Anatoly. He and Boris will not be missed. But your search for Sergei Ivan off proves fruitless."

Juan wants more, "How do you mean?"

Anna replies like a repeating pistol. "There is no such person. Although we suspect there is a military person involved, Sergei is a code name. His real name remains unknown. Why are you here in St. Petersburg?"

Mannie grabs a batch of papers; "we photographed some of the bills of lading from Anatoly's barge and traced the shipping through Germany to St. Petersburg. We don't have an address but we know it is from St. Petersburg and we know it is in a heavy industrial area that was at one time considered secret."

Anna peruses the copies and notes some Cyrillic markings in the upper right-hand corner of each billing. She recognizes something. "This is a symbol for a company operating out of Moscow."

Mannie jumps on the news, "Ok. So, we have a company shipping here to St. Petersburg. Let's go look for what is here now."

Anna replies, "I know the location. The area includes many small plants that acted as suppliers for the former tank plant."

Mannie's eyes brighten, "Tank plant? Yes, Mikhail said something like that to us yesterday."

Anna offers some history, "It used to be one of the largest buildings in the world with no windows. It was totally secret then, but it started out making cannon balls and cannons in the Czarist era. In the Bolshevik era it was Plant No. 323 mainly building tanks and artillery. Now it's Korovsky Zavod, they manufacture tractors, escalators and still cast and machine artillery."

Juan offers a thought, "Maybe we can go inside these places as inspectors?"

Anna counters, "Your clothes give you away and how is your Russian? We would be better off putting on pipe fitter's coveralls and take along a complete tool chest on wheels, so that the operators know we mean business. All of those buildings have steam lines and we can go from one to the next looking for leaks or frozen valves. I, of course, will be your boss and all you have to say is "Da" to everything I tell you in Russian."

Mannie and Juan, obviously impressed, chime in, "That sounds like a doable plan."

Anna nods agreeably, "Good, wait for me here. I will get a plumbing vehicle from the steam plant and coveralls and boots with dirty hats, greasy gloves, safety glasses, and scarves to camouflage your identity."

With Anna back and Mannie and Juan suited up, they load up on the maintenance truck and drive to a bridge crossing the river to the north side of the city going east on Arsenalnaya Roadway, a six lane that runs along the river and fronts on major industrial developments.

Just a little late in the morning the traffic is light with Mannie and Juan already very much impressed by the breadth and depth of this very big city when Mannie sits up straight, "Hey slow down. What is that, a pharmacy company?"

Anna looks and comments, "Oh yes they produce generic drugs for our country and also for Europe."

Mannie has to ask, "Do they produce drugs for veterinary medicine too?"

Anna snaps back, "That I do not know, but the Georgian Mafia is heavily involved in the pharmacy business and they have mafia brothers here in St. Petersburg."

Mannie thinks out loud, "Hmmm, the pharmacy business and the Russian mafia, very interesting."

Anna interrupts, "But now we are approaching the rail station and beyond that we get to the older buildings around the tank plant."

Anna then slows down to make a left turn into a gated driveway with an open court for loading and unloading, some with docks and doors and others with just concrete platforms. Anna looking at Mannie and Juan, "Now you play dumb."

They slouched down with their hats low on their brows as a gate guard questions Anna. Things aren't as difficult as might be expected. The guard walks away, opens the gate and Anna drives in and parks at a ramp.

Anna looks at Mannie and Juan, "Now we get out and inspect. Get the tool dolly out and carry this temperature gun. We are going to work."

As they unload their gear, Mannie starts looking around. "This place is really decrepit, a big brick clearstory plant at least a hundred years old. But it has top of the line cameras and motion detectors on the exterior walls, modern exterior lighting, electrified fencing, as well as angled barbed wire and a very functional radio antenna running up that old 100-foot chimney."

Anna is quick to comment, "Very observant and that is why I have stopped here. There are only two cars in the shipping yard and one gate guard. But a lot of rubles in security equipment tell me it is more than cheap storage. And along the roof there are modern ventilators on old square brick oven chimneys for this abandoned long ago, metal treating plant."

Once on the loading dock, the guard comes up to open the door for us and then walks back to the gate house. The building interior is totally open steel framed space, black carbon coated with dust, dirt and rust covering everything including ten- and twenty-ton bridge cranes on rails running along this deep column free, high bay corridor building from front to back. Aside from loose wiring for refitted lighting, all of the original copper cable is stripped out. Now hanging loose, former water pipes for fire control and cooling hot metal, ruptured from winter freezing.

Juan remarks, "This place is spooky, so still and dark."

Anna corrects him, "Nonsense! What you see is the devastation caused by the failure of the Soviet system. There are whole cities dedicated to the military, that are empty and falling apart. This city in fact is doing well except for recent closures of a Ford Plant. GM and Nissan are also leaving. All of this happens because of the imperial behavior of his majesty the self-anointed czar for life, Vladimir Putin. Our decline starts when he annexed the Crimea. Western governments, financiers, and industrialist no longer trust Putin's Russia, and we the Russian people are once again paying the price for his criminal megalomania as he steals billions of rubles from our treasury to make himself the richest man on earth. Yes, and going back to Stalin, people are still disappearing and all we can do is say that it is good that we have a lot of people."

Mannie is floored, "I am so sorry for your troubles. Juan and I hope we can help you with stopping this evil, wealthy, and powerful drug ring from sending drug poison all over the world."

Juan walks down the wide and high corridor, "Hey. Over here, this is a steel enclosure with a heavy-duty lock on it."

Anna checks it out, "This is not a cheap lock and the door has an alarm system on it."

Mannie adds, "I don't think we need anything yet but we do have the tools to jimmy the door open. But let's keep looking."

Now halfway down the corridor, Juan spots something else. "Look! Here is a rail line and those tank cars on a side line are like the ones in Madrid."

Mannie goes up to one, "These are benzene carriers."

Anna whispers, "Hush, we are not alone. Listen, at the end of the building. See the lights. Hear the machinery?"

The three of them with a tool dolly in tow creep to the end of the building where active steam pipes are visible including main lines with high pressure safety valves. On the left side is a heavy steel door slightly ajar.

Anna looking in, "There are people in there and we can follow these mainlines in there as inspectors."

Anna pushes open the door and they walk in looking for pipe shut off valves and leaks. Anna whispers, "Now is your time to play dumb. There are many workers here."

Dressed in a black silk suit and black silk shirt with no tie, a short, squared off, wide man with no neck, a heavy black mustache, and black hair in a knotted pony tail, standing between two bigger men also in black silk suits, march up to Anna, "What are you doing in here. This is a restricted space."

Anna calmly and bureaucratically states, "I am a steam inspector searching for the loss of pressure in our system. What are you doing with our steam here?"

The no neck man is short, only five feet four inches, with short arms and legs he shapes out with an equally short face. He stomps up to Anna, face to face within inches, "That is none of your business! Our work here is secret. We have permission from the Polo Pharmacy. Take your peasants and leave now!"

Not giving up so easily, nor easily intimidated, Anna continues, "You have steam condensers, boilers, and copper kettles all for distillation, and ovens, I see your conveyor moving pellets that are in a semi-solid form laid on a conveyor, running through the oven and coming out quite hard."

The square man with his hand on her arm and the other two standing beside her yells, "Enough! Go or we will drag you out as he pulls a pistol out of his pocket."

After that dangerous comment, Anna realizes she is giving away the game, so she now plays up the 'I'm scared routine.' Mannie and Juan already have their hands in their pockets holding their Makarov's, "Oh please, please, I mean no harm. I will not report you! Please let go of me and we will leave."

The black suited bully smiles. Being pleased with her fearful pleading, without a word, he spins around and bobbles away as the two bigger bullies push Anna to the tool dolly and Juan and Mannie start moving back into the empty part of the building. The steel door slams shut behind them.

Anna is now committed to finding out more. "That man is a Georgian gangster, part of the mafia that runs illegal trade in his province. We are definitely on to something."

Juan is now happy to talk, "You bet something is up. All that equipment isn't in storage. There is an automatic bagging machine with one person mounting the bags, placing them on another conveyor going to pallets then being loaded on a truck. On the bag it says, Formula, with the pallets labeled intestinal treatments for horses, cattle and pigs and it has a red shipping band on it like the others in Madrid and Bogota."

As they get back to the ramp outside the building Mannie notices, "The extension of the building we were in has offices with floor to ceiling glass windows on a second floor that look like laboratories."

Anna grabs her telephoto lens camera, "Yes I can see two Russian officers, one is a general, the other a colonel and another with his back to me is a civilian."

Mannie blurts out, "Could that be Sergei Ivanoff?"

She looks at him sideways, "It could very well be. I cannot recognize any of them."

Juan asks "What are they doing here?"

Anna now smiling, "Well, they are having an active conversation. Their arms are flying around. They seem to be yelling at each other. They are looking at the civilian. That is that Georgian pig that nearly broke my arm."

Mannie wanting to move, "Juan, stay and watch for us. Honk the horn if someone is coming. Anna, lets climb this outside side stair case to get in and listen if we can."

Juan disappointed with not going, Anna drops her camera in Juan's hands, "I am the translator."

At the top Mannie tries the door, "It's open. Come on, I see no one in the hallway."

Anna trying a hall door to the next office whispers, "This door is open!"

Mannie smiling with another whisper, "This is like a front row seat!"

They slipped into the room, leave the lights off and move up close to a paper-thin wall. With their ears up tight to it they hear, "Why is this shipment late?"

"My general", sounding like the black suited Georgian, "we have had shipping problems. Our middle man in Paris is dead. We don't know why."

The general with disbelief, "You mean Anatoly?"

The Georgian answers respectfully, "Yes. He and Boris were shot at the barge. We no longer have a middle man to ship to Paris." Until we get a new man in place, we must withhold our shipments or compromise our network."

The General demands, "We must find out who is behind this attack on Anatoly. I want you and your brothers looking hard to find them and I want all of our locations guarded more closely. Check our intelligence out of Moscow including the police." The colonel interrupts, "General, our people in Moscow indicate that the police have been tracking an

American and Columbian investigating our shipments to and from Columbia. We are also under suspicion because of our monopoly of pharmaceutical production in Georgia. We know they sent a covert agent here to trace our shipments to Paris." The foreigners may have been the ones who killed our people in Paris.

"We will have our way," said the Colonel. "Our contacts with the Georgians are working with the other mafia groups in Moscow, all of them will be very interested in a capture and kill reward. Put out a contract on the three of them at 200,000 rubles each and we will get them, especially the officer in Moscow involved in the investigation." Ah," with a sigh of satisfaction the General concludes, "Increase the payment to 300,000 rubles. Somebody in the Moscow police will help. One of their own kind will betray that person for this kind of money. Go to our national and international intelligence agency and find out what information they can get about the American and the Columbian. Our military hacking office may also be of assistance."

"There is more, my General."

"And what is that?"

"A Spanish agent for drug enforcement in Madrid revealed the location of Anatoly to the two investigators."

"And what has happened to him?"

"He is eliminated. They will never find his body parts. We sent them to a pet food factory."

The General then goes on, "If there is cooperation between governments, we have a problem. It is not the first time we have encountered this, but we must deal with it quickly, efficiently and ruthlessly. No loose ends, all dead ends"

While Mannie and Anna are still in the room listening to the comments about organizing a new middle man in Paris, Juan decides to do some investigating of his own on the ground floor. He goes in front of a still bagging machine and collects a sample of the hard nuggets. He also goes to the storage area for the tank cars and draws a sample into a bottle container. As he goes back to the office warehouse, he passes a lab and notices a notebook open on one of the counters and grabs that to boot.

The meeting ends abruptly in the next room and Mannie and Anna sense that something is wrong. A plant alarm rings loudly as they hear footsteps going down the stairs and the sound of gunshots down the corridor towards the back of the other side of the warehouse. A firefight grows intense with rapid weapons. Juan has been trapped in the corner of the warehouse by three guards with machine pistols. He is desperately hiding behind stacks of barrels that are being pierced by the bullet's inches away from him.

Mannie and Anna, after seeing the occupants of the room next door go down the stairs, come out and run down the opposite stairs of this mezzanine space and work their way around the other side of the warehouse to rescue their friend. They open fire as they see the backs of their enemies. Two short bursts from both Anna and Mannie put the three assailants out of commission. The people in the upstairs are gone. Now the warehouse is quiet and empty.

Juan comes out from behind one of the perforated canisters with a smile on his face saying, "Gracias Amigos. Once again you have saved my life Mannie."

Anna stops for a moment as they are smiling, "It took two of us to save you and you are supposed only to be a look out."

Juan said, "Yes, but I have found samples of their shipments. They are in my back pocket."

Mannie impatient now, "Time to go folks. More are coming."

Once in the truck with Anna's lead foot breaking through the entrance gate and leaping on the highway, Juan bounces up and down trying to hold on to his booty. With light traffic after hours, Anna gets to the bridge across the river to get back to their hotel in good time. All the while Juan keeps talking, "I have recovered quite a bit. Look here. This is a lab manual for combining compounds and processing the benzene. With the samples that I have recovered, we can have them tested in a laboratory."

Anna shows appreciation, "Good idea. But now we need to get out of here fast. There is a price on our heads."

Anna drops Mannie and Juan at their hotel and parks the truck a block away. Now back in their room with the samples stacked alongside each other on the table in front of them Anna's muses, "What are they doing here? This smells like gasoline. This smells like cleaning fluid."

Mannie, "I'll bet you anything that's toluene. And these nuggets, they are hard like calcium preformed before casting in a pill mold."

Anna adds, "Yes. But the preformed unit looks like a prescription medicine for stomach problems for horses and cattle of all types."

Juan volunteers a slant on that, "But look at this booklet of formulas."

Anna notes, "They are refractory formulas for distilling and drying. This is a simple process for extracting heroin from the gasoline. Another formula uses the toluene byproduct for an insecticide for barns, stables, and animal enclosures. This is simple, not difficult, and hardly a secret formula"

Mannie concludes, "Ok, we know one leg of the trip, but what about the cocaine going to Russia."

Juan takes the butt of his gun and crushes one of the nuggets. "This is a simple compound. No smell or taste of cocaine. There is nothing else to it. So, at this point, we can possibly nail them for transporting heroine in gasoline. But we don't have anything for distributing cocaine from Columbia or Argentina."

Mannie raises the anti, "We need to go back to Bogota to see what they do with the nuggets and follow their shipments out."

Anna agrees. "Da, if we live that long. They will seek us out and kill us as soon as they can. Our lives are short if we don't move immediately. And I think we can kill two birds with one stone by going to Finland by train and stopping in Helsinki and the University. I have a chemist friend that can help us with the nugget's buried compounds."

Mannie agrees, "Great idea Anna, we do need to confirm our suspicions with a laboratory analysis. Sounds like the safest way out of here and still getting something done."

Anna thinks for a moment. "I am sure if we send these samples to the labs in Moscow the results somehow will slip out the back door into the hands of the Georgians along with our ID's and location. We should go now while we can get past their check points and the Finland train station is just across the river. We would never make it out by plane or trains going west. They will be watching for us everywhere, even on the roads at gasoline stations."

Juan also agrees, "We are the birds already out of the cage as far as that goes. Let's chance Anna's run, with roadblock adapting as needed."

Chapter Eleven

Let The Games Begin

Back at the Hacienda after an allowed loss to the Columbian team at Parma, a famous Argentine barbeque is in progress with guest team supporters from the Buenos Aires district. For Josephine, the past month melted away and all the sixteen horses, now trained ponies, and the team, able and ready to play for the championship, have proved themselves ready for the challenge.

Julio's grandfather, Damian, raises his wine glass to the crowd, "Senors y Senoras y Senoritas, I wish to toast our team. They won the regional in Florida to participate in the International Championship play-off here at Parma. Nineteen countries have competed regionally to come here. Only eight teams have advanced to come to this final playoff. There will be two brackets of four teams. The winner of each bracket will play for the final championship. May our team for Argentina once again be a winner, to victory and my grandson Julio and his team, Salud!"

With the evening full of party noise, Julio sitting alone is nudged by his aunt, Alessandra, "Julio why are so lonely here?" Julio with his head down, stares at the ground, "I cannot help it, my heart and soul burns with my passion for Josephine. I feel like I am on that barbeque pit being roasted with every turn."

Alessandra with her hand on his shoulder sits next to him, "Julio, it is the burden of love and be glad you have it. For without love, your life would be empty. She has fulfilled you more than you know. I have watched you grow, and it has been all good since you have met her."

Julio, "But I don't know where our story is going. My mind pains me beyond reason just thinking I might lose her and never have her as my partner in life."

Alessandra, "You have no choice. You must always be here for her as best you can be. Our lives are a mystery from day to day. Enjoy each moment with her. She is already a good friend and has risked her life to safe you."

Julio, "I know she wants me. I can feel it. I want to kiss her, hold her, and give her my heart and soul. But she stops me, and not so gently."

Alessandra, "The both of you have a predicament. You can't fit together the way things are. Don't you think that she too is in pain with her willingness to protect you and work with you? I am mystified by her and your mother hates her for having such a spell over you, especially after fruitlessly sending the Niña to you to distract you."

Julio, "It is true, I felt obliged to accept my mother's gift. But it was nothing and left me empty. I wished it was Josephine. She is already a part of me and because I respect her and I trust her in every way, I must hold myself back. On the ponies and with everything we do, we are so much alike and liking it so much."

Alessandra offers her final council to Julio. "Be patient. Be the hands-off good partner that you are. Many people have no partner at all. And with her you will never be alone. Look, they are dancing with the mariachi band. Go ask Josephine to dance. Soon you will be on the field from where all your happiness stems."

Julio gratefully accepts her advice, "Si la Tia! Mucho Gracias!"

Alessandra, heartfelt for the two, watches them dance. Her past is locked with a lost love and she feels a very real sympathy for Julio. She also fears for the two of them amid all of the family intrigue with Lucia and Adolpho.

The next day, Julio speaks at the first game breakfast meeting, "Today our first set is with France, a team from St. Tropez in the south. The captain's name is Dax. He is a wonder boy with electronics and is said to have trained his ponies with electronic signals. They also have a woman on their team playing offence. Her name is Alexi and she has a goal rating at 8. This team ranks among the top ten in Europe. Our challenge is to employ our new team plays. Josephine, you are riding against a lady much smaller than you, likely weighing just ninety pounds. Her speed will count but her agility will rely heavily on her pony, likely to be a mare. And Bandit will definitely want to dominate her steed and by all means you are encouraged to show off your barrel racing and calf roping skills in our practiced two- and three-way passes. Carlos, you, Pedro and Alejandro will work up our defense with your great stealing and pass practices. Guillermo, Alvaro, and Armando will be our back-ups."

Alessandra interrupts, "A moment of prayer to our Lord, bless us dear Lord, we pray for your strength in the course of our game today. Our faith remains with you at all times. Amen. And by the way defense means offense."

All respond, "Amen."

All stand up and leave for the stable with ponies already trailer loaded. The next stop is Parma. Their cavalcade through the city is uneventful? Not bad this time. The people lining the streets are waving and cheering them on.

As the Vega de la Dega cavalcade of trailers pulls onto the field, the grandstand, filled shoulder to shoulder, stands up and cheers. For the oncoming French team, thousands of fans from around the world and Europe vigorously provide a very competitive cheer. Without hesitation the ponies, unloaded and saddled, are warming up with their riders on the field. The game horn announces the beginning of the game as the two teams line up in center court. The first chukker begins as the umpire and his pony moves to bowl in the ball for play.

Julio and Josephine are facing Dax and Alexi. Bandit is already stressing, so jumpy at the ball drop that he bumped Alexi's pony and gave Josephine a dead-on 100-yard shot toward their goal. Carlos and Alejandro move out behind Josephine's line when suddenly Dax and Alexi cross ahead of them and close in on Josephine. Julio moves off for a pass with the pressure now on Josephine. For some reason Bandit falters and kicks, and Josephine is quickly passed by Dax reaching the ball with a backward pass to Alexi. She establishes a line with Carlos closing on her despite her defense riders, and is pacing her all the way. Alexi fifty yards out takes a shot and scores for the first point of the match.

Back at the side lines for a break, Alessandra, face to face with Josephine yells, "What happened with Bandit?" Josephine stutters, "I...I just don't know?"

Julio barks, "That Dax is wearing a headset radio under his helmet. Somehow, he got to Bandit's ears. Ready for your pass I saw his ears reverse to the rear, his anger mode, and then he bolts."

Carlos thinking a bit, "Could it have been a horse fly, hornet sting or something in his eye?"

Alessandra concludes, "If there is some interference from Dax, Carlos, you and Allehandro keep him busy, distracted, and crowded.

Keep blocking his vision of our team working the ball."

Saddling up for the field they yell, "Si! Mucho Gusto!"

Back in center court with the bowl of the ball, the players bunch and Julio hit the ball loose with the side of his mallet. With a break away, Carlos rides alongside Julio at speed tapping the ball to set it up for a single thirty-yard shot between the goal posts. Dax is at speed riding between Carlos and Allehandro as Josephine paces Alexi. As Julio expertly taps the ball between the goals the sideline referee waves his hands for a score. The crowd roars with pleasure at the sight of a most artful play on the field.

With time for another play and with no calls for penalties, the umpire calls for a second bowl in. Upon the toss, Carlos backs away as Julio slivers his way into the middle of the bunch and back hits the ball to Carlos. Alexi then swivels into Carlos's side and hooks his mallet as the ponies kicked the ball a short way from the tussle.

Julio paced by Dax, has a right-side clearance and makes a deep hit to within thirty yards of their goal. Dax yells, "Mon Dieu, Alexi se charge!" Alexi faster than Josephine to the ball makes a defensive hit to the boards on the side line. Josephine makes a neck braking barrel turn and Bandit recovers with due speed. Julio and Dax race to Josephine who sees no advantage hitting to Julio. Carlos is free on the opposite side of the court waiting for one of their practiced routines. She hits across to him literally free of interference. Carlos almost walks the ball to the court for another gentle tap for a score. The grand stand shakes with cheers madly waving Argentine flags.

At the break for the next chukker, Carlos speaks quietly, "This tough team doesn't know our moves. This is fun!"

The second chukker proves a stalemate as the French team anticipates Julio and Carlos and watches for Josephine's fantastic equine moves with Bandit.

With the third chukker, the French team is getting desperate and makes an illegal move crossing Josephine's line of movement after hitting the ball. The umpire blows his whistle and places a Penalty 3 on Alexi giving Josephine a 30-yard shot to the goal at an angle from the center where the penalty occurred. Looking skyward, taking a deep breath, Josephine calmly whispers to Bandit, "Easy boy" as she gently pressed her knees against his withers. She slowly road up to the ball in place and off the right-hand side hit the ball hard, but low to the ground. It bounced a couple of times going the wrong way and then the final bounce put the ball between the goal posts.

Julio's grandfather watching from the grandstand exclaims, "What a game to watch. This is fantastic."

Lethal Lucia has more slime to toss, "There she goes again, grand standing for the crowd!"

Adolpho speaks covering his mouth, "Lucia, stop it. We need to win this tournament or we may be grandstanding somewhere else, just to be safe!"

Lucia agrees, "Si, and we put our little friends with the Columbian team to also help us win?"

Adolpho grins, "Naturalmente, mi amor."

The fourth and fifth chukkers proved stalemates in this low scoring but evenly matched competition. At the last chukker, Dax and Alexi brake away with the ball between them rushing from center field to the Degas goal. Bandit catches up to them and Josephine bumps Alexi's pony to no effect. Dax, now in control, takes a shot to score a goal to make the score two to two. With no time left for a second bowl in, the umpire calls a tie game that automatically goes into sudden death. The first to score from this point on wins the match.

At the break, Alessandra looks silently skyward with her hands in prayer. Julio looks at Carlos and Josephine and calmly describes a winning maneuver. "Now is the time to try our three-pony pass. We have not used it yet today and we can rush the field with side to side passing in a zigzag formation. It will throw them completely off balance."

The French team leader Dax exclaims, "C'est magnifique. Nous avon la balle se passer troisieme chose. Allez, Allez!" It looks like the French think like the Degas team.

In the center and set four to four on each side, the umpire bowls the ball in the center of the set. Instead of the scramble both teams back off three up-front and one back. Bandit rears and charges to the ball and Josephine hits under his belly to the left at Carlos. Already the French team anticipates and intercepts the ball with a drive to the Degas goal. Julio, Carlos and Alejandro race to the goal with the French, both teams with their three positions, side by side.

Josephine now at the rear with a squeeze whispers to Bandit and he leaps into racing gate for Josephine to execute a classic cavalry move. She drives to the right boards and out flanks the French three pony drill and cuts between them in a three second standoff to hit the loose ball under Bandit's belly back to the French goal. She is already on the way to recover it for a second shot when the remaining players are just pivoting for a reverse run. With a great break away and now within thirty yards for a head on shot, Josephine drills the ball between the goal posts for a score. Although the French protest Josephine's cross cut between the two sides with a two or three second standoff, the umpire declares her to be hitting a loose ball with no line established.

The crowd dominated by Argentineans is ecstatic with paper cups, papers, and hats in the air and hugging everywhere. And then a song erupts that all know by heart, "Himno Nacional Argentino." Back at the trailer station, all team members, after such an exhausting duel, hug each other with a great deal of energy. Julio and Josephine are the last to embrace and without a thought they kiss and hug again and again without a word. They then look at each other with a smile as if it was their first meeting after a long time apart.

Alessandra gently with a smile breaks them apart, "Now, now. That is enough. We must care for the ponies and return to the hacienda for another party!"

Enough said, Josephine and Julio break up, nodding yes, and go to unsaddle their steeds for loading on the trailers. The next match occurs in four days.

Back in St. Petersburg, Anna fears discovery. "Mikhail knows your hotel location and they will get to him. We must leave now. Package our evidence on ourselves and carry a small overnight bag. We can still get to the rail station going to Finland before the traffic builds up.

We'll use the steam repair truck."

Mannie counters, "Maybe we can set up a new location and sit it out?"

Juan looks reality in the eye, "No, Mannie, they are hunting us big time with lots of rubles on the street. That kind of news travels like wildfire! They, the general and the Georgians want us all dead, and the only way to save Anna is to get her out of Russia too. We are a black op with no branding and no official sanctioning. They can accuse and kill us for being a terrorist arm of any convenient real or fictional organization."

Mannie shakes his head in disgust, "Great! So, there is no safe place in Putin country. Once again, we are off to apply our back door skills.

Spaciba, Anna, we go to Finland and knock on a few more back doors"

Anna agrees, "Da, and my old school mate in Helsinki at the University will help us. We can get our lab results with her unofficially and then seek out our most trustworthy contact to disclose this drug ring evidence and its distribution network."

Mannie then suggests, "Should we go as tourists to Helsinki? That way they can't expect us to speak Russian and Anna you can be our guide?"

Anna shaking no, "Get on plain street clothes. No plaid shirts. No tennis shoes. Wear your work hats. Carry your guns in a pocket. Leave your luggage here. When they get here, they may think we are hiding. Not running."

In a few minutes, Juan looks at Mannie and Anna, "Ready to go. Let's take the back stairs."

As they are just down the hall to the stairs, the elevator stops on their floor. Mannie motions to Juan and Anna as they head into the stair door, "They're here!" He quietly closes the door, "Double time, down the stairs. It will take them a few minutes to check out the room."

Opening at the back of the hotel, they skirt around to the truck parked in the alley. Anna takes the wheel of the truck and she slowly moves out onto the road when she notices, "That's their black van. I'll turn left to get back to the next corner to get on another street going north to the Liteyny Prospect and bridge to the Finlyandskiy railway station."

Mannie turns to Juan, "Get to the back door window. We may need you there if they spot us."

Making all the turns, traffic going north was lighter than going south. Anna breathes easier, "They would never suspect us going back to the tank plant area. I am going to follow this electric bus across."

Juan looking back and to the side traffic, "None of the drivers are giving us the once over. Looks good, uh oh, there's the black van farther back. They don't see us yet."

Anna replies, "Our turn off onto the river road is just ahead."

Juan barks, "They are moving over to the left lane to go faster."

Anna cranks the wheel, "Turning now and speeding up to get out of their view."

Juan with a big exhale, "They're going straight."

In a few blocks Anna turns to come back on the split road to enter the train station plaza with its clock tower over the entrance.

Mannie exclaims, "Wow, what are all these people and military with canons doing in front of the plaza?"

Anna, "It is a display of all of the artillery produced in the tank factory" as she parks behind a bus in a bus only parking zone.

Mannie, "They have everything from mortars, rocket launchers, anti-tank guns, and 125 to 250 millimeter cannons."

Unloaded, Anna leaves the keys, "Now we are to walk just like we are separate. I will walk ahead. Mannie, stay just behind me toward the curb. Then Juan moves closer to the building in the shade. Stay this way as we enter the station and sit near me but separately as I buy the tickets. Follow me the same way as I go to the train platform. Come up behind me when I go to the boarding counter and I will provide the tickets to the conductor as he asks for them. And we will then board and stay together. We are going to the University and you two are visiting professors from the US and Columbia. Correct?"

Mannie can't resist, "Let me see, I specialize in human behavior, psychology!"

Juan laughs, "I did graduate with a degree in science. I like the idea of being a professor of chemistry."

All done with no problem, Anna followed by her tourist friends walks up to the conductor at a first-class coach with steward services. She pulls out three tickets for a private compartment with a toilet. The conductor takes off a tab from each and points to cabin number three's door.

It has been a long day. Once on board and in the compartment with the door shut, thinking how they are going to make their next move, they just sit and stare out the window.

Back at the international polo tournament, the Vega de la Dega team handily defeats the second and third round opponents to survive as one of the last two winners to compete for the championship. The other survivor, the Columbian team, pulls onto the field. The grandstand divides evenly between these two South American teams and all stand up and cheer waving their national flags. With tension and binoculars glistening everywhere in the stands, the ponies start warming up with their riders on the field. Then the game horn announces the beginning of the game as the teams line up in center court. The first chukker begins as the mounted umpire moves in to bowl in the ball for the first play of the game.

Julio and Josephine are facing Fernando and Sanchez, and Bandit is already jumpy with Fernando's chestnut stallion. A dual bump from both ponies put Josephine out of reach for the ball. Fernando then hooks Julio while Sanchez moves in to slam the ball to the Degas goal. Carlos and Alejandro move out behind Sanchez's line, while Julio sprints with Fernando to meet the ball. Josephine pivots back to the action. With Bandit's fast gate she soon is back to act as a pass receiver if Carlos or Julio make a hit. Rodriguez seeing the play catches up to Josephine and paces her as she almost rides in circles waiting for a chance to receive a pass. Julio's pony, trying to back up, kicked the ball out of their play, giving Fernando a dead shot to the Degas goal. It is refereed as a score for Columbia.

At the break Alessandra admonishes, "Fernando has a 12-goal handicap. Carlos, you and Alejandro have to double your guard efforts with him. Don't interfere. Just always be with him on each side as much as you can. Josephine, make your break away without looking, just go. You can count on Julio to match you for a pass if needed. Remember our practice passes and double carries down the field to avoid interference."

The Columbian team is happy about the first goal and plans for an all-out victory. Fernando opens with a shout, "Bueno, we showed them how to play. Sanchez, we may not have to employ Raul's magic pin. If things get tough, I will signal you to sandwich that crazy woman for a pinch of our needle juice to slow her down and oops fall off her pony."

Rodriguez interrupts, "Si Patrone. Yet my pony, playing so well these last games, now gets temperamental when I need to turn hard right or left."

Fernando orders, "Change ponies now. We need complete control playing this team, on to the field."

Back in center court with the bowl of the ball, the players crowd and Josephine sneaks a bit hard hit bouncing off of Fernando's pony's boot and ricocheting to the side boards. Carlos pointing in the right direction brakes away to meet the ball while Julio rides to the Columbia goal for a pass. Carlos just gets the ball away as Sanchez bumped him to shake his hit. Fernando alongside Josephine snuggles up to Bandit, but Bandit shoots away like a missile launch. Julio plows the ball to a 30-yard shot and swings a hefty hard mallet hit to score with a referee's flag. The game is one to one.

Fernando grows angry and confused with his pony's refusal to reign, and can barely get him back to their stand as the seven-and-ahalf-minute chukker ended with the horn. Sanchez and Fernando call to the stable mates. Fernando yells, "What is wrong with our ponies. They are acting as if they are in pain. Call a vet here now!"

The veterinarian on duty comes and examines the ponies for cracked or split bones, torn muscles and finally examines their teeth. After removing the bit and harness he opens the mouth of Ferdinand's pony and gasps, "My God, this pony is massively infected with bot flies. His gums are soft and the teeth are moving every time you put pressure on the bit." It will take a week to get the pupa out with medication to avoid infection. This pony can no longer be ridden."

Ferdinand screams, "How does this happen? Our ponies were inspected before we left and when we arrived. They had no such infection then. It had to happen over the last week."

Looking back at the vet, Fernando pleads, "Will you check all of our sixteen ponies to see if they are similarly infected."

The vet nods affirmatively and goes from pony to pony. The umpire inquires of the delay and with pony injuries he extends the break.

The announcer discloses a bot fly infection and the crowd hums with negative tones as bot flies are common throughout South America.

The vet returns with a sad face, "I am sorry Senor, all of your ponies are infected and I cannot allow them to be played on the field."

Ferdinand screams, "This is insane. We must be able to play."

The two umpires and referee meet and come back to Ferdinand with their decision, "Senor, if you cannot field ponies for the next chukker in the next hour we will declare you in default and award the championship to the Vega de la Dega team."

Ferdinand desperate to stay in the game calls the French team, "Dax our ponies strangely became infected with bot flies during the last week. Can we ride with your ponies for this last match?"

Dax replies, "I am sorry my friend our ponies are at the airport in a hangar waiting to be loaded onto a 747-cargo plane. There is nothing I can do for you."

Several more calls produce the same answer, "Sorry!"

The umpire announces on the grand stand speaker, "Ladies and Gentlemen, we regret that the Columbian ponies are unable to play on the field due to serious bot fly infections. The Columbian team is unable to field alternative ponies at this time, thus incurring a default. The Vega del la Dega team is hereby declared the winner and champion of this tournament."

The crowd is utterly silent. One onlooker declares, "This is no way to win or lose a championship." The rumors run rampantly from row to row of seating. "How does this happen? Those ponies were at the same stables with all of the other ponies. None of the others who played here had this trouble?"

Suspicions gather momentum and Columbian fans begin pointing at the Degas team and their fans stand in defense declaring the Columbians are incompetent at caring for their ponies. The arguments get louder and collapsible chairs started flying.

The chairman of the international polo committee announces, "Ladies and Gentlemen. The rules prevail regarding this tournament. However; the umpires, referees and veterinarian believe the infection deserves an investigation. The Degas team tied the Columbians in the second chekkar. If our investigation warrants it, we will call a new match within a week. If not, Degas is the champion."

Rioting quells, and the crowd disburses thinking sadly for the ponies suffering what they know is a painful and weakening infection. On the other hand, it means another week of partying. One fan gets philosophical? "Why not party, this is Buenos Aires?"

Back at the side line for the Degas team, Alessandra truly exasperated screams, "How can we win without winning. This is no victory and the infection announcement smells of malicious intent to wipe out the Columbians."

Josephine is also shattered with disappointment, "We are ready to win. We want to play."

Julio in anguish, raises his hands to the sky, "I just don't know? Something always goes wrong with what we are doing."

Carlos is angrier than ever, "I had them on the field. They are gone but not with their tails between their legs."

Alessandra knows that there is no pride taken in this default. Her team can't be better without proving it on the field. She quietly relents, "We must care for our ponies and return to the hacienda. The match may still be scheduled and as always we will be ready, until then, no party."

In a very quiet way, Josephine, Carlos, Alejandro, Pedro and Julio nod agreement and unsaddle their steeds for loading on the trailers.

Julio's grandfather, Damian, watching from the grandstand exclaims, "This is most perplexing. It is no great win for our name. And we know stable keepers are well trained. Bot flies are always watched for and brushed out from their hides and around their eyes. How could this happen?"

Lucia offers a back hand on her own work, "I have heard that their stable keepers are on Paco."

Adolpho whispers in her ear, covering his mouth, "Lucia, stop it. That has not been announced yet."

Damian looks at Lucia, "Your pharmacy has antidotes for bot flies, does it not?"

Lucia agrees, "Si, that is a large part of our business."

Damian is getting curious, "So you must study bot flies in your labs and keep pupae on hand for testing your antidotes and antibiotics for fighting infections."

Lucia forcing a smile, "Desde luego, mi padre, we are very knowledgeable about their reproduction and timing from insertion of an egg to pupa development and flying out when ready."

Damian is now accusative, "So you know how long it takes for an egg to pupate and infect at an insertion. How long would that be?"

Lucia responds evasively, "It depends on the egg location, body temperature, exposure to sun light, and other variables including Ph levels and alkaline levels in the diet."

Daminan still persists, "So how many days does it take for an egg to mature to a pupa or larva?"

Lucia replies, "One to several weeks. Look! Julio and the trucks are leaving. We must go."

Chapter Twelve

Surviving The Ride

After a rewarding nap on board, the movement of the train awakens Anna who alarms Mannie and Juan, "Hey you can sleep later. I am going to the dining car to pick up some sandwiches. The steward will bring us coffee."

Mannie jokes, "What, no wine for this luxury compartment?"

As she walks out, "Privacy is a luxury; alcohol is the loss of an edge for survival. We are not free from danger yet."

Mannie apoligizes, "Yes Anna, you are right, just trying to have some fun."

Once the door closes Juan couldn't hold himself quiet, "You have a thing for this very good-looking lady? Don't you!"

Mannie tries to be professional, "We are lucky to have her on board."

Juan replies, "You mean we are lucky that she takes us on to help her investigation!"

Mannie faces a different reality, "Ok, we are all professional but her face keeps appearing in my mind when I close my eyes. That black hair, that critical smile that sticks with me, and her skills and confidence attract me beyond professional appreciation."

Juan now getting wise, "You mean you are falling for her."

Just then a knock and whisper, "It is me, Anna."

Juan opens the door and Anna rushes in and quickly shuts the door. With utter surprise and fear she announces, "They are looking for us on this train. Two Georgians are cruising the seats in second and third class. How did they know we are here? Did either of you contact anyone?"

Juan replies, "No, I haven't used my cell phone since we took pictures of documents in Paris."

Anna falls to the seat, "Oh Bozhe, that is why everyone knows about you two. They have been tracking you with your cell phones from Columbia, Madrid, Paris and Russia. Our military hacked your cell phone system data base for movements in Russia. They know we are on this train!"

Mannie sheepishly adds, "We should know better. We didn't think our system would track here."

Juan answers, "Yes, but at least it helped us with photographing documents in Paris."

Anna now the teacher, "All good spies carry cameras, not self-locating cell phones. Take out your cell phones. If you cannot remove the battery throw them out the window"

Mannie interrupts, "Wait, do we have several stops before Helsinki?"

Anna, "Yes we are coming up to Gavrilovo, a stone quarry town just before we enter Finland at Vyborg. The people getting off are lined up at the 3rd class coach."

Mannie, "Juan, lets lock out our phones. Anna, take them to third class, walking past them, drop them into the carry-on bags of the people leaving."

Anna with a clever smile quickly agrees, "Blagoy! It will be crowded and shoulder to shoulder bumping. Oh, and not to worry. I have a pocket camera with video that also registers time, date, and longitude-latitude."

Anna takes the phones and walks back to third class as the train starts to slow down.

Mannie hopes. "We only have a couple of hours to make Helsinki. They will likely figure out that we got off at Gavrilovo to hide out and will leave at Vyborg to come back here on the return train."

Juan, "That's great. I'll bet Anna will keep her wheels moving." Mannie now starting to clutch reality, "Yeah, She's great. We have to watch out for her and cover her back. Come hell or high water, the three of us are in this together."

Juan half asleep, "Si Sinore. Mucho Gusto, a pleasure especially for you. For me it is the need for another nap before anything else goes wrong."

At the Hacienda at the morning breakfast after the big match, Julio, Damian, Lucia and Adolpho are already seated and eating when Josephine comes in and goes to the buffet and gathers some eggs, bacon and some fruit with toast and sits at her now accepted place next to Julio at the table. The news about the match on TV points to stable keepers influenced by the use of Paco leading to carelessness for the bot fly infection of the Columbia team. The Degas team is declared the defaulted winner and the party in Buenos Aires ends. No parades, no flags, no glad handing at all. They all mumble, "Maybe next year."

Julio affectionately looks at Josephine, "I have made the arrangements for our ponies to be flown back to Miami for stabling in West Palm. We need to leave soon. I have to get back to my practice and my patients are upset having to wait for me. We also need our ponies for the next tournament."

Josephine is in agreement, "This has been a lifetime experience. Getting back to the beach parties in Florida will be like wading in a still pool of stale water. But that is where I must be, when my husband arrives."

Lamenting Lucia grins with a crooked smile, "Yes, at this hacienda, there is no time to meditate. Adolpho and I need to go back to Bogota to carry on our business."

Julio's grandfather Damian then volunteers, "Julio, I have arranged for a caravan of trailers to arrive tomorrow morning to deliver your ponies to the airport. It is a bit of a ride so Lucia and Adolpho will help with the stop at the veterinary just outside Buenos Aires to have them checked and give them the appropriate inoculations for the trip and for entry into the United States. You won't need to come along. They can arrange for that all on your behalf and meet you at the airport." Julio agrees, "Yes that would be fine. We will meet you at the airport and fly with the ponies in a cargo plane. I believe we have a 747?"

Damian continues, "Yes, I have arranged for a Federal Express plane to come in and make the delivery for us. They have the cargo bay set up for properly fastening the ponies in netting and so forth to make sure they are not harmed on flight takeoff and landing. The whole cabin is pressurized so they will be comfortable and warm as well."

Julio happily replies, "Wonderful," as he gets up, he asks, "Josephine would you like to join me for a walk in the garden?"

Josephine rising and looking at Julio, "I would be very happy to. Would you excuse us?"

Julio opens the French doors onto the veranda and off into the garden they walk.

Lucia and Adolpho walk to the library and shut the door. Adolpho punches his phone for his call, "Olah, General Menendez, it is Adolpho. How are you doing?"

General Menendez briskly replies, "Fine Adolpho, why are you calling?"

Adolpho in a low voice, "We want to make a shipment. Can we meet you with a troop convoy on the outside of Buenos Aires to escort us to the border?"

"Of course, Adolpho, I will bring a platoon of soldiers along with an armored vehicle. You have my usual fee?"

"Yes, we do. We have received it from Bogotá. Adios Amigo"

Lucia concludes, "He's expensive, but we couldn't make it to the border with two tons of product without him. And we may be doing more business this way. A US Army unit arrived in Bogota to help the federal government reduce Columbia's higher coca production at 951 tons this last year, meaning to cut it by half in a year by again going out and destroying growing fields."

Adolpho asks, "Where did you learn this?"

Lucia's devilish smile, "I have friends at the US Embassy and the Russian Embassy."

Adolpho concludes, "Si, Sergio always knows both ways."

In the garden, while walking casually, Julio abruptly stops, looking at Josephine, and begins in a very soft voice. "Josephine, I can no longer hold back my feelings for you. I love you very much. I would like to make you, my wife. Would you marry me?"

Josephine looks at him with a wonderful smile and a soft passionate face. "My dear Julio, marriage is not on my calendar. Much remains to be done that I cannot tell you about at this time."

Julio persists looking for her answer, "What is your secret? In Florida you can easily arrange a divorce from your always missing husband."

Josephine tries to stave off the issue, "Yes that is very possible. Believe me; I cannot surrender my heart to you at this time, only when the time is right."

Julio now certain of Josephine's affection for him, pauses a moment, then solemnly replies, "I also have a problem to get out of our way. And I am afraid it may cause us more problems."

Josephine is ready to listen, "What kind of problems, and how can I help?"

Julio cries out, "It is my mother, her business. It is where the money comes from. It is too much for a pharmacy business. It is too far spread from where things come and where things go. Something is wrong. Why are gangsters after me? Who wants to kill a dentist? They try but they can't keep me out of it. I believe she is dealing with an international drug cartel, and using her pharmacy business as a cover."

Josephine notes, "Lucia's business survives with her brutal attitude, one needed for that kind of enterprise. And your father's military connections may help to carry a network. His friends are respected, outstanding citizens. These relationships eliminate a lot of trafficking hazards."

"Well, that's just it," said Julio. "They're all military. All his friends are generals, colonels and majors in the military of Spain, Columbia and Argentina and," then he paused, "Russia."

Josephine is surprised with a broader horizon. "What do you mean Russia?"

Julio follows up, "I have heard my father speaking to a man called Sergei Ivanoff. I looked his name up with the Russian Military. There is no such person. But the Russian military for ten years has had access to one-third of the world's opium in Afghanistan. And that kind of bad habit could carry-on long after they left. I don't know how, but my mother with the help of my father is somehow trafficking in the opium trade, as well as cocaine which she collects here in Argentina by the tons."

Josephine playing the non-devil's advocate, "No, that can't be. There are a lot of shipments of medicine components from Russia to Europe and the Middle East. Perhaps your mother uses materials from Russia for making their medicines."

Julio agrees but, "Oh yes there are such shipments and materials. Besides generic pill making, some shipments that come from Russia have a statement – 'FORMULA' branded on the cases."

Josephine's wheels are now turning, "I get it. Given all the obvious pharmacy business, your mother is running a hidden, likely illegal, sideline, covered by a legitimate, intricate shipping and receiving web typical for a pharmacy business."

Julio is exasperated, "Exactly! It is not so obvious and it is impossible to penetrate and prove what is happening."

Josephine now shows a heavy concern, "Julio, how can I help you out of this predicament? What do you want me to do, spy on your mother?"

Julio now backs up, "No, I cannot ask you to do that. I want to be free of her, but not that way. She is still my mother. But what she is doing will go wrong someday. So far, on the surface it seems just a business, but if it is worse than just business, as I suspect, the end of it will come by itself with much pain to us all."

Having survived Russian Mafia discovery, the train pulling into Helsinki wakes up Mannie and Juan, while Anna, diligent as ever, comes back to the compartment after going through the train to ensure no Georgians remain on board.

Anna speaking up, "We no longer need to play separate. Mannie you have Euros to pay for taxi, meals, and a car rental to drive to Sweden? I only have rubles and cannot use my badge and cards." Mannie wonders, "Why don't we just take a ferry?"

Anna shows impatience. "Do you want crowds to see the three of us with some people on board already alerted about 300,000 rubles apiece for us, a reward now all over the continent?"

Mannie sufficiently chastised ends with a friendly compliment, "Anna, you are right. The men would have trouble keeping their eyes off of you."

Juan cutting in, "Time to get off this train and take a taxi to the University, right?"

Once out of the train station, Mannie walks up to a cabbie, and lets Anna give him the address. They keep quiet until they reach the University campus by the Science building. Mannie pays the cabbie and they walk into the building. On the third floor Anna knocks on a heavy steel door. As it opens, she smiles, "Olga Kakuty? It has been two years since we met in Moscow over a chemical forensics class. I am so happy for your work here at the University with the anti-drug enforcement agency of Helsinki!"

Olga with a similar smile and equal enthusiasm, "Anna, it is amazing how our paths cross working to stop criminals from ruining our societies. What new challenge do you have for me? Is it more of the many transformations of drugs to escape detection by the anti-drug inspectors of Moscow?"

Anna opens up, "You wouldn't believe how they try to hide opium and cocaine shipments by plane, truck, ship, and cars using donkeys carrying bags, shoes, medicine caplets, even wine bottles with false bottoms filled with liquid cocaine easily recovered with simple evaporation and filtering."

Olga agrees, "Ha, they can't easily hide the cocaine scent from a good dog no matter how hard they try. Yet here in Helsinki we fear some drugs are getting through without detection. And we are anxious to cooperate with you on any detection methods to be uncovered with the how, when and with what. Who are these handsome men that you have with you?"

Anna slightly blushes, "These are my two comrades, Mannie is from the US and Juan is from Columbia. We are a team investigating an international cartel smuggling drugs all over the world, a ring that waltzes past shipping points without question and transports thousands of tons of heroin and cocaine each year worth billions of Ruples, Dollars, and Euros, as well as Yuans."

Mannie graciously asks, "I am so glad to meet you and I hope that your knowledge in forensic chemistry can help us with distinguishing a simple medical pill from a treated medical pill containing otherwise undetectable drugs."

Juan adds, "And in our country the success in growing over 200,000 acres of coca leaves continues with the ability to export cocaine always at arms with our government. We are very successful at airport discoveries of passengers or packaged shipments. But what we find hardly makes a dent in our crop production. Again, we are getting help from the US to train our troops to destroy the crops in the field. But that will not end the trade."

Olga with a smile confirms, "I am so glad that you have joined Anna in this great struggle to defeat this cartel, no doubt very powerful, and well connected in government with millions in payoffs. We here in Finland struggle with the runners and sellers but not the makers who flood our country with their social and physical poison."

Anna warns, "Olga, we are here undercover. The Georgian Mafia is looking for us with a price on our heads. I cannot go back to my office in Moscow. One of them, I am sure, is ready to inform them of my location. So, what we do here is completely secret from your people, their people and my people, until we know enough of the story to go to our embassies and the World Health Organization with our evidence. I must warn you that working with us may put you in danger."

Olga hardly frightens, "Give me what you have and I will see what can be done."

Juan handing over a clear plastic bag of hard, very large, oval, white pills, "These are what I snagged at one of our unauthorized inspections. I took them because the box packaging compared to all the others in storage had a stamped red word "FORMULA".

Olga begins, "Let's get to it now. Crushing this pill in my mortar and pestle, I add some water and test it with our trusty strips. For cocaine, it will turn blue, if heroine, which is a morphine base, it will turn brown."

Anna watching, "Nothing has happened for either test. How can that be?"

Olga adds curiosity, "Let's try a strip for fentanyl. Aha, it shows up, but with no intensity it could only be contamination. This combination of compounds has blockers in it that work against our standard tests. It will take some time to break down the compound and independently define the test for its components. This is the first time I have ever seen such a proprietary disguise of medicine to prevent pirating for generic copies. Anna, here is my VPN protected email address. Contact me in three days. There are several tests to perform. Tell me no more and leave me to my work."

Anna speaking for all three as they walk out the door, "Olga, spasiba."

The next stop for this threesome is the cafeteria to plan for safely traveling out of Finland.

After a heavy moment about love and their future Julio and Josephine walk back to the hacienda. By that time, his grandfather and Adolpho are preparing for the transportation of the ponies. Josephine goes back to her room and begins to pack her belongings for the trip. Lucia knocks at her door. Josephine answers, "Come in."

"Josephine", a big greeting from Lucia with her straight lipped all teeth smile, "I am so happy that you have made my son happy. He is so different with you than he has been with other women that we have known. Is there something good coming from your relationship?"

Josephine blushes a bit, "He wants to marry me."

Lucia loudly rejoicing, "Oh, wonderful! My son needs a wife. And we need grandchildren. Family life settles a man down. It will help him to grow in the business."

Josephine with controlled intensity looking Lucia straight in her eyes, "Julio wants me to divorce my husband as soon as we return to Florida."

Lucia now shallowly speaking with hollow concern, "Divorce is an emotional event that has many pulls and pushes in doing or not doing."

Josephine now increasing in confidence, "I told him I had many things to do first and cannot leave my situation right away."

Lucia now showing her colors, "Not to be rude but, it is obvious to me that you married for wealth and prestige. It would be hard on Julio but I think you should break away from him as soon as you return to Florida. My son deserves better than a second-hand marriage with a gold digger."

Josephine keeping her anger in check and for another reason relieved by her rejection, "I married for love. Julio remains my friend. I don't know where our story goes but I remain his friend, no matter what."

Lucia callously insists, "What plans have you made?"

Josephine getting careful, "Going back to Miami, working things out with what we can or cannot do. That is our plan."

Lucia now getting fiercely obsessive, "Leave my son now. I have plans for him without you. I will not let you stand in my way. And I will do what I need to do to get you out of the way."

Josephine couldn't help herself, "Have you told Julio your plans for him without me?"

Lucia now in a rage as she moves to slam the door behind her, "You bitch! You will regret the day you met him."

Josephine now packed and walking down the steps meets Julio's father Adolpho catching up to her and beginning to speak, "Josephine, I want to apologize for my wife. When her mind gets fixed upon an issue, she sees no other point of view."

Josephine sees an opportunity to do an inquiry of her own. "Oh then, you know what plans she has for Julio, about his business?"

Adolpho meekly admits, "In our culture it is not machismo for a husband to consult with his wife about his business. But my business, now Lucia's business, came to our marriage after I chose and lived a military career. For three generations my family, before migrating from Spain, practiced as veterinarians as well as developed new pharmaceuticals to help with the maintenance and the health of livestock and horses that are so important to our people in our culture."

Josephine encourages him, "Oh, so the business must require a lot of work to keep ahead of the competition from other countries like Spain."

Adolopho now showing sympathy for Lucia, "Oh it is not easy. Our laboratories discovered and patented new medicines preventing a lot of diseases. It all goes to the healing of broken bones and controlling infections. Many of our medicines are taken from human pharmacology. I call it horse medicine but my wife objects to that. She has discovered many things. That is why she goes to Russia."

Josephine now shows interest, 'To Russia? What an exciting thing to do."

Adolpho now exhibits pride, "Oh, we import primary ingredients for our medicines from Russia, ship them to Spain, do processing there and then ship them here to South America for reshipment all over the world."

Josephine now gets complimentary, "It sounds like you know more about your wife in the business than she thinks you do."

Adolpho admits his back door knowledge, "I keep quiet but I listen and I learn. There are many things that I know that I don't speak of because it is my wife who is in charge."

Then Josephine steps lightly, "Then you probably get some idea of how things work."

Adolpho smiles, "Yes, I am getting better at understanding how the business runs, materials storage, and special shipments."

Josephine thinks of an exit, "Well, I must get to Julio for the trip to the airport. I am glad we have had this chance to talk."

Then Adolpho changes his flag as she starts to walk away, "Josephine, I have come to like you. I help Julio in any way I can but many times he won't even accept it. He is stubborn like my wife and I tolerate it. But Lucia and I always watch out for him, wherever he goes. And I must warn you. Do not disappoint Lucia and her plans for him. I am her enforcer."

Josephine now thinks Adolpho's concept of machismo includes his power wielding with no sense of responsibility, without the consequences of such behavior. Perhaps it has always worked that way for him as the enforcer in the business with his wife.

Josephine after arriving with Julio at the restaurant at the airport steps aside to make a phone call back home. In Dallas, Matt is again wondering about Josephine while having a million other problems.

Getting ready to leave his 41st floor office, the phone rings.

He tersely answers, "Matt here."

"Matt, this is Josephine. How are you?"

Matt replies "I've missed you, how is it going?"

Josephine opens up, "We won the tournament by default and the problems here are coming out of the wood work. Julio's mother and father just told me to break from Julio or they would deal with me. It was no idle threat. They mean to kill me if I don't get out of her way dealing with Julio."

Matt's voice hardens, "That doesn't surprise me. I've been checking up on the Verelez pharmacy operation. They are indeed very dangerous people."

Josephine agrees, "With all of the attempts on Julio and now his parents threatening me, my working with Julio's polo team is getting more than difficult."

Matt goes on, "Keep this on the QT, I've got a retired DEA agent and his friend from Bogota, a Columbian Anti-Drug Agent, checking up on Julio's family, and their business. The last time I communicated with him by email he was in Paris. Two men are dead and they were almost dead themselves."

"From Bogota?" said Josephine.

Matt narrows his voice, "Yes, Bogota. Heavy drug trafficking is a problem there with increased production of cocaine and even heroin. There is a smuggling network that covers South America and traffickers in Mexico. Some very powerful, well placed people in government quietly guarantee undisturbed operations with money laundering and some army leader involvement expediting issues such as protecting or turning their backs on tonnage shipments."

Josephine gets the picture. "It all sounds possible knowing Julio's mother and his father's military background including friends in Spain and Russia. But that's all speculation if you don't have any facts."

Matt snorts, "We are getting the facts, slowly. But we are disturbing a hornet's nest. The warning you got today is for real. People disappear. This is a billion-dollar operation with no problems eliminating lives that threaten it. You may be an unfortunate accident falling off a balcony twenty stories up. Tread carefully. Carry a pocket gun with hollow points. You won't get a second chance."

Josephine relents. "I know. I know all of that. Julio also confided in me about his parents."

Matt surprised, "You mean he is not involved?"

Josephine very emphatic, "No, he is not involved. He tries to stay away from them. They won't let him go. Even in Florida as a dentist they keep him on the hook with polo and his team which costs a fortune. His aunt Alessandra and the polo riders watch over him when in Florida. Their vehicles carry automatic weapons and are bullet proofed. Now they are watching me too, even as I am talking with you from the airport here in Buenos Aires."

Matt roundly replies, "Let's end this for now. Don't be afraid, but remain openly uninterested in their business. Sooner or later, we are going to need to put this all together, hopefully helping Julio at the same time."

"Yes, I hope we can keep him safe, take care."

After hanging up with Matt, Josephine goes back to Julio, "My husband knows about your parents." Julio taken aback "How did he find out?"

Josephine with pride answers, "Matt has connections, a former DEA agent is prying into an international organization that includes your mother and father."

Julio admits, "Yes, it is more than my mother, but she is there at the top. I am concerned for your safety as well as mine. My mother has control but not so much that she can save us if the organization decides that we are a threat. Even though we won the tournament for added prestige, living like this in a dark hallway with only one exit is no fun."

Josephine helps out, "Julio, you have done nothing. She wants you to take over her side of the organization with her insistence on your MBA at Harvard, your brains to run the system."

Julio refusing to fall into an 'I can't help it attitude', "Yes, I am trying to stay clear of it, staying busy with polo and my practice. If I ignore them, they try to humble me with my dependence on my trust money for polo, and when Raul tried to kill me, my mother or her enemies killed him for failing to kill me. What a mess. Somehow, I have to deal with it. Trying to run from or ignore their business anymore is useless."

Josephine offers comfort and support, "I'll help you. I'll get Matt to find out what we need to know. He told me he would help us."

Julio looking at his watch, "Thank you. This is good to know. More for later, we must be going."

Julio and Josephine carry their bags to the 747 on the offset runway already loaded with the ponies with Damian there to see them off with Alessandra, and Carlos already on board.

Chapter Thirteen

A Volvo

Ending up at the Helsinki University cafeteria, Anna, Mannie, and Juan sit at a table to have a bite to eat and plan their travel going west as secretly as possible.

Anna speaking up first, "From here going west to Denmark we do not need to show our passports crossing borders. This way we cannot be tracked by driving a car across three countries. We can buy our food at a grocery and avoid restaurants as we picnic across the country side. And we can stay at hostels each night if needed."

Mannie shows enthusiasm, "We can't rent. We need to buy a used car for cash with a legal plate on it."

Juan suggesting with a grin, "If we can't get a plate, we can always borrow one at a parking lot."

Anna getting positive on the plan walks over to the student advertizing cork board and finds a notice of a vehicle for sale, takes it down and begins reading it to Mannie and Juan. "This notice for sale is a 2004 Volvo wagon, petrol powered at 104 kW (141 HP) with 288,600 kilometers on it for 936 Euros. It is located at student dormitory A across the campus square."

Mannie's ready to go for it, "Wow, what a deal, a Volvo for 936 Euros. Let's get it!"

At the student dormitory they meet Olaf, a fourth-year student. Anna introduces herself, "My name is Anna Melankinov. These are my visiting friends and we would like to buy your car."

Olaf with an appreciative smile, "Wonderful, I am graduating soon and I need the money. Do you agree to my price?"

Mannie introducing himself, "We do if your car is running properly. We are touring and would like to visit Sweden while we are here."

Olaf replies with pride, "Yah, you can be sure. Before coming to university, I was a Volvo mechanic."

Anna interrupts, "We will need to keep your plate on the car."

Olaf, "I will give you a bill of sale but I will need my plate for my next car."

Anna looks for a compromise, "We don't want to keep your car, just to tour Sweden. How about if we rent your car and leave it for you to pick it up in Stockholm?"

Olaf asks, "You mean you will pay me my price just to rent it?"

Anna looks for confirmation from Mannie and Juan, "How about we rent it for $500 Euros to go to Sweden?"

Olaf is quick to answer, "Good. Give me your ID to copy and a phone number. Here is my address in Stockholm. Leave it there when you are done. Say hello to my parents. I will tell them you are coming in a week or so."

Mannie shaking his hand with 500 Euros, "Good, we have a deal."

Olaf now dancing around in the room, "Aha, I can still have it for graduation. Yes. The car is yours in the front side lot. Here are the keys. The ownership papers and insurance are in the glove box."

Once in the car with their tote bags the question remains who is to drive. Anna opening the driver side door, "I can read their road signs We do not want to get stopped for anything, not even a parking ticket."

Mannie up front with Anna finds a road map in the glove box while checking for all the documents. "I guess you are Olaf 's sister's friend and you are taking the car home for him while touring with your foreign friends visiting at the University. Oh, did you give him your real ID?"

Anna offers a grin. "It is so nice of you to help with a believable story. No, I gave him one of several back up ID's. May I see the map?"

Juan asks, "How long is this going to take?"

Anna figures out the mileage going around the Gulf of Bothnia, "It is a bit of a trip at about 1500 kilometers. We could take a ferry going slower for 400 kilometers at 15 knots for 26 hours or going an average of 70 kilometers per hour by car for 22 hours. We could be more easily spotted doing the ferry."

Mannie looks at Juan and agrees, "Driving sounds better. Too many ways to have spotters on ferries loading and unloading, plus ticket counter exposure and services on board. When you think about it we are slightly obvious with a beautiful woman like you."

Anna smiles with a naughty wag of her finger, "Well, one of you could play my husband whom I met at a US Embassy party in Moscow and Juan could play our business partner from Columbia. But driving an old Volvo, I am not sure it will stick."

Juan begs, "Why can't I be the husband?"

Anna smiles back, "We need each other far beyond a marriage. To survive, we go up Highway Four. With the rear seat folded down, one of us can sleep while the two up front drive and watch. We'll stop for groceries and picnic along the way wherever we can stop. Buying gas is our biggest problem. That won't be a problem with me. But you two should pretend to be asleep when I stop for gas. Gossip will start along the way, hopefully for us as just tourists in Finland. Fortunately, our plates are for Sweden."

On the road stopping for gas once in Finland, driving on into the night, they reach the border with Sweden and drive through unstopped at an abandoned check point. Mannie takes over driving and Juan comes up to the passenger side while Anna goes in the back to sleep.

Juan starts thinking over shipment billings, "While driving up here I went over every billing in detail and found another interesting shipping point, Copenhagen. It looks like it's a warehouse, but the address looks more commercial than industrial with a fourth-floor suite for a location."

Mannie mumbles a bit, "Not another stop. We need to get to Interpol in Brussels and unload our evidence to take this off of our hands."

Juan is astounded, "Don't you want to make this the bust of the century? Did you know there is also an Interpol station in Buenos Aires?"

Mannie gets frustrated, "Problematically, we might never make it to Buenos Aires."

Juan smartens up, "Yeah, Interpol is not law enforcement. They merely coordinate law enforcement between 192 member countries."

Mannie still sees a light at the end of the tunnel, "Yes, it includes Russia, Spain, Columbia, and Argentina, the key countries of this trafficking cartel."

Juan is getting serious, "By going in will we be protecting Anna or giving her up to the mafia influence in her own agency?"

Mannie not thinking twice, "Ok, let's keep her undercover with us. We go and meet with the Interpol and see what they want us to do, at least with Columbia or the US and the DEA knowing what is going on."

Anna now awakes and listening, "Gentlemen, thank you for your concern for my health, but I also have a duty to perform and I will see it out with you to the end."

Mannie then pulls over to give the wheel to Juan.

After driving a while with the sun rise breaking over a forest along the highway, Anna straightens up startled, "I hear the roar of a helicopter. Pull off the road into the trees."

Mannie opens the sunroof, "Wow that is a turbo-prop sound. But I don't see anything."

Anna now looking along the highway, "We cannot take chances. We are lucky with this heavy weekend traffic. We must assume they know we are here but just can't drop down on this road. All we have is pistols. They will have AK's and a door mounted machine gun. They may be circling for a landing area in this heavy forest. If they come back, they are hoping that we make a run for it. Here it comes. I am right! It's a Ka-62, Russia's newest and fastest, used by the Special Operations Forces, the Security Force, and for commercial transport. It will carry a squad of at least ten, but with three for rifles and a machine gun they only need four."

Mannie figures, "They could go back in the woods and lower the shooters with a drop line."

Anna thinks it out, "They could try. But the woods are very heavy. That helicopter has Russian markings probably passing as a commercial transporter. And a gunfight on the edge of the highway could expose them to the public."

Juan suggests, "I say we move into traffic and get between a truck and cars and stay there. We are still 400 kilometers from Stockholm and they flew here from Russia or Helsinki. Their gas must be getting low by now."

Mannie and Anna agreeing, "Ok, after their next pass we move out."

While waiting Juan speculates with a sinking voice, "Olaf, the college student, probably bragged in a beer garden about renting his black Volvo station wagon to three strangers, one American and so on. It must have spread like wildfire as a joke about those crazy tourists."

Anna is not upset, "We still are making the right move. That helicopter is coming back. There it is and it's returning to the woods, probably to make a drop. Hit the road Juan and speed up to traffic. Once in Stockholm they can't track us by air without violating air space limitations."

Mannie now thinks technology, "Anna, now that they spotted us and radioed our position, they can track us with their satellites."

Anna does some mental plotting, "That will work depending on the time of day. I think we still have a margin, but you are right. We need to change the color of this car and put some mud on two of the numbers on the plate."

Juan smiles, "Here is a smalltown turn-off, lucky us. We are still on track for Brussels with no shots fired. Oh, can we at least get some hunting rifles along with white spray paint cans?"

Back in the US, with the 747 hangers at the cargo side of the Miami airport, Pedro and Allehandro show up with four trailers to take the ponies to customs holding pens for two weeks quarantine. Pedro rented a car for delivery to the hanger for Julio and Josephine. When Julio pushes the remote-control button to unlock the vehicle, no lights go on and there is no beeping sound.

Julio, disappointed with such poor service, loudly complains, "The battery must be dead!"

Carlos offers, "There is a vehicle assistance service here in the airport. I see a phone on the wall. I'll go over and make a call."

As Julio starts to put his key into the door lock he notices, "Hey, there are scratches on this door next to the handle. Why would somebody try to unlock this rental car to steal it, to bug it, uh oh, or to plant a bomb?"

Josephine shouts, "Don't put your key in the lock! Get back! It could be an IED! Somebody may have tampered with this vehicle and could have planted a bomb. Let's wait for the vehicle assistance person to show up."

In two minutes, the airport guard drives up in a pickup truck with a battery charger in his hand. He comes up to Julio, "Open up the hood and we will put a charge on that battery."

Julio disagrees, "No. I'm afraid somebody broke into this car and placed a bomb there."

The guard simply frustrated, "Oh come on. Are you the President? Are you the mafia? What's the story here? Maybe it is just somebody trying to steal the car. This car has warning devices to discourage that."

Julio answers with certainty and conviction, "No, I am not the mafia, but they know me and my ponies. I don't want to charge that battery because I think it's tied to an explosive that depends on the turning of the ignition switch. That is how it works isn't it?"

"Yes." The guard is finally getting Julio's drift. "That's the way it works. I am not in the mood for fooling around. But before we open the hood, I'll look under the car first."

He lies down on the ground next to the driver's door and looks up towards the front of the car underneath the engine. "No, I don't see anything, no new wiring, nothing unusual, no black boxes, and nothing in the way or out of the way." He gets back up and says, "Stand back about ten feet."

He puts the key into the lock and turns it. Nothing happens. "Ok, we are in, at least at this point. Now I need to get under the hood." He reaches over to the lower left side of the dashboard and finds the hood release latch and pulls it. The hood pops up. He goes around to the front and opens the hood to look into the engine bay. "Oh my God, what have we here?"

Julio, "What is it?"

"There is a little package of C-4 plastic explosive tied in with a detonator and wires running right to the distributor and capacitor line. I learned to use this in the military. There is enough here to disintegrate this car."

"Damn it," cries Julio looking at Josephine. "Why are they still trying to kill me?"

Josephine attempts to quiet Julio, "They are still trying to get to your mother through you!"

The driver of the airport vehicle assistance truck cuts the wires, removes the C-4, and announces, "I'm reporting this to the sheriff as an attempted homicide. You must remain here for their investigation.

They'll need to tow the car and dust it for prints in their shop."

Julio gets nervous, "No, I can't have that. Are you arresting me?"

"Oh no, but our chief of operations will have the police here in about ten minutes."

"Ok." Julio finally accepts his plight, "I have no choice in the matter. In the meantime, can you get me another vehicle from the rental ramp?"

This attempted homicide involves Detective Harland along with a forensic explosive tech and a sergeant, arriving with two vehicles, one drove to check the rental garage, and one on-site. The detective thoroughly questions Julio and Josephine while checking passports and getting contact information. The forensic analyst gives out with a laugh, "The boob that put this together tied in a short on the battery that ran it down in an hour."

At that point the detective smirks, "Amateurs are everywhere. You two are very lucky. Go home with this safe rental car. I will be in touch after more checking on the rental operation."

With things settling down Alessandra calls Lucia apprehensively, "They tried to kill Julio with a bomb planted in the car we rented here at the Miami airport."

Lucia frantically screams, "Is Julio alright?"

Alessandra calming her down, "Yes Julio is fine. I suspect Raul's old gang, Sanchez and Rodriguez, did it for revenge on Raul's murder."

Lucia laments, "We don't need a war now! But we have to put a stop to this. Our friends in Florida can help us. Where is Julio now?"

Alessandra is ready for an outburst, "He is driving Josephine to her beach condo on the Gulf. He will be staying at his dental office to get back to work."

Lucia now a dragon breathing lethal fire, "That woman, she has to go."

That ends the conversation and Alessandra drives back to the ranch with Carlos and the others. The next morning Lucia calls Julio at his dental office, "Tell me what has been happening there? Alessandra said somebody tried to kill you. Oh, and did you finally sleep with that loathsome woman?"

Julio still half asleep, "No mother I dropped her off at her place. It was a long drive and we were tired. The police are investigating the car bomb as an attempted homicide. The detective suspects us as drug users or dealers because of the timed attempt to kill us. They searched our plane and luggage and my passport from Columbia is a red flag in Miami."

Lucia, "I see. And the ponies are they safe in the Customs Service Quarantine"?

Julio, "Yes, Carlos placed them in the holding pens before the car incident."

Lucia, "What did you tell the detective?"

Julio, "That we are returning from the Buenos Aires Polo tournament which we won. Then he asked me why somebody wants to kill me, again sniffing around my background in Columbia. And mother, it's time I asked you! Are you involved in drug trafficking?"

"Why do you ask that son?"

"Everything seems too controlled. You do make a lot of money.

You sell....."

Lucia interrupts, "Are you still with that woman Josephine? I want you to part with her now. I helped you win the tournament. You don't need her anymore."

Julio now gets more than curious, "Mother! How did you help us? Did you cause those bot flies to infest the Columbian team?"

Lucia replies defiantly. "Of course, I did it to protect you, to help you, to get you away from that adulteress woman."

Julio now very angry, "How could you? Josephine has not committed adultery like my father or you. And we could have won that tournament honorably. How can I respect you when you so arrogantly interfere with your crude cheating in a fair competition?"

Julio's mother now losing this verbal match, changes the subject, "We sell pharmaceuticals. That is a very lucrative business."

"Yes, I understand that. Just what kind, I wonder, always to the point of being secret."

"We have a lot of secrets to keep in our business and we have a lot of formulas for the patents on our medicines. We do not disclose formulas. They are even secret to our employees. If we did not keep our secrets, we would be out of business."

"Then why are people after me? Why am I being threatened?"

Lucia falls dead silent, motionless, and without emotion, "They are trying to get to me through you. Somehow, they think they can force me to give them what they want, whatever it is. I don't know for sure but I think it is because I am a woman."

Julio's jaw dropped, "Madre mia, por favor. I don't think so. I am so disappointed in you. You have no honor, and without honor, I cannot trust you. Your whole life is a matter of convenience for you and that is what I have been all along, a convenience at best. I pity you."

Julio's phone crackles and they lose their connection. Lucia did not try calling back and Julio threw his cell phone down on the counter going downstairs to prepare for the day's appointments. He wonders as he rides the elevator. "Is this some kind of simple industrial espionage? The pharmaceutical industry is very competitive. Is spying going on or is my mother involved in drug trafficking in some way that nobody can detect and somebody wants to take over from her? That must be it, a stupid cartel war, but obviously over billions. That's my mother. Something I am sure she relishes, but I cannot abide. It is over for us." With this sad and depressing decision, his heaviest thought goes to Josephine, "How do I keep Josephine out of this mess? When we have to go through all of this to find out the truth about ourselves and the way we are going, how can we be together?"

As Josephine awakens from a long sleep and stretches out on her condo balcony twenty stories up overlooking the beach and Gulf, she's asking herself a similar question, "How far can I go with Julio. I don't want to hurt him and how do I stop myself from feeling the way I do about him. He is with me whatever I am doing."

A moment later her door chime rings. Matt appears on the door camera patiently waiting. When she opens the door, he simply says with a great deal of relief, "Josephine!"

She responds with a tired smile, "Yes Matt, I'm here at last."

As always Matt inquires, "How is it going?"

Josephine fumbles for a moment in her mind and with relief, "It's good to be back, but they tried to kill us with a bomb in our rented car that we hired at the airport."

Matt is dead serious, "You are into very heavy stuff. Got any angles to keep you clear?"

Josephine is also dead serious, "I think something very big is really going on here that is way beyond our ability to help Julio. But we have got to try and do our best to deal with this."

Matt now questions Josephine's neutrality, "How do you know that? How do you know that?"

Josephine marshals her full faith, "I believe him. He suspects his mother of drug trafficking. He is not sure. But I believe him."

Josephine then walks up to Matt asking for a hug, "I don't know what to do."

She melts as Matts arms now accept his fatherly role for his best agent in the field. "Well, whatever it is that got it started, we have to use nimble fingers to deal with it. I have had Julio investigated. He is clean. I have had his family investigated. His grandfather appears clean but his history goes back to Juan Peron. His mom and dad run a very successful pharmacy with interesting connections in Spain and Russia. I have an old time DEA agent and his friend from Columbia in the field now with a third investigator from the Moscow anti-drug service and they are on the run from the Russian mafia and Sergei Ivanoff, a cover name for maybe "The Brain" who supposedly runs an eight billion dollar trafficking ring in Russia."

"They have already been in a firefight and two of the traffickers are dead. There is a great deal going on here that is way beyond our ability to control but we are learning what is going on with every step that we take. And now that you are in it, you need to be taking more steps until we can figure out a way to defeat the system, not the mafia, but the system."

Josephine is ready to fight, "What do you want me to do?"

Matt emphasizes continuing to exercise caution, "You have already been in danger with Julio and doing well thinking on your feet. Despite Julio's mother and her talented duplicity, her people are watching you now. But what you can do is go along with what is happening, get closer to everything that is happening and find out how it is happening through Julio. Maybe once we know how things are happening, we can stop the practice cold, hopefully without any losses."

Josephine looks for direction, "You are talking like a general developing a battle plan. Are you expecting to bring in the federal government?"

Matt starts to hem and haw, "Well, in the end that is true. That is what we may have to do if we can't get enough going on our own. But getting into their system through the back door is our strongest suit. Yes, there is still time for the undercover route. If we let loose now with accusations, we will only be mere pawns in the political and legal games that they play. We have to be able to set the game up in our favor and then turn it over to them when we are ready. At this point I plan flying to Bogota to meet with Mannie and Juan. Then we will all be working undercover to find out how their system works chemically."

Josephine now thinks positively, "I think I can do that with Julio. He wants to free himself from his mother!"

Matt smiles, "Yes, but keep your emotions in check. You are no longer a passive observer of what is going on. You and Julio will be taking risks together."

Josephine bravely affirms, "Yes."

Matt with admiration, "Josephine, there is no turning back. And what you are doing is high and mighty in my book. We are a team working a thin line. God help us."

Chapter Fourteen

Changing Saddles

At their interchange stop, desperate to change the color of their car, Anna spots a diesel truck hauling a drive-on trailer loaded with new cars. Anna breaks out with excitement, "Look! That car hauling truck has Belgium plates. It is getting dark. And the driver is in that restaurant at the fuel station. Let's leave this car here with the keys in it and sneak a ride to Belgium in one of those cars in the middle of the trailer."

Juan jumps on the idea, "Yes, that SUV with heavily tinted glass is a great choice."

Mannie chimes in, "I agree. They are onto us in this car, especially with a satellite. In the dark we have a chance to sneak on board."

Anna grins, "And who knows, somebody may take the Volvo to lead them to who knows where?"

Mannie asks, "Will the doors be locked?"

Juan thinking back to his earlier police officer training, "We had to learn how to jimmy locks with a band of steel, or a metal hangar. I can still do it."

In complete darkness they approach the trailer. Juan warns, "The interior lights will go on as the doors open so we have to make it fast." He climbs up and finds the driver side door open and unlocks the others as Mannie and Anna quickly climb into the back with their gear, food and water. With the interior lights out they set down the last row of seats and make themselves comfortable.

Juan sitting smartly in the driver's seat announces, "This vehicle is loaded with extras. It has satellite radio, GPS, self-driving routines for parking, and a notebook computer with WIFI. I think I can bypass the ignition to activate some of it. The fuse box is just under the dash next to the firewall."

Mannie is now on the same channel, "If you can do that, I can email Matt and catch him up on our progress and learn how things are doing with Josephine."

Anna chimes in. "And I can get back to Olga for her lab results."

Just then they hear the heavy turning of the diesel starter motor on the semi-tractor. With the standard deep knocking sound of the running motor, a gear drops down and they start moving with gears switching to get to highway speed.

Juan proclaims with a smile, "Great, here we sit in utter comfort on leather seats travelling for free and undetected. Life couldn't be better. And it will get better when the sun comes up so I can see what I am doing without turning lights on. That trucker has a radio, a satellite tracking dish and cameras front and rear to keep an eye on things. No sense taking chances."

Anna feeling pretty good opens up with a smile, "We still are making the right move. No helicopter, no satellite, and no spotters or tracers to worry about. 'Slave Bogu.'"

They slept well with the hum of the diesel. The next morning Juan finds a hot wire to the fuse box and ignition, crosses it over and activates the radio which has telephone service, a computer, and GPS.

Still on the move almost to Stockholm, Anna looks at Juan, "Olga. We need to email her to get her lab results. Here is her email address. Try that computer, we may get Wi-Fi from the truck or it has a Wi-Fi roamer."

Juan activates and types in a message, "Do you have the lab results for us?"

Juan gets a reply, "I do not know your address. What is your project?'"

Juan reads this to Anna who answers, "I don't want to give her my name. Her system may be monitored, type in "Pharmaceutical Safety Check".

Olga replies, "Safety check indicates suspected contaminants using overlaps from multiple testing. No single test is effective, used Gas Chromatography with methanol solvent, including fentanyl and methyl palmitate. Compounds are identified, but closely related peaks are of unknown origin, which masks contaminants otherwise offering easy detection. Infrared Spectroscopy could not identify the noted spectral pattern with a reference library. Various applications of chloroform, acetone, ether, acetate, xylene, and hexane as a solvent did not improve results. Final tests include Solid Phase Spectroscopy, Liquid Phase Chromatography with Potassium Hydroxide, and Capillary Electrophoresis looking for phenethylamine isomers, and Mass Spectrometry examining a powder sample for ionization. The product is well formulated for shipping and reformulation for separation of components."

Juan emails back, "Report received. Thank You."

Anna looking at Mannie and Juan, analytically concludes, "Those pills are difficult to detect. The only way to sabotage their system is to sabotage the pill making or the method of reformulating the pill for local heroin or cocaine consumption. If the Russian pills are made for bulk shipping of material, the reformulation must be happening in Bogota and reshipped to all distribution points throughout the world. The only way to defeat the system is to sabotage the reformulation in a way that self-destructs after shipping. We don't need to know the formula. All we can do is try to contaminate the reformulation. Then the whole system collapses. But what we do has to be apocryphal at the same time worldwide and hopefully leading to local investigations seeking cause and effect and exposure of the illicit subsystems."

Mannie wide awake with questions, "Brilliant, What a plan! No crime fighting outfit has ever publicly succeeded at destroying a criminal organization this way. Indeed, we are probably illegally acting as commercial espionage agents without any approval by any government. For them we provide deniability. We are at this point in our own cold war with truly covert actions. My black box fund from Matt who asked me to do him a favor has no name or official approval. Wow. How did this happen? Did Matt plan this as a rogue operation?" Juan now getting shaky, "Do we even want to go to Interpol?"

Anna now backs off, "No, now I don't think we should go to Interpol. That is a public member country transparent organization run like Congress or Parliament."

Mannie tossing in his two cents, "The DEA, my old shield, is also limited, requiring complete co-country approval on any operation. That's a big crack in the armor of covertness to worry about. So far, we have Argentina, Columbia, Spain, France and Russia involved here. What do you think it will take to build a sting operation that can be kept secret with them? And we think at least the military is compromised in at least two of the countries."

Anna now shapes the next move, "We have another 1,200 kilometers before hitting Brussels. We can make Hamburg tonight and I say we get off in the dark and get a taxi or tram to Hamburg Airport. Juan, check for flights to Bogota tomorrow."

Juan reports, "Tomorrow American Airlines departs at 18.00 hours for Bogota, non-stop. There is a subway S1 and S-Bahn that goes directly from the city network to the airport."

Mannie sees the light, "Taking the subway is most covert with keeping our hats down. Getting tickets at the airport will be our only exposure and I will buy for all three of us. We will have to show our passports with tickets to board. With our carry-on we have nothing to be checked in; we will still have to dump our weapons."

Juan patting Mannie on the back, "Not to worry, when we get to Bogota I can get you whatever you and Anna want including the latest Russian AKs."

Anna bragging a bit, "Yes, worldwide we sell more of those guns than any other."

Mannie makes one last request. "Juan, send an email to Matt giving him our arrival time in Bogota. When we arrive, he will want to be there to meet us."

Back in Miami, for Julio's ponies, still safely quartered at the Custom's Bureau in quarantine, Lucia usually asks a local veterinarian to check them out. That is Dr. Hernandez who appears at the customs confinement area and begins inspecting the ponies for illnesses of one kind or another.

The customs agent normally witnesses the inspection but for some reason was called away to another duty. With the customs agent cleared off, the veterinarian opens his case, pulls out a set of scalpels with a local anesthetic, and makes an incision under the right front leg quarter of each pony, inserts a muscle separator, and out drops a plastic pouch with a little over 310 grams of cocaine. He seals the wounds with super glue. To the deft incision he adds skin anesthetic as well as a germicidal coating, making it undetectable. In fifteen minutes in the false bottom of his case he places sixteen packets. He then goes back to the control desk asking for a release. The customs agent does not search the bag or question the veterinarian. Dr. Hernandez opens the electrically released gate and leaves.

Back in his office, Dr. Hernandez, makes a call, "Senora Verelez, I retrieved your delivery with no problem. There is enough medication to make 6,200 caplets."

Loathsome Lucia with her greedy caw warns, "Be sure not to miss any doses. My payback for errors will not accept excuses. Your fee is only the doses we give you until the next shipment."

Dr. Hernandez, an addict, happily replies, "Si Senora Verelez."

After a week of getting settled from day to day with his practice in Sarasota, Julio calls Josephine on her cell phone, "I have great news to get us out of my family rut for a while."

Josephine's ears perk up with the phone close to her head, "What is that, Julio?"

'We will be competing with the west coast polo teams from California next month and we need to work our team to prepare our ponies and get them into shape for that competition. It's a trophy competition, one of the most cherished trophies we can get in our field."

Josephine now falls into the totally committed and helpful person for the Verelez family, "Wonderful! How much of this exercise and training will be involved?"

Julio now trying to work up a schedule, "I have my practice three days a week now, so I will be coming to the ranch at West Palm on Thursday and coming back to Sarasota on the following Monday. Would you join us at the ranch for these training sessions and help with the grooming and training of the new ponies that we brought with us from Buenos Aires? Some of our riders are new from Argentina. You would help a lot in making them feel comfortable on the field here in the US."

Josephine strokes Julio's ego for the kind of fight he really likes, "Julio you can also be teaching your hard riding, your dead aim with the mallet and pass on your competitive drive to win a match."

Julio speaks deftly, "But winning without you, just doesn't work for me. Those luncheons, dinners, and post-game parties are empty without you."

Josephine comes back with polo philosophy, "Julio, it is not a crime to be competitive and although your competition carries a very strong message, it always comes out very gentlemanly. The captain of the French team in Buenos Aires came up to me afterwards and noted how tough you are on the field. He said you never let up. He asked where you learned to be that way. With your drive none of us ever let up, and we do win. Our tactics are all legal, although the Frenchman complained that you beat your ponies, knock riders down, and give no leeway while crowding opponents out of the ball run."

Julio is quick to defend himself, "We won that match fair and square."

Josephine with a slight grin in her face, "Well, I think that's what Polo is about."

Julio almost pleading, "Will you come to help?"

Josephine doesn't hesitate, "Of course."

For the next two weeks Josephine has her hands full. The new riders, all young men, ambitious to make their name in the game, work feverishly with all of Julio's and Josephine's guidance, including Alessandra's strong sideline coaching. The new riders know Josephine is more than just a friend of their boss and want to do everything to please Mrs. O'Conner. And Josephine is more than just slightly pleased to work with these handsome young men. At times she had some difficulty maintaining a lady-like posture.

Alessandra is quick to notice Josephine's fleeting looks at them, "Those young men are the cream of the crop and handsome all day long, oh, to be young again."

Josephine appreciates her knowing comment, "Oh, you saw me looking. They are beautiful men. But in polo it is always look, but don't touch. Am I right?"

Alessandra answers with a soft smile, "I know your feelings for Julio, the side lines can be innocent fun for me too." And they both have a good laugh.

After a week, the ponies, which had already had training in Argentina, are beginning to coalesce into a team with the riders. Josephine often rides with the team and coaches from one side of the field to the other. She often plays as an opposing team rider with some of the stable boys and the second string of horses. While Julio restores his dentist practice, his hope that Josephine will work the team into playing shape proves very well answered.

In preparation for the big tournament the next day, Julio arranges for a scrub match with a local team. But in getting the ponies up into the trailers, Julio detects more nervousness and refusals to move up the ramp.

Julio speaking churlishly to Carlos, "What is wrong with these ponies? They are limping, not moving their front right leg."

Carlos turns back to Julio, "They were just fine yesterday. Let me look at them. Aha, the upper part of this pony's right forward quarter is swollen. It is leaking white puss from a break in the skin up on the inside of the quarter."

Julio checks another pony, "My God, this pony's right forward quarter is also swollen and leaking puss on the upper inside." Josephine with Carlos now moving about all of the sixteen ponies, "These horses have all been cut on the inside of their upper quarter. The workouts of the last week must have stretched the seal of what looks like an incision."

Julio now incensed, "Who did this and for what purpose? Was this sabotage?"

Carlos is loudly defensive, "We have stabled these ponies and watched them constantly since they left the customs confinement. No one but our people have been near them."

Josephine notes, "These are precision cuts made with a surgical blade. Did anyone visit the ponies during their confinement?"

Julio remembering, "My mother always sends her veterinarian friend in Miami to check our new set of ponies and see if they made the trip without injury."

Carlos is now suspicious, "There is no reason to make this kind of incision unless there is something to be removed, perhaps for Senora Verelez."

Julio screams in a rage, "My mother! Smuggling drugs with my ponies! How dare she!"

Josephine moves to calm Julio, "I'm calling the scrub team to cancel the match today and you as the captain will need to withdraw from the tournament."

Julio boils with anger, "Yes, withdraw due to unforeseen difficulties, my mother! Tomorrow we fly to Bogota and confront her!"

Josephine remembering her promise, "Yelling at her will do no good. Let's go there for a nice visit claiming problems with training for missing the tournament and you need a break from your dentistry doing so well. We both need to work at being compatible with your mother and you must show an interest in her business and how it works. She wants you on the inside. She told me so. Once on the inside we can quietly search for what she is doing wrong, and figure out how to stop it, so that you can be free of her, and give her a chance to go straight."

In the meantime, the pressure on Mannie, Juan, and Anna continues to mount. Every contract killer in Europe is on notice through the Internet. They search every point of travel and place to stay to claim three hundred thousand rubles, Euros, or dollars on each of their heads depending upon the country. As a threesome, even disguised, they might be discovered. At the airport, video monitors are everywhere and facial recognition software goes to the mainframe that can be hacked.

After jumping from the SUV trailer ride, they board the subway in a crowd with no problem, standing back-to-back carrying their bags. Stopping at the airport ticket building they meet with their backs against an entrance column. Anna leads the next trying journey, "We go in one at a time, look at your feet, don't look side to side and give away a profile, and keep your cap low on your face. Mannie, we don't need passports to buy a ticket but we need to show picture ID at the security check before the gate"

Mannie adds, "I'll leave first and go right to the counter. I'll meet you at the security check."

Anna, "Wait, I need to work on your face to improve your appearance."

Mannie is confounded, "What?"

Anna, "We undercover people carry disguise kits. Put your arms around me and embrace me face to face."

Mannie complies with undisguised pleasure, "I am your slave!"

Anna now slightly miffed, "Be quiet, I will darken the bags under your eyes, lighten your cheeks, draw on a light mustache and stiffen your hair straight down on your forehead. There, now you look Slavic."

Mannie is now smartly committed, "To make this real may I kiss you?"

Anna shrugs, "Da!"

Juan breaking in, "Ok you two, you definitely make a couple. I'll wait at the security check in."

Mannie holds out his arm, "My darling, shall we?"

Anna with a little more sweetness, "Da, and keep your hands to yourself."

Mannie dutifully murmurs, "Da, Moy Dorogoy!"

All goes well. They pass the security gate with their tickets and walk to their departure gate. The flight to Bogota is a non-stop on a 747 with Anna playing Mrs. Mannie and Juan on his own account in his row of seats was a Columbian in conversation with other Columbians on their way home.

Chapter Fifteen

Back To Bogota Undercover

Too much too long in the dark, Matt receives an email from Mannie flying from Hamburg to Bogota. "This thing is going way too big too fast."

He gets up from his desk, walks to the door and slams it shut as he starts leaving. His astonished secretary asks, "Where are you going sir?"

Matt speaks quietly off the record, "I am flying to Bogotá. I need a non-stop flight as soon as possible. Tell no one about this excursion. I am just in the field. Do you understand?"

With her secret "I-know-look", she demonstrates her speedy computer talent, "I have a flight that leaves at 4:00.P.M. Do you have any luggage?"

Turning around to leave Matt replies, "No, I'll be in touch in a week or two."

With all things happening simultaneously in Bogota, Mannie, Anna, and Juan walk down the ramp from the plane and enter the gate corridor. With Matt waiting on the other side of the security line, they wave and meet each other. With a broad welcoming smile, he helps Anna with her carryon and greets them all, "I am glad you made it back." Then in a hushed rough whisper, "It sounds like you had one hell of a time getting here."

Mannie is utterly blunt, "Yeah, they've got us made. They are after us with a vengeance. I don't know where to go from here because wherever we go there is going to be somebody around the corner ready to blow our heads off."

Matt looks at Juan, "You made it too. How is your wound from Paris?"

As they walk down the corridor, Juan replies, "Mannie patched me up like a doctor. He even stitched the wound shut. I am glad to be back but not as a member of the Policia Nationale. I am definitely staying undercover with a new identity to get me into the Verelez pharmacy operation."

Then Matt addresses Anna, "My name is Matt and I want to thank you for shepherding these two through your country and bringing them here with yourself to carry out this incredible mission."

Anna with her stern police posture, "We are on a joint mission to rid the world of these criminals. I am committed to add my best skills to bring this battle to a successful conclusion."

Matt very much impressed, "I thank you. We are indeed a team bound to succeed and we thank you for your commitment with your very much appreciated talent."

Matt opens with details as they enter his rented SUV, "The Verelez operation is peanuts in Bogota. Ten of the world's largest Pharmaceuticals employ over 90,000 people here. The smaller companies like the Verelez's Tridexan Pharmaceuticals specialize to survive. Juan, you can shave your mustache, cut your hair close, and wear glasses with a slight yellow tint and offer yourself as a chemist assistant."

Anna volunteering, "Yes, with my degree in chemistry at the University of Moscow I will teach Juan all the basics of lab operations."

Mannie suddenly bursts in, "Anna, I didn't know you are a chemist?"

Anna is startled by Mannie's interruption, "Mannie, my position with the Moscow police started with my forensic ability to perform inspections of suspected drug-producing labs."

Matt suggests, "Can we get Anna in as a chemist without being spotted? We can get her a new passport with her make-up kit, dye her hair, and so on. Anna, your English is good. Do you speak any Spanish?"

Anna replies, "Nyet, spasiba. Iche spreche Deutsch!"

Mannie understands a path to action, "Perfect, I know the perfect person here to make for you a German passport, how about a name like Marlena Dietrich!"

Matt now smiles, "Hmmm, Anna you certainly look the part."

Anna is sweet but curt, "I will not be a movie star, but no sense going in looking like a washing woman. Start me out as Greta."

Matt now traces out a working plan, "Aha, to get on the inside of the reformulating drug process, the two of you can apply for jobs on different days and hopefully will be working in the same or nearby labs."

Now driving in the fancy well to do Chico district of Bogota, Matt reveals his preparations, "With my old cover as a building contractor, I have rented a five bedroom apartment in this high rise building on the right where the Verelez family owns the penthouse covering the whole top floor with balconies, patios, a tennis court used for parties, and a pool, all with a view of the city on one side and Montserrat on the other."

After parking behind a gate, going up an elevator to the 41st floor, and entering a palatial apartment with balcony, they rest for a moment. Then Matt adds, "Mannie and I can work on the owner side perhaps as regional dealers or investors with Josephine already inside. As for our movements, keep separate outside, avoid coming and going together, and stay at least ten minutes apart. The bus transportation here is great and their operation is a fifteen-minute ride from here. By car the rush hour is bumper to bumper, just like Dallas or Miami.

It is going to be a touch and go road to hell uncovering how they are smuggling cocaine and heroin around the world. What we don't know is the formula they are using to get their stuff through and then converting it back to heroin and cocaine."

"You mean we are setting up a sting?" crows Mannie.

Matt jumps back, "No, we don't really want to sting them."

Anna sees the light at the end of the tunnel, "Stinging would be just a one-time injury. It would not do us any good to get one person or one group. This is a world-wide organization and it stretches from Russia around the world to China. We must do more than that."

Mannie is now energized to start planning, "We have thought about drawing them out into the open in a way that will get them caught and exposed at all their system delivery locations all at the same time."

Matt agrees, "That is a tall order and tough to carry out, but I believe doable with stealth, cunning, and silent efficiency."

Mannie punts on Matt's statement, "Hmmm, just like a CIA covert operation. And they never answer for that and neither will we. But Matt you just may lose your job with the DEA."

Matt replies calmly, "Hah, I will cross that bridge when I come to it.

But whatever we do outside the law we are never to be above the law."

At Matt's rented condo the team confirms the details of their plot to invade the system undercover. It looks like a play of characters developing to deceive and beguile the system operators, already at the top of the social and economic pyramid. Matt, well trained to melt into the glitter and glory of plenty of money and power, looks forward to charming his way into the Verelez social life via some kind of business con.

At the dinner table, now a thinking circle, Anna develops a platform for their invasive undercover behavior, "We shall act like cats. We pick and choose with aggressive friendliness the people we need to know. At the drop of a hat, to emphasize our self-confidence, we walk away with style from an acquaintance going nowhere. But we never ignore the cleaning lady for review of gossip and her trash barrel. We are experts at expressing loyalty, and the most loyal friend our targets can have. Getting inside the top of the pyramid as well as the bottom is what we need to do."

At that point Matt's cell phone chimes, "Josephine!"

Without formalities she starts like a machine gun, "We defaulted on the West Palm tournament. We are now in Bogota at the Verelez penthouse. I have finally found favor with Adolpho and at least superficially with Lucia."

Matt looks at Juan for where to meet, "Meet at the Simon Bolivar Monument statue tomorrow at 2:P.M. Mannie will be wearing a red shirt." With no other word Josephine cuts out.

Anna was surprised as ever, "There is another woman on our team?"

Matt proudly admits, "Yes, Josephine is undercover working with the son of the owners of the pharmacy that we are after."

It is a bright, sunny, but heavily humid morning dripping with dew at the Simon Bolivar Monument on Calle 13 next to a Parque De Los Periodistas where Mannie meets Josephine asking, "Why are you wearing a red shirt?" Mannie replies, "I am here to meet Josephine."

She can't help being impressed, "So you are the Mannie just back from Europe?"

Mannie starts to turn away, "Yes, let's start walking in the park."

Josephine opens the conversation quickly, "I know we have a lot to say and do but we do not have much time, I have to be at the beautician in a half hour. They are still suspicious of me and I have to account for my time. A stroll in the park before the beautician is ok and the beautician is on the other side of the road, so I am reasonably safe for this meeting."

Mannie is to the point, "We need to know the formula they use for disguising drug shipments. Samples we have taken show that there is no specific formula for converting the cocaine and heroin into liquid or hard pill form for distribution as veterinary pharmaceuticals. Is there a safe place in the penthouse for keeping the formula? On the plant side, we have two people to hire into their lab system, and will get at their preparing their special shipments, but segments of the components are made elsewhere."

Josephine plaintively asks, "Can't the Columbian government get a search warrant for this?"

Mannie empathetically asserts, "Josephine you must understand, your friend's father has very hard Columbian army connections. The Columbian government is very concerned to keep the billion-dollar pharmaceutical business in Bogota unhampered for the country's prosperity. The army is part of a drug enforcement system and not always without influence from the drug rings. If we bring our investigation out into the open our efforts will be washed over."

Josephine now understands, "It was in the paper about the massacre of Columbian police making a raid on a drug establishment, they had been attacked by a platoon of heavily armed men dressed like soldiers."

Mannie confirms, "That was a setup. Someone in their own system betrayed those policemen."

Josephine feels more positive, "Well if we can't use the Columbian government what is it that I can do?"

Mannie now encouraging, "While you are in the penthouse, when Adolpho and Lucia are gone, just saunter around the place and look for things that seem out of place, hidden doors, or concealed safes. Look in or around bookcases, you can always pretend to be looking for a book. On our end we will look for hidden labs even in their warehouse."

Josephine drones a negative, "That penthouse has an alarm system, cameras with sound and infra-red lenses, along with motion detectors. How can I avoid them?"

Mannie is firm on safety, "I don't want you to take any more risk than you need to. Here is my phone number and a dead-end flip phone. It is connected to my satellite cell so you don't have to worry about being traced. Call me if you find anything. If you hear anything, even of meetings, let us know. Their place likely cannot be bugged with the old technology. I'll check on that and they probably have bugged their own phones so don't use them."

Josephine eager to get to the beauty shop ends with an affirmative, "Both Julio and I will do what we can."

Mannie adds, "In the meantime Juan and Anna will keep working on penetrating the warehouse and the lab and figure out a way to poison their distributions with some kind of chemical that cannot be readily traced."

"Who is Anna? Is there another woman involved in this mess?" demands Josephine.

"Oh!" Mannie apologetic to the point of a genuflection to a queen, "I am sorry. Yes, Ann Matrinov is a Moscow undercover policewoman who met up with Juan and me in St. Petersburg. She has saved our skin getting us away safely from contract hits posted on us by the Russian mafia. She has a degree in chemistry and is now applying to work in a Tridexan Lab along with Juan who is a lab assistant."

Josephine is much pleased by the news, "She has my prayers working in their lab. I hope to meet her someday. It is nice to know that Matt is an equal opportunity employer."

Mannie laughingly replies, "Yes, even me, the physically disabled. Juan is presumed missing, as is Anna. And Matt is literally away without leave running this rogue operation. All of us are on his expense black box. Juan can't even go back to his family until this is over. So, we are incognito my dear. We will be in the shadows, but be assured when you need us we are ready to help you and Julio."

Josephine now happy with new partners on the job, "Thanks Mannie, I must go now."

"Good luck," said Mannie, "We will meet in a week, same time, same place."

"Yes, same time, same place, I'll need to get my nails finished." "But of course," jokes Mannie.

Lucia now worrying about preserving their reputation for providing undetected product, "We must consult with a trustworthy chemist to create a real formula, one that shows some sophistication in everyday dissolving of the cocaine and heroin into solution and the precipitation of it back into its pure form."

"I agree," smiles Adolpho. "And I have just hired a chemist for our pharmacy lab. Her name is Greta Dietrich. She just came over from Germany and is new to everything."

Lucia reading into Adolpho's selection of female employees, "So the chemist is a woman. Is she young and good-looking?"

Adolpho stuttering a bit, "She is gorgeous, in her twenties, and brilliant. I tested her for some basic components and interactions of chemicals to produce alkaloids. She even corrected me as I read to her the basic components."

Lucia now showing interest, "Yes, Germans will do that. Call the lab and have her come up here immediately."

Ten minutes later Greta knocks on the office door.

Lucia answers, "Come in." As Greta walks in, "Am I speaking to Greta Dietrich?"

Anna stands at attention in front of Lucia, "Yes I am the new chemist in your lab. You wish to speak to me?"

Lucia starts to fish, "Why did you leave Germany?"

Anna gets creative, "I was bored and my boyfriend left me."

Lucia is now inquisitive, "Why did you come to Bogota?"

Anna shows some art, "My boyfriend came here. He works at the German Embassy."

Lucia gets more comfortable with Greta, "Well, I am glad you came with us to work, and I look forward to meeting your boyfriend at one of our celebrations. In the meantime, I have an interesting assignment for you. We process a lot of ingredients for our medicines that we wish to keep secret. Some include TLC from marijuana, heroin, and cocaine derivatives for pain pills with special activators that reduce side effects and minimize addiction."

Anna replies positively, "Yes, just like codeine for cough syrup." Lucia gets to the point, "You have an inventory of our medications. Those labeled formula, I want you to examine and improve on their chemical combinations to basically prevent the ready detection of our components. Do you understand?"

Anna agrees enthusiastically, "Yes, with your permission I will begin immediately."

Lucia commits to Greta, "Fine. I will pass on your special assignment to the staff giving you complete access and cooperation. You may go and I expect a report on your progress weekly."

Anna, compliant as she backs to the door, "Yes Madam Verelez, I will do as you wish."

Juan is also accepted as a processor and Anna is now a lab chemist. At their lunch break far from the lab building, they begin to discuss how they might sabotage the distribution system.

Juan ventures a thought, "You know if we place diethyl ether into their system as part of their solvent and they use a reacting agent, fortune may be smiling upon us."

Anna waves a caution flag, "That is highly volatile even adding it up front in the lab, but we could do that if we could get them to create safety ventilation and a pressurized lab formulation room."

Juan adds, "Oh, I am temporarily assigned to the area with the vats and overhead hoppers for filling shipping containers. These machines basically fill the 5-gallon plastic drums for the hard product and for the solvent they fill metal lined plastic bags placed in card board boxes."

Anna drops a bomb on Juan, "Guess what? There is no formula for shipping drugs in liquid form. The hard form is by the Russians in St. Petersburg. We can only create a problem one way with the liquid form. But we could insert the reactant in the hard pills that goes volatile with the solvent containing our additive. As for your diethyl ether, we can temperature sensitive the caps to go off when heated for evaporation of the solvent."

Juan is jubilant, "Yes at that point we create a lot of mischief."

Anna adding fuel to the fire, "Suppose we can inject the diethyl ether as part of the solvent, what would cause that to be a problem?"

Juan getting practical, "It seems that when they go to solidify the drug after receiving a shipment in liquid form, they could also put in a precipitate as well as heat to evaporate the carrier liquid. If they use the right kind of precipitate there might be another explosive reaction."

Anna seeing a possibility, "We need to know that precipitate or offer a newer more efficient one. Maybe then we can cause a back-up problem."

Juan still searches for alternatives "There is one other solution." "And what would that be?" inquires Anna.

Juan coolly offers, "We simply contaminate all the samples with arsenic."

Anna sternly rebukes him, "That would be murder. They only typically test their entire product before distribution after distilling it."

Juan emphasizes, "But do they test it for poisons or just for the quality of cocaine or heroin?"

Anna discounts the affect, "Arsenic would do the job well, just once. It would not destroy the system, just delay it for a correction. What we need to do is cause the hard product to self-destroy on liquidation for separation of product and the liquid product to explode with distillation. At one time the whole process becomes suspiciously unreliable and a very loud fire and explosion occurs, typical of badly run meth labs, and easily identified and followed up by the authorities at hand."

Anna is counting on the temptation for Tridexan to increase its supply following the increasing cocaine and heroin production, as production camps and outdoor labs move to denser jungle areas or across the border. When growers cover 330 square miles of land devoted to the production of cocaine as well as poppies for heroin, the fields prove difficult to locate and once eliminated, they just appear elsewhere.

And as Anna hopes, to take advantage of increasing demand along the world system, Lucia moves to negotiate a merger with Don Fuego a major supplier growing in Columbia, Peru, Chile, and Argentina.

Lucia boldly confronts the man by herself, but not without a squad of heavily armed paramilitary behind her. Standing tall, powerfully delivering her message, "We have to increase our production of shipped quantities, the bounty of our business and our partners requires us to accept more and distribute more of your product. Merge with us and you will be free of managing the distribution with dealers that come and go, requiring a field army for enforcement, and the loss of product through unreliable smuggling. We have a formula to disguise your product and ship it all over the world without detection."

Don Fuego, a tough guy with a boisterous demeanor, "I expect payment in full on delivery for every delivery. None of this 'wait and see' for the sale to a dealer in Miami. Hah, I doubt you can do that."

Lucia now acting like an accountant goes on the offensive, "Senor Fuego, I presume you have an account in Switzerland, or are you still dealing in cash?"

Don Fuego responds harshly, "I only deal in cash."

Lucia laughs, "And where do you hide it, in a garage to keep it safe from thieves, fire or confiscation? When you deliver product, we will immediately transfer the funds to your account in Geneva, Switzerland, where it will be safe and no one can take it away from you."

Don Fuego born of poor farmers now thinking of a regular flight to Europe to check on his bank assets, begins to see the light, "Lucia, you will be giving me the going price at the door?"

Lucia, still the business woman, "Mi Senor Don Fuego, since we will be relieving you of your many-sided tasks for disposing your product we will apply a discount on the door price of 25%."

Don Fuego just a little perturbed, "Bah, I'll give you 20% or no deal."

Lucia calls it like an auctioneer, "Done, we have a deal. This is a verbal agreement. Open an account in Switzerland and give us your number and approval code for making deposits. You have my protected email address. We will expect deliveries of your entire product year-round."

Adolpho hardly believes, "He agreed to 20%?"

Lucia chants in absolute bliss, "Yes, our deal with Don Fuego for our system doubles our profits over cost and then we get a 20% discount on field product prices. All this money goes to our Swiss bank before our product hits the street mark-up. What a business! On top of that we also make a legal living!"

<h1 style="text-align:center">Chapter Sixteen</h1>

<h2 style="text-align:center">Getting In Deep</h2>

With Josephine and Julio now comfortably settled in the Verelez penthouse, Adolpho offers to show Julio the company plant operations over several days. Lucia spends at least half a day at the plant offices but returns for lunch and a chance to better size up and attempt to mold Josephine into an acceptable member of the club.

Lucia pleasantly suggests to Josephine, "What do you think about a nice shopping trip this afternoon?"

Josephine smiles lightly. "Yes, I would like that very much. Where would you like to go?"

Lucia amiably suggests, "Oh I think the shops downtown would be wonderful now. They have some new clothing in from Paris. I think it would be a good idea to start thinking about dressing for the season."

Josephine is friendly as ever, "Wonderful."

Lucia replies casually, "We will be leaving in about a half hour. Our limousine will be waiting at the door."

Josephine is one hundred percent compliant, "Fine."

Back at the plant, Adolpho continues with Julio's education over the plant operations, and is quick to inform Julio of a new source of medical additives, "The volume of our business from our sources here in Columbia and overseas has increased considerably and the demand has not gone down one bit. We need to process more and more each day and it is getting difficult because we are running out of space. We have to change our formula to reflect some exclusivity that we thought we had kept secret. We are concerned that our partners may easily squeeze us out of our distribution system if they learn our secret."

Julio shows genuine concern, "Ah yes. So, the formula must truly be made an impenetrable secret?"

"Yes. We have discussed things with our new chemist. Diethyl ether is a new chemical that we will use as a solvent starting next week. The chemical comes in bulk from China and Russia and Germany. We have made our orders for it and it shall be arriving soon. Our first shipment will be by air and the rest will be by ship."

Julio interjects, "But isn't this the chemical that explodes in labs?"

Adolpho asserts, "Yes, it is dangerous. It is highly volatile and is subject to temperature changes and could be very much of a problem in our processing. So, we have to increase our ventilation and air conditioning in the warehouse and in our production facility. We have to make sure our containers are much tighter and are able to handle the pressure that is caused by gasification."

Julio is in agreement "Ah, more problems in production, no doubt needing more space. Is there any more room in the warehouse or for an expansion in the yard?"

"Yes," Adolpho now gets down to specifics, "We will probably want to do one other chemical. We have not been exactly sure what to use yet but we will call it a red herring chemical, one that cannot be readily discovered, but one whose presence will be known. In the end it will actually do nothing to impede the process of solvent and precipitation in our product."

"Ah," goes Julio. "I remember from my days in the chemistry lab when I was studying to be a dentist. The most complex organic chemical compounds are perfumes. They are very difficult to replicate and are subject to so many variables and tests that analytical chemists cannot breakdown their composition to recreate the exact same thing."

Adolpho is eager to explore his thought, "This could be very interesting. A perfume! What a wonderful camouflage to confuse our distributors. For them to share their wealth for our processes and our protection, for a formula that they do not even need to have. Your mother and I love it!"

"You know," suggests Julio, "I think we could use Josephine in this matter."

Adolpho questions, "How do you mean?"

Julio explains, "I think maybe we could ask Josephine to pick a perfume for us to give as a gift to our favorite female employees."

"What a wonderful idea!" We have a new lady chemist and a present for her would be good business."

Julio laughing, "That sounds like she is a new side business for you!"

Adolpho grumbles a bit, "Oh of course, that aside, I agree that we need to get Josephine involved with our business in an innocent way. Eventually she will learn more. And we will bring her in slowly so that she feels the wealth and power that we have generated. When she becomes accustomed to it, she will be seduced by it, just like your mother and me."

Julio is a bit disconcerted, "I hope you are not thinking of Josephine as a gold digger."

Adolpho denies the hint, "Nonsense. I will check with Lucia. She and Josephine are shopping this afternoon and we can suggest it to Josephine at dinner."

With Julio off to the warehouse to look for expansion space, Adolpho at the office makes an important call, "Generalissimo, so nice to talk with you again."

The Generalissimo starts the conversation about business, "How are you doing?"

Adolpho answers with candor, "Fine. But you need to pull back on your running interference of the Bogota Policia Nationale. Attacking our own police trying to raid a drug facility is not good? We cannot handle that, too much publicity."

The General admits, "Ah, but it had to be done and the troopers had no IDs and wore masks. We need to keep these police out of our special business places."

"Yes," Adolpho almost pleads, "But we need to have a meeting to discuss slowing down the police without killing them."

"Aye," the Generalissimo brags, "We did a good job though. They all died and it didn't cost us any money. They got our message!"

"Yes." Adolpho gets irritated, "But they pleaded as they died and you brutally killed them with condemnation as terrorists."

"But there is more to it." The General goes on, "We are dealing daily with terrorists supported with donations by wealthy Americans. Our message is broader to include the social disrupters and communists funded for this kind of sedition to create chaos and disorder."

Adolpho gets out before getting in too deep, "Yes, we will have to talk more, until we meet at the Club."

Matt meets Mannie at the Simon Bolivar Park to minimize their traffic at the condo.

Matt opens with a start, "What is the situation now?"

Mannie is eager to announce good news, "We have Juan working in the warehouse close to the lab where they do the formula mix and the shipping. We have Josephine in the penthouse and becoming very trustworthy. And Anna met with Lucia who ordered her to devise a new formula to protect and keep secret the components of Tridexan medications. We now have three operatives on the scene to implement our self-destruct plan. The question is, what do we use as a perfume in the formula and should it be the catalyst for diethyl ether volatility for dissolving the cocaine and distilling the heroin in their shipments. According to Josephine, Julio's father told him they are going to be starting to use diethyl ether and improve ventilation and cooling in the processing areas."

"Diethyl ether?" said Matt, "What a stroke of luck for us."

Mannie enthusiastically suggests, "Perhaps the perfume can be contaminated with time released perchloric acid mixed with diethyl ether causing an explosion in all of the 55-gallon drums side by side.

Matt avidly agrees, "It sounds like a good way to go. To avoid discovery of our additive, we have to insert it before filling the barrels. For the hard pill packages Anna will have to insert our additive under a false name as part of her new formula."

Mannie adds an idea, "For the hard pill packages Juan thinks capsules cannot be large or they would be easily spotted in the solution. Instead, he wants to use a timed release coating for very small nano sized particles, almost a dust, mixed with the formula and not visible to the naked eye."

Matt is now energized, "Ah hah, we mix the nano perchloric with the perfume that Josephine chooses in the lab for delivery to a pill mixing and fabrication line with packaging for 5-gallon containers put on a pallet and all the way up to 55-gallon drums for the liquid."

Mannie focuses on the results, "That would create a fairly big explosion and fire."

Matt qualifies, "I think we can minimize the explosion effect to the point where the packages would simply burst. But diethyl ether being volatile would still cause a fire."

Mannie backs up, "Well, somebody might get hurt. We might have some innocent casualties in this kind of arrangement."

Matt points to the dealers, "There might be some casualties tied to the drug rings themselves. There are already numerous casualties with the meth labs. When will you next meet with Josephine?"

Mannie with his undercover tone, "Josephine, has an appointment for her nails to be finished tomorrow at the salon across the street. She will be here in the park at 8:30 A.M. We will see each other on different benches on the other side of this open square."

Matt is slightly amused, "Well how are you going to meet with her then?"

Mannie, smarts with a grin, "We actually don't meet. I gave her a communication devices about the size of your watch. It is good for fifty feet. What she is going to do is sit on that bench and I am going to be sitting here with a newspaper over my face. We will be talking with each other that way with ear buds on a very high frequency channel that is not accessed by normal radio devices."

"Hah, hah," laughs Matt, "As usual you are up to your latest tricks."

Mannie is very protective of Josephine's cover, "We have to keep in touch this way. She is very high profile now. People in this area know her as she is viewed as intended for Julio and their family is very powerful, politically recognized, and highly respected by the well to do aristocracy in this district, let alone the politicians, and the giants in the bureaucracy."

Mannie continues, "Anna now has a free hand to start working on the micro time capsules. Josephine will start looking for the perfume that will suit their needs. And Juan will stay cool in the warehouse production area."

"Right," said Matt. "We'll coordinate all this tonight back at the condo. I will meet you here at three o'clock again tomorrow. I will find a warehouse shop space for any off site work we need to do."

Mannie agrees, "Steady as she goes. We are on course."

Matt finds a small warehouse with a machine shop if they need a place to manufacture the timed-release nano caps of perchloric acid for mixing with Anna's new formula for Tridexan. Best located among outlet stores and warehouses, he chooses a rundown industrial area along Carrera 65.

The next morning Mannie meets with Josephine at the park near her beauty shop. Looking around and at the sky with her new transmitter, Josephine speaks with amusement, "Things are looking much better than I thought. They are beginning to trust me to do things for them that before would have been impossible."

Mannie is concerned about Julio's continued commitment, "Is Julio still on track with you to get him up and out of his family's business?"

Josephine is acutely aware of Julio's problem, "Julio is getting the 'my son is taking over the business' treatment. Adolpho is showing him all the processes of the business on site along with the kinks and need for improvements. And he is behaving like a perfectly interested son. He can't really start working the system yet but he thinks he will be managing something in a week. Adolpho, after checking with Lucia, asked me and trusted me to provide them with a perfume to add to their medications. So, I am working the market for a perfume mixed with a spice that might be acceptable."

Mannie tries to be helpful, "Where are you going and how are you going about it?"

Josephine is unperturbed, "Us women know how to shop perfume. It is in our genes, both kinds. Perfumes are highly concentrated and it does not take much to change the character of a chemical. Basically, I have been trying to find a perfume that is not overpowering, but is pleasing to the senses, and yet quite subtle, so as not to attract too much human attention but which will overload the senses of a sniffing dog and won't register on spectral analysis."

Mannie laughs behind his newspaper, "Well I guess that is a woman's approach to the problem and that's fine. The scent that you provide is what we will use to insert our little time bomb that can't be seen with the naked eye. We will provide that in fifty-gallon drums and will need you to supply the laboratory with the perfume for insertion in their shipments."

Josephine qualifies, "That's all easier said than done, but I will do it. I think I have got the scent."

"And what kind of scent is that?" said Mannie?

Josephine with a bit of cache, "I like watermelon"

Mannie shows wonderment, "Watermelon?"

Josephine now eager to find it, "Oh, you will love it. I will be shopping today for it. I will have it sent to your condo when I find it."

"No," he said. "Don't do that. Matt is getting us a warehouse to produce our mayhem."

"Ok, I can wait and send a sample to you and of course am required to send a sample to the lab at Tridexan." Looking at her watch, Josephine frowns, "I must go. My manicurist is waiting at the beauty salon."

Mannie thankfully offers, "Let's meet the same time next week. We will have a shipment ready at that time."

"So soon?"

"Yes, timing is important with a price on our heads."

"Ok,"

"Next week at 8:30 A. M. same place?"

"Yes," as Josephine walks away unnerved over the speed of everything happening.

Chapter Seventeen

And Deeper

At the Officers Club, Julio thinks to have a simple lunch with Adolpho. While at the bar waiting to be seated, Adolpho's friends' gesture to him to join them in the adjoining private meeting room. Adolpho gives Julio a sign to wait and eat at the bar.

The Generalissimo speaks tersely, "We need to discuss your plans for increasing production and about how, when, and where to meet Don Fuego's requirements and our need for cashing him out for each transaction."

Adolpho now exhibiting considerable leadership, "Gentlemen, we must look long and hard at what we are doing and come up with improved production. We need to provide faster conversion and a wider distribution system that will meet a greater demand and higher profits for ourselves"

"Yes", agrees the Generalissimo. "We need to do it, but it is not so easily done. We need to acquire a new and bigger facility. We need to bribe a new set of local police. We need to bring in another brigade of soldiers commanded by another colonel that we do not have on our pay list now. Every time we do that we increase our exposure to the risk of discovery and prosecution. Things have been running well for us. Why do we have to go this route?"

Adolpho builds his case, "We have no choice. We either expand and cooperate and make more money or we suffer a war, a war that we are not likely to win."

"How can that be?" The Generalissimo forcefully emphasizes, "We have the guns. We know the dealers. We know whom to kill."

Adolpho exploits reality, "Oh so easily said, but assassination is the 60% owner's specialty. Each one of us is a target. Without showing our value to the operation, we become expendable. They work behind the scenes, not out front. Their methods are ruthless. To make their point you know they will kill our families, our children, our grandchildren, our brothers and sisters, our uncles, our parents. If we will fail to provide value, one by one, they will have somebody to replace our unfortunate loss."

"Easily said but it is not so easily done. I say we fight. They are and will stay under our control."

Adolpho announces loudly, "Fight? As soon as we start fighting what happens? We get exposure. We get newspapers. We get reporters. We get investigators. They are all waiting for us to make a mistake. A cartel war makes no sense!"

Adolpho concludes, "I have put our future on the table. Go and think about it in terms of added local police bribery and tougher enforcement squads for receiving deliveries. We will meet again next week to vote to become a larger part of a multi-billion-dollar business."

They agree and end the meeting walking quietly out to the dining room, some to use the facilities and some just stretching legs. With the doors open, Julio walks up to Adolpho, "Father, your meeting proved very noisy, but nothing said could be heard."

Adolpho is now at odds with himself, "We must begin expanding our space to increase our production. Let us drive to the industrial zone and look for a new plant location. Those men are our partners in this business and we will need to make them happy with a better, bigger plant."

The next day after Matt rents a warehouse, to start the ball rolling, he decides to begin the setup of the manufacturing process for the nano sized time released perchloric acid. He discovers that new machinery is not available immediately but used equipment might be available from a pharmaceutical company. Matt then contacts the Verelez business and asks if they have any used equipment, they are willing to sell, as he needs it for his production of hard-shell coated chocolate wrapped candies.

"And what kind of candy is this called?" said the purchasing agent for the Tridexan company.

Matt aptly replies, "Oh we call them Global Wonders. We sell them all over the world."

The agent with little hesitation volunteers, "We do have a piece of equipment that might apply and we are thinking of replacing it. In fact, we are not using it right now. It is on standby in one of our lines. If you would like to come over and look at it, please feel free. I will be available this afternoon at three o'clock. We will need also to get permission from our president, Senora Verelez to conclude an agreeable price."

"Fine, I'll be there. Your name again is?"

"Miguel Piniendo."

"Ok Senor Piniendo, my name is Mark Monahan, I will be there."

After cutting off, Matt rubs his hands in self-congratulation, "Wow, I can't believe it."

At that point Matt's cell phone rings and it is Mannie. "How is it going with the machinery we need?

"Amazing," replies Matt. "I just made arrangements to view and hopefully purchase from Tridexan the equipment we need to make our timed capsules."

Mannie is happy at that, "Great. We can get the warehouse up and running ASAP. The meeting with Josephine went well, but she did not have much time. She has a chauffeur driving her to all the perfumeries looking for a relatively low-cost perfume that can be diluted and mixed with the formula. She likes watermelon!"

"Huh, watermelon?" Matt now wonders, "That could be interesting. I will be back to the warehouse tomorrow. Now I am going over to Tridexan to look at the equipment and will be meeting Lucia, "la presidenta," to close on the price of the machine."

Mannie adds, "Good luck. In the meantime, Juan will be working up how we can automatically mix our capsules into their formula." Matt concludes, "Well I will have to suit up for the unexpected opportunity to meet Julio's mother. Who knows how that will go?"

Anna snuck back to the Condo for a lunch break when Matt shows up to dress for his occasion at Tridexan. She is quite fashionable in a long white, well pressed lab coat with her Greta name plate. Her attractive pearly smile, and hypnotizing eyes never fail to stun Matt with a magnetic attraction way beyond friendliness.

As he comes out of his room with a suit on, Anna inquires, "Where are you going?"

"I am going to meet Miguel Piniendo and then Lucia Verelez to look at and hopefully buy a coating machine for my candy business." "Ahh, yes. But I don't think you should wear a tie."

"Ok, no tie."

"Yes, an open collar and no t-shirt either. Do you have any gold to wear for yourself?"

"I don't really like to wear jewelry."

"I think maybe this time you should. What do you have in your bag of tricks that would make you look like a grandee?"

"I have a gent's three carat diamond ring that I could wear."

Anna's eyes grow wider, "Yes, that works to impress her a bit. Don't you think?"

"Well, ok. I will wear the diamond ring."

"Ok," she said. "One more thing, I have a gold earring that I think you should also wear."

"On my left ear," he said.

Anna now laughing lightly, "Whatever ear makes you a man and not a crossover."

Matt gives up, "Ok"

With that and his gray-streaked red wavy hair combed neatly back and behind his ears, Matt definitely makes Anna's eyes pop with a new appreciation of her comrade in arms.

Anna goes on, "You will be meeting a tigress. She will definitely admire your rugged demeanor with your square shoulders and sturdy physique. And your height is above average for this place, but what about your boots?"

"What about my boots?"

"You don't need to wear cowboy boots."

"Well," as Matt backs off on that question, "I don't really like to wear other kinds of shoes."

"Ok," Anna thinks a second, "We will go with the boots as your Mexican heritage, a caballero?"

Matt confirms with pride. "Yes, my Mexican heritage. They are handcrafted with ostrich skin. Thank you for your help Anna. Now I must go."

Anna smiling as he closes the door, "Indeed your boots and you look very nice!"

Matt uber rents a Mercedes XL with a chauffeur. At the entrance to the plant with a gate keeper coming out to enquire, he gives his name and after a call, the gate opens and the guard directs him to building number three. At the front door stands a man waiting for his arrival.

Out of his vehicle Matt asks, "You are Senor Miguel Piniendo?"

"And you are Senor Mark Manahan?"

They shake hands and walk into the back of the building where a shut down and empty forty-foot line conveyor dispenser, dryer oven, and separator for packaging stands. Miguel turns a main switch and the machinery runs faultlessly with all wheels and belts moving and the oven warming up. Matt examines the moving parts, "What electric amperage rating is required to run this equipment?"

Miguel opens a switch box and notes, "We have a mainline rating of 500 amps with no problems with conveyor motors using capacitors for starters. We purchased this line ten years ago and have recently increased our production requiring a larger system. If you buy it, for a small fee I will have it disassembled, delivered, and installed at your location, as I gather you are new to Bogota."

Matt answers coolly, "Yes, we are expanding into South America from Mexico City. And with your assistance I would be happy to purchase this equipment."

Senor Peniendo opens the door at the rear of the building, "Let us go to meet our president Senora Verelez. She is expecting you."

They walk across a parking lot to a four-story glass building with offices and laboratory arrangements including vent stacks and heavy duty air handling on the roof. On the fourth floor a receptionist greets Matt and Senor Peniendo and ushers them into a large office with continuous floor to ceiling glass windows. Behind a large glass covered desk a high back chair facing the view of the plant area suddenly swivels around to face Matt.

Peniendo speaks. "Buenos Dias Senora Verelez, with me is the gentleman wishing to purchase our coating machine. He is from Mexico City and is expanding his Global Candy Company here in Columbia. His name is Mark Monahan."

Lucia warmly greets Matt, "Welcome to our facility Mr. Monahan. So, you are a candy man. What kinds of candy do you make?"

Matt now talks like a salesman. "Madame Verelez, we make the finest chocolate coated candies in the western hemisphere. Our surprises are behind the best chocolate made in Switzerland and blended in Mexico City with our special ingredients including fillings with marshmallow, caramels, and soft cherries in their juice, chocolate truffles, and assorted creams including blueberry, brazil nut, coffee, maple, nougat, orange and my favorite raspberry cream. All of our creams are made from scratch with our special recipes."

Lucia now looks Matt over from head to toe. "Peniendo, you may go. Mr. Monahan please be seated. Monahan, that is an Irish name, but I see you wearing caballero riding boots."

Matt gets back to his heritage, "My mother is from Mexico and my father is from Dublin, Ireland. I was raised in Texas and moved to Mexico City to start my business."

Lucia shows considerable interest, "You are making a good choice locating here. Bogota is a very prosperous city and a good base for South America. I am willing to sell you our machine for one million pesos. Do you find my price agreeable?"

Matt is diplomatic, "I think it is agreeable if the price includes reinstallation of it in my newly rented warehouse."

Lucia in a pleasing mood, "I agree. In fact, I would consider it a compliment if you would join our family for dinner tonight to discuss the delicacies of doing business in Columbia regarding regulations and employment of workers."

Matt seeing more opportunities, "Senora Verelez, I would be honored to join you and your family for dinner."

Lucia can't stop asking, "Do you have a wife to bring with you?"

Matt hesitates, "No, my wife died seven years ago."

Lucia now gets aggressive, "I am sorry for her loss to you. But an attractive man like you must have a lady friend."

Matt feels he is falling into a trap, "Ahh, no, my business has kept me free from any liaison at this time."

Lucia now becomes obvious, "Would you find it difficult to have a liaison with a married woman?"

Matt walking a rail gets philosophical, "No, I have had several. They were very lovely affairs. They did not last for various reasons. No hard feelings. But wonderful times they were."

Lucia hits the concrete running, "We have just met and I cannot help but like you very much."

Matt looks at her with a possessive grin, "I also find you very attractive."

Lucia concludes, "Good, I will see you at seven at our penthouse. My assistant will give you the address. And the payment for the equipment you can set up with Peniendo whom I will inform to include set up in the price."

Matt standing and slightly bowing graciously like a knight in shining armor, "My thanks to a beautiful lady. I look forward to dinner tonight."

Lucia, as Matt turns to leave to the door, "As do I."

A moment later Adolpho enters Lucia's office, "I understand that you sold our old coating machine for a million pesos."

Lucia, "Yes, and I invited him to our pent house for dinner tonight."

Adolpho, "Wonderful, since we are having guests, I would like to invite our new chemist to help fill out the table. It would be good to know her better socially for what we want her to do for us."

Lucia looking at him sideways, "Adolpho you have eyes for her, I am sure. But by the same token I have eyes for our candy man. And I agree that it would be good to bring her closer to the possibilities for her betterment with us, and not with her German boyfriend at the embassy."

Adolpho, "Good. I will go to the lab to check on her progress with the components of our formula and invite her for dinner at 7."

Matt is in his room getting ready for the dinner party when Anna knocks at his door. "Matt, are you going to the Verelez penthouse for dinner tonight?"

Matt opens the door. "Yes, Mrs. Verelez invited me after she agreed to sell the coating machine for a million pesos. Why?"

Anna adds herself to the party, "That pompous Adolopho put his arm around me at the lab and also invited me to dinner tonight at their penthouse. He said they were having another guest from Mexico City, a candy manufacturer. Is that your new cover?"

Matt fills Anna in. "Yes, this has all happened today after we got our warehouse and I started calling around for equipment. I had to make myself up as a person needing it for something so candy felt like a good idea at the time."

Anna offers a hint of humor, "You certainly know how to develop a line."

Matt now feels a plan coming on, "This is very interesting. We know Adolpho will be chasing you. He'll love to talk to impress you. Dress in your best shoulder showing dress and just be your vivacious, pert, and very curvaceous self."

Anna shows her shoulders with a smile, "Now you are being funny. I will let down my hair and prop and expose my bust a bit and prance my feline figure like a prostitute. That hardly matches my lab technician character, but it will certainly produce results with Senor Verelez."

Matt does not joke. "Ahhh, but that will get you on the inside of this guy's head and all I want you to do is tease him just a little. It will also distract his wife who will be chasing me. We will both be playing at our best, me as a candy man attracted to her and you as a sexy bombshell for him."

Anna now falls into the plan, "And after tonight, how long will this be going on?"

Just then Mannie walks into the condo after working on getting material for the new line to be installed at the warehouse the next day.

Anna calls him over. "Mannie, Matt and I have been invited for dinner tonight at the Verelez residence."

Mannie, "What? You will be meeting Josephine and Julio before dinner for cocktails."

Matt still firm on the commitment, "I trust her to figure things out. She is quick on her feet."

Mannie, "I am sure she will be there to talk about her perfume assignment. If she looks like she recognizes you, the game is up. You are risking our whole project. We are off the grid. If something goes wrong with total denial from Russia, the US, and Columbia, we are fair game for the cartels"

"Mannie, I got the machine and I had to accept the dinner invitation from Lucia. It is for the better that we are literally shoulder to shoulder with the owners of the operation. This evening may be hard. But all of our moves have included the same danger. We cannot stop now. As they say in the theatre, for us 'The play must go on.'"

Matt and Anna go to the first floor of the condo to access the private elevator to the penthouse. They give their names to the operator who calls the penthouse for permission to send them up. Granted, they arrive on the sixtieth floor with the doors opening to a butler standing in a two-story open foyer with a giant crystal chandelier hanging from the center. Along the walls are busts of Julio's family, a few generals including Juan Peron, and a few past Presidents of Columbia. The entrance is hanging and dripping with statements of who they are, on the top of the social and economic pyramid in Columbia. Matt is not impressed with such a show of connections.

Coming from the main reception room, Adolpho with his arms outstretched and a broad smile on his face, "Ah my friends, Mark and Greta, thank you for coming. Welcome to our wonderful home in the sky of Bogota."

"Yes", remarks Matt, "This is truly a palace in the sky with an unending view of Bogota and Monserrate."

"Please, let us go to our lounge area to have some drinks and talk. Don't you think?"

Anna walks in to the room rather coyly, displaying herself very well, but not doing it in a flaunting way. She cannot help but be noticed by Adolpho, twice, three times and definitely to the irritation of Lucia who is waiting to meet them.

Lucia lights up looking at Matt, "El Senor Mark, I am glad you are here to make our evening interesting with your business. And Greta, I am hoping you may enlighten us a bit about your latest progress in the lab."

At that point, as they are discussing histories of their families, Julio and Josephine arrive from their rooms.

Matt's back is turned to Josephine and she does not notice him as she and Julio are hailed and greeted by Adolpho. "Ah, you are finally here, the two of you. What a lovely couple you make. Come, I would like you to meet our guests for dinner tonight."

Julio brightly responds, "Wonderful, and whom do we have to dine with us tonight?"

Adolpho primes his words, "Some very special people. Greta is our new lab chemist working on our special formulations. She is from Germany"

Greta extends her hand to Julio, "It is a pleasure to meet you and your friend Josephine."

Adolpho, points to Matt talking with Lucia who gestures to Matt to turn around to face Josephine and Julio. Matt turns around and is stunned speechless as he stands a few feet from the face of Josephine. He does not hear a word of Adolpho's introduction. He is becalmed and frozen in place by her beguiling image.

Josephine smiles elegantly with her arm folded into the arm of Julio. Seeing Matt frozen and needing a breaking word to free him of his trance, with a very loud and boisterous greeting. she blurts out, "Ah yes, did I hear something about chocolate candy?"

Adolpho adds a cheery quick pick up, "Women always seem ready for an opportunity to enjoy chocolates."

Josephine nudging Julio on his shoulder agrees "Yes. How did you know?"

By this time, Anna picks up on what is going on. The electricity between Matt and Josephine that is so obvious to her is beyond Lucia, Julio or Adolpho. Lucia focuses on Josephine nudging her husband, and Adolpho still can't take his repetitive glances away from Anna. Matt's meeting with Josephine barely goes well.

Thankfully, at that moment the butler opens up the doors to the drawing room, which leads to the dining room. "Ladies and gentlemen, dinner is served."

Adolpho invites the guests, "Let us move then to the dining room,"

Josephine and Julio nonchalantly lead the way talking about his day at the plant with his dad. Adolpho carefully places his right arm around the waist of Anna including a slight but intended hug, and follows the first couple in.

Lucia, with her arm in Matt's, gently leans her thigh into his with her shoulder resting on his invitingly, with a suggested firm command, "Come, you will sit next to me." She then looks at him quizzically and asks, "Do you dance?"

Adolpho, with Greta closely held, hears Lucia and announces, "Of course he dances. He is a Spanish gentleman, all Spanish gentleman dance. He then looks at Greta with a "Will You?" smile.

"Good!" agrees Lucia, "I would like for us to dance after dinner. I have some street players coming to entertain us."

Adopho jubilates, "A capital idea. We all enjoy music, and evening drink, and dancing to lift our hearts and pursue our dreams of love and friendship."

"Josephine, will you join us with Julio?"

"Julio looks at her and commits, "Of course she will. She needs her heart lifting too."

Looking at Greta, Adolpho queries again, "What about our lab lady Greta?"

Greta unperturbed but slightly pressured to go along, "Well I don't have a lot of dancing experience but I will try."

"After dinner then, we will celebrate with dancing!"

By tradition Adolpho sits at the head of the table with his Lucia to the right with Matt next to her and Greta on the opposite side next to Adolpho. Julio and Josephine sit side by side at the other side of the table. Being Adolpho's son and only heir, Julio rightfully should sit at the other end of the table, but for a small dinner meeting, he and Josephine sit at the middle.

As the dinner progresses Josephine finds her eyes wandering over towards Matt, amazed at his grand presence as a candy man. She no longer wonders how Greta fits in with Matt and the others of his team, but remains utterly amazed at their brazen presence. Of course, as planned, Adolpho is constantly staring at Greta, with her frozen smile and stiff posture.

Josephine becomes more at ease as she notices lustful Lucia looking with hunger in her gaze at Matt and concludes that Matt has Lucia on the hook, or could it be the other way around, when Lucia's shoulder drops next to his as she puts her hand below the table and strokes the inside of his thigh.

Adolpho gets conversational, "Josephine, how have you been planning your perfume research?"

"Perfume research?" pops in Matt.

"Oh yes, Josephine is joining our family business as a market and product researcher."

"Oh, what is that she is working on?"

"She is going to help us make our products smell better. We use carbolic acid as an antiseptic for scratches, wounds, bites, blisters, sores, cankers, whatever might occur on a horse or a cow or a bull. The carbolic acid is not a very good smelling product so Josephine has been going to all the perfumeries to find a scent that we think would be appropriate for our products."

The evening drives on with chattering at a cheerful pace. Then as the meal comes to an end, Lucia claps her hands for the dance music to proceed with the clearing and moving of the table.

The first dance begins with a tango and Lucia moves chest to chest with Matt inquiring, "Do you Tango?"

Matt takes her hand, swings her around to hold her waist as he begins the choreographed two steps to the chanting beat and violin's sweet song of attraction melting the two together as one. Only the two take the floor and move with the smooth, embracing turns, arched backs and finally a deep dip to a sexy ending.

Lucia is almost breathless, "I have never danced so well, thanks to your fine lead. May I have the next dance with a Mambo?"

Anna and Josephine were taken aback by the suave dancing led by Matt. They would never have guessed he could dance so well and with such a manly appeal, reminiscent of the bull fighters in the ring.

For the mambo, Adolpho grabs Greta holding her tightly while grinding his hips as she barely moves to make an attractive statement of her torso with inviting motions, with an almost distant look on her face. No doubt the direction of her look at Matt reveals her distaste for her job this evening.

Without speaking, Josephine and Julio dance quietly with a controlled, very personal and gentle small step movement to the music.

The night ends with an invitation from Lucia to Matt, "I would like very much for us to meet for lunch tomorrow at the restaurant in our building to discuss how I can help you market your candy in Bogota." Her kiss on his lips at the end was more than an invitation to lunch.

Adolopho makes the same move on Anna who accepts his slovenly kiss with a quick take away. He ends, "Thank you for coming to our dinner. I look forward to working with you."

Anna replies, "I have had a wonderful evening."

Retiring to their rooms, Julio acknowledges to Josephine, "That Mark Monahan overwhelmed my mother. I have never seen her so overcome by a man, almost as if he is a magnet."

Josephine adds her observation, "And your father certainly showed his attention to Greta quite a bit without even looking at your mother." Julio then looks at Josephine quizzically. "I saw you staring at Mark. Do you know him from some place? It seems you are familiar with him."

Josephine willingly admits, "It is not that I am familiar with him but I did find him fascinating. He is a bit of a handsome fellow just like you, when you are on the polo field. And your mother is definitely enamored with him."

"Yes, I saw that too," admits Julio. "He is an older man for sure but he certainly seems to be able to attract women."

"Yes," she agrees, "That is what it is. At some point I have to admit that I was jealous that it was not us on the dance floor doing the same."

Julio apologetically admits. "Jealous? Ohh, yes, I should have asked you to dance the tango. That is one dance I have not learned."

Josephine approaches the door to her room. "He is a distraction for her, just like I am a distraction for you. We need to be getting back to Florida. How long do you think we will be here?"

Julio shakes his shoulders without an answer. With blank faces, they bid each other good night with a hug and a kiss on the cheek not knowing what fortune the next day will bring.

Chapter Eighteen

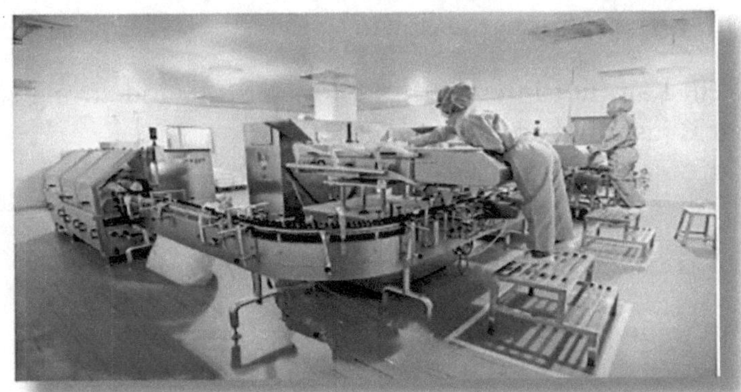

Building The Bomb

Josephine spends the next day going from luxury perfumeries in the major department stores to the specialty shops looking for a scent that she thinks ought to smell like fruit. Approaching one of the clerks in a major department store, Josephine asks, "Do you have anything that would smell like watermelons?"

The clerk politely replies with some skepticism, "Water melon? No, senora. But we do have something that smells like oranges."

Josephine is ready to explore other scents, "May I smell it?"

"But of course. Let me bring it to you."

Josephine whiffing the scent off of a drop on her wrist, "It smells like oranges. But it is too citrusy. Do you have something that smells like pears?"

"Ah, yes we do, bring out La JurD'Amour for the lady."

Josephine thinking it smoother and appropriately subtle, remarks, "This is very nice, how much is it?"

"Oh, it is very reasonable," said the clerk, "only Twelve Hundred Fifty Pesos an ounce."

"Oh," Josephine looks a bit shocked, "That seems a bit much. Do you have it as a cologne?"

"Oh, you mean watered down?"

"Well, I am not interested in a long lasting and strong scent. But one that is just mild and lingering."

The clerk brings out a pint bottle of La Jur D'Amour Calogne.

That is exactly what she wants. "I'll take a case."

"You want a case, Senora?"

Without hesitation, "Yes, a case" she said.

The clerk goes back to the storeroom and brings out a case. "I will have my assistant take it to your car."

With the case placed in the back of the Verelez limousine. Eduardo, the Verelez chauffer who acts as a bodyguard when Josephine is shopping on her own, remains unimpressed. Josephine now getting ready to go back to the penthouse asks Eduardo in a friendly way, "Have you been a driver for the Verelez family for long?"

Eduardo makes a slight grin, "No, Senora, I am a general associate. I am from the military and am paid well as a body guard, driver, and for odd jobs. I am responsible for your well-being and that of the Verelez family."

Josephine replies in her ingratiating way, "Eduardou, Mucho Gracias for being with me and watching for me. I appreciate it."

Eduardo still very formal, "De nada, Senora O'Conner, I am happy to keep you safe."

And of course, Josephine consoles herself with the thought that he is told to watch her every move, and reports back to Lucia.

At the warehouse, Matt checks out the power service for Mannie, as workmen unload the coating machine with conveyors, dispensers, baking, and collecting components. "It looks like a 1000-amp service, with starters we can handle heavy duty electric motors and heating elements. I am wiring a million pesos for the equipment in the name of Global Candy Company. This is getting to be an incredible pursuit."

Mannie senses a problem with Matt beginning to stumble, "You worrying about something in particular?"

Matt, "I am having second thoughts; as a safety net, maybe we should bring Columbia and our government into this action."

"Don't bother," barks Mannie. "We know some of the army is bought and paid for and a lot of the politicians even on the inside circles of good intent would let loose with something that would basically give warning to the people we are dealing with. The bad guys could then come at us any way we turn. No, we are never going to stop them if we use the governments. Governments are too entwined with legal issues and criteria and especially in Latin America where the economy of the actual legitimate and illegitimate drug business itself is so immense."

Matt feels pangs of guilt, "Yes, but the DEA is always hard at work trying to control illegal drug distribution and drug production."

Mannie holding on to the ladder, "Yes, but you started this rogue operation out of pure frustration with the system. I am not questioning my brothers in the field that I worked with for years. I am questioning the world system of government with laws that stretch and yawn to meet political goals. Some are getting into the drug dealer supply and distribution systems themselves. What we are doing is attacking their whole system by thinking of a way to cause a massive failure leading to its demise, not on the outside but by exposing them from within. Trying to prosecute them with legalisms and court systems that take years and jail terms that are met with penthouse accommodations for drug lords just don't work too well. Let me see, "The war on drugs" has been going on for a while, and the consumption, supply, and distribution of drugs is diminished?"

Matt now getting back on track, "No, we want them to defeat themselves. I believe we can do it with sabotage. That will put one network drug dealer against the other. I never doubted our intent and I never thought that what we are doing is wrong. We are the underground underdog doing what is right. I just thought maybe we could get more help."

Mannie wisely concludes the subject. "Sometimes too much help can hurt. We are doing well. There is you, there is me, there is Juan, there is Josephine and our lady from Moscow. That's it. And with Anna, aka Greta with her special assignment at the Tridexan Lab we can do it. And when things get tough, she alone can take on three guys and come out ahead of the game."

Matt strongly agrees, "That's good. And for arms we better get Juan onto pistols and bull pup automatic rifles for concealed carry. I am a little rusty but I can still shoot well. I have not had any hand-to-hand combat for a few years, or should I say decades, but I remember, when I was a Marine, how to deal with close quarter situations."

Mannie now surprised, "Great, I did not know you were a Marine."

Matt proudly proclaiming, "Yes, Once a Marine, Always a Marine, Semper Fi,"

After setting up with Mannie, Matt goes to lunch with lovely Lucia, fully posed with a tight fitting open top blouse and elastic slacks. In the dining room, lunch goes quickly. "Oh Mark, you must see our separate apartment for visiting dignitaries like yourself. It is considered the Presidential suite and you may stay there until you get your plant in operation here. Come. Let me show it to you."

Matt knowing the routine agrees. On the forty second floor she opens the door and waltzes him through the living room to a room with a large king-sized bed with bed posts and cover. She moves to a sitting area and lowers the top of her blouse to expose the full measure of her breasts."

"All the latest is here for you. As she reclines in the chair, "Won't you invite me to rest with you for a while?"

"Oh, I would be delighted."

She continues her advance, "I like you very much."

Matt looks at her with an agreeable hunger, "I find you very attractive."

They reach over to each other and embrace. Lucia and Matt spend the afternoon together wrestling in bed like a bull fight. When they leave, she gives him a key to the apartment with a smile, "You know how to make me very happy!"

Matt happily replies, "There is an art to making love, isn't there?"

Adolpho is busy at the plant looking over the shoulder of Greta as she examines the perfume cologne purchased by Josephine. "Ah, my dear, here is the scent that we may add to our medications but we need to test it out some way. I suggest we take it to our visiting workers room, close it up and turn off the lights and wait for the scent to reach us across the room." Anna agrees and when they enter the room, she is amazed to see a large covered bed and comments, "Oh, what a wonderful room. Do visitors also sleep here?"

"Yes, I think with me you will enjoy it a great deal. We have a lot of things to do and talk about."

She then offers encouragement, "Won't you turn the lights off. I'll put out the perfume and we can rest on the bed waiting for the scent to reach us. We can talk while we wait."

Adolpho almost salivates, "But of course my dear."

Anna has one of those knowing Mona Lisa smiles. The lights go out. The perfume is wafted and they talk awhile in the darkness with Anna leading him on about his great leadership of the company and her many questions of how he runs the company. The test lasts several hours and Anna dresses to conclude their interview. Adolpho comments, "That perfume is perfect for an addition to the formula medications."

Anna agrees again with her smile, "It works so well!"

Later at the condo after working hours, Anna turns to Matt, "Did you have a good time at the luncheon with Lucia?"

Matt smiles, "It was ok."

'So you spent a few hours with her?"

"Yes, for God and country of course."

Anna now more than a bit interested "I assume it went well."

Matt now on Anna's experience. "So, what is the status working with Adolpho and the perfume?"

"Josephine found the right item. I think it will work well. It has no color to it. It has a pleasant scent and is relatively low cost and may offer a good cover for our self-destruct input. Otherwise, it meets the Verelez need to have a phony formula to protect the secret of their smuggling system. In the meantime, you need to provide the nano crystals. Josephine purchased a case, so I can make up a healthy batch of perfume that will need the final mixing addition from you. Then I can order the prepared perfume to be placed in the medication treatment process."

Matt confirms. " That's fine; we will just call our perfume "Friendly Fragrances." Anna agrees, "The name is acceptable."

"Ok," Matt now very curious about Anna's other experience, "How did it go with Adolpho, otherwise?"

"Oh, I took care of Adolpho's lust for my body, like you, for God and country. He immersed me in the family business. They have friends in the President's cabinet. They have friends in the legislature, they definitely have partners in the military, the national police, and the municipal police are all social and economic friends of the Verelez family and business. More to come on their distribution system at our next visit to their visiting worker's quarters to test our batch modified perfume. He also offered me an apartment to live in, clothing and a car to drive as well, if I would be his girl."

Back at the warehouse, on into the evening Mannie and Juan are getting the nano-crystals ready for dilution with the perfume that Josephine shipped to Anna for mixing and placing within the Verelez medication lines.

Juan is concerned. "Are you convinced now that Julio is ready to run from his family's business entanglement?"

"I am not sure." Mannie questions his commitment, "Josephine believes he may be sitting on a fence. He still wants to be clear of them but not knowing by going how far. Josephine is not sure, because Lucia, after all, is his mother. Josephine will keep emphasizing with him the need to eliminate this drug ring with its distribution all over the world. Fortunately, Julio's parents are very friendly and nice to her, but deep down I know they are ruthless and only consider her a temporary convenience for future elimination."

Mannie gets practical. "At some point we are going to need to make a clean getaway, nice and quiet without a gun fight, if not, we are going to be outgunned."

Juan equally concerned, "True, what do you have in mind?"

"I have been in contact with my old buddies at the CIA. Their weapons lab has come up with a very interesting self-defense mechanism for getting past guards."

"How does it work?"

"It attaches to your wrist like a bracelet. It has a little rectangular box with a microscopic barrel facing outward towards the palm of your hand."

"Ah, some sort of mini-gun?"

"Well, not even that," Mannie speaking quietly, "It launches a mini dart with compressed air that the person being hit by it can barely feel it. It might be a slight twitch."

"Then what happens?"

"It is loaded with that famous Carrere poison. It only takes a mini amount to immediately paralyze a nervous system, long enough for a get-away without killing the victim. The interesting part is that the release of the poison is controlled by a radio frequency. It has a small receiver and the broadcaster is a verbal command picked up from our ear communicators."

Juan is impressed. "That is an interesting device that allows us to use stealth for our getaway instead of noise and fire."

"Yes, it is silent, it is instantaneous, and at some point, we are going to have to arm ourselves this way, including Josephine, Matt, and our Russian colleague."

On his way to again visit Greta at the lab, Adolpho receives a call from the Generalissimo. The partners are receiving an unannounced surprise visit by Don Fuego to inspect the factory for manufacturing the medications carrying his product. Don Fuego does not come alone anywhere. He spots bodyguards before he gets there, has an entourage with him once he is there, and he usually makes his point by killing someone before he leaves. Informing Lucia, she warns, "Adolpho. We must be careful. He will want to know the formula."

Adolpho is literally shaking, "Yes, but we don't have the mixture ready yet. We will have to show him our regular production and use one of our old samples for him to check. Josephine now has picked the right perfume and we are waiting for our lab to get one more element to include it in our production within a day or two."

"Fine, be extremely careful. There is no reason why at this point he cannot just kill us all and take over."

"Yes, I am afraid our partners, the generals and our civilian politicians, would readily fall in line if Don Fuego's push comes to shove. He has his own labs in the jungle with more than one chemist at hand."

At the plant Josephine tells Julio, "Your father received a call and said there was some kind of emergency and that your mother has to

be with him. And I have urgent business to take care of."

Julio slightly curious, "What is that?"

"Well, I need to get this perfume finally treated by a company called Friendly Fragrance to the plant today if possible, tomorrow at the latest. They need to get a new formula perfected very quickly for new shipments of the pharmaceuticals."

Julio with flippant approval, "Ah, well, off you go then, business is business. We have to be careful not to let it go,"

"Yes, I should be back by dinnertime."

"Wonderful, we will see you then, I love you."

Josephine hesitates for a moment. She finally admits she loves him too. But there is that moment when she thinks and says it abruptly. "Yes, I love you too. See you then. Bye."

Josephine picks up five gallons of perfume from the lab and using a company pick-up truck that she borrows from the plant, drives it to the warehouse where Matt and Mannie are waiting. With her honk at the door, the overhead opens and she drives in.

Opening the truck door Matt greets her. "Josephine, it is good to see you again. You look well."

"Well, I am doing well enough. But this is getting a little scary and I am becoming more suspicious of Julio every day. I know, at least I think, they are getting suspicious of me as well. But they keep having me do more and more of their business to get me involved. I don't understand it."

'Well, maybe they are not that suspicious," said Matt. "What have you got for us?"

"Here is the five-gallon jug of very strong cologne from the lab prepared by Greta, I mean Anna, and once diluted, it will be very mild and pleasant. It is a refreshing fruity cologne with a light fragrance similar to pears."

Mannie declares, "In less than an hour we will have a mixture ready for you." He takes the five-gallon drum and dumps it into a mixing hopper and Matt brings over a bag full of crystals. "Ok, we are going to make twenty-five-gallon drums from this mixture." Matt proceeds to mix the crystals with the cologne and diluting it with water.

"Ah, said Mannie, "now we have eau de cologne. What a wonderful brew we are making here."

"Yes, now let us get the other twenty-five-gallon containers and mix this with water and go from there," said Matt.

The twenty-five-gallon drums are quickly loaded on Josephine's truck. Mannie gives her his dummy company bill of laden for the perfume of Friendly Fragrance. Josephine drives off. The nano-sized time caplets mixed in with the perfume are delivered to the Tridexan mixing and formulation plant for immediate production of waiting worldwide orders. At the loading dock, Juan, whom she had never really met, has a knowing smile, as he loads the containers on to a pallet and picks them up with a forklift to take them to a mixing room. There, the containers are immediately opened and emptied into a large hopper to mix with new shipments of cocaine to go out with carbolic acid as part of a treatment for wounded horses and cattle. The other drum soaks the heroine processed base pills before crushing and reformulation as finished product for packaging pain pills in the same packaging.

Adolpho and Lucia are also at the lab at the time that Josephine shows up. They come out to the loading dock to greet her and ask her to join them in the lab. Josephine does so with a great deal of attention and a little bit of stiffness. She is very nervous and uncomfortable. Lucia and Adolpho note her nervousness and think it as part of her being unfamiliar with the lab.

"How are you doing Josephine?" asks Adolpho.

Happy at doing her job for the company Josephine replies, "Oh, I am fine. I hope this shipment of perfume will meet your needs in mixing with your carbolic antiseptic."

Adolpho pleasantly continues, "Yes, I think it will, but of course you know that it is more than that, don't you?"

Josephine has sort of a small smile, "Well, I think we are doing more than just selling veterinary pharmaceuticals. Aren't we?"

Adolpho begins his benign lecture, "Well, it is interesting that you use the word 'we' because that includes you and that is what we want – you to be included. We are doing this as a defensive move. We have to deal with drug lords that are ruthless, murderous gangsters. We are not that, but we are seeking the wealth and power that they have. We have obtained it and we have it above and beyond their ability, because of our social and economic connections in the financial and elite world of this country and other parts of the world. You, like Julio, make a good representative of our effort in the right circles. You have the charm. You have the presence and Julio has the charisma that we foster and want to keep with this organization. Don Fuego, our unwanted partner, forced himself on us with all the attempts he made on Julio's life, and partly on yours, as well as on ours. He did this to force us to join with him. We have no choice. Their last effort was to kill Julio on the polo grounds and then the car bomb."

Without a word other than a nod of agreement, it all makes sense to Josephine.

Adolpho continues with his reasoning. "We want you and Julio to be married and be partners with us to keep our organization and our pharmaceutical company running soundly and safely. We have worked many years to reach this level of distribution without discovery by the authorities, or without their interference. In fact, we do have the army on our side and some of the generals in this country are our partners. As well, we have partners in other countries where we rely on their protection to prevent our discovery and interference with our distribution."

Lucia is not one to be left out of the 'welcome to us' lecture, "Josephine this is a business. We do not seek violence. We do not want violence. We simply provide goods to people willing to pay a lot of money for their use. The goods are here, they are part of our national economy, they are part of the economy of South America, and part of the economy of other parts of the world. We have no morality about what we sell. Ten percent of the population in our opinion is always going to be corrupted by drugs, alcohol, and tobacco because they need or want and must have escapes from realty. The only difference between the alcohol manufacturers and us is we don't pay federal taxes. We don't pay the taxes upfront; we pay them at the back door to all officials that must be paid."

Adolpho proclaims, "We are sending our next shipment out tonight and tomorrow to all of our customers worldwide. We have our formula in place and we have the raw product already in the warehouse."

Lucia is pleased, "Very good, how many tons do we deal with today?"

Adolpho proudly reports, "It is actually twenty tons in forty pallets of a thousand pounds each, all distributed within a week after our loading from the warehouse docks. Most of it will be going by air, some by ship, and mixed mode with train and trucks."

Lucia grasping Josephine's hand, "With our new formula we ought to celebrate. I suggest we adjourn to our penthouse for a party and invite Greta and Mark the candy man. In a week the big checks start being wired to our banks everywhere."

Chapter Nineteen

Penthouse Party Disaster

Back at the condominium on the 41st floor, after a very long day of hard work mixing ingredients for a bomb in each container set for shipping, a party of self-congratulators is already at hand.

Mannie can't help it, "Gentlemen and lady, my glass is up to you for a magnificent job. We can now get lost while it is still safe because their system will carry our bomb to their product to self-destruction with shipping in five days, our scheduled interaction for our IED. So cheers and now pack up, because we are leaving."

Anna interrupts with a wary thought. "Matt and I have been invited to their party at the rooftop mansion. If we don't show up, they may suspect us and go back to the plant to check things out?"

Matt thinks a minute, "Although our trap is sprung, they could still save the day until at least tomorrow. So, Anna and I will go to the party. Pack now and load our vehicle so we can all leave tonight after the party. Juan and Mannie, you wait in the parking ramp for us to make our getaway. But just in case, Anna and I will take our small caliber pistols and conceal them well."

Anna also congratulates. "We are now at the last point of succeeding with our great mission. Hra Nee Vas Bohl."

Juan also has a salute, "We have turned many corners and survived many trials, all, I believe, with the help of the Lord. May his good grace continue to keep us, Que Dios os bendiga!"

Mannie is not to be left out, "I agree, my Russian and Spanish tells me to say God Bless us all and keep us safe for this battle is far from over. We will be hounded retreating to safety."

As the elevator door opens Matt and Anna are greeted by Eduardo, the family chauffer and bodyguard and his two companions that are plant guards. Senior Peniendo, the shop manager, is also present. "Welcome to our company party to celebrate our new shipment."

Matt with a firm grasp shakes the hand of Eduardo as Julio and Josephine arm in arm walk up to the hallway. Julio gestures, "You made it and what a great time we will have. We have plenty of food at the table and our bar is ready for making your favorite drink."

Adolpho is not far behind looking for Anna, "Greta my darling, you are ravishing, allow me to escort you to a table and bring you a drink."

Lucia is quick to follow looking at Greta, "Where is your boyfriend from the Embassy?"

She then turns to Matt, "Mark, I am so glad you are here. I have missed you since our last acquaintance and hope that we may carry on at our Presidential suite, tonight? I hope you still have the key."

Matt holds his smile, "Lucia, you warm my heart just thinking of you. I see you have included Senor Peniendo, your plant manager.

Come let us have a drink to celebrate your company's great shipment."

Just as everybody begins to adjourn from the entry hall to the lounge, an alarm goes off at the elevator. Eduardo yells at the two plant guards, "Go to the door with your weapons ready. Stand at each side."

Eduardo pulls out his HK MP7A1. Slowly, one side of the elevator door opens only six inches. Then the barrel of an automatic rifle points out. In a second, the roar of automatic gun fire brings everybody in the place to the floor. Eduardo flattens and roles over to spray the elevator entrance while the guards back off of each side to shoot in at an angle with their Glock 18 9mm pistols. Adolpho behind a human sized statue points to Julio and yells, "The gun cabinet at Simon Bolivar, get all the AK's out for us. We can't hold them back without our guns and ammo. "

Lucia, Josephine, Anna, Matt, and Peniando lay flat behind sofas and turned down tables. Julio crawls to the painting at the end of the corridor and with a light pull, the frame swings out exposing six AK 47s with straps of banded clips for each, two hand grenades and a flash grenade. He looks over to Josephine lodged between a crevice and fallen statue base, and yells as he slides an AK with a clip belt on the floor, "Grab this gun and suppress their fire so I can pass to Dad and Eduardo."

Amid the ricocheting rounds, many just missing Julio, the hall walls are exploding with flak plaster, glass, and marble shards off of fallen statues, and streams of lead rip across hundred-year-old paintings. In a five second break of fire to reload, Julio slides two AK's over to Eduardo and Adolpho and then slides the two AKs, the hand grenades, and a smoke bomb over to Matt. From the elevator door opening a hand throws out a smoke bomb followed by renewed automatic firing in a circular direction destroying anything and anyone not under or behind some kind of cover in the corridor. Adolpho hides behind a fallen marble pylon supporting a broken statue while Eduardo makes due in a shallow enclave for another fallen statue.

Over the next minute of gunfire, Eduardo pelts the elevator doors with his bull pup which only keeps the attackers at bay. Adolpho motions to Eduardo to use the AK with heavier vest piercing rounds that may also get through the doors. The attackers get bolder with a move to widen the elevator doors to make a charge down the hallway with heavy automatic fire.

Dressed in full military camouflage with bullet proof vests and helmets, Adolpho stares at them in disbelief. "Have I been betrayed by my Generalissimo, they are behaving like Special Forces?"

Eduardo takes advantage of the opening doors with renewed fire. With the AK 47 rounds hammering the opening, Eduardo hits one of the four attackers and the doors start closing again with the heavier rounds forcing them back in and to the floor creating a ten second break.

Suddenly with heavy pounding sounds coming from across the other end of the hall leading to the locked double doors to the fire escape staircase, Matt looks as the doors begin to bend inward. In a high crouch running down the hall, he put a few rounds through the door. The banging stops only to end with an explosion blowing the doors apart. In a few seconds, a calculated flanking operation on the Verelez party occurs with a screaming charge into the hall spraying fire in all directions.

Anna fast at Matt's back yells, "Into the hallway doors. I'll go to the other side to start an angled crossfire." The constant fire keeps Matt and Anna leaning in and out of those hallway doors to return an on again off again testing barrage of fire from the invaders who have also retreated into bedroom doors.

At the elevator, Julio along with Adopho again open-up with their AK's on the elevator door. The guards keep turning their guns in, but from the side wall, angle fire and ricochets hit one in the shoulder while the other falls unconscious with a belly wound. Lucia stays under cover lying flat behind a sofa but dares to raise her head to see where she can go to be safer.

Adolpho, Eduardo, and Julio continue to hold their ground, but the three shooters in the elevator continue returning fire.

Lucia calls for help, "Julio! Help me to the kitchen!"

Julio replies, "I can't leave Dad. The guards are down! They will outgun and kill Eduardo and Dad."

Matt and Anna listen to Lucia's pleas and wonder why the kitchen.

Lucia then calls to the hallway for help, "Mark help me to the kitchen. We can escape!"

Matt looks to Anna, she nods, "Yes, there must be another exit. I will cover you."

Matt agrees, "Ok, use this smoke grenade and follow."

Adolpho looks back and knows what Lucia is about to do with Mark and Anna and looks at Julio, "My son, make for the kitchen with your mother, I will cover you."

Julio shakes his head no, "Father I can't leave you. They will overwhelm you."

Adolpho, an old military man to the end, assures Julio, "Not to worry, Eduardo and I have four clips and help should be coming soon." Eduardo standing at the other niche returning fire nods with agreement. "Go, when the firing slows, we will back you up to the kitchen. As Julio makes his run Adolpho opens fire and yells, "Aha, I just got one of those bastards."

The battle continues for two minutes with flanking on the stair hallway moving up door to door. The plant manager Senior Peniendo slithers back to the glass patio doors remaining in a prone position, silent and distant from the fire fight.

With Anna's cover fire, Matt on a high crouch run zigzag to the kitchen looks around for a door and sees nothing. Amid ricochet bullets Julio grabs Lucia's arm and slides her on the floor to the swing doors of the kitchen. Matt asks Lucia, "How do we get out of here?"

Lucia quickly stands up and rushes to the double door refrigerator and pushes a fire alarm button on the side. With a great deal of relief, she whispers looking at Matt, "The refrigerator will slide out to a door leading to an enclosed passage way to the Presidential Suite on the 40th floor!"

Matt, with an uncontrolled smile, yells, "Ok! We can make our getaway.... Now!"

Anna tosses another grenade down the hall and makes her way to the kitchen, while Eduardo and Adolpho provide cover fire for Julio and Josephine who shoot and scoot. Adolpho and Eduardo barely hold ground with their last clips at the elevator and Anna empties her AK down the hallway as the invaders leap frog close to the kitchen.

As Matt takes a last look, "There is no chance for Adolpho and Eduardo and the guards are down."

Anna agrees, "We do not have any more time or a better chance than now."

As they make their move to go in to the corridor with steep stairs, Julio yells out, "What about my Dad and Eduardo?" Just as he speaks, the elevator attackers over run Adolpho and Eduardo. In a heavy barrage of fire they fall with a mass of bullet wounds as they turn and finish off the two wounded guards. They then focus their rounds on the kitchen, with lead bouncing off the walls and blowing everything into pieces as the refrigerator starts to come back to the wall.

Matt, the last to enter the passage, grunts, "Ah, they got me with some flying glass. Keep going."

They close the door and the refrigerator quickly returns in front of it. The alarm stops. And the attackers charge into the kitchen spraying automatic fire in every direction. With no one there, a sudden silence leaves the attackers going berserk looking for the escapees, tearing up the kitchen and shooting holes in all of the cabinets and the refrigerator.

As the five escapees make their way down the stairs to the 40th floor, the attackers roam around the penthouse looting whatever they can carry and then discover Senor Peniendo hiding behind a table near the balcony. The leader of the invaders, wearing a captain's bar, asks him, "Are you the plant manager of Tridexan?"

Senor Peniendo replies with a weak smile, "Yes, I am"

The captain smiles back, "Good, the Generalissimo thanks you for letting him know about this celebration, an excellent opportunity to attack the Verelez family at one time, and per our agreement with Don Fuego you are now the new president of Tridexan. We never expected them to shoot and fight like predators, as if special force trained. Our only regret is that Senora Verelez and her son Julio have escaped by some secret passage and we cannot invade the entire building to look for them. But we have posted roof top snipers around this building to catch them escaping."

A sergeant approaches the captain, "Sir, the policia nationale have surrounded the building what should we do?"

The captain replies with confidence, "Take our troops, wounded and dead, to the tennis court on the roof. You will find a helicopter waiting to take us away. Senor Peniendo will wait for a rescue and be declared a miracle to have survived our attack. Excuse my rifle but you need to shed some blood." He strikes Peniendo across his head with his rifle butt yelling, "Bueno! Vaminos!"

Matt finally entering the suite on the 40th floor and looking at Anna let go a deep breath, "I have been in this apartment before with Lucia. I think we are safe enough for now, but we need to keep going tonight. I know the first floor quite well and there is a basement accessed by a service elevator that leads to a loading dock at the rear just behind the parking ramp."

Julio volunteers the family armored SUV parked on the ramp. "It is on site 32 and the key code is 1642."

Anna calls Juan on their flip throw away, "Get Mannie and meet us with all our stuff at the SUV, spot 32, lock number 1642."

Lucia adds, "We can take a local elevator at the end of the corridor. It is actually next to a service elevator that goes down to the basement.

Here, Mark, or is it Matt? Let me wrap this table cloth around your arm"

Matt acts a bit sheepish, "Yes, thank you, Lucia, no apologies, it is Matt."

Lucia almost with a smile, "No problem, Matt."

Wasting no time, Anna checks the corridor and they all double time to the elevator and reach the basement in a few minutes.

As they make their way through a door to the loading dock, Matt bumps into a tall rack, "This thing is awfully heavy with the wine bottles in place but this rack will stop this door really good." Just in case, they lean the rack over, to block the entrance to the dock after the vintage reds crash to the floor creating a pool of wine on the floor.

Lucia stops and looks at Julio. "What is going on? It does not make any sense to me. We are fighting to be alive after a cocktail party!"

Matt replies, "Keep on running because we can't wait to figure this out!"

Julio quickly gives Lucia a reality shock, "It could be Don Fuego knowing that with us out of the way, the whole organization is up for grabs."

Lucia murmurs, "Yes, we were the stop between the drug lords and the distributors and our investors and with us gone they can control our plant distribution, but with whom?"

Julio jumps in, "Senor Peniendo, what happened to him?"

With no time for sorting things out, they quickly make it to the SUV with Juan and Mannie ready to roll. With all of the gunfire and grenades, many residents are wildly evacuating and a line of cars is jamming at the gate, taking time to get to the street with the policia checking for the shooters who killed the penthouse elevator staff in the lobby.

Matt looks at Juan, "Keep calm. There are watchers looking for us trying to get away and we are going to have to make a break for it." Juan agrees, "We play it cool and ask the policia what is going on and show them the key to our condominium on the 41st floor."

Julio looks at them, "Not to worry so much once we are in the vehicle. It has bulletproofed glass and the car's sides and bottom are armored. I don't think anything they are shooting could penetrate.

And there are Uzi's in the center console."

'Well thank God for that," said Juan as he exhales his held breath.

All present, they jump in the car and Juan fires the ignition and motions for everybody to look happy. Juan puts the wheels into reverse to back the vehicle out of the ramp and does a spinning wheel turnaround. He then peels rubber towards the gate. There are two policia guarding the drive to the street. They signal Juan to stop. "Who are you and where are you going?"

Juan shrugs his shoulders, "We live in unit 22 on the 41st floor. We are going out to dance the night away."

The officer looks with his flashlight at all the passengers who are all well dressed and not at all looking like terrorists. "Si, you may pass."

Now past the policia the worry begins with the contract killers on the lookout for their escape from the penthouse.

Halfway down the street, from nowhere, a sniper targets the windshield with bullets pinging off the glass, starting to shatter and crack the metal framing. Fortunately, the gas tank is armored as well as the rest of the vehicle. Taking a lot of hits, Juan just keeps going for two hundred yards before making a turn on the road and out of the site of the shooter, speeding along a winding road back into the downtown area.

Lucia now under control, "With all this gunfire, the policia and the army will be looking for us instead of Don Fuego's gangsters. They are no longer our friends."

Mannie agrees on the defensive, "Yes, we need to ditch this car fast."

Matt looks to the side and sees a small restaurant with about twenty vehicles parked out front. "Let's go to that restaurant. Pull in behind where this vehicle will not be noticed." "Ok." Juan makes the move with speed.

Careening through the parking lot at a fairly fast pace and slamming the breaks at the rear, Juan and Mannie get out of the vehicle. "Wait here, we will be back with another car in about three minutes."

With their Uzi's at their side, they walk into the restaurant, raise their guns, fire a few rounds, and simply state, "Put your keys on the table."

All the people now silent and frozen compliant, quickly put their keys on the table.

Juan examines the fobs and asks, "This set is for what?"

The owner answers. "A four door Chevy Suburban."

"We'll take this one. Here are the keys to a Cadillac SUV."

As they start walking out the door, Juan turns around as they exit, "Put your keys back in your pocket. Do not move or speak for five minutes." Without a sound all owners grabbed their keys and remained quietly seated at attention.

Juan and Matt find the Suburban, pull it back to the family SUV and load Julio, Josephine, Lucia, with all the gear including extra guns into the rear of the vehicle.

Juan is ready to roll with Matt as navigator. "Ok, we have another hour or two of freedom before this vehicle is given an ID and the police and army start searching for us again, where to next?"

Matt figures on a break spot. "Let's go to the warehouse lab. Nobody knows about that and we can pull this vehicle into the garage."

"Right," said Juan.

Lucia disagrees. "Senor Peniendo knows."

Mannie agrees, "You are right, he is definitely compromised. I was thinking of renting the adjoining building. It is still vacant and I have a key to inspect it for expanding our operation."

Matt finally concedes, "Well it is some place for just a while."

Driving south in one direction with sirens and lights of army cars and policemen going in the other direction is pleasantly tedious until they come to a raised drawbridge and have to stop. At the front of the bridge there are army personnel routinely guarding the bridge from night time rebel attacks, typical kidnappings and robberies. The guards start walking towards the back of the line looking into each vehicle. At this point, they look casually without any kind of special search in mind.

Matt quips. "Just behave normally and smile, Juan. Try to act like a chauffeur."

"I think I can do that but I have no cap."

"That's ok. I think we will be able to get by with this."

The guards saunter past the Chevy Suburban, look in, smile at Josephine and waived at the chauffer, and keep walking, but they did have walkie-talkies at their belts. The gate opens and the cars slowly begin to move up to cross the bridge. Juan is looking into his side view mirror, watching the guards as they continued to walk to the rear. They are about five cars behind them, almost six when one of them grabs his walkie-talkie from his belt and starts talking.

It is obvious to Juan that they are getting a call for a pickup on the vehicle. The traffic starts inching forward across the bridge. The guard nods in an affirmative action, points to the other guard, points in the direction of the Chevy and they start coming their way.

Juan punches his alarm button. "Get ready, the guards have us identified. They are coming after us with guns drawn. Lock and load. Make sure you are ready to shoot. Take your windows down as soon as they come around the side. Don't let them get a chance at you. Just pull out and shoot."

"Ok," Matt hands an automatic to Josephine. "You understand what to do!"

Josephine gets the automatic pistol that was in the case that Juan had carried from the SUV. She pulled back the receiver, loaded it and was ready to shoot.

Lucia is dumfounded, "Josephine, where did you learn to do that? Are you a Green Beret?"

"No time now. I'll tell you later, if we get by."

Lucia freezes with fear. "Not again?"

Juan traces their movements in the mirrors, "The guards are approaching slowly with their guns cocked and at arms. They are not fooling and they are not going to come right on top of us."

Juan sees a chance to get away. "Ok, our line is starting to move across the bridge. The guards are still moving cautiously and aren't doing anything to stop the traffic for fear of alarming us. So, let's just keep inching forward. Maybe they will have to start running to catch up with us."

"That would be good," said Matt. "We would have some advantage."

As the cars start moving faster, the guards open fire at the rear tires going flat, then at the back gate. Because of the double paneling, their bullets did not penetrate but the shattered glass went flying. Everybody is head down and Josephine, inched up, turned around and opened up with her Uzi. She wounded one of the guards immediately. They both jumped to the rear of another car returning fire.

"Good shooting," said Matt. "Juan just keep moving."

"What luck, the drivers on the bridge are panicking and speeding across the bridge and bumping into each other. We are clear to cross now!"

Once across the bridge, they turned into one of the older residential commercial areas with single lane streets. In these narrow streets in a semi-poor area, anything and everything happens with little police involvement.

Juan spots a chance ahead. "Would you believe it?"

Matt now looking for something, "What?"

"Look ahead; there is a car rental place."

"Oh yeah, three cars on a lot on a corner, not a big dealer means we can negotiate. Let's get one."

"You got it." Juan pulls up with the Suburban, which by this time looks like a wreck. The owner of the rental place comes out. Juan did not hesitate to pull his handgun out, point it at his belly and say, "We need a car."

The owner holds his arms up, "Take your pick."

Not to be meagerly about it, Matt pulls out ten thousand pesos, and hands it over, "Gracias Amigo."

Leaving the Suburban for salvage, they start driving back to the warehouse. Five in a four-door sedan is a bit cramped but they make it.

Juan advises, "I think we can all relax now because I don't know of anybody who is going to bother us. We gave that owner money for this car and he is definitely going to want to chop up that Suburban for parts. I don't think he will be calling the policia."

"I think you are right on that one," said Matt. "I think we are in the clear. Once we get to the warehouse, we can make arrangements to get out of the country because that is what we are going to have to do by tomorrow."

Julio looks at his mother. His mother looked back at him. She begins to talk. "Your father was afraid of this happening. He tried to prevent it. But with the attempts on your life and ours it was only a matter of time. I had hoped this would work but it didn't. There is too much money involved. But we can go to Mexico City and be very comfortable there. Or even Spain, if you like."

Julio is stunned. "This is all because of you. And my Dad died protecting us and I am not going anywhere without Josephine and Mexico is not on our agenda."

Lucia looking out the window, "Given we are still alive we will go where we can survive."

Chapter Twenty

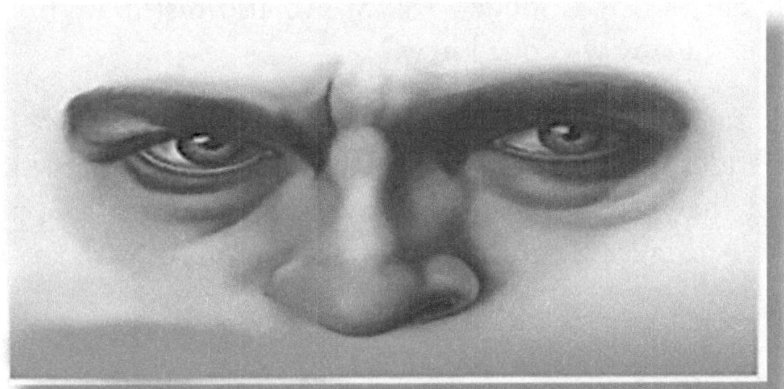

A New Boss At Tridexan

Back at the pharmacy lab, Don Fuego explodes with a fiery temper. Informed by his enforcers that Julio and Lucia with Josephine escaped with the help of two unknown assailants, he immediately contacts the Generalissimo, "I want those renegades dead, not alive. I offer you a million pesos." Still steaming, he turns to his chief henchman, "We must kill them immediately. They know too much about this organization. What we don't know we can find out. What they know they can use to destroy us. We must find them and kill them."

"Si, Patron, we can do this without any trouble. Yes, a million pesos on the streets is worth a lot of money in Bogotá to a lot of people. I am sure we will be able to get them. In the meantime, we have to oversee this first shipment. I have made all the contacts with all of the suppliers."

Don Fuego wants a number for his trouble. "And what is the value of this shipment to us?"

"Oh, Patron, I believe we are talking a hundred million dollars."

Don Fuego responds with his ruthless, greedy smile. "Ah, that is the kind of payroll that I like to see. And look, we did it with shooting only four people so far." He then laughs.

"Shooting with my gun that is," said his henchman with a grin on his face.

Don Fuego laughs louder. "Si, Si, we also distribute free needles that kill how many we don't know."

Back to business Don Fuego dictates his first order as the new head of Tridexan, "Si, no time must be wasted. Ship immediately all containers that were finished yesterday. I have agreements in place. We don't want the takeover of this organization to occur with any ripples."

'Si Patron."

At army headquarters in Bogota, Generalissimo has issued orders for the capture of Julio, Lucia, and Josephine as criminals in the drug trade. This is very unusual because the Generalissimo himself was a friend of the Verelez family until of course Don Fuego changed his mind.

He makes the capture "dead or alive". "Lucia is a very smart woman. She will seek to leave the country. We know they have money oversees in many banks. It is not enough to think they would go to Switzerland or try to go to Europe, Spain, Mexico or even Brazil. They might even end up in Japan. I want the entire border crossing locked and checked for their passage. I want all the air, rail, and bus depots guarded and checked. I don't want them to be able to squeak out of this country. Not even a rat or a mouse can escape without our approval."

"Si, my general, we will implement your orders immediately."

"Fine," said the Generalissimo, "in the meantime we must wait and see how Don Fuego succeeds with this new venture. Now that Adolpho is dead, we still need Julio and his mother eliminated. Don Fuego knows that the rest of the organization right here in Bogota and by now the rest of the world in terms of the dealers, are watching him and waiting and seeing. If shipments don't go well, there will be a death squad also at his door."

Back at the next-door warehouse Juan pulls the car safely into the garage where everyone steps out and goes to the office for a rest at a conference table. Matt breaks the silence with an optimistic note. "This attack coincides with the shipment from your company tomorrow. The deliveries will be completed in five days. There must be a great deal of money involved for this kind of violence to occur."

Lucia is full of anguish, "Ah, so you are telling me that our biggest and best shipment ever is the reason for that murderous attack at our home?"

Anna assertive and happy to answer, "Correct, I have analyzed the finished mixing of the shipments. Nearly all are impregnated with cocaine and heroin."

"Right," asserts Juan, "I am with the policia nationale of Bogota and Greta is Anna with the Moscow police drug prevention department."

Lucia "You mean, you two have been planning to destroy me and my family?"

Juan leads with his chin. "Absolutely, what you do is evil. You hurt so many people. You cause so many deaths and you sit there with your gracious manners and presume to be above it all. It's not that way at all my dear lady. You are guilty of the highest crimes in society and your son, although not actively involved, has benefited immensely from your crimes."

Julio with a sad face glances at Josephine and his mother. Josephine opens up, "Julio has wanted no part of Lucia's evil. He and I have come back to Bogota to learn the operation to give his mother a chance to change her ways. He would much rather have spent the rest of his life in Florida but has wanted to free himself of his mother and get her out of this covert drug business."

Lucia looks at Julio in disgust, "How could you do this to me. We have given you everything and you have everything. This is insanity. We took a generation to get this system properly disguised and operating. Even if it is not now in my control, I don't want to see it die."

Lucia then looks at Matt. "Mark who are you? Are you part of this conspiracy to destroy my business?"

Matt not ready to give up his ghost or that of Mannie, "Lucia, I am here caught in the middle of some kind of gang war. All I know is that it is not safe to be in Columbia. Those people killed your husband and they very much want to kill you and Julio and Josephine. And because we are witnesses to their attack, our lives are forfeit as well."

"Your company will go on, probably under the control of the drug king pin behind the attack. Is it Don Fuego? Did you have dealings with him?"

Lucia backs down, "Well we did have an agreement. I still want my company back!"

Julio is no longer dismayed and shows his determination to stop her nonsense before it goes too far. "Mother I want to be with Josephine in Florida instead of fighting for our lives here. My father died honorably. The assets you and Dad worked so hard to develop are gone, and Dad told me that you only owned 40% of the company to begin with."

Matt looks at Mannie and takes him to a side room in the warehouse. "We've got a problem with Lucia. She is just as bad as the minute we saved her. She is not interested in seeing the system taken over and doesn't need to know about our self-destruct time bomb. She wants it back if she can get it and whether we like it or not, we need to get her out of the country."

Mannie agrees and adds. "We cannot let her out of our sight until all of the shipments are gone. Then we have to keep her quiet so she doesn't warn anyone on their distribution system. That means no phones and we keep her away from a computer for sure. I know she has internet codes for the immediate access to the entire system, especially Russia."

Matt can see things going wrong fast. "Amen, I see where you are coming from. Maybe Julio knows those codes."

"That's a thought," said Mannie. "We are going to have to talk to him."

Then Mannie thinks of a quiet approach. "What we should do is watch on the sidelines, and wait for our little nano-bombs to take effect while we are on the run with Lucia. Maybe we can turn her around to help with any clean up after her system is wiped out.

To check on the waiting time for the bomb, Matt brings Juan into the room for an update. "What is the story on the batching?"

Juan sums up the process. "The assembly technicians and warehouse people are batching now as we speak. I carried in the final order from Anna. For the liquid product there will be a hundred thousand gallons batched and shipped by tomorrow with five days to go before the nano particles interact and explode."

Matt then asks regarding the rest of the shipment. "What's the story on the delivery system for the nano timing on the caplet bombs?"

Juan "Well, we are talking about a distribution time that is fast, at five days on average, and we've got caplets to explode and interact with the chemicals on the hard product within three and a half hours to five hours of mixing."

Matt with his fingers crossed. "A great umbrella coverage, Tridexan will have almost all of the material delivered to the distribution points where and when we want the explosions to occur. It will expose the entire distribution system and make national headlines worldwide."

Juan goes on with confidence, "That's the interesting part. We looked at all the bills of lading and the delivery dates and it's amazing how their system has become so sophisticated that any one delivery would pretty much reach any part of the world at about the same time as the others, either by air, freight, ocean going or rail."

Matt continues to be amazed, "What an incredible genius with their delivery system. Hopefully this will expose it completely."

"Well, we would hope so," said Mannie. "All we have to do is sit and wait. But we can't wait here. How do we get out of Columbia, away from Don Fuego?"

There is a kind of moral code with Don Fuego and his cutthroat henchmen. As Lucia surmised, Don Fuego covers himself locally and in the provinces. Even in other countries he keeps platoons of body guards and enforcers watching and able to move to enforce his will, including revenge upon his dealers. He does not allow his dealers to be addicts, otherwise, they disappear and new dealers are installed. He also has sales quotas. Each dealer has to distribute so much volume a month. If they fail to do so, they too disappear. Parts of their bodies might be found in places where other dealers might find them with name tags and little descriptions of what body part did not succeed in meeting Don Fuego's quotas.

Without discrimination, Don Fuego directs his anger against his own henchman if they fail to provide him with the bodies in parts or the whole of Julio, Lucia, Josephine and the gangsters that helped them escape. Don Fuego speculates with his lieutenant, "They could not have been government. They have to be something to somebody else. All of my snitches in the government, even the U.S. federal government, know nothing of any program or mission against Tridexan."

Don Fuego's lieutenant reveals equal frustration. "I am getting somewhere with information about the American Mexican person. His name is Mark O'Manahan from Mexico City. He presented himself as the owner of the Global Candy Company. He purchased a line machine from Tridexan through Peniendo with the approval of Lucia who interviewed him personally, and met with him later for lunch. Peniendo told me the name of the bank in Switzerland that paid for the machine. He even installed it for him in a warehouse here in Bogota. We checked Global Candy and there is no such company. We have the address of the warehouse. And the lab technician, with a German passport, displayed the fire fight skill of a Russian Spetsnaz, and the older American Mexican also held such skills as well as those of Julio and Adolpho and his body guard Eduardo and two plant guards. It was a battle and without their secret escape we would have had them as soon as they ran out of ammo."

Don Fuego's face lights up. "At least we now have a location to check. And knowing Lucia she probably made a personal friend of this man to invite him to her cocktail party for what reason was it?"

The lieutenant smiles, "To celebrate the shipment of our product."

Don Fuego thinking up a ladder, "Why does this man with an obvious military skill, goes to all the trouble of spending one million pesos to install a candy machine for a company that does not exist? That is a lot of money to fool Lucia, and for what reason? This plot begins to smell. Find them!"

The lieutenant added, "We sent different men back to the condominium tower. With some pesos, they were able to trace all the new arrivals over the last week but had no picture of any of them, except by the lobby camera and hall cameras. We saw no groups coming and going and the timing reflected hours for people coming and going to work. The hours before our attack we did get a video of people going up the private elevator to the penthouse, including Senor Peniendo. We have no good facials but one was an attractive woman, no doubt the Greta lab person. I believe Aldopho, had eyes for her, otherwise a lab technician would not likely have an invitation to a cocktail party at the Verelez palace. The other man in the elevator was older, at least in his fifties. All we have is top-down facials. We checked the parking ramp and the Verelez armored vehicle is gone."

Don Fuego concludes, "They are on the road with a vehicle and they have a warehouse. We don't know who they are but we have a start for where they are."

In the meantime, Don Fuego's crew of enforcers with automatic weapons quickly infiltrated the plant warehouse and pharmaceutical mixing batch plant immediately intimidating all the staff and workers and weeding out suspicious looking workers which they thought might lack in loyalty to the new boss, El Patron.

Back at the warehouse, Matt, Juan, Mannie, and Anna are brainstorming furiously to determine how they might leave the country without being discovered. Matt's first thought is how Mannie and Juan escaped with Anna from Russia with workmen's clothing.

Anna's disguising skills are important to Julio and Lucia. Both of them are often photographed and seen in the newspaper, especially after the attack on their rooftop palace.

Anna thinks of a closer alternative. "Well, I don't know if I can help you but why don't you go to the American embassy?"

Mannie goes back to the risk of government exposure, "No, that's not likely to work for us. There are spies everywhere, including inside the embassy. I found that out when I worked with the DEA. We would be dead as we left the place. Or we would be shot on the way to it at the gate where I am sure they are waiting for us. But they would not be looking for us in the Russian embassy. Is there something we can do at the Russian embassy to get out of the country under some kind of cover?"

Anna replies, "Spies lurk in our embassy also. More on the economic side, but they have as much to do with the problems they are having with the drug trade too. No, we need to do something totally different."

Matt nervously answers, "We don't have much time. They are probably three to six hours behind us. They will find out we rented the warehouse next door. They will be here with full arms. Probably including the army with 50 caliber machine guns, there is no way we are going to get out of here if they find us here."

Being spotted on route anywhere, certainly Josephine would have to be disguised. Matt knows he is clean except for videos at the condominium tower, but Anna's photograph was copied from her passport when getting her lab job. Juan is not really known as part of a gang that helped Julio and Lucia escape. Mannie only dealt with the warehouse operation set up and didn't even meet Peniendo.

Mannie speaks up about Juan's quandary. "We have to worry about Juan's family. For his own safety with Tridexan under Don Fuego, Juan must leave the country and we should arrange for his family to discreetly visit relatives elsewhere."

Matte adds another problem. "For us to succeed we have to break up and leave Columbia in different directions in different ways. There are seven of us. Matt and Lucia can go to Mexico City as husband and wife or girlfriend. Mannie and Anna can go to Dallas under the same guise. Julio and Josephine can't go back to Florida yet. There must be another safe place for them. And Juan can meet his family going on vacation and relatives in Rio de Janeiro."

Juan has a thought for the theatrical, "Let's have a funeral. Let's put Julio in the casket and make him dead. Let's make Mannie, you and me as pallbearers. We can be Julio's brothers and of course, Julio's mother can be his weeping mother and Josephine can be his weeping wife."

Mannie winks. "We would get attention for doing that. We would be less suspicious if we tried to be innocuous and try to slip through a crowd. If our makeup and disguises work well enough, we can do it, just like we did in Russia."

Juan offers help to keep his thought alive, "I have a friend. We can get a hearse from him. He can be our chauffer. He can drive us to the airport and we can ship Julio by…."

Anna interrupts Juan. "No, he will freeze to death in that casket in a jet airplane at thirty thousand feet. It is not going to happen." "Right, we'll skip that one," said Matt.

Agreed on disguises with just plain street clothes, Mannie, Juan, and Anna decide to take their stolen vehicle to the market square. Seeing the policia national at every street corner into the square they park outside the square and split up in different directions to buy daily use average clothing, hats, carry-on bags, toiletries, and packaged food and bottled water. Juan picks up a newspaper to catch up on the attack at the Verelez pent house palace. After loading up their vehicle with enough goods to last three to five days, before they leave, Juan opens the paper to read the front page. "Well, we are not the only ones to suffer El Patron. There are two generals, one visiting from Argentina and the other one an adjutant to the Generalissimo in Bogota. The generals are blown up in a staff car, attributed to some kind of rebel activity near Monserrate. Don Fuego is putting pressure on the local system to insure it's his."

With Juan, Mannie, and Anna gone, at the warehouse Julio speaks with a great deal of excitement. "Josephine, to hell with the billion dollars in assets in fifteen banks around the world, we can work our way back to Florida. We will be freer than ever without the system, whether or not it survives or is destroyed by Don Fuego, who may end up assassinated for his treachery."

Josephine replies with caution, "You mean his perceived treachery. We don't know what happened to Peniendo, the plant manager, and what about the other general friends of Adolfo? Have you ever heard of the term frozen assets for crimes committed and the testimony of past cronies?"

Lucia walks in from the office space and speaks up. "But you saw what we can do. If Don Fuego fails with his brutal takeover, we will still have the system in place. We can start it up again."

Josephine looks at her in earnest, partly convinced and partly just being realistic. "For you, it's over, and Julio has only a family connection to the business. With your reappearance, all of the past and ongoing criminal actions including smuggling are now easily traced by the authorities back to Bogota and your pharmaceutical company. As the previous president and owner, you won't have that innocence that you now feign for your protection. And we have yet to see what Don Fuego does, if we can escape his death squad."

From the office, Matt comes forward waving his arms to break up the argument.

Lucia is not easily discouraged, "We shall see."

As Juan approaches the warehouse with their load of escape gear, Mannie shouts, "Pull over. There are armed guards at our pill machine building. They don't look like regular army or policia."

Anna adds, "They look like the hitters who tried to take us down at the roof top." She quickly opens Juan's gun chest, "Wow, we have three silenced nine-millimeter sixteen round HK semi-auto pistols. Thanks Juan. Let's split up and hop scotch to the grounds of the building. At the building entrance I see two guards and one each at the front corners. I don't see anything going back to our location in the rear. They all have AK 47s. I'll take the big tree at the southwest corner of the building to provide flanking fire. Juan, you take the center on your belly. Mannie, you come along the next building wall to get crossing fire on the other corner."

Anna surmises, "We can take these guys out on the corners while Juan opens up in the middle. With silencers they won't know what hit them. But don't miss. We are shooting at thirty of forty meters."

Juan agrees, "Yeah, I think we have a good chance there. Let's take them out."

Mannie emphasizes stealth "Alright, get as close as you can before you fire. Set up for the best shot you can get. Anna, you take the first shot. When he drops, we drop the rest with our shots. Clear?" "Clear!" from Anna and Juan.

They begin their moves with Juan crawling on his belly and Anna and Mannie slowly stoop walk up to the edges of adjacent buildings. As Mannie comes closer, a corner guard turns around and spots him ready to shoot. As he raises his weapon to shoot, Mannie double taps him with the silencer. He falls silently to the ground. The two entrance guards, not hearing him fall, fail to turn to shoot, as Juan opens up on them from a hundred feet, making multiple hits, slamming those two paramilitaries back into the door, while Anna takes out the other corner guard with a single round in the head. All are down without a sound in five seconds.

Mannie and Anna rush to the entrance, slowly opening the door looking for more guards. Anna goes in first, "The lights are off except for the office. No one is in here."

As they are standing inside Juan comes to the entrance and picks up the ringing cell phone of a dead guard and answers, "Si, nothing is happening. We are secure. Si, I will report every hour."

Mannie and Anna join Juan moving the bodies into the warehouse, then returning with their stolen vehicle to the rear warehouse. Once in, Mannie announces to Lucia, Julio, Matt and Josephine, "We have an hour to get out of here. We just killed four Don Fuego guards at our candy machine building. Here are the street clothes we bought to get out of our formal ware. Change clothes now while Anna starts helping with her disguise make up."

Lucia frantically changes her black silk diamond studded garb and with survival in mind finally rubs off her makeup. She looks at Julio and Josephine, "Yes, if we go to Mexico City, we can pick up our funds there and move on until we finally lose our pursuers."

Julio "We have no choice but to run." He looks at Josephine. "They have put death warrants on us and they will stop at nothing to kill us now. But going to Mexico is not my choice. Josephine and I can make it on our own to Florida."

Josephine looks back at Lucia, "Why don't you go to the authorities? Why don't you expose them all and seek protection from the government? Julio and I could then go back to the United States, our home. If needed, the federal government would give us witness protection. We would get changed identities and be hidden amongst millions of people in the big cities of Chicago or Los Angeles."

Lucia objects, "No, we still have friends in the system and we cannot betray them. My husband's friends in the army, the government officials, all of them must be protected."

Josephine lashes back with disgust. "Hah, that is truly what you are. You are still a crook. Just like the crooks that you deal with. You are no different from them."

Lucia looks with the eyes of an attacking vampire. "I cannot be holier than anybody else. This is a business and it is a business with relationships. I want to keep those relationships. I am not a mafia. I don't have blood trusts. But I have my pride and I have esteem amongst others that I must maintain."

Juan laughs while pulling up his jeans, "Lucia, here is a newspaper. Two of your generals that you hope to protect have been murdered today by Don Fuego."

"Hmm. I am shocked." Lucia now a bit humbler and suddenly ready to change tack and musing to herself. "Maybe I should be counting myself out of this prideful organization of ruthless killers, thieves and liars, holding themselves up to society as leaders and good persons."

Josephine's face, while changing her dress turns red with rage. "So, think you can just count yourself out without guilt. You are part of a world cartel. Huh. Look at your system. It is full of hypocrisy, lies, thieving, cheating, and murdering for convenience and comfort. Corruption is a game for you. Not in the doing of it, but just worrying so much about the cost of it."

Josephine shuts down with a stiffer lip. Then Anna starts darkening her skin as she joins in on the debate. "All human societies are subject to weakness and corruption. But we don't ignore it. We don't hide it. We expose it and we get rid of it as soon as we find it. We cut it out like the cancer that it is. If we don't stop the cancer, it will engulf us like it has engulfed our countries and enslaved our people to a system of corruption and evil that leads to the death and destruction of society itself. Of your own society, you survive because of power and killing. In the end, you will be dead too for the same reasons. And as history tells the story, corruption leads to failure of not just one but of all in the death of a civilization."

At this point Josephine was about ready to spill the beans about her working with Matt. But Matt looks at her sideways and nods very lightly, but significantly, to tell her to shut up. It looks like Matt has more plans for her yet.

Chapter Twenty One

Day One At Monserrate

Juan is the only person in the group who has any ability to walk the streets without discovery. There are no warrants or wants for him by the local policia, army, or the criminal rings in the city.

Matt looks at Juan, "We need you to get us out of here, any ideas for right now?"

Juan looks back and answers. "I have it. We now have the perfect escape. Tomorrow is Sunday, the day of the biggest tourist crowd on Monserrate. We leave here and drive up to the cable station and wait until it opens in the morning and take the cable car to Cerro de Monseratte. They have two restaurants and tourists from all over will be there. You pick your destinations from there and join the tourist group coming back. From there you can separate yourselves into twos, hail separate taxis, and go to where you think you can leave the country by private tours to a new destination like Mexico City or the US or charter private planes or boats for isolated places. "

Mannie likes melting into a tourist crowd full of foreigners. "Great, your timing is perfect. But what do we do for money? We can't use credit cards."

Matt opens a briefcase that he brought from the warehouse. "That is not a problem. Here is fifty thousand pesos for each of us. We can do it!"

Anna shows a smile, "So this excursion is going to be as tourists. Acting as a tourist is easy and we can readily melt into a crowd of people with English, German, Russian, and street language Spanish. But we have no cameras?"

Juan "Yes, at the cable house there are stores selling everything including cheap cameras. The view is fantastic from Monserrate."

"Yes, of course, but what about policia?"

Juan answers, "With millions of visitors each year, Monserrate is one of the best police protected tourist points in the city. They do not want the area invaded by hoodlums and pick pockets. The policia typically carry billy clubs and radios. And the crowds are so heavy on Sunday, they spend their time keeping walkways open and giving directions."

Matt catches on. "Of course, we can sign up at the cable station for private tours. We just pick the group we want and go our separate ways. Juan will drop us off, abandon the vehicle in a lower neighborhood on the other side of the City, and meet his family; Juan, how about a vacation to Impanema on the beach by Rio?" Juan happily nods without a word.

Matt then checks his watch. "Ok, load up in the vehicle before they send new guards for next door. Stuff all of you want in your carry-on back packs. Leave nothing behind here. We will leave all else in the vehicle."

Just as they are leaving, the cell phone of the dead guard rings. Juan answers, "All is well. Oh, I forgot about the time. Si, I will not forget to call, gracias."

With all on board, Juan acts like a conductor, "Fasten your seatbelts please."

Anna answers "Just get us to the cable house without a gun fight."

On the road Mannie raises the destination question. "We split up at Monserrate. Where are we going to go as pairs, or singles?"

Anna opens with her citizenship. "Of course, there are trustworthy people at the embassy that I have known for years and whom I believe will help me. And I have the authority through my investigation to command the services of the embassy."

Mannie counters, "But can you do it in a way that will not attract the attention of potential spies in the embassy?"

Anna answers matter of fact, "Of course, it will be a back door operation, but there will be a bureaucratic slowdown on approvals."

Mannie suggests a diversionary trip. "As tourists Anna and I can take a taxi to the airport and fly to Las Vegas. I am a real estate broker there. Also, there is a Russian Consulate to provide assistance to any Russian citizen. As a couple leaving from Monserrate, we would not attract any attention and many people go to Las Vegas from South America."

Matt thinks of another location, "That's a good idea for you two. Lucia and I could go to a travel agency and book a trip to San Antonio for their annual festival. From there Lucia can fly to Mexico City and I can get back to Dallas. I think we can do well without being noticed."

Lucia looks at Matt with a small smile. "Why Mark, oh I mean Matt, I think it would be fun for us to travel together and I do believe we would make a fine tourist couple. Your Spanish is good as a foreigner, I mean your Mexican accent, and I can play the loving wife always holding onto your arm, always smiling and wanting to buy things."

Josephine looks at Julio with a smile and Julio, looking away from his mother, gave her a small smile back. Josephine noticed the look and was warmed by it. Their wheels are turning for their adventure to escape Don Fuego and his mother.

Julio offers an interesting alternative, "Not far from here is the home of my father's faithful servant. He was with my family for forty years and was getting old, so my father bought a house for him here and provided him with a retirement. His name is Pedro and he will help us."

Josephine grows skeptical. "But that won't get us out of Bogota!"

Julio goes on. "Pedro is just a stopping place. We can rest there and he will drive us to a Berlinas bus terminal in Facatativa. From there we take a bus to Cartagena, a seventeen hour ride where I have a sail boat moored at a marina. We can sail to Cuba until it is safe to go to Miami and hopefully to Alessandra and the ranch at West Palm or otherwise dock at Venice to go to Sarasota."

Juan jumps on his suggestion. "That is a great idea and definitely low profile on a bus from a small town. But I didn't know you have a sail boat. Are you a good sailor?"

Lucia gets a chance to brag. "Julio has sailed the Caribbean to Puerto Rico and Cuba where we have done business getting herbs for our medications. From there he can easily sail a few hundred miles, when it is safe, to return to Florida."

At that moment, Julio and Josephine looked at each other again with the confirmed love that they suspected of themselves earlier and somehow had been overwhelmed during all the turbulence of the last month. She now feels the fires of love in a very warm heart with her passion growing the way it had done when she was with him at the estancia.

With the rising of the sun, the first day on the delivery of the time bombed drug shipment, the perpetrators continue their escape with determined obfuscation. The Monserrate cable trip line forms at the cable house and breakfasts are being served at an adjoining restaurant. All leave the vehicle, except Juan. Mannie, Matt, Julio, and Josephine salute him. "Juan, God's Speed. God bless you for all your help. Be safe."

Juan grins and waves as he starts moving out, "I am always safe and will be seeing you again. God bless you too."

As the group separates into couples, they walk at a distance from each other to explore the tours available on the street and get into line for the cable tickets to see Cerro de Monserrate.

Matt and Lucia encounter no problems getting a tour with a group of retired Americans. They then walk through the various shops on the street waiting for the cable car call for boarding. Problematically Lucia's shopping addiction is beginning to raise Matt's alarm.

Matt pulls her aside at a dress isle. "Lucia, you can look, but don't buy anything. I know how well you like to dress but we are not here to impress anybody. Do you understand?"

Lucia replies with pouting. "Matt, I like it when I look good for you.

Do I have to look so sour and dour?"

Matt in a mellowing voice, "Lucia you always look good to me. But I am a jealous man and I don't want other men looking at you by the way you walk with your gentle sway, the way you dress showing off your lovely body, and with your articulate and enticing voice. There is an old song in America, it sings "marry an ugly woman and you will be happy the rest of your life." The reason is that other men will not try to sneak you away from me. In our case, I do not want any policia or cartel paramilitaries to be attracted to you for one moment. Maybe you should also cover your head with a scarf to help conceal your beautiful hair."

Lucia holds Matt's arm ever more firmly and in a very soft and pleasant voice. "For you, I always want to look pretty. I feel warm all inside when I am near you. And I cannot forget how you made love to me with a passion I have not known from my husband and short acquaintances."

Matt chooses not to ask about the short acquaintances.

As the call comes for boarding the cable car, Matt offers a compromise. "Ok, I like you too. But now you must act like my ugly unattractive wife who doesn't talk much and acts bashful. You are to play my good old wife, not a girlfriend. We are not having a tryst. That is all over with in our marriage."

Lucia gives up with her flirtation, "It is without doubt that your wife must be a loser and that is what I will be, just for this trip. Do you understand?"

Matt gives up. "When we make it out of Columbia you will no longer be a loser, and you will have my most willing adoration and attention."

As they board the cable car, Lucia offers a nod of agreement and acceptance. "Si, I didn't think of that, but you are right. We need to be a happily married couple taking a tour."

Matt confirms with a lower voice as they move to the window corner overlooking the city. "Yes, it is rather pleasant, isn't it? Despite our problems, just this moment alone together in a crowd of people after all of our running and shooting, it is not so bad."

Before she can answer Matt wants to change the subject. "Ok Lucia, look and oooh and ahhh over the view of the city. We can talk more at the top."

Julio and Josephine come aboard with a younger group of people from New York, including a few teenagers. They are unseen by Matt on the opposite side of the cable car with Mannie and Anna lodging themselves shoulder to shoulder standing in the middle of the car. The ten-minute trip occurs with mild chatting with almost all looking out the windows as the steep climb opens a massive view of the wide expanse of the city with door-to-door white stucco and red tiled roof tops ranging into the green hills beyond, totally enhanced with shadows from the sun light just breaking over the top of the mountain.

Anna and Mannie find their choice of a group of Germans in a tour, a very clever move as the guards at the cable car and on the street ignore them for their loud and heavy foreign conversation. Anna's

German does well enough and her husband with his broken English does well smiling and saying hello.

Once at the top, each group goes their separate way to view the church and grounds of the monastery. Several broad stone walkways and narrower lanes are explored in the conservation areas to view the wildlife including deer, mountain goats, and birds of many kinds with Columbia having more species than any other country in the western hemisphere.

After two hours and in time for the cable car going back down, the tours adjourn to one of two restaurants for a short lunch. At a small table Julio and Josephine are alone. Julio moves to calm Josephine about their next move at the bottom of the mountain. "Josephine, as soon as we leave the cable car, we will take a taxi to my family friend's house."

Josephine looks at Julio, "I am getting tired. Will it be far away? Oh, it would be so nice to sleep in a bed."

'Yes, his home is in a nice quiet neighborhood. I remember the number. My father took me there many times. They were more than just employer – employee, they were good friends. I played with his sons and we rode the ponies together in polo."

Josephine sighed, "Great, can't wait to get there."

Matt and Lucia are sitting alone at another small table unseen on the other side of the restaurant in a window corner. Lucia feels free to speak with a smile. "This trip is rather nice and of course, being with you is not bad either. But of course, I am sorry about my husband's death."

Matt consoles her. "Oh yes, it is very sad for all of us and he was a hero sacrificing himself so that we could get away. Of course, Don Fuego will someday have to pay for his murder. There is revenge in Julio's eyes that will someday be satisfied if we ever get out of this alive."

Matt elaborates, "Unfortunately, with the effort they are going after us, we all have much to worry about. With you and Julio still wandering around, the question of Don Fuego's supremacy is at hand. Without the Verelez family extinguished along with us foreign legionnaires, the other wolves at the table will start looking at Don Fuego as a weak disorganized leader who cannot run the organization."

Lucia believes the story is far from over. "He is a ruthless person, but he has weaknesses. He assumes people will just lie down and die for whatever he wants. When people start fighting back, he becomes careless and loses his judgment. And like all bullies he shows his cowardice with failures and relies on other people to carry out his ruthless commands. His time will come if he bites off more of our organization than he can chew."

"He has made as many enemies as he has friends and he knows that his friends are only friends because of fear or money. We have been in this business for twenty years and our family goes back generations. He came from a poor farming family, so there is much for him to overcome and little to work with other than force as an answer to his success. He has little in terms of education, culture, or even knowledge of the market here and how it works. In his all iron handed, feet stomping behavior, just like Pablo Escobar in 1993 he will be betrayed, hunted and shot down. That is not the way the real world works beyond the streets to the level of society where things get done more efficiently with less human cost."

Lucia then stares at Matt with the look of a Spanish Inquisitor. "Why are you here and why are you doing this? You came to process candy, buy our equipment and then you very professionally save us with the use of our automatic weapons? You came from nowhere and yet you are helping us at your life's risk. What is your motive for being here?"

Matt bounces back at Lucia, sternly with some admiration. "You are part of my problem, because your organization is my problem."

Lucia pursues her question. "You are obviously not the U.S. government. Your connections go worldwide because you have a Russian officer in our midst. She has power and influence as well. You have all these abilities, the weapons, tools of the trade, and money buying my equipment for a million pesos."

Matt stops Lucia for a moment, looks her straight in the eyes and puts his hands on her shoulder. "I think I can tell you this. We are freelancers. But we are not here to take over your organization. We are here to destroy it. We know we can't change the world, but we are trying to fix a part of the drug disease infecting the world. We believe we are doing the right thing and are willing to go outside the protection of the law system, undercover, on our own, and fight the fight."

Lucia breaks out with a smile and a laugh at the same time. "Superheroes? You are superheroes? You work for the good? You receive no pay? You risk your lives? And travel around the world doing good? I don't believe it."

Matt goes on. "Well, that's the story. We believe it is worth it. I am an agent for the DEA running a rogue operation. Whatever happens to me, the agency will disavow me and what I am doing. But my job now is to get you to safety. You will be on your own, once we are beyond the reach of these murderous criminals, and we will be on our way back to our official positions, Anna to Moscow, me to Dallas, Mannie back to his real estate brokerage in Las Vegas and Juan back to Bogota's Bureau of Narcotics."

"Good," she said. "I am glad that you are helping us and I thank you for it. As for the organization, it may or may not survive on its own account. Julio and I may be back to take it over, or not. We don't need it to survive. I have millions of dollars in banks around the world. When I get back to Mexico City, I will retrieve some of it before Don Fuego finds out how to get it. No matter, maybe it is time for me to look at another side of life, but I just cannot live without running a business of some kind."

Matt agrees, "Life expectancy in the drug business is not very good, even when you are sitting on top of the heap, and in your case, the social heap as well."

Lucia shows signs of compromising. "Maybe, I should go from the dark side to the good side. Maybe I can join you and become a superhero too. Hmmm. Maybe, maybe."

In the middle of the restaurant Mannie and Anna sit with the German group at a table for two next to a window. Anna is looking out the window with a view of the city. "Mannie are you married?"

Mannie is stunned by the question. "No, my wife left me ten years ago when I was active with the DEA."

Anna continues being forward. "And what have you been doing with your love life since then?"

Mannie is totally disarmed. "After my disability and removal from the DEA I have spent most of my time starting a new career in real estate sales and hopefully development. I have gone out on a few dates but finding a woman in Las Vegas that is not too fast for my blood, is difficult. Why all of a sudden your interest in my love life?"

Anna places her hand on Mannie's as his heart beat rises from 70 to 90. "You look at me the way I like to be looked at. You respect me as an officer of the law but also as a woman. From all of our experience together I have been thinking of you as more than a friend, to be with more than just on business."

Anna opens up Mannie's held back feelings for her. "Anna, our meeting and work together awoke in me a long dead feeling for any woman. You are special to me and I am leading with my chin right now. I love you and would like to spend the rest of my life with you. But given our doubtful circumstances, for now, how about just being engaged?"

Anna continues with a light laugh. "Oh, so you are not making a marriage proposal, but a let's get acquainted engagement?"

Mannie is honestly dealing with reality. "We are not out of hot water yet. You have Moscow to deal with. For now, we can seal this engagement with a kiss and keep on with our mission."

Anna turns to embrace and kiss Mannie, "Ja, das gut! For now, I am very happy to play your wife. When we arrive in Las Vegas we can decide on our future together."

As lunch is finishing up, the call for the cable car returning to the street begins with an agent ushering the groups in the restaurant to head out. The Tridexan escapees stay as couples with their groups as they pass policia on each side of the walkway every forty feet to the cable car. They see them looking in all directions but are well camouflaged within the crowd almost jammed nearly shoulder to shoulder. They pass them by without notice. The trip down in the cable car is full of mild chatter while the escaping couples remain quiet and anxious to make for a taxi for their separate destinations, for Julio and Josephine to a friend's house, and for the other two couples to the airport with different planes, one for Las Vegas for Anna and Mannie, and Matt and Lucia via a private charter for Dallas.

Once at the airport, Mannie, unknown to Don Fuego's hunters, uses his Las Vegas driver's license and Anna's Russian passport with no problem to purchase their tickets. Yet the tension is not over as they sit in the gate room waiting for the boarding announcement. Anna notices policia and army guards patrolling the halls and the waiting rooms looking at pictures in their hands and scanning the people in the rooms as they pass. Anna quietly warns. "Mannie, try to act natural, bored, relax and cross your legs and lean back and look at the ceiling while I fuss with my hand bag"

Mannie provides a slight nod. "Ok. I'll pretend I don't notice them."

Just then a guard walks by. "I don't see them here. Let's try the next gate."

With the announcement for boarding to Las Vegas, the entire room of fifty people immediately stands up and jockeys for the best position in the line for boarding.

Since Lucia is easily spotted in a waiting room and even getting a ticket would get her spotted with the video facial recognition system, Matt takes her with him to get an expensive but safe charter operation at the other end of the field. At the office entrance Matt holds her back. "Lucia, wait out here and wear your scarf across your face. The clerk will recognize you and we don't want that."

Lucia agrees with a nod. "Of course, just one phone call will get us killed."

Matt walks into the charter office up to the clerk. "Do you remember me?"

The counter clerk replies with a smile. "Si, you are Senor Matt O'Conner with the DEA. You hired our charters two years ago flying back and forth to Dallas."

Matt gets to business. "Yes, it is good to see you again. We are back to help out your special forces with cocaine control. And I need a charter today to fly me and my lady associate to Dallas. Do you have any planes available?"

The clerk looks on the schedule board. "We only have a Lear Jet Challenger 350 gassed and ready to go. Its range is 3200 miles. I can have a pilot here in ten minutes. Shall I bill your office?"

Matt pulls out his carry on. "Today I am paying cash in pesos."

The clerk's eyes pop and he checks his pricing schedule. "Let me see, the charge for Dallas at 2,500 miles is 40,000 pesos."

Matt agrees and passes out the cash on the counter. "If that is the plane in front of your hangar, I'll take my associate to board it and enjoy some of your well-known refreshments."

The clerk expresses a macho smile looking at the female figure outside the glass door. "Si Senor, take your lady associate to relax in our fine passenger cabin and enjoy our cocktail service."

Chapter Twenty Two

Making Cartegena

Julio and Josephine take a slow cab ride to Pedro's house at Santa Barbara Central, 11Z-37, Calle 118. The cabbie punches the meter and Julio and Josephine quietly enjoy the scenery driving through the city as the sun starts to set. Once at the address, Julio pays the cabbie and they walk up to the entrance of Pedro's house, side by side with other houses built to the narrow street, some with shallow small fenced gardens at the front and an everpresent garage door with no parking available on the street. As they approach the dimly lit entrance of this modest two-story home with a tile roof and a heavy wooden door, they note no first-floor windows to the front of the street. Julio pulls up a large, heavy knocker and bangs on the door with it.

In a moment Pedro answers, "Who is it?"

Julio speaks up. "It is Julio."

An old man bent forward from his back, probably in his sixties, frail but very much with a kindly face with deeply drawn lines, opens the door with a curious look.

"Julio, what are you doing here now?"

"Por favor, Pedro, let us in, we need your help."

"Si, Julio. Please enter my humble home."

Pedro in his usual stance ushers Julio and Josephine safely in and quickly closes the door.

"You have heard?" asked Julio.

"Si, your father's death is a big shock to me. I am very sorry. He did so much for me."

Julio is upfront with him immediately. "The army and Don Fuego are looking for us. The drug cartel has contracts out for me, my mother, Josephine and several strangers, who from nowhere seem to be helping us."

"I know little of what is happening, except what is reported in the paper calling it a terrorist attack on a pharmacy company owner. And yes, the word at the coffee shop is that there is a reward for locating you and your mother and the two strangers. How can I help you?"

"We need your help to go to Facatativa…"

Pedro cuts him off. "I know from years ago that trip. You take a bus to Cartagena to go sailing on your family boat. It is too late today. Stay here tonight and I will drive you there tomorrow morning for the 9:00 A.M. run. Have I met your lady friend?"

Juilo apologizes. "I am sorry. This is Mrs. Josephine O'Connor. She is a friend of the family and has been helping me with the company business. She is also our best rider on our championship polo team."

Pedro now recognizes Josephine. "Yes, I have seen you on TV. You are indeed a beautiful woman. Julio's father spoke very highly of you. He appreciated all that you did for Julio and the family name in the polo world."

Josephine smiles politely. "Gracias senor."

Pedro continues. "It is very nice to meet you. So, to get back to business, my wife and I are going to evening mass at Santa Beatriz. She will set up a table for you two to enjoy her delicious cooking. We only have one extra bedroom but there is a big bed to share. We will leave you to yourselves for any sharing agreements." Pedro offers a prim smile and a wink to both.

With Pedro and Maria gone to church, they sit and dine at a candle lit table. Julio looks at Josephine and speaks to her with tears in his eyes. "When I am with you my past means nothing. When we are together my life is whole again. My future is your future. We can find our way by ourselves. We are separated from my mother and those other men and I don't think we will see them again. The city is on alert and the only way we can survive is if we can get out by ourselves. We can sail to Guantanamo where we conducted our herbal business with the farmers. The organization knows about our business there but not where my cousin keeps a house on the farm we use for growing. We can go to that house and stay there until it is safe again to move."

Josephine looks at Julio. "It seems like every time we turn there is something there to help us. I think that we have a guardian angel or two"

"Yes, my father was a careful man. Wherever we would go, whatever we did, he always planned for an alternative with escape routes and safe places. His business was never certain."

"And what about the others, how can we find out about getting back to Florida?"

"We spent many months there and we have many friends. But, because we are going there to hide, we do not wish to contact any of them. On my sail boat I have a short-wave radio and can contact grandfather at the hacienda. He will check with my aunt in West Palm. She will have her ear to the safety issue."

Julio is ready for a heavy reply but cannot hold himself back any longer. "But here and now, I am thinking of us and our happiness and my proposal of marriage which you have for-stalled. There is no room, no time, and much that could forever end the beauty and happiness you place in my heart."

Josephine leans forward and looks hard into Julio's eyes. "I have a confession to make. First of all, I am not married. Second, I am an undercover agent for the DEA sent to involve myself with you and your family to find out about your possible involvement with the Columbia drug cartel. It is our Karma that my job brought me to you and as I worked with you, the more we liked each other and now I feel the same heart warmth when we are together. But I could not ignore my commitment to my job. Matt, formerly Mark, is my boss, not my husband, and our intent has been to destroy the drug trafficking at Tridexan, which also seems to be happening with Don Fuego."

Julio leans back in his chair and stares at the ceiling fighting a tug of war between his love and his disgust with Josephine's duplicity. "My God, I have fallen in love with a spy!"

He then pauses. "But this spy has made me the happiest I have ever been. She has risked her life and saved my life and helped my polo team win a championship. How can I hate a woman who has done so much for me; and her spying has helped me cut myself away from my mother and father's evil business?"

Julio gently holds Josephine's hands across the table. "Josephine, I love you. Will you marry me still? I ask nothing more of you now, just an engagement till we reach safety to build our lives together forever." Josephine faces up to her own deep desire to have and hold Julio. "Julio, YES! I love you, and yes, for us to be together forever."

As they stand up from the table, they embrace, kiss, and hold each other with tenderness beyond passion. Josephine admits to herself. "This is wonderful and it feels good to have my love's flood gates open and flowing."

As they take their carry-ons to the second-floor bedroom, Josephine looks back at Julio who picks her up and carries her through the bedroom door. The next morning Maria knocks on the bedroom door for breakfast. Pedro gets the car ready to hide Julio and Josephine under blankets as they leave the garage in front of the neighbors and walking traffic. The trip is only about thirty miles. After breakfast Pedro rushes Julio and Josephine to the garage. "I am taking the back road. It will take about an hour. We should be there a half hour early for the nine o'clock bus."

They arrive from the back road at the Berlinas bus station without incident. Julio and Josephine both hug Pedro and wish him a healthy goodbye with many thanks. Pedro cannot hold himself back. "God Bless and keep you on your new adventure. Maria and I will pray for you. But always be steady as she goes on the helm. Your love will make you strong together, the best sailors on the Caribbean."

With Pedro pulling away Julio is already purchasing tickets just behind a group of American tourists and getting seats just behind them. With all aboard, the bus leaves on the beginning of a seventeenhour trip with a half way break in Medellin, the second largest city in Columbia, formerly the world's most dangerous city run by Pablo Escobar and cruelly harassed by FARC-EP guerillas. After eight hours on the road, listening to endless chatting of American tourists, many from Florida, Julio and Josephine welcome a break, when the bus stops at the station in Medellin. Julio notes it not being the same city he remembers everything looks new with people moving about freely without fear. Even the food is good. With just enough time to get a meal and a decent bathroom, all board the bus for the last part of the journey.

Josephine looks at Julio and asks, "Is it ok if I break our quiet time on the road to ask some questions about your boat?" Julio's eyes widen and he sits up straight. "My boat, I named her Papillon. She is our flight to freedom. On the seas we are our own masters and free from the rest of the world. She is a 56-foot catamaran with two equal sized hulls parallel to each other connected by a center island above the water line, all to create a very stable sailing platform, with a single mast for a main sail and a jib. She is older, but a finely mature maiden, a 1978 model and very much overbuilt. We have accommodations with four staterooms, four heads, two with baths, a full galley, a commodious lounge and dining area and a fantastic enclosed pilot house. She is all finished in teak with seamless craftsmanship. All of her sailing gear is electrified. I can sail her all by myself and that I have done. With you as my first mate we will be better than ever, just like on the DC-3."

Josephine is a bit overcome. "Julio, I have never sailed. I know nothing about seamanship. I have spent my life on the prairie away from lake water, let alone the Caribbean."

Julio is not concerned. "Do you know how to cook?"

Josephine is quick to answer, "Of course!"

Julio is more than sure of Josephine. "We will be at sea for three days and your cooking is part of sailing. But by the time we arrive at Guantanamo Bay on the fifth day of our escape, you will be an excellent first mate and pilot."

Reaching Cartagena at midnight, Julio waves an uber at the station for a ride to Manga, marina Calle 24. In twenty minutes, they arrive. Julio walks Josephine out on the docks where Papillon awaits them. Josephine marvels, "She is beautiful." As they board her, Julio points out the master stateroom for stashing their carry-ons and they go back to the galley for a snack and a glass of wine. Josephine asks. "Shouldn't we be going to buy groceries for this trip?"

Julio laughs. "You are forgetting my father's insanity with safe places and safe ways. We have enough packaged food on board to sail to the Mediterranean. We have a fresh water maker, and solar panels for battery upkeep, a unique air conditioner, and double fuel capacity for two diesel engines and a generator. We will leave with the high tide this morning at seven. So sleep is number one on our agenda." After a toast to Adolpho, they adjourn to the master suite for instant sleep with a smile.

Chapter Twenty Three

Day Three Sailing On Papillon

Up at 6:00 A.M., Josephine cooks powdered eggs and frozen sausage and muffins for a meal. On deck the captain names shows and names the specific tools and functions for leaving the dock. "On board we don't have ropes we have lines. Those lines attached to the dock cleats must be untied and thrown on board from the dock. After that you jump on board as the boat starts to drift away. Then I will engage the motors and the bow and stern thrusters to push us away from the dock into the open water between the docks. After that, join me in the cockpit for an electronics course and I will head us out to sea on our diesel engines. Once in the open we will raise the sail and cut the engines"

Josephine smiles with enthusiasm. "So far this is easier than flying. I am ready to go."

Julio offers encouragement. "Once a sailor you will always love sailing on the open water with the breeze at your back, getting a free ride, away from a world of worry."

Josephine agrees. "I can appreciate knowing that feeling with the freedom of the skies."

While motoring out, at the console of the pilot house Julio begins the electronic lesson. "Ok, Josephine, instead of having a gauge for elevation, we have a depth gauge to hard bottom. If we hit hard bottom, we sink. Keeping in at least five feet of water we float. We have a magnetic compass which is about 2 degrees off True North." True north is available from this satellite GPS which also includes our location on navigation charts for all of the Caribbean. We also have a link to all on shore weather broadcasts. Our radar is good to the horizon about twenty-eight miles off the top of our mast with 360-degree coverage. And this is our marine radio, also with a double sideband shortwave to get back to the estancia and to monitor local traffic. The remaining gauges include electrical services including an anchor motor, engine gauges, and wind, temperature, barometer, and a marine clock."

Josephine is impressed. "Wow. What is that brass thing with scope and mirrors?"

Julio reflects his father's two of everything for safety. "In case all goes to hell in a basket electronically, that is a sextant, and it can help us navigate with the paper charts that I have on board. It helps us find longitude and with a compass, and a marine clock, we can determine our location and latitude and distance travelled from horizon to horizon as long as we can see the sun, the moon or stars."

Josephine is thinking. "So just like on an airplane this boat has a backup for everything."

Julio smiles with her perception. "Right, we also have an auto pilot same as an air plane. We have solar and generator power, two engines instead of one, two sales and jibs for wind power, one for replacement, three radios, two for long distance, an extra anchor, extra line for sail rigging repairs and replacement, and fishing and diving gear for fresh food."

Josephine starts looking into every cabinet and corner of the pilot house and stares at a hatch with a number combination lock. "What is inside that floor hatch with a lock?"

Julio gladly answers. "Oh yes, on the high seas there is no law enforcement. Remember the number 717. Go ahead and open the hatch."

Josephine hits the mechanical moving numbers and the latch opens. "Well, I assume we may have to defend ourselves. Let me see, here is a flare gun for emergencies, a sniper rifle, an old M-1 Garand with clips of 30-06 armor piercing rounds, two twelve gauge semi auto shotguns one with led slug clips and the other with double ought buckshot clips, two 1911 forty fives, an AK 47 and two RPG's made in Russia. What is this all about, a war?"

Julio is dead serious. "The Caribbean is crawling with pirates, some for looting recreation boaters, others hunting for smuggling with recreation boats, leaving no witnesses, to use in transporting drugs. When done with the use, they sink or change the appearance of the boat."

"If I am sleeping and you are at the wheel, if you see any boat approaching us, or by radar on the horizon, moving fast or slowly like us, wake me immediately. Without a radio call from it, if they get within two hundred yards, I fire a warning shot with the M-1. They know its rounds will pierce their hull. I also have a megaphone and tell them to stand off. If they fail to reply or come up with a lame excuse like asking for cigarettes, then ..... "

Josephine gets the message. "You mean you have to fight off a boarding attempt? Has this ever happened to you?"

Julio answers reluctantly. "Yes. We are away from the cartel, but we are still in hot water till we get to Guantanamo Bay. We have to have one of us on watch day and night. They can approach silently or on fast boats. We will relieve each other on six-hour watches with breaks for meals in the daytime. Our radar at night will be very helpful. I also have a high beam light on the top that we can operate from the pilot house. And here are two sets of high-powered binoculars for horizon scanning and a night scope using infra-red, also made in Russia."

Josephine tires herself out just thinking of what can go wrong. Julio senses a need to change direction and he stops the engines. "Come, let's get on deck and rig the sails and we can use the wheel outside and enjoy our first cruising day."

All of the commotion in Bogota does not escape the attention of the U.S. embassy and attached DEA and CIA intelligence officers in Columbia. Their routine monitoring of drug traffic and terrorists is catastrophically turned upside down.

John Whitney is in charge of affairs for the DEA and receives a memorandum from one of his informants at the army headquarters in Bogota. Speaking to one of his subordinates he said, "This memorandum is kind of hard to understand."

Charlie, a burly, tough looking, mean son of a gun in the DEA blurts out, "What do you mean?"

"The local barracks are on alert. They are out on the street patrolling the warehouse district and monitoring the airport, and checking hotels everywhere. They are searching for a group of foreigners and citizens. It is kind of garbled. It does not seem to make sense. But it kind of goes with this latest newspaper article with the assassination attack on the Verelez family at their penthouse with Adolpho Verelez and his guards murdered. Our other informants on the street tell us there is a contract out for a million pesos a head for the death of Adolpho's wife, his son, Julio, his girlfriend and two unidentified foreign individuals."

Charlie chooses to clarify. "There is more to it than that."

"Well, what do you mean?"

"Don Fuego is in town and big time. He has brought in about ten hit men as well as his usual mob of paramilitary goons."

John Whitney sees the web. "I think there is some relationship between Don Fuego and the death of Adolpho Verelez. We need closer tabs on this. These foreigners that are being pursued have upset the apple cart someway and we need to find out who, how, and why. I think they are doing some kind of damage to the drug cartel in this town. Are they trying to take it over? Are they trying to subvert it somehow? I don't know, but we need to find out."

Charlie agrees, "I'll get on it. We have six people on the street right now talking it up with our informants. I will have a report for you on your desk tomorrow."

Whitney gives Charlie a nod. "Let's see what we can do to mix up the pot more."

With every passing hour on the third day since his take over, Don Fuego is more and more nervous. He paces his suite at the top of the grand hotel in Bogota and grinds out a question to his trusted second in command. "What have you found out?"

"We know they went to the warehouse district. They killed the guards we posted at the candy factory pointed out to us by Senor Peniendo. Our people are combing through the district now going from building to building. We will find them."

Don Fuego disagrees. "Ah, I think it is too late. We would have found them there by now. They slipped out into the other districts to hide. But we must stop them from leaving the city. Airport, car rentals, buses, what about those places. We need to have them eliminated, now!"

"The policia and the army are at the airport since yesterday. They check car rentals but did run into a stolen car incident at a restaurant. But that happens all the time. Two men came into the restaurant with pistols and demanded all to place their car keys on the table. They took one set of keys and left."

Don Fuego's eyes widened. "That is a great way to get out of town unseen, just steal a vehicle? Check it out. Send out our search to all of the surrounding villages along the highway from town. They will need to buy gas. Also check the cabbies and ubers. We need to put our new partners at ease both here and overseas. Unappreciated leadership does not last long in this business."

With engines off, Julio and Josephine make sail after her quick education about watching out for the boom, raising and lowering the main sale and working the jib from full to a storm setting. She handles the wheel to maintain a compass course going north toward Jamaica. Julio remarks as he sits beside Josephine, "Ahh, to be at a sea, the open air surrounds our seeing, the gentle breeze caresses our face, gently swaying us over the waves, and lifting our souls beyond our senses."

Josephine picks up on Julio's dreaming. "From time to time, from place to place, we take a few curves ending up with a sigh of relief and together we survive. On this full blue, bright sunny day, light with clouds, this trip is truly a change of pace, to one of pleasure and relaxation."

Julio smiles, agrees and then as a matter of habit, scans the horizon for other boats and ships. "Oh my God, there is a trawler. She has spotted us and is coming our way!"

Josephine asks. "Is that a problem?"

Julio growls, "They have not contacted us by radio. That makes me suspicious, as if they might be sneaking up on us. They could be pirates."

Josephine grows with concern. "Can we out sail them?"

Julio judges their distance. "They are about ten miles and closing on our starboard side from the east. We are doing about twelve knots under sail. The most they can do is 16 knots. Start the engines and let's add some speed without using too much fuel."

Julio takes the wheel. Josephine starts the engines and goes to the pilot house to watch their distance with the radar screen.

Josephine yells back after an hour. "They are getting closer, now only about two miles. How can that be?"

Julio notes with his binoculars the trawler getting closer, a newer boat likely able to get 18 to 20 knots. "Josephine, open the weapons hatch and bring up the rifle"

Josephine hands the M-1 to Julio and takes the wheel. "They are still over a mile out. Can you hit them with this rifle?"

Julio shoulders the rifle and steadies on a rail. "This double hull platform is fairly steady relative to a single hull. They haven't called us on the radio. They mean trouble and hope we aren't prepared for an onside boarding after raking us with gunfire 200 feet from our starboard side. All I want to do is let them know we can shoot first."

Julio takes one shot for distance and sprays water near the trawler. "There, that will give those bastards something to think about." Julio squeezes the trigger five times, milliseconds apart, and a line of hits spray near the trawler which suddenly turns to avoid a hit.

Josephine marvels the result. "Good, we can continue our course."

Julio minimizes the result. "It is a good thing we are on sail and saving on fuel. They have us on their radar. It is getting dark. They can see our radar but may hope that we fall asleep. To test us they will move closer to us a little by little. No sleep tonight for either of us until they move off for good."

As Julio predicted, the trawler runs parallel with their northerly course after dark. Both are in the pilot house watching the radar screen when the dot starts moving closer.

Julio breaks silence. "Hah. They think we are stupid. They are coming in."

Josephine readily admits Julio's suspicion. "Ok, what shall we do next?"

Julio develops a plan. "I can turn on our million-candle spot light and shine it on them to let them know we know they are coming. They might think we are just trying to scare them off and will keep on coming, or they might just move on. But pirates are greedy, often just desperate if we are the only victims spotted this far out. And they always assume that we are afraid of them and they are fearless, especially with their AK's. In all fairness, I will give them a chance to leave. Josephine, grab the light control handle and shine it in their direction side to side as in a search warning. Let's see what they do."

Josephine scans with the boat light, its deep beam easily seen by the pirates. Julio, for fifteen minutes stares at the radar screen. "The fools are staying with us and moving in. In fifteen minutes, they will spray us with gunfire. Josephine, get out the RPG's."

Josephine hands one to Julio. "Do you want the other one too?"

Julio. "No. Take the wheel and start the motors. When I say now, turn Papillon's bow into the trawler at full throttle. I want to cross their "t", and hit them on the broadside and give them only our bows to shoot at. Do all this from the stern wheel and lay low, OK?"

Josephine is steady at the ready. "Aye, Aye, Captain!"

In less than a minute Julio yells, "Now!!!"

Josephine guns the engines and hard wheels Papillon's bow into the trawler now exposed by Julio with the high beam light. Automatic fire from four flashing guns starts hitting the water and walking up to the bow of Papillon. At that moment Julio runs forward, rests his elbow on a railing ready to fire the RPG.

Josephine yells out. "Go for the pilot house. Take that out and they lose control."

Julio yells out. "Yeah, you bastards, take this home to your momma."

Julio's RPG fires with a flash, then a streaming red trail runs straight to the pilot house. With a dead on hit the attached grenade demolishes the pilot house, radar and radio equipment including antennas. Josephine instinctively turns the boat hard to port resuming the northerly course to Jamaica at full throttle.

Julio jumps back to the stern wheel. "You handle Papillon just like you handle a pony. Great steering, mi amor, I am proud of you!"

Josephine gives way with a heavy sigh of relief. "Si, mi amor, el capitan. You handled that RPG like an expert. I am glad you did and am equally as proud of you."

Once clear of the attackers, Julio puts Papillon back to sails, turns on the auto pilot and they adjourn to their state room for the rest of the night. While just settling down from their adrenaline high, Julio thinks out loud to Josephine. "I am wondering what it is that they are doing, that Matt and my mom. She has taken a liking to him from the first time they met. I wonder how they are working out escaping together. She knows our contact in Guantanamo and our safe house there. My mother would probably go to Mexico City."

Josephine adds. "I know Matt is already in Dallas. Lucia said she would go to Mexico City from there. Mannie and Anna are in Las Vegas. And Anna has choices to stay or go back to Russia. Where they go from there, I don't know. But they will have to be in touch somehow. We will get together. I know we will."

"I hope so," said Julio. "This is all such a mess. We don't know where we are going to be and what we are going to be doing even thirty days from now."

Josephine now breathing confidence, "That's true, but we are alive and we are together, that means a lot." Then, looking at Julio with tender eyes, Josephine places her hands up to his face gently stroking his cheeks. "Julio, for all that we have been through" with her jesting smile, "believe it or not, I still love you."

Julio smiles, they kiss, and then fall dead asleep.

Chapter Twenty Four

Day Four Mexico City

It's nearly morning now and Lucia is at the airport waiting with Matt at her gate to Mexico City. Their talk, more than ever reflects the tone of lovers, as if their differences past and present never existed. Lucia sweetly murmurs as they sit side by side, "Will you come to visit me in Mexico? You told me your mother was from there?"

Matt with simple sincerity, "You know I will. Going away from you now is like leaving me half a man. But I don't know exactly how and when yet. The question is, do they have your system records to find you in Mexico?"

Lucia puckers with a sly smile. "Do you think I run my business like an open book?

My Alphonso, the backup man of all time, always makes sure to keep the hard contact set of books out of the country with our safe place in Mexico."

Matt is getting back to his DEA job. "Really, well that will keep you on the safe side when Don Fuego gets taken down."

Lucia firms up again as a business woman. "Well, I'll just turn that corner when I get to it, with or without you." As she rises to enter the gate, Lucia promises, "There it is. I hope we can make our lives work it out, good bye my darling."

Back in Las Vegas, Anna and Mannie are staying at Mannie's condo just off Fremont Street next to down town. After a fun time, last night getting in from Bogota, Anna needs to get in touch with the Russian Embassy. Anna is using Mannie's lap top computer. "Mannie, there is no Russian Embassy in Las Vegas, no consulate and no diplomatic mission, just a place to help people here on visas. I can't talk to anybody here face to face. I need to find out if I am safe to go back to Moscow."

Mannie offers other places. "Well, we know there is a Russian Embassy in Bogota, and in Buenos Aires, there was a Russian Embassy and Moscow police raid on smugglers from there. Maybe you can trust somebody there?"

Anna is doubtful. "No, I will call my friend in Finland, you know, the chemist we met on our escape from Russia. Maybe she can help me."

Mannie backs up a minute. "No, in the end you are going to have to call Moscow to make a report. I suggest you wait for the end of the fifth day which is tomorrow. Give our demolition of the system time to reach back to the Russian mafia. You know all hell is going to break loose in Bogota and all over the world with the demolition of this last shipment."

Anna is again thinking chemist. "Yes, it will certainly be one big set of fireworks."

Mannie sees the disaster playing out. "After that it won't take long for heads to fall and the right people will be in charge to clean up the corrupt mess including government insiders like possible members of your squad. Everybody will be squealing on others to save themselves. It will be like a tsunami of squealers lapping on top of each other."

Anna thinks it over. "Well, there is no place for me to report here. And you are right, I don't want to set off any alarms before our chemicals do their damage to a worldwide shipment. Ok, I will wait and see."

Mannie decides to get Anna's mind distracted. "Great, in the meantime I have some condos to show in this building. Would you like to assist me with your talent and beauty to sell real estate? I cannot pay you a commission, but I certainly will reward you with my gratitude and maybe teach you a new profession, just in case!"

Back on the Papillon, Josephine and Julio are sailing in following seas to Guantanamo Bay, a U.S. Navy Base. There they can anchor and take the Cuban border gate leaving the base on to the city of Guantanamo. As they approach the base, radio traffic never ceases. Julio notes to Josephine. "Guantanamo is only a temporary place to stay. But we will be plenty safe with my cousin who lives there on our ten-acre farm in the mountains where we grow herbs."

Josephine looks at Julio. "Will there be any more surprises?"

"Well, because of our Tridexan business we will have no trouble entering Cuba to check on our herbal crop. We will approach the U.S. base as American citizens travelling to Miami and ask if we can anchor for a rest. I know that they have dock facilities for small boats and we can pass through their heavily barbed wire guarded gate to enter Cuba proper. I will find my cousin and he will escort us to the mountains where we will be safe for as long as we need. No one but my cousin knows me and I trust him."

Josephine worries. "Won't people recognize us or know about us because of the attack in Bogota?"

"Cuba doesn't get much on world news, except communist propaganda from around the world. They have me on their files for the farm and fly over privileges. You are an American I met in Florida and we are engaged to be married. And we have our passports. I don't think we will need visas or we'll get one at the Cuban side of the gate house."

Josephine is amazed at all the pre-planning that Julio's family goes through to find places to hide. She looks at him. "I just find it hard to believe that you have all of this ready for this kind of problem."

Julio looks at her not wanting to answer. "Yes, my father, Adolpho the general, knew they were trying to get us for several years. My mother, ambitious as ever, downplayed his concern. I know he was having trouble with the other general partners at his last meeting with them at the officer's club. Several attempts to poorly planned assassinations were defeated by Eduardo, their body guard, and thank you again for saving me as well. Adolpho planned for this inevitability all along and Lucia, maximizing her greed, hid funds in different countries, just in case he was right. Yes, thanks to my father, the great Adolpho, bags of cash, caches of weapons, false identities, clothing, and food are planted everywhere, so as needed, we can easily choose alternative escape routes to different parts of the world."

After a moment of silence, Julio prepares for entering the bay. "Ok, we are fifteen miles off shore. Mount our US flag on the stern and move the Columbian flag to the bow. Throw our last RPG overboard. Don't lock up the gun locker. We will be searched."

Julio makes a call to the base. "US Guantamo base this is Papillon, a 52-foot catamaran single masted sail boat with US registry seeking temporary dockage en route from Cartagena to Miami, Over."

"Papillon, Papillon we have you on radar. A coast card cutter will meet you shortly for boarding, a vessel search, and papers."

"Message received. We have lowered sales and are standing down. Over"

In fifteen minutes a fast, small cutter approaches. A lowered power dingy comes along side with four armed seamen and secures to the stern swim platform of Papillon.

A second lieutenant approaches Julio and Josephine at the stern cockpit after two men go below deck and one goes across the hulls of the top deck. "Your passports, please."

As he examines them, the top deck seaman approaches. "Sir, the bows of this boat and along the pilot house have bullet holes. "The lieutenant looks at Julio with a hard face. "Are you the owner of this vessel and from where did you get those bullet holes."

Before Julio could answer, another boarder reports, "Sir, there is a weapons locker with shotguns, pistols and an M1 Garand."

The lieutenant looks at Julio and Josephine with a tight smile. "So, you are the ones."

Julio answers promptly. "We were under pirate attack last night. They sprayed us with automatic weapons. I returned with the M1's armor piercing bullets and tracers and got lucky with a hit on the wheel house. It blew up and their engine stopped. We motored at full throttle until we lost them and then raised sail to get directly here."

The lieutenant responds. "Our air search for traffickers located a damaged trawler. They had no radio but waved our plane off. I am sure they wouldn't want a boarding party to help them out. Why didn't you radio us for help?"

Josephine breaks into the conversation. "It all happened so fast." The lieutenant turns and looks. "And you are Josephine O'Connor. What is your relationship to Mr. Verelez? And how did it happen so fast."

"I am his fiancé. We are planning to be married in West Palm, Florida. We saw them at sunset and watched them on radar. After dark, they suddenly turned into us and started shooting. I took the wheel and Julio asked me to turn into them at full throttle. He started shooting with the rifle and something blew up. They stopped shooting. In the middle of nowhere we escaped as fast as we could."

Another boarding member comes up. "Lieutenant, the sniffers are negative. We checked all spaces, including the bilge. The boat is clean."

The lieutenant now has a broader smile. "You are indeed lucky. Your weapons saved your lives. Your boat is an ideal snatch for traffickers. The owners are usually forced overboard, making them jump with their hands tied. They use the boat to smuggle under the owner's papers, change the name with false papers or just sink it. This is not the Bermuda Triangle; it is the "pirates and smugglers triangle" between Columbia, Mexico and Florida. You are welcome to port with us for repairs and fuel. I will pass on your clearance."

A seaman receives a call. "Sir, an emergency call back on board, our aerial spotter found a submarine trafficker."

As the lieutenant left from the swim platform he waved and yelled, "Safe Trip and congratulations on winning one for us, that far out, they probably won't make it."

For better control and making no wake, the Papillon approaches the mouth of the bay under slow motors, and Julio wheels to starboard to the harbor master designated parallel dock position number eight just ahead of another Coast Guard Cutter. Although restricted to the port area because of the prison portion of the base, Josephine and Julio are happy to see American men and women in uniform.

Josephine marvels. "Look there is a McDonalds. This place is like a small town in the US. And there is a night club. Let's go and have a hamburger. Uh oh, they don't take pesos here. I guess we will have to sit this out."

Julio answers with a smile. "Once again we may thank General Verelez. On the road, the US dollar goes everywhere and he put a safety cache in the galley freezer in the frozen fish package. That will pay for our fuel at the Marina and from the Commissary we can upgrade our food supply. I'll get permission from the Commanding Officer to use the Northeast Gate since they closed it for Cuban traffic after the locals worked their jobs out in 1993. There are also Cuban exiles under protection here since the revolution."

As they begin their walk to McDonalds, at the sound of a trumpet for 8:00 AM, loud speakers start playing the Star-Spangled Banner as the flag is raised at the port commander's office.

With permission to go to the guarded barbed wire gate, Julio and Josephine walk through the base's border to a check point on the Cuban side to enter Guantanamo.

After passing through obtaining a temporary visa, their passports are stamped with a smile and "Guantanamo is safe for shopping and the food is great."

Julio and Josephine take a short walk north along the road to a rundown apartment building formerly used for base civilian workers. Julio looks and finds apartment 6 on the first floor and knocks.

Upon opening, the occupant answers "Julio. My long-lost cousin, what are you doing here out of season in Guantanamo?"

Julio looks at him grimly. "Alonzo, I am seeking your favor. We are on the run."

Alonzo guesses, "It has happened?"

"Yes, my father is dead. My mother is with another man heading in a different direction. This is my wife to be, Josephine. We need your help. We need to hide."

"Of course, I'll take you to the farm now."

He ushers Josephine and Julio on to his jeep wrangler and immediately heads into the mountains. At the end of an unpaved gravel road that winds its way up to the mountaintop, there sits a small farmhouse, inconspicuous and surrounded by a chicken coup and small pens for pigs and goats.

Alonzo admits, "This is where I really live; the apartment is for my girlfriends. I thank you so much for letting me stay here all these years."

Julio looks at him holding his hand. "Alonzo, all these years you have been my best cousin. Do you still have the short-wave radio working?"

"Yes, and there is a hard-line phone. And it has the encryption your father installed. You can call me on my cell phone. Here is the number." As Alonzo leaves, "There is a scooter in the shed if you need to get to the city or back to the base."

With Alonzo gone, Josephine recognizes an opportunity to call out. "Julio, I can use that phone to call Matt in Dallas. We can find out how everybody else is doing and with this number they and your aunt can call us about the safety for sailing to Miami."

Julio agrees. "Yes, I would like to know how my mother is doing."

Josephine calls Matt: "Hello Matt. This is Josephine with Julio. We made it to the Navy Base at Guantanamo and are waiting for the fifth day to make our next move."

Matt responds with a healthy surprise. "Josephine. It is so good to hear your voice. We have wondered how you two are making the trip by water. Has it all gone well?"

"We were attacked by pirates but Julio fought them off with an RPG and his rifle. We left them stranded with a missing pilot house"

"Not that I am jealous, but you two always get the action, and I am glad you hang together so well. I will call Lucia to tell her that you two are well in Cuba. Are you staying on the boat? How did you call on this line?"

"It is an encrypted line at Adolpho's safe house that he put in a year ago at a small farm for raising herbs. We have a temporary visa from Cuba to be here but our boat is permission docked at the Navy base for fuel and repairs of a few bullet holes."

"Well, you two wait out tomorrow and see how things settle out. Tell Julio his mother is in Mexico City lying low for now, but I am sure she will be planning how to deal with Peniendo, reported in the news as the president of Tridexan. Mannie and Anna are ok in Las Vegas, also waiting for the fall out. Juan and his family are covered with the Bogota policia, as I will be notifying the DEA there that he is undercover for me in Brazil. He can go back without any fear after the meltdown."

"Ok. We will wait it out. God Bless."

"Copy that my dear and say to Julio, I thank him for bringing you back safely. God Bless."

Receiving another call, backlash confronts Matt a few minutes later, this time from the D. C. Office of the DEA.

"Matt, I just received a call from our director in Bogota that a major cartel battle has been going on with the takeover of a minor pharmacy company. Is that true and is that what you have been working on over the past month? Have you been running an undercover rogue operation without my approval?"

Matt opens up, honest and true. "Yes, I want to give you the opportunity to disavow what I have been doing. Undercover, we infiltrated a small veterinary pharmacy company in Bogota and mixed explosive material with their last shipment bound for all the ports that they deliver their drugs to."

"Without our local DEA and Bogota policia, that is impossible."

"Yes, it is, four of us did it undercover. Beginning in St. Petersburg in conjunction with a Moscow Drug bureau officer also under cover we devised a nano-bomb. We mixed nano particles mixed with their drug cover solutions for hard pills with cocaine, and their heroin shipped in liquid form that resists sniffing and the usual chemical testing. Recovery of the drug involves creating a solution and then drying. In the solution those nano-particles are dissolved, with carbolic acid and the liquid will explode. Typically, we don't know where, but they will explode in the hands of the shipment receivers tomorrow as they work to recover the drugs from the hard pills and liquids."

Matt's director speaks coldly. "You are destroying what took a long time to build, and that is good. The way you are doing it is definitely illegal between the countries you involve. My God, you have somebody from Moscow? No way can we get any extraditions from any of the involved countries. You are disavowed and terminated if this comes out the wrong way. You may also face criminal prosecution, which we will fight to prevent or co-opt."

"It's not over yet. At the time of the cartel fight, myself and the Moscow officer saved the lives of the operator of the pharmacy, Mrs. Lucia Verelez and her son Julio, while her husband Adolpho gallantly held off the attackers to help us escape. He and his guards were killed in the fire fight lasting just a few minutes. But Mrs. Verelez knows all of the who's, how's, and what's of the operation. And I and our team escorted her and her son out of Bogota to avoid a death squad. I chartered a plane to fly her with me out of Bogota to Dallas. She just left to Mexico City where she has a back-up office with all the data and a cache of money to start up the operation if it fails, which it will with the nano bombs."

"Let me see. You saved her life and her son. She owes you. I am ignoring your undercover operation for disavowing potential and you can go back to her and find out more about her contacts. If she helps us, we can make a deal on protecting her and keeping her off the hook with us. Can you turn her to the good side?"

"Well, a week ago, just to get on the inside of her operation I made the ultimate sacrifice and it wasn't all bad. We are getting to know each other better. So, keep my black box open. I don't want any information about her and her location slipping out in any way, including monitoring my activities."

"Unofficially I am ignoring your rogue adventure. I don't want to see what good that comes from your attack on the system go to waste, especially with easy and often quick replacement. We are having enough trouble just reducing cocaine production in Columbia. Ok. We have never had this conversation and I will ignore any continued absences in Dallas. Understand this. You could still get burned. And if it works, we still can't recognize your subversive success, but be assured, your job is safe and you will be rewarded with my approval." "Understood director, this conversation never occurred." Click.

Matt calls Mannie. "Mannie, I have good news. We are still in undercover business with a black box. Has Juan called you?"

Mannie is stunned. "Matt, I thought you'd be fired after all of your time undercover. How did you survive? And the fifth day isn't till tomorrow. Yes, Juan called me at my office to see if we made it. I clued him in on you and Lucia, but told him Julio and Josephine are still somewhere in the Caribbean."

Matt breathes out a very happy relieved tone. "Julio and Josephine are safe in Cuba. I laid out our rogue operation to our section director in D.C. He still can disavow but he wants us around to clean up the pieces after our great event tomorrow. He even wants me going back to Lucia to try and turn her to our side, work with us to put finishing touches on our great effort, and be free of DEA prosecution. Juan is covered with our DEA manager in Bogota on a DEA investigation working on a trafficker follow up in Brazil. So he is safe to go back after tomorrow to help them clean up."

Mannie comes back. "That is great news. Anna is holding back until after the bombing. There will be a shakedown in her office, the army, and with the Mafia. Now we wait, until tomorrow, bye."

Chapter Twenty Five

Day Five Death And Destruciton

It is day five and all hell is breaking lose all over the world. Container ship High Dough in the port of Hong Kong offloading container number 19274 is being lifted by a crane on the dock when a gigantic explosion in midair rocks the boat and collapses the crane. A precipitate shop in Tokyo, where the offloaded chemical from Bogota is being heated to precipitate back to cocaine, explodes in a warehouse building where it causes a conflagration, killing all the lab technicians and the distribution leadership.

Madrid, Spain also has a warehouse explosion in a precipitation lab that spreads fire in the industrial district. All of the processors and distributing management are killed.

Beijing, China has an explosion of a small precipitate shop in the basement of an apartment building. The explosion causes a weakness to the building and collapses killing forty residents working for the distributor.

An air cargo plane landing in Paris approaches the tarmac and explodes at the rear and the tail falls off the plane. Nobody is hurt.

In Miami, a precipitation shop located in the warehouse district explodes and catches on fire. Fire inspection indicates cocaine on the site and no one is hurt but all of the people on the site are arrested.

In New York, a veterinary pharmaceutical distributor experiences a fire in one of their testing labs. Investigation reveals cocaine on the site. All the people on the site, including the president of the corporation are arrested.

Los Angeles, a semi-tractor trailer and truck explodes on the interstate. Investigation indicates veterinary supplies on board. No one is hurt.

Up and down the coast of South America, explosions and fires are occurring in every major city. The authorities are beginning to see a pattern and note that at each explosion site, traces of cocaine and heroin, packets of cocaine, and drug distribution evidence is at every site.

Interpol, DEA, and government drug agencies, forty-two in all, coordinate their assessment of the explosions and fires and begin making arrests through connections not only from each point but from point to point and through intermediaries that are noted in business records for all of the locations.

In Bogotá, the Tridexan main mixing warehouse and distribution center explodes with a large conflagration, burning down an entire city block. Military as well as the civilian forces to contain the fire immediately set out to explain the situation as an accident with natural gas.

Don Fuego receives calls and Internet emails from all over the world. He immediately evacuates his offices in downtown Bogota. As he is leaving in his limousine, three military vehicles surround his vehicle and soldiers with automatic weapons step out and fire upon the vehicle completely destroying it and killing the inside occupants.

Mexico City also has its share of fires. There are actually three at different locations. The authorities explain them as accidents. As Julio's mother watches the television, she notes each location as being a distribution point for the delivery of the carbolic acid used for veterinary treatment.

Matt flies to Mexico City to confront Lucia with the results. Lucia greets him at her condominium with a stern comment. "You meant what you said. It is happening."

"Keep watching the news," said Matt. "It is happening all over the world. Your empire is now nothing. All of your distribution points have been destroyed. The credibility of your distribution system is destroyed. Even your warehouse in Bogotá is destroyed and the people associated with your distribution system are either dead, arrested, or fleeing the country. Flight from arrest, flight from suppliers, flight from buyers, and yet monies have transferred without goods being provided. You know what happens in the drug business when one buys something and gets nothing."

Lucia smiles to answer. "It is a lifetime of effort. But I don't feel bad about it. In fact a heavy load has been lifted off my shoulders. I am beginning to feel the weighty wrong that I have committed. I never realized it is a sin but now I know it is a sin,"

Matt agrees. "Yes, and you have the wonderful luxury of knowing it because you are still alive."

Lucia looks at Matt with love in her eyes. "Yes, and it is because of you."

With the same affection Matt looks back at her. "I have feelings for you. But I have more to tell you. You have to know everything before I can say the words I want and yearn to say to you. With Don Fuego dead, the million-dollar contracts fizzle. Lucia, the death squads have disappeared in smoke and carnage. With the collapse of the system the supply for cocaine dries up to nothing from one of the largest tonnage distributors of cocaine in the world. You are free to start a new life."

"But how will you start it? A drug vacuum ensues and the price of cocaine doubles, then triples. The supply dribbles to nothing as the old smuggling techniques come back into dominance. The DEA and Coast Guard double their efforts at the boundaries of the United States and each government is overwhelmed with petty smuggling of small amounts because the price of cocaine has gone so high the risk of the reward is now being accepted by petty criminals."

"But, because of the high price of the drug you wish to start up again, alternative drugs become even more important and even more in demand and cocaine may be dying in the fields of Columbia with a dying demand. Methanol, crack cocaine, and alternative pharmaceutical drugs all will become substitutes for cocaine and at a lower price. Corruption in Columbia comes to a wane as there is less to be corrupted about. With less trafficking the drug lords subside in their business locally and begin to branch out into other areas of drug distribution. Some even leave Columbia to set up new bases in the Caribbean. Some buy their own islands, set up ports, airstrips and helicopter pads and the traffic patterns changed significantly. Heroin is still on the table and it is still in demand and can still be made reasonably affordable to the addicted population, but who will trust you after what happens today."

"Day five and all hell breaks loose. Massive arrests of tens of thousands of drug dealers, distributors, primary leaders are handcuffed to each other and being led out of buildings as their nests of production and distribution are exposed by explosions one after the other everywhere. Is this what you want back?"

"Lucia, the violence only gets worse. In the world of South America and the Caribbean, the favorite weapon of punishment, the machete has found its way to many of the people exposed by the explosions. Headless bodies are found everywhere from small villages to large cities."

Matt couldn't know it but even in Cuba where Julio and Josephine are hiding out, Julio's cousin is a marked man. That evening as he is leaving the coast to go into the mountains to see his cousin, he is ambushed on one of the mountain roads, pulled from his jeep and with no ceremony, his head is cut off with a machete. Everywhere, the criminals are bewildered looking to blame each other for the massive destruction of one of the biggest economic traffic systems of the illicit drug industry that ever existed.

Yes, Julio anxiously waiting for his cousin and watching the news on television looks at Josephine and screams without hesitation, "We need to leave now. The boat is refueled and ready to sail. We have to get to the coast and make our escape."

"Where will we go?"

"We need to be on the water away from all of this. I will use our short wave and radio grandfather to find out where to go. But I think we should go to Venice. Right now it is safer to be on the water."

Josephine looks at him. "But they will be waiting for you there. They are taking out everybody. It is an insane reprisal. Anybody who had anything to do with the organization is being killed."

Julio responds in anger. "This is no time to argue. Get our carryons while I get the motor scooter in the shed."

With his headlight finding shaded turns etched against the late noon sun, Julio leans the scooter with one leg out to steady the turns. Josephine's legs wrap around the bulky motor housing as Julio presses on with each turn rising, rolling and listing from side to side in dangerous twists. Shifting up and down, the engine roars, as Julio turns with his knee burning on gravel. Then close to the bottom of the hill the curves turn to caresses. Josephine holding on tightly sometimes with eyes closed and with a prayer to be heard, Julio slows down at the bottom where the road splits to the left to the Naval Base and looks to the right to Guantanamo. As he makes the turn, he notices an approaching vehicle and moves off the road and turns off the motor.

Josephine whispers. "Is that Alonzo's jeep?"

Julio very much angered speaks with tight lips. "Yes, it is his jeep, but I believe his murderers are driving it, and they are turning up the mountain road to the farm. We got out just in time."

In ten minutes, Julio and Josephine, making the northeast gate at the base, are passed in and run to Papillon.

Once on the boat, Julio thinks out loud with a great deal of doubt. "I need to talk to my mother."

Josephine looks sternly at him. "You don't need your mother anymore. We need to survive on our own, not with your mother and all your family's money."

Julio's training in sports, his willingness to accept the responsibilities of leadership between the two of them stiffens his resolve, showing the courage that Josephine knows he has, one of many reasons that keep popping up in the love data bank in her heart.

Josephine holds Julio's arm. "Julio from day to day I don't know if we will be alive. And now we go back on the sea. Our love sings on through tragedy and joy. It is a deep song in my heart and it goes on and on. I love you with all my heart and want us to sanctify our belief in each other in the eyes of our Lord."

Julio doesn't think twice. "The base commandant can marry us in the Chapel of Our Lady Gitmo. We still have time to do it today and can leave tomorrow morning on the tide. He takes her hand and with a ring he has carried for some time asks. "Josephine, will you be my wife?"

Josephine with tears of joy and a most happy nod. "Yes, my darling. You are forever my darling on this Fifth Day in our lives that joins us with freedom and wonder."

Julio gently nods. "Yes, Josephine, you are indeed my Fifth Day Lady, forever!"

The Commandant agrees to have the Chaplin perform the marriage. The Coast Guard cutter captain that met them on the water asks if he and his crew can stand up for the wedding. The Commandant aware of Julio's' defense against the pirates, notes that Julio is also a boat captain, and hails the crew of the cutter for its offer and it is indeed a time for celebration on base as he orders up the band for the wedding music.

Julio and Josephine in their best dress with Julio wearing his captain's hat are amazed when they leave the boat and find a uniformed escort to march them to the chapel.

The petty officer approaches. "Sir, I believe I am addressing Captain Julio Verelez. Please allow us, the crew of the Coast Guard Cutter Baiyner, escort you and your lovely wife to be, to our Lady of Gitmo for your marriage ceremony."

Julio nods and salutes. "Chief Petty Officer, my wife to be and I are truly honored by your escort and presence at our wedding. Thank You."

Julio and Josephine hold hands as they walk to the chapel. But they are not alone. Half the base has turned up along the walk wishing them the best. "Congratulations, you are a lovely couple. Happy, Happy Marriage. You look great." As they approach the base the band assembles at the door and strikes up the American Anthem. All stop to salute or take their hats off and hands on their hearts to honor the flag.

At the altar, Julio and Josephine make their vows. Hand in hand with complete devotion in their eyes and with their words they pledge their lives to each other. The Chaplin asks for special thoughts from each. Julio begins. "My present to you is all that I am, your husband, each day for me, is waiting to say how much I love you in every way." Josephine with complete commitment softly proclaims. "Our hands hold firm to share our lives. Always here in my heart and soul, each day your gift renews me whole till the end of time."

The Chaplin then finishes. "I now pronounce you man and wife. You may kiss the bride and go with the blessing of the Lord."

The chapel full from row to row gives out with a hoorah as the band plays the wedding march. Once outside, streamers fly as the guard salutes. The commandant with his post vehicle is waiting.

The Commandant holds the door, "You two are my guests at the mess hall for all to celebrate with you. Have a good time"

Josephine couldn't hold herself back as she rushes to kiss and hug him. "Thank you so much. It means so much to us."

As the Commandant closes the door he adds. "You are most welcome. I have a daughter and I gave her away like this last year. Your wedding has been a great reminder. Keep safe on your journey with tomorrow's tide."

After the celebration dinner, Julio and Josephine walk to the beach. The calm waves shine like day with a full moon. The glassy reflections lap on the shore with layer upon layer of curved lines looking down the beach, teasing the sand coming to shore and backing away. As Julio and Josephine wander along that way they hold each other's hand in delight as they gently bathe their feet. Returning to Papillon, they smile good bye as the waves wish them their dreams delight.

Anna and Mannie in Las Vegas revel over all the destruction they see on the news. In Bogota, a city full of dealers is fighting over drugs suffering hundreds of murders in the street and end up being quelled by the national military. Accusations cascade on some government officials, now condemned as corrupt for sheltering the drug distribution system within the legal system and protecting it by looking over their shoulders, for a great deal of money. And in Bogotá the greedy generals look at each other in disgust.

"I cannot live on a general's salary," speaks the Generalissimo. "I cannot even afford my second or third girlfriend. We must do something to recover our financial position."

'Well," said another general. "We have to restore the system. There is nothing else we can do. But we cannot step out of our roles to do it ourselves. We need to find another leader. It was all Don Fuego's fault.

If he would have left well enough alone, we would still be living in our glory."

"I know," said another general. "But the cocaine fields are going to rot for now. The crops are nowhere near being distributed. They are going out in small bundles and small dealers and they are all fighting each other for control of small distributions. The supply is dwindled and other drugs are taking the place of cocaine. We need to restore the value of this crop. It is for our good! We need to move forward."

"Well spoken," said the Generalissimo. "But we don't have the system anymore. We don't have the secrets that the Verelez family had and so well protected and so well distributed our product throughout the world."

"It is terrible," said another general, "the way our system has been destroyed by malicious mischief of those malignant people, wherever and whoever they are. We know it is not the DEA. We know it is not the FBI. We know it not the CIA. We know it is not the Russians. Who are these people who destroy our system? They are ruining our economy!"

The question mark is big. But it is hardly the national economy, just that of the drug lords and corrupt supporters. But that is happening all over the world. All the drug agencies, tried and true blue, trying to stop the drug distribution system, are amazed at the destruction of the system they have been chipping away at for decades. How had it crumbled so easily and so quickly leaving all the evidence they need to prosecute the survivors of the collapsed system? How had human greed made itself best known with everything to be greedy about? Is self-destruction a self-fulfilled prophesy of greed?

The official lines of communication are busy with questions. Who did this and how did it get done so efficiently at one time? Some in the press are calling them unnamed Super Heroes, disappearing in the woodwork. No one is coming forth to claim their fame. There is no trailing evidence, no smoking gun. Gone into flames, there is no residual evidence of the nano-bombs mixed with the carbolic acid used to dissolve the cocaine for distribution.

The news by the hour on the fifth day with Lucia and Matt listening intently continues to be amazing. Safely behind the doors of her non-descript dwelling in a modest part of Mexico City, long into the evening they continue to watch TV news sometimes laughing, but more than once Lucia would cry, "That took me two years to set up." Matt approaches her as she watches news of Bogota, the failure of the crop distributions and the crumbling of the drug empire in Columbia is so welcomed by the people who wish to walk the streets safely and without fear.

"It is for the better," said Matt. "Your country needs to get itself away from that crop; away from the corruption and death that it causes. It has a new independent and strong economic base, and doesn't need an elicit one, that causes so much pain, for your own country and for the rest of the world."

Lucia gruffly growls. "Oh, if we just made it legal, we would not have these problems. The drug would be cheaper. It was legal a hundred years ago. Why all of this trouble?"

Matt sizes it up for Lucia. "It comes down to good and evil. Yes, it is that simple. There are things that are good and there are things that are evil and there are things that tend to be abused and become evil. Drugs are one of them. Human beings are no better or worse than any other animal in this kingdom that we live in. We can lose control of ourselves easily without discipline, without law and order, without morality. We can be scrambling animals working over the dead carcass of another animal in the field. That's what we can be and that's what drugs and no controls can lead us into."

Lucia rebounds with the thought that human nature is its own fault. "There are weak people everywhere. They look to drugs as an escape from their own reality. They can't deal with it. They want to die but they are too cowardly to kill themselves. So, they go to drugs to escape and eventually kill themselves anyway. Why doesn't the government just buy the drugs from me, feed the drugs for free to people who want to kill themselves and let them die? And of course, give them a place to die. Make a giant resort, a free drug resort. I will make a deal with the government. If it buys my drugs, I will build a resort for the users to live in. We will have gambling with play money. We will have free drugs and the more they win in gambling the more free drugs they can have so that they can die faster, I mean overdose for their ultimately desired maximum high."

"Matt, we won't need to have prostitutes. The user men and women prostitute themselves for their drugs. It does not matter. Drug use is a self-corrupting, self-destroying pursuit, freely pursued by choice. The abuse is self-cleaning. We just carry out the bodies and process them like the Germans did with giant furnaces."

"My God!" said Matt. "Won't you want to try and save these people from themselves? Where is your heart? Where is your compassion?"

"I have had my experience with drugs and drunks. They don't want to be saved. We try so hard to save them time again, over and over, but the 'save yourself' sell wears off. They don't want to be saved. They just want to get high. I don't have to prove myself on this. You go find the statistics."

"But there are people who do save themselves. I know that myself," he said.

"And how do you know?" she said.

"Because.., I am a former drug addict. I became one recovering from head wounds suffered as a Marine in Viet Nam. I saved myself with the help of a drug use anonymous organization. On the side I am a mentor helping others in Dallas. There is a future for those people caught by a medical as well as mental need that you are talking about. This is not a world where only the strongest survive. The difference between humanity and the animals you talk about is the compassion we have for our weaker members and what we do to help them survive and to live a better life. That is the reason for calling ourselves civilized, for calling ourselves above the animal kingdom. What you want, what you see, is us falling back into the animal kingdom away from the one thing that places us above it."

It was like a light bulb turning on in Lucia's head. Her eyes widened. Through her whole life, her whole training as a catholic, her own corruption through her business, her own skeptical views of humanity, she suddenly realizes there is a path to follow, to climb even, to become better than she had ever been with her own thoughts of her soul.

There is a bottle of water on the table. Matt takes a swig. As they sit there in the little kitchenette off to the side between the stacks of boxed records from the business, Matt could not help but gaze into her eyes and her face thinking. "This truly is a beautiful woman, a confident woman, an organized woman, a very intelligent woman, and one who has much love in her heart. I can feel it. I think she needs a hand to hold. I hope she will take mine."

"So," Lucia brandishes resentment. "You must tell me now. Why are you helping me? Did you think I was trapped in Tridexan? I suppose it was because I invited you to our penthouse and we enjoyed ourselves at my presidential suite."

Matt is wholly honest. "It's possible, some things happen without us getting prepared and that is one of them. We could have saved ourselves with Julio and Josephine and left you behind with Adolpho."

"But I was the one who showed you the way out. You convinced me to seek your help with the way you and Greta and even Josephine handle weapons like they were your friends. You all know how to kill."

"Well, I have been truthful with you on that. Mannie is a former DEA agent and I am a DEA agent."

"I see. So, your intent was not on me. Your intent was on our system."

"Yes, I will admit that. And your system will not recover from our nano bombs latched to all of your shipments all over the world. Too much has already occurred. Your husband has been murdered and your life and your son's life are in jeopardy as well as Josephine's. I basically believe that destroying your system is in the end saving your lives."

"I cannot believe it," she says. "And I know that my husband's death is not your responsibility. We have been under attack for several years with attempts to try and kill us or take over our business."

Matt responds diplomatically, "Yes, that is apparent from what's happened already. Our intentions to destroy your Tridexan ended up saving those of you we could save while trying to destroy a system that somebody else has already taken from you. But like that little glimmer in your eyes, it is not all over for you. I will need your help to clean up the mess we have left behind."

"Well, I must admit. This is a time for me to pay back. My mortality weighs heavily on the scale and with what good is left of my life depends upon admitting that my past is not a good reference. Because of my blind ambition, I travelled a deadly path leading to self-destruction just like a drug addict. And you are saving me from the precipice. I want to thank you for saving my son and myself, and Josephine as well.

She is a lovely woman and she is very good for him."

Matt stiffens up. "Yes, it could not be any other way."

The conversation stops right there as Lucia puts her hand on Matt's. She melts in his arms as they stand up and look at the door to the bedroom.

Lucia seeks Matt's warmth. "Let us sleep together. My heart is warm for you."

Matt smiles. "My heart is yours tonight my dear, and it has been for some time."

But Matt holds back on his assignment to convince Lucia to join forces with the cleanup and become a consulting agent for the DEA, with no jail time forthcoming for past alleged crimes. He bites his lip as she walks to the bed disrobing herself. He likes this woman and yes, feeling the pangs of love all along. Although his job is still in his heart, he just can't cut her out so he can be the cunning undercover agent he is supposed to be.

Does he love her so much? He now understands the torture suffered by Josephine with her growing love for Julio. Although he needs to use her, he wants her to be happy with him regardless. Hopefully they are safe for each other but neither one has a way of knowing. Yet Matt knows Lucia is the only way that he could possibly follow through with the massive cleanup around the world. What is left now between the two of them is a matter of seeking and finding each other regardless of the deep chasm between them. And with that, they make tender love and fall asleep contented.

Chapter Twenty Six

What's Next?

On the ending of the fifth day, Anna makes a phone call to her friend in Finland. Olga reports to Anna with a great deal of pleasure. "Anna, you wouldn't believe it. In Moscow, labs are bursting into flames. The mafia grunts running the operations scattered and are netted immediately by the Moscow metropolitan police. Thousands are arrested. The leadership including some army officers and police officials are also arrested as the thousands who fled, expose their leaders and the 'never do well' dealers quickly try to fill in the gap, exposing and killing each other in the streets. Never in the history of drug enforcement has so many criminals been captured and will be successfully prosecuted with evidence and testimony than with what is happening, on this the fifth day you designed for your nano-bomb. Congratulations. You are a hero."

Anna is thankful for the nano bomb success in Moscow. "Olga. Do you think it is safe for me to return to Moscow?"

Olga comes back with a sour note. "My friend in Moscow's drug test lab told me that your immediate superior in the drug enforcement department has been arrested as well as three other investigators like yourself. Even if they are gone there is no assurance that the barn has been cleaned out. You could send a report to the police chief. But there is a problem with higher level politics including Putin, who is the richest man in Russia for many undocumented reasons. You assisted on a drug bust with no authorization to leave Russia. You may be disavowed, which in the end makes you a criminal of the state. My dear friend, I think you should defect to the US. And I would be very happy to come and visit you if you do."

Back in Mexico, Matt checks his watch. "No more days to go." Lucia looks at Matt. "Why are you saying no more days to go? We have many more days to go. I have to move at least every three to seven months wherever I go for years to come if I am not to be found. They will not stop until they find me. I know too much. I have done too much."

Matt agrees with a nod. "You might as well know."

Lucia demands. "Know what?"

Matt lays out her source of fear. "Although we sabotaged your distribution system, the people behind the operation are untouched."

Lucia admits but minimizes. "Hah!" she said. "That could be! But they are all over the world."

Matt prods on. "Yes, that's true. But don't you think if we eliminated the backers, the 60% owners, you could then be safe?"

Lucia starts to think. Matt hopes the wheels are turning clockwise. He does not know how far he can turn this woman.

Lucia looks at him. "It is a business, like any other business. They can find another medium for the same kind of distribution."

"I know," said Matt. "You have isolated yourself from the destruction your business is causing to societies all over the world."

Lucia back on the defensive using her worn out rational, "Don't people cause problems for themselves? Drugs are just a part of it. If there are no drugs, they would create drugs. It is an escape mechanism for people who cannot or will not deal with the reality of their lives. They become escape artists."

"Some lives are so bad," Matt agrees. "You are right. There are weak people out there. For thousands of years drugs of one kind or another have been at hand. More recently it has been in the west, alcohol, rum, tobacco, heroin, and cocaine. Bought and sold and distributed legally or illegally for money, and creating unbelievable wealth."

"Yes, I am a mere supplier and have made a fortune for myself and my backers. But I don't tell people to take these things. I don't tell them to abuse it. I don't tell them to kill people for it. I simply sell it."

"Yes, you are just a purveyor. Just like the people who sell weapons and ammunition to African nations who slaughter each other in their own ignorance because they have modern weapons and mass tools of destruction."

"Exactly!" she said. "Human nature is what it is. I cannot cure it by denying it, if it wants to destroy itself. It will destroy itself in any event. You think I am a silly fool. I planned this operation following any business course. I am very much a part of it and I maintained it. It has nothing to do with religion, or goodness, or badness. I am simply a purveyor."

"Yeah, you are just providing a product. But your product has disappeared in the last 24 hours. The system crumbles at your plant and at all of its distribution points and Don Fuego is also dead because of it. Shouldn't you be worried that your backers conspired or agreed with Don Fuego to take over your business? They killed your husband, and then killed Don Fuego, because he failed, and you are next because they can't restart with you knowing the whole story. The money is great and they want you dead today."

Lucia is waking up. "Yes, I will be on the run unless I can stop them like you stopped me. I will think about that."

The wheels in her mind are finally turning in the right direction.

Back on Papillon, Julio and Josephine start early on the first day of their honey moon cruise with mild following seas, blue skies and the wheel on auto pilot as they lounge in the sun and kiss and hug again and again. Suddenly the weather radio whales like a siren. Julio checks it out as Josephine goes below to cook some breakfast.

Julio yells back. "Oh, no! Josephine! We have a tropical storm heading our way. It is six hundred miles due east of us moving at fifteen miles an hour."

Josephine runs back to the pilot house. "Can we miss it? What should we do?"

Julio checks his charts. "We are heading northeast as we are now passing the bottom coastline of Cuba. The Bahama islands are going to be to the east of us. We have 600 miles to go all the way up to Key West to get to the Gulf and then straight to Venice."

Julio thinks up a plan. "We are making 15 knots. We can raise our racing jib and add five knots. And we might beat the storm by racing along the frontal winds likely at 30 miles per hour. The storm could literally push us all the way to Key West."

Josephine comes back. "Ok, we are back on our six-hour shift day and night with breaks for meals."

Julio agrees. "Yes, and like any storm, things on board or the storm can change without notice. We need to prepare for surviving the storm. Batten all hatches and secure all lose items from flying about. We have high freeboard, but we will play rock and roll in high waves and deep swells. I'll secure all deck lines, the dinghy, and check the reefing line for the main and jib sails. I'll back up the boom line and attach a crank to the halyard winch in case we lose power."

Josephine helps Julio raise the racing jib. Julio then opens a deck locker to bring out a drogue.

Josephine asks. "What is that giant plastic float with vanes and holes in it?"

Julio explains. "If we lose our sails tacking, we need to nose into the wind. We can use our power but it may not be enough or we might lose power with the cradling of the hull causing a problem with oil or fuel flow. We can use this toughly built drogue as a sea anchor placed on our long anchor line as a drag. It will pull our bow into the wind no matter what. That will keep us from cap sizing on the broadside. If we find ourselves on course but cannot control for high waves in the following seas, we place our drogue to the rear to keep our stern from swiveling broadside to a wave or indeed just tipping us over or sinking us with a massive flood of water pulling us down from the rear."

Josephine shutters. "This is like flying without enough fuel in a storm. Can all of these things happen?"

Julio replies, "Many sailboats disappear in these kinds of storms. The Bermuda Triangle has taken many without a trace."

Josephine comments. "Great, nothing like being ready for the worst. I'll break out the self-inflating life jackets with lights, helmets, gripping gloves and satellite beacons."

Julio consoles her. "Josephine my wife, we are a team, and we shall survive this storm."

After sailing for ten hours the storm front is in view coming up from behind. Julio notes. "According to our GPS we have made 250 miles. In four hours, we can make a protected Cuban bay at Villa La Brujas and wait out the storm, or if we can handle the winds, we just keep on going."

Josephine checks the latest storm report. "The front is approaching the Bahamas with winds circulating on our side to the northwest. Why don't we race to the protected bay and wait out the storm in safety?"

Julio agrees. "Yes, we need a place for a safe anchorage. Now is the time to let everybody know where we are. I'll radio our short-wave transceiver frequency at the estancia."

Josephine looks up the chart. "Do you want channel seven at 5.7 megahertz? The same channel on the DC 3?"

Julio nods affirmative and once again speaks charged with authority, "Estancia Vega, Estancia Vega, Estancia Vega, this is Delta Charlie one zero one, over."

Julio waits for a response but hears nothing and calls the same message again.

Estancia in a tone of utter disbelief, "We read you Delta Charlie, over."

Julio coolly replies, "Please put Ricardo on, over."

Estancia returns in a vibrant voice, "Ricardo on, we worry about you. Where are you? What can you tell us, over?"

Julio confidently replies, "The lady Josephine and I are safe. We married at the US Naval Base at Guantanamo. We are on Papillon and there is a tropical storm coming our way near Cuba. Inform Don De La Vega that we are safe, over."

Estancia's Ricardo reliably confirms, "It will be done, over and out."

The drug cartels in Columbia pretty much evaporate with the leaders running and hiding with their money to different parts of the world. But on the horizon Matt knows, and now Lucia appreciates that the ugly system could rise again. The rumblings are strong and firm as they listened to the feedback from the DEA office in Bogota adding to Lucia's long pause to think.

Then Lucia, a once loathsome ruthless person, waking the next day after breakfast with Matt, comes to a solid conclusion. "Well, there is still time for me to pay back for all the offenses that I have committed. I am facing the fact that the life and the power I had is not good. In the end, by hiding and trying to survive, I am destroying myself and my son. By working to expose the backers, the 60% owners, I am saving myself and my son from the precipice and reinforcing the demolition caused by your sabotage. If I am to be a turn coat for a good cause, I commit myself to help as much as I can. I am not going to hold back on this. My mortality is closer than ever and in the hands of you Matt, you are the first man I have truly come to love."

Matt just melts with tears flowing down his cheek. "Lucia I am going to make you a super hero. And yes, you bind my soul with my heart. It yields warmth and yearning I have never known. We will make a great team."

Now impulsive with her energy, Lucia cannot wait to get the ball rolling. "Matt, get the car out of the garage. We are going for a ride."

Matt most willing asks. "Where are we going then?"

Lucia with apprehension directs Matt. "Head towards downtown and the train station; I will know exactly where to go after we get there."

Once by the train station, Lucia yells. "Turn left here. This is the street where we keep our records hidden from everyone. Nobody knows about this records storage building that we have had for twenty years."

Matt is more excited than Lucia. "Really, where is it?"

Lucia jests Matt with a know-it-all tone. "Well, we turn just down the next street to the right."

As Matt turned the car Lucia screeches. "There it is, that two-story building over there."

Matt scorns, "It is just a plain old building."

Lucia elucidates, "Exactly, it has a plain old iron door on the front and a padlock. But I know how to get in secretly. We always had secret ways of getting into things because we never were sure if we would ever have keys for anything either. That was my husband with back-up, a military thing of his."

Matt volunteers. "Thanks to Adolpho, yes, we had a secret passage out of your roof top condominium palace."

Lucia daintily leaves the car and walks past the front of the building to a short narrow passage between the two buildings. "Follow me to the rear," as she slid almost sideways between the two buildings, with just enough space to offer light for a window on either side. As she comes to the rear there are stairs going up to the rooftop of the building. "Up the stairs, quickly!"

Lucia practically leaped up the stairs to a second-floor door. "Here is the door."

Matt replies caustically, "Yes, there is another steel door with a padlock."

Lucia going back to duplicity "But we always leave a key to the rear door." She reaches up high around the edge of the roof that covers the door entrance and there in a magnet box is a key. She pulls the magnet box down and unlocks the lock and Lucia announces, "Santa Maria, we are in our warehouse filled with our records."

Matt counters, "There is no electricity in this building."

"Not to worry, here are white gas lanterns for lighting, but we have no air conditioning."

Matt ignores this minor limitation, and gets serious very quickly with a filing cabinet containing records for the last five years. Opening the top drawer includes last year's billings, payments, and special invoices labeled confidential.

Lucia sees Matt's eyes popping. "That invoice file is for our 60% owners. An impressive list of notables, wouldn't you say?"

Matt activates his cell phone to get a GPS fix on the building. "I need to send a recovery team here to get these records back to Dallas. But this top drawer I will carry back with us to our charter plane at the airport. Lucia Verelez, you are now a consulting member of the DEA.

And we are flying back to Dallas and putting you up in our local safe house."

Lucia begins to purr. "Matt my darling what is your hurry. There is a bedroom down the hall with some fine champagne and a king size bed, and I would like to take a rest. Will you join me?"

Matt resigns himself with a grin. "My dear Lucia, I will join you for love and country."

Lucia smiles as they walk down the hall. "Oh, Matt! You are so diplomatic."

On the Caribbean, the storm catches the Papillon after sailing for three hours into the dark. At 10:00 P.M., black clouds, cumulus nimbus, towering 30,000 feet highlighted by continuous lightning strikes getting closer starts to raise the waves to plow over the bows and onto the cockpit at the rear. Julio announces, "I think we are still an hour from the protected Cuban bay at Villa La Brujas. Hold onto anything near you. Attach your life line. This is going to be a whiteknuckle trip to the bay. This storm's wind, driving rain, and waves are treacherous"

No sooner said, now in gale force winds, Julio yells to Josephine. "Lower the spinnaker and raise the storm jib."

What a job for Josephine as she bundles the spinnaker with the boat now rocking and bouncing worse than a roller coaster. "Where are the sheets for the spinnaker?"

Over the howling wind, drenching rain on their faces Julio yells. "The sheets are tied to center the jib. Just raise the sail with the other line in place and tie it to the cleat."

On her knees Josephine grabs the line to raise the storm jib which offers just enough sail to make headway without heeling the boat.

With the wheel locked in place Julio jumps up and also quickly reduces the main sail size with reefing lines for the same reason.

Josephine just getting away from the jib rigging almost gets washed overboard by waves breaking over the bows. "Where should I go?"

Julio struggles with the wheel yelling as loud as he can. "Come back here to the cockpit grabbing onto the railing. The wind is shifting. The swells are getting deep and wide. We are making little headway." As Josephine grabs Julio's arm and the wheel just to get into the cockpit against the rain and wind, Julio continues screaming. "We are barely making 5 knots. I'm going to change course to sail off of the wind and keep our bows into the breaking wave tops."

The water in the cockpit can't drain fast enough in the heavy wash and down pouring rain. It is up to their knees. Julio starts tacking into the wind to make better time.

Josephine looks at the compass for the direction to Cuba. "Look to the west. I can see the lights of our bay."

Julio agrees. "Ok. I'll start the motors to get us there faster while I continue to tack port to starboard."

As they reach the mouth of the bay the wave height goes up to fifteen feet with following seas into the bay. Julio looks at Josephine pointing to the bow. "Josephine, go forward. Get the drogue and coiled rode, and bring them back here. We will get swamped going in and I'll work the motors to keep us up on the backside of the wave in front of us."

Fighting the wind's, driving rain, with balancing against the pounding and swaying catamaran, Josephine takes one careful step at a time as she makes her way to the drogue and coiled rode. Julio yells. "Tie one end of the rode to a cleat and the other end to the drogue and drop it over the side."

Stressing herself to near exhaustion, Josephine took fifteen minutes struggling from the bow thirty feet back to the cockpit.

Julio reaches out of the cockpit for Josephine as she approaches. "My darling hand me the line and take the wheel. We are on a slight port tack. Hold this until we heel and then turn the wheel to a starboard tack."

By this time Josephine knows the routine. "Julio be careful. Tie this line to yourself. I don't want to lose you or the drogue."

"Julio senses her humor just like in the airplane landing. "Ok Josephine. You are now the skipper. When I drop the drogue in the water, slowly steer this cat around on a course west to the bay light." Josephine yells. "Go for it."

Julio drops the drogue and comes back to the cockpit to play out the rode and start the engines to assist the reverse course with the port engine in reverse and the starboard engine forward.

Riding the back of a heavy wave with the motors and the drogue keeping the stern from being flipped by an approaching wave, Josephine gladly confirms, "Wow. Getting this way is scary but the ride now is like a cruise."

As they get past the bay's break water, the waves calm down and the wind slows as Julio brings the engines to neutral as he recovers the drogue. "Now we need to find an anchorage."

Josephine points to a series of docks while Julio checks the depth gauge. "Julio. There must be ten catamarans docked over there."

Julio agrees. "The cats are a clue to shallow water. We are in five to ten feet of water. Steer at low rpms and no wake towards the docks."

Josephine nods. "Aye, Aye, Captain Verelez."

Julio raises his hand. "Stop engines. We drop anchor here." Julio walks forward to release the anchor with a lengthy rode. As they recover from exhaustion, the storm moves farther north leaving behind calming waters with some stars appearing between the clouds. Julio returns to the cockpit, embraces Josephine and kisses her tenderly. "Great job my darling. We did it again. I love you."

Josephine continues her hug and kisses Julio twice on the lips, on each shoulder and on each side of his neck. "That's for being a great captain and my great husband. I love you."

They kiss the catamaran on the deck and retire below deck, totally wiped out to sleep in each other's arms.

At the Mexico City scene, Matt brings in two agents to empty the records in the warehouse into a van truck to drive to the airport and ship by air to Dallas for deposit at a new address. It is to be delivered to IBA, Inc. or the International Brokerage for Agriculture products. The office and all relevant furnishings and equipment are in place and await occupancy by Lucia and clerical staff.

Back in Dallas, Matt helps Lucia getting out of their charter plane. "This is your new home, your new safe place to work, to become a super hero."

Lucia almost smiles. "Where are we going now?"

Matt answers quizzically, "You are a business lady are you not? Well, you are the new manager of IBA, Inc. All of your old records are waiting for you to begin your work. But before we go there we need to go to your new safe house, a condominium in a high rise near downtown."

Lucia laughs. "Wonderful, maybe we can take a rest while we are there?"

Soon enough Matt turns the key on Lucia's new living space.

"Welcome to your new home. Kali."

Lucia jumps back. "Who is Kali?"

You are now under a witness protection program. Here on this table is your new identity, a driver's license, a US passport, a bank account, a debit card, a special cell phone with a VPN address and the keys to an economical car parked in the basement ramp at stall 32. Your new name is Kali Ramirez."

Lucia accepts with some reservation. "Matt. Thank you for all of this, but Kali, that name is not my style and Ramirez is too common."

Matt agrees. "Yes, Ramirez is the 28th most common name in Spain, 42nd most common in the US and 9th most common in Mexico. It is exactly what you need to stay safe and lost, without detection. No more fancy clothes or fancy cars and your new job is to stay below the radar with no publicity, no public interviews and no patronizing of places for the rich and famous. Or you will get spotted."

Lucia rebuffs Matt. "You mean I have to stay bored?"

Matt disagrees. "No, you will be running and participating in an undercover operation, an extension of the rogue operation that we ran against you."

Lucia perks up on that. "Who will be my agents?"

Matt goes on. "Well, I could be one and I include rest period's part time. I am thinking of Anna and Mannie part time, Juan in Bogota part time, and your son Julio and Josephine, also part time."

Lucia adds. "Does that mean I am also part time?"

Matt nods no. "You are the president of IBA, Inc. And I am the chairman of the Board of Directors and you will report directly to me.

When not running an operation for your staff, you are consulting with other agencies fighting drug cartels in the US and elsewhere. And your consultations will be based upon your record collection with lists of distributors and the 60% owners at the top end, wherever they may be worldwide."

Lucia shrugs her shoulders. "Ok. I can handle that, but Kali. What does that name mean?"

Matt is amazed. "I thought you would never ask. Kali is the name of a Hindu goddess. She is the destroyer of evil forces to protect the innocent. I thought you would like that instead of a common name like Susie."

Lucia with hesitation accepts the compliment. "I do like the goddess part of it. I guess I can handle it."

Matt concludes. "That's it. You are Kali from now on. I need to get back to my office and work on getting our team on track. Take the rest of the day to build a business-like wardrobe as well as typical street clothes. I'll be back to take you out to a family restaurant at six."

As they embrace and kiss, Kali replies, "See you tonight my darling."

In Las Vegas, Mannie just closed on the sale of a $400,000 condominium sale. Anna, as the office manager, schedules showings, meetings, and advertising for the listings. Mannie, at returning to the office drops a $16,000 dollar commission check on Anna's desk. "Well Anna, it is time we sit down and think about our future. We can make it here or you can go back to Moscow, but you already know I love you and want us to be married."

Anna answers. "My life in Moscow is not over, but it is not safe for now. I have unfinished business there and I cannot let it go. I love you too. And yes, I accept your proposal to marry. That is a proposal that you just made, is it not?"

Anna stops to think out loud. "Some political problems for me will be solved with you making me an American citizen. I will not have to seek political asylum and when the time is right, I think we, not I, can go back to seek closure on the cartel people and corrupt military and other government appointees in Moscow. How yet, I do not know." Mannie is amazed. "You always put our problem together so clearly."

The phone rings and Anna answers. "Hello, yes, is that you Matt?"

Matt starts his spiel to sell Anna and Mannie. "Anna put this call on the speaker. I want to talk to the both of you at the same time. Hi Mannie. I have great news. Lucia has come over to our side under a witness protection program. Her name now is Kali Ramirez and she manages a new business called Independent Brokers in Agriculture, Inc. She has a budget from my black box. She has turned over for our use, all of her secret records and is ready, willing, and able to go undercover to expose the 60% owners who are escaping our melt down."

Mannie pops in. "Wow. Those records are invaluable. We could do a lot with them."

Matt agrees. "Exactly, and the key word is we. I want you and Anna to team up with us as part time agents. You will be doing what we have learned to do under cover. But the work will be spaced to give you a part time status to develop and maintain your daily lives together."

Anna agrees even more. "Well, our lives are shaping up. Mannie proposes marriage to me and I accept. And with us going back to work undercover with you and Kali gives me the opportunity for closure on my work in Moscow, (with Mannie nodding yes) we accept your proposal."

Matt adds more frosting on the cake. "Great. Lucia, now Kali, will be sending you a notice of engagement from Dallas. I will continue recruiting our past team including Julio, Josephine, and Juan. Congratulations on your forthcoming marriage, the sooner the better. Keep safe and God Bless. Bye."

Mannie looks at Anna. "Uh, oh, you know we are never going to get bored working undercover again, just part time. Ha, sure, part time. It's a deal?"

As they kiss and walk out the door Anna agrees. "Yes, it's a great deal. Let's get a marriage license today!"

With a well-deserved rest overnight after the storm, sailing from the Cuban anchorage without incident, Josephine masters tacking and sail trimming earning a bona fide first mate rank. Heading for Key West they enjoy calm seas with a decent wind to move them along at 12 to 15 knots to stop at the port in the channel at Key West. Julio brings Papillon under motors into the marina at the Coast Guard and Ferry docks and the Marathon fueling station and rents dock space for the night. With the boat fueled and secured, Julio escorts Josephine for a walk to a prime steak house on Carolina Street and then they tour for the evening along Front Street with a stop at Hogs Breath and Island Dogs Bar.

The next morning on high tide, Julio wheels out onto the Gulf, due north to meet and follow the coastline of Florida to Venice. By dinner time he navigates Papillon under engines in the intercoastal waters of Venice at Snake Island and docks at the local yacht club. After securing Papillon for a lengthy stay, they grab their carry-on bags, call an uber, and ride to Sarasota to stay at Josephine's condominium.

At the door to Josephine's place Julio barks a command. "Stop! My dear lady, allow me to carry you over the threshold of our new home."

Josephine with a sweet affirmative, "Hurrah. We have a place we can call our home. And no one knows about it except us and Matt."

After several loving embraces they sit out on the balcony and wonder how everybody else is doing. Josephine jumps up. "Let's call Matt at his office in Dallas. It will be on his private line, a safe connection, to find out how all is going and that we are ok here in Sarasota."

Julio agrees. "Yes, I dare not call Alessandra at the ranch yet, but Matt can get some feedback from her through his channels as to when we can return safely there to care for our polo ponies."

Josephine looks at him with a slight grin, knowing polo is never out of the picture, and makes the call.

Matt answers. "Josephine you and Julio made it! Fantastic!"

Josephine is full of energy and confidence. "Yes, we beat the storm out of Cuba, made it to Key West and on to Venice yesterday. All is well with us. Our marriage in Guantanamo was in a chapel with a minister and a full guard from the base and a wedding dinner as well. How is it going with you and Lucia?"

Matt unloads the changes. "Lucia is now Kali. She is here with me. She has turned to work with us under a witness protection program. And Anna and Mannie are joining us part time under a dummy corporation to use Kali's Tridexan records, which we recovered from Mexico City, to clean up on the heavy-duty owners that survive our demolition of their delivery system. Kali is now living in Dallas and starting to organize the records with our staff to create a case file for all the major locations around the world."

Josephine looks at Julio. "Julio would like to speak with his mother can you put her on?"

"Mother is that you? This is Julio."

"Julio, my son. Are you safe?"

"Yes."

"And Josephine?"

"Yes. We are safe and together."

"Where are you now?"

"We are in Sarasota. We sailed the Caribbean with Papillon and got married in Guantanamo. My cousin is dead. The fifth day of our escape, I believe he was hacked to death with machetes as he was coming to warn us in the mountains."

"Oh, that is so sad to hear."

"What should we do mother?

"My son, it is for you to tell me. You are the head of the family now. It is your leadership that I look to."

"Josephine and I are together and bonded solidly. We don't want anything more than to live in peace and raise a family."

"That is good. For me I am truly in love with Matt and wish to make him my husband and live out our lives together, also in peace. But I have changed. I have a need to make up for all the ill that I have caused through my business."

Julio speaks hesitantly. "I have always felt guilty, always felt it was wrong. What can I do to help?"

"I have a new identity and I am working with Matt. Mannie and Anna will work with us part time to carry out our future missions. Matt and I agree that in Bogota we became an unbeatable team. And we invite you and Josephine to work with us part time while you continue to pursue your business and polo teams at the ranch with Alessandra."

Josephine nods as she listens on the speaker phone. "I say, we become fighters for freedom from drugs and drug dealers."

"Julio, my son, and my daughter Josephine, I am proud of you. We can do so much. We know so much. We can quell the cocaine business. Other drugs too. We know the heroin tracks. We can fight that as well."

Julio agrees, "Yes, it is a worthy cause. It is one I should pursue and Josephine agrees."

"Good. Let me speak with Matt and see what we can do to get you involved part time in our undercover clean up after the demolition event."

"Fine. Josephine and I are willing to be part timers. We love you. God bless you for your help."

"I love you too. Give my love to Josephine. God bless and keep you both. Goodbye."

This is probably the first time in twenty years Julio says he loves his mother. It is probably the first time Kali ever said 'God bless' to anybody. Things have changed a lot for Julio and Kali. Feeling thoughts of doing goodness not just from believing that they ought to, but from feeling in their heart that this is what they want to do.

Kali approaches Matt. "With Julio and Josephine in Sarasota, they can pursue a normal life with Julio's dentistry business on the side. They can also continue pursuing their polo competition in the many places we have delivered our products. Their cover is the polo games just like it was for Josephine. They are safe and now we can get them involved in our continuing undercover program."

Matt thinks for a moment. "Well, I agree our escape bonded us and proved ourselves as a team. Juan is back in Bogota and has been promoted to the head of a drug investigation program outside of the bureau. The only way we can tell what he can do is call him about our new under cover office in Dallas. I think we should all meet here in Dallas for a day to celebrate our survival, and then we can decide how and when we can continue our mission. They can all come as economic consultants of some kind by invitation from our new corporation. From this point on we are doing everything with our new cover."

Kali is expansive. "Yes, I will employ my corporate development skills and set up an off-shore subsidiary, and make up fake credentials for all of us to get back into our best skills as undercover agents with a mission."

Matt responds positively. "Yes, and your off shore idea is a must for us. An out of country location is necessary for us to be disavowed by the DEA. And you can set up your banking there to network with other working locations. Do you have any ideas as to where to go?"

Kali reminisces. "I once took a cruise that included Jamaica. It is a sophisticated place with a good banking system. It is also central to the Americas. The downtown is very modern with office towers and condominiums. The air terminal is busy with flights everywhere. And cruiseships stop there all of the time in season."Matt salutes Kali. "Go for it."

Kali starts her corporate engine. "All overseas transactions come through my bank at Kitt in the Caribbean with deposits in the Verelez name with coded access. That way we may legitimately do business from Jamaica to and from different parts of the world and operate with an excellent credit rating for our cover that is, in fact, a true business."

Before calling for a meeting, Kali and Matt make it to St. Kitts. They transfer the papers and set up appropriate funding arrangements for an agricultural purchasing company and a brokerage firm for agricultural goods for private sellers around the world. They then fly to Kingston to purchase a condominium, rent a furnished office space, and open an account at an international bank in Kingston. The new company gives members of the company the opportunity to travel from their locations to all parts of the world with an excellent cover.

With Juan back in Bogota and safe at his new post he makes a call to Mannie in Las Vegas. "Mannie, I just want to update you about Columbia. Things are very quiet. Every seller is leaving town to set up shop elsewhere including Argentina. We are looking hard at the generals but have no evidence to implicate them. And the policia nationale is having an internal investigation."

Mannie replies. "Call Matt on his private line, Anna and I are getting married and we are doing fine selling condominiums. As an American citizen she won't have to go back to Russia. More for you to talk with Matt; can't talk on this line. Bye."

Juan makes his call to Matt. "Matt, Mannie said to call you about happenings that might be of interest to me. I told Mannie things are quiet now but I can't find evidence to get back to the generals."

Matt loads Juan up with potential. "Lucia turned to work for us. We recovered all of her side line special files that she kept in Mexico City. She has a new identity in our witness protection program. And we have set up a dummy corporation to research her ton of records where I am sure a general or two can be found. Our mission is to clean up the 60% owners that survived our implosion effort. This is an undercover operation hopefully with the same team, including you if you are willing, on a part time basis. You know, a month or two at a time."

Juan doesn't think much. "Count me in, where to next?"

Matt almost falls over. "Wow. You are on for a big ride my friend. We are building files for now, but it looks like Argentina is a good start. The cocaine trade diminished significantly out of Columbia but is beginning to creep back in with small operators. Significant damage is done worldwide. Even China is on our list. Honest government is filling in the cracks on the distribution side but top-drawer operators remain untouched. Tough nuts to crack include Russia and Southeast Asia."

Juan replies, "Argentina is a good first step on digging deeper. What is our cover and what do we call ourselves?"

Matt goes deeper. "Our cover is a worldwide agricultural product broker. Lucia, now Kali, the goddess destroyer of evil forces to protect the innocent, employs her corporate skills to the hilt. You, Mannie and Anna go undercover for a specific location. I come in as a buyer/broker for the company. Julio and Josephine will come on board part time with their polo cover where they can fit, from buying horses in Romania to regional competitions in India."

Juan begins to marvel. "Big is getting bigger. But from Dallas?"

Matt counters a good question. "Aha. We are set up in Kingston, Jamaica, a fairly neutral ground with good banking and a relatively central location for the western hemisphere."

Juan replies. "Good thinking."

Matt continues. "Our motivation is not giving in to this persistent evil. We will never stop fighting to keep it in check, diminish it, and keep it in a morally responsible framework in society. We must never give in, for evil to win. We are an undercover business, undercover guardian angels, as Kali now calls us, super heroes, ready willing and able to carry on the fight for justice and freedom from purveyed addiction."

Juan, Mannie, and Anna, with all the risk that they had taken crossing from Europe to Central Europe, to South America, knew that on the fifth day there would be a lot of cartel failures all over the world. The effort was worth the results. And for them there is no greater satisfaction than defeating an evil infecting the world.

To establish closure on the Bogota operation and discuss the potential of investigating further with Kali's records, Kali has extended paid invitations to Kingston to meet for a day and map out what to do and where to go.

Matt opens the meeting in their new office conference room. "Welcome to Kingston and thank you for coming here. It warms my heart that we are all here, safe and sound, and indeed we have congratulations on two marriages, and Kali and I are engaging each other to that point also. And Juan just keeps on having more kids with his wife. So, at this stage we all have a lot to lose facing danger the way we did just a few months ago. Kali is organizing her files and has something to say."

Kali looks around at all with a confident smile. "I plan on becoming a super hero to make up for my past. You are already super heroes. And your commitment to accept danger to get a job done to make the world a better place is now my commitment. To make a long story short I have organized and researched a file on Argentina. My contacts while there have always been with a man named Sergei, a Russian who ran our operation going west to Bogota while I ran our operation going to all points. But Anna has confirmed Sergei is a cover for another person who is definitely a leading 60% owner in the whole operation. That person remains a mystery but to my great surprise, shock, and disappointment one other person has been buried deep and long in this system for over twenty years. With your support I believe we can expose that person along with many of his cohorts in government, the military, and cover businesses. What! Damian Vega de la Dega."

The room contains a stunned silence. Matt calls for a vote on Kali's report. The motion to investigate is unanimous.